Isolating Contact
The Contact Series: Book 1
Ash Remington

D1715484

Contents

Chapter 1

Mirrors and the Lies They Tell

Emilia Vera

"Nuclear Explosion in the Pacific," was the headline on the morning of August 4, 2032. At any other time in human history, this would have been *the* world news event of a person's life. For those of us who lived through the times that followed, the catastrophe would barely warrant remembrance. I can excuse the idiot majority for their lack of foresight, but of all people, I should have known better.

I read four articles covering the disaster from my top-floor, corner office of the One World Governance Chicago building. The incessant pinging notifications of panicked emails from my colleagues and subordinates drowned out the Pink Floyd in my headphones to the point where I could no longer consume in peace the news of impending war.

I stood at the window of my oversized, executive office, examining the city while the people below rushed from one pointless endeavor to the next in a mad scramble to have any agency over their simple lives. The city skyline populated my view from that elevation, but I was rarely ever able to see past my reflection when it presented itself. If I looked hard enough, I could see the woman I pretended to be. A caramel-kissed, Argentinian beauty. A Latina black shine to her straight, natural hair, cascading symmetrically over both sides of her face. Perfect attention to detail in her makeup, style, and wardrobe. A tiny body, small in stature, but carved out of steel in ways that can only be achieved through discipline. Confident, postured, and fearless. She was right there in the reflection if I could ignore the scars, both perceivable and buried under the surface.

The daily stress of wearing the face of a better woman, along with my general distaste for mankind, took the fear out of a potential nuclear war. I stared past my reflection and daydreamed of the sky flashing white and orange in the distance. The sun blacked out by a mushrooming cloud of nuclear destruction. The shockwave swept through the city as it destroyed steel and flesh indiscriminately. I imagined the fools peering out their windows at impending doom before the glass exploded in their faces. The blast radius expanded slowly enough for them to experience mangled deformities like mine before the nuclear surge turned them to ash. I welcomed that end if it meant not having to stand before my subordinates to engage in dreaded human contact once again.

I killed the world in my imagination, and far too much time in the process. I turned off my music, closed the web browser, and sent a group email to my team to meet in the conference room. To further procrastinate, I switched the audio feed for my headphones from music to my intercom monitoring and eavesdropped on my employees as they gathered to wait for me.

"Has anyone talked to her today? Know what kind of mood she's in?" a nervous male voice asked.

"I wasn't aware she had any variety of moods outside of judgmental-resting-bitch-face," a female voice answered.

"She makes me so uncomfortable. Look at me. I'm sweating. We're on the brink of World War Three, and the only thing that scares me is a ninety-pound sociopath."

"Nod your head, avoid eye contact, and speak only when spoken to."

"Avoid eye contact? Has she ever done that staring thing to you? It creeps me out. I can't tell if she's trying to force me to notice her burns or birthmark or whatever the hell it is on her cheek, or if she's trying to guarantee that I'll never look again."

"Oh, yeah. Everyone's had the stare. She did it to me in my interview. There's no amount of foundation in the world that can Maybelline her problem away. I think the stare is a more effective concealer. The wig is a nice touch though."

"That's not her hair?"

"Of course not. I bet there's burns all the way up into her scalp. She's styling the hair close to her face to cover it up."

"It's certainly not stunting her career, nor is her toxic personality, for that matter. Apparently, being a prodigy genius has its perks."

"I don't care how smart she is. Emilia can't be a day over thirty. How did she get this job? I've been OWG for fourteen years, and she waltzed her way right by me, up the corporate ladder."

"She must be connected, because there's no way she networked her way up the food chain. That girl has the social skills of Hannibal Lecter."

"Pretty sure she didn't bang her way to the top either. Not with that face."

"She's probably somewhere on the spectrum. You guys should cut her a break. Whatever you think of Emilia, you must admit that her methods are effective. She flipped the mayoral race when we were dead to rights. She led us from controlling four school board seats to seventeen of the twenty-one. She literally created the blueprint for social media propaganda. DC and LA are both copying her bot farms."

"Well, I wish the figureheads would promote her already. I can't take much more of this. I'll go back to the think tanks or get into field recruiting. I don't care."

This conversation was not out of the ordinary. It was one of many that I had eavesdropped on over the years through office bugs, telephone taps, and hacked email accounts. I don't know why I bothered listening in on the opinions of the sheep. I never acted on them. I wasn't about to change who I was, treat anyone differently, or even terminate the employment of those who spoke ill of me. If anything, I heard their complaints and antagonized those making them in the hopes that they'd avoid future unnecessary contact with me.

If untrained, I would have marched into that conference room and unleashed holy hell on those peasants who dared let their negative thoughts reach their tongue. How quickly they'd appreciate the walled-off and muted version of myself they found so detestable.

I discarded my headphones, closed my laptop, and collected my yellow legal pad before exiting my office and stomping down the hallway toward my audience. I could hear their voices dying out as they were alerted to my presence, whispering their distaste for me right up until the moment the door swung closed behind me.

They sat quietly at the long, rectangular, wood-finished table. Some with hands folded, others with their gaze averted. Rather than sit and get comfortable, I lightly kicked the rolling office chair away from the head of the table towards the corner of the room. I rifled through my notes while occasionally looking towards the weaker of the bunch to intentionally give them a microdose of my discomforting stare.

"All right kids, here's the rub," I began to address them. "At 4:42 a.m. central time this morning, there was a nuclear detonation at an estimated water depth of fifty feet in the Pacific, two hundred and twenty miles east of the Philippines. This corner of the Chinese blockade of Taiwan was said to contain five naval cruisers carrying fifteen hundred and sixty-six sailors and officers, who have all been wiped out by a twenty-one-kiloton nuclear warhead. Satellite imagery suggests that the blast emanated from the Changzheng, a Jin-class submarine that appeared to be surfacing to launch depth. The CCP is denying that the blast came from a warhead. They claim that the nuclear reactor from the submersed vessel went critical, even though all the preliminary evidence says otherwise. Everyone following so far? Questions?"

"Do we think the Chinese government is lying?" Josh asked.

"Oh, for fuck's sake. Any *intelligent* questions?" I specified as I stalked around the table behind my subordinates.

"What's our play here? What's the next move?" Abdel asked bravely as I stopped behind him with my hands on the back of his chair.

"That's more like it. Good boy." I scratched the top of Abdel's head and tossed his quaffed hair as if I were praising a dog. "You paying attention, Josh? Pass Abdel a cookie." I nodded toward the plate of community snacks on the table.

Josh humbly placed a chocolate chip cookie on a napkin and slid it towards Abdel, but I snatched it just as Abdel reached out for his prize. I returned to pacing around as I broke the cookie into bite-sized amounts, and I put my pet on the spot. "What do you think the next move is?" I asked as I held up the first chunk of cookie and mocked a toss motion toward Abdel.

"Well, the CCP is definitely lying. The size of the blast suggests it came from a nuclear warhead. The fact that the Chinese are warding off the U.N. from assisting in disaster cleanup insinuates that they've got something to hide."

I tossed the first bite of the cookie underhand to him, and he leaned forward slightly to catch it in his mouth. "Go on. Keep going," I instructed as I taunted him with the next bite.

"We could use social media and our plants inside legacy media to paint the CCP as evil or incompetent at a minimum," he continued amid chewing.

"Look at you go. You're on a roll," I teased as I tossed another chunk of cookie intentionally off-course, forcing him to catch it in his hands. "Can anyone tell me why that would be beneficial?" I taunted the group with the next bite of cookie. "Anybody? Monique?" I asked again, this time forcing an answer directly.

"Ms. Vera, with all due respect, shouldn't we wait until the OWG takes an official position? We could be fanning the flames of World War Three," Monique stated as a misplaced voice of reason. She had barely delivered her well-intentioned position before a nugget of cookie hit her square in the forehead and crumbled all over her blouse and the table in front of her. "That is so uncalled for," she groaned as she dusted the crumbs off herself. "This is a tragedy, not a game."

"It's neither," I said confidently, completely unphased by her frustration. "It's an opportunity and a rare one at that. You think our directors don't see that? They're in boardrooms and on Zoom calls at every OWG office around the world right now. All gleefully plotting and scheming how they're going to further the agenda in the wake of current affairs. I'm not going to sit on my hands and wait for the bossman to instruct me. I'm going to get after it, and I'll drag you halfwits with me kicking and screaming towards mission success if I have to."

I wheeled my chair back from the corner and into position at the head of the table. My tolerance for the team's laziness, stupidity, and altruism was running low, and I wanted to return to the solitude of my office as soon as possible. I took a seat, along with a deep breath, and tried to address them calmly to wrap things up. "The mission is the same as it's always been. It's right there in the name, people.

One World Governance. You don't work for the United States, for the benefit of North America, or for the damn CCP. We don't mend fences, broker trades, or prop up nations. We topple them. If that's too overwhelming for your delicate sensibilities, you can go work for Google or the Tribune or Burger King for all I care. Now, get on the phone with your contacts. Work social media. Put my bot farm in play. And I swear, if a single member of your team leaves this building for a lunch break today, you might as well join them and never return. Understood?" I asked coarsely. They answered with affirmative head nods and hustled from their seats to make their escape from me as quickly as possible.

If I had less self-control, I would have exposed my eavesdropping capabilities and fired one of them on the spot. A warning would be served to the rest of them to keep my name out of their mouths or face the same fate. It would have worked too. They'd spend the rest of their days at the OWG looking over their shoulders, knowing that my digital ears were all around them, but I would lose my direct line to the intimate truths that they only dared to speak in privacy. This was the first of many important tactical lessons I had learned from my mentor, Penelope.

I returned to my office, shut the door, closed the blinds, and drowned out the noise of the world in my headphones. I had more than enough to work on, but my mind wandered back to the day that Penelope came into my life, taught me the practice of restraint, and changed my course forever.

I was thirteen years old, living near the port of Buenos Aires. My father worked on the docks and my mother at a food processing plant. They did the best they could with what they were given, but it was never enough. The slums were our home, and there wasn't a single thing my parents could do to change that fact.

We lived in relative filth. Shacks for homes, stacked on top of one another and crammed into every available piece of real estate. My childhood abode was surrounded by poverty, crime, and despair. The sounds of my mother crying were a frequent nighttime lullaby through paper-thin walls.

I escaped the toxic environment that I called home in name only by spending my time in school and the local public library. I scanned every book I could get my hands on like there was a hidden ticket out of that life lost somewhere in the pages. While my peers were obsessing over the latest installment of Harry Potter, my attention was swirling between studying the Holy Roman Empire and educating myself on how to hack and format code. It was my abuse of the latter skills that put me on Penelope's radar at a young age.

My youthful misadventures had placed me in the care of local therapist, Maria Cruz. My time with her was assigned in lieu of traditional punishment, but I would've rather had the belt or detention than spend another moment bored to tears in her presence. Mrs. Cruz was dreadfully tedious with her tests, questions, and constant psychological examinations. Her very existence was a slight to me. I was doing everything I could to not end up like my mother, and I feared that the best the world would let me become was someone as bland as Mrs. Cruz.

I was with Mrs. Cruz for one of our after-hours punishment sessions in the high school library when Penelope walked in and changed everything. I was doing a repetitive line writing assignment of, "No se debe abusar de los talentos excepcionales para vengarse," which translates to "Exceptional talents are not to be abused for revenge," in English, when I heard the library door close. Penelope strutted in with the tenured regality of a woman in her fifties, but the fashion sense of a woman in her thirties. She was a tall, thin woman whose presence was expanded by heels and confidence. Her skin had the palest of white tones like she was the mortal enemy of the sun. Her hair that day was in a bleached blonde bob, and she rarely ever wore it in the same style. Her fashion toolbox was full of short, shaggy, choppy, and layered bobs, with or without the bangs. One day she would have curly flicks and the next, she would have an asymmetric side part.

Her flat chest, abs, and ass gave her an androgynous look that wasn't traditionally sexy, yet she carried herself with the boldness of a curvy woman. Her posture was upright, and her non-existent hips switched when she walked. She carried a legal pad and pen, which made her present as a no-nonsense businesswoman.

Mrs. Cruz was quick to tend to Penelope like an underling who had been caught taking an unapproved break. I kept my head down, pretending to write my lines while I listened in on their conversation.

"Hola, Senora Martin," Maria said nervously.

"English please," Penelope politely ordered in a smooth British accent. "This is the girl?"

"Which girl?" Maria asked with a confused tone.

"Emilia Vera. The test results you sent me last week. Is this her?" Penelope pressed with what little patience she had running low.

"Yes, this is Emilia. She's of no consequence though. Gifted, but severely troubled. You've come all this way; you should meet Ramon. He's a brilliant student. Best in the program. I could make arrangements..."

"Forget Ramon," Penelope interrupted sharply, which further caught my attention. "Tell me about Emilia."

"She's a child sociopath. Aggressive. Damaged. A selfish, socially stunted, narcissist. If you want my professional opinion, the girl should be institutionalized. She's a danger to herself and those around her. It's only a matter of time before she creates the brand of trouble that turns detention into prison time."

"What this trouble she's embroidered in?"

"We advanced her from middle school to high school in the hopes that she would socially adapt when surrounded by children more akin to her intellectual level. She sabotaged those around her at every opportunity and isolated herself from her peers, though."

Penelope frustratingly waved a hastened hand. "Save the bollocks, woman. Spit out the short version."

"There was an altercation at school with Ana, a senior valedictorian front runner. Allegedly, there was some schoolyard bullying concerning Emilia's scars, though the little psychopath won't confirm it for some reason. Kids will be kids. She should have notified a teacher if she had trouble with her classmates. Instead, Emilia took it upon herself to hack into the school's database and change Ana's grades. If that wasn't enough, she snaked her way into the poor girl's email account and sent unspeakable messages to the Dean of Admissions at the University of Sao Paulo. We're trying to sort things out, but it seems Ana has lost her scholarship. The menace taught herself how to navigate the digital world and used that knowledge for malicious purposes."

The moment I heard Mrs. Cruz bad mouth me; I began to substitute my instructed writing assignment with one of my choosing. She thought she could speak freely in English, but she had another thing coming. I removed the sheets from my notebook and walked up to the two of them without speaking a word. I shared a glance with Penelope before focusing my gaze on Mrs. Cruz so I could collect a mental snapshot of her examining my work.

She shifted her weight from one leg to the next as she sighed deeply with equal parts embarrassment and anger. "This is what I'm talking about," Mrs. Cruz said as she handed my homework to Penelope.

"I speak English, you dumb busted cunt," she read aloud before pausing to compose herself and clear her throat. "You may fool everyone else with your pseudo intellect..." she switched from reading aloud to skimming over my slander for herself. "Charming," Penelope said as she returned the pages to Mrs. Cruz.

"You see? She's a hostile monster."

"That's very well, Mrs. Cruz. Thank you for bringing this to my attention. You may go now." Penelope dismissed her.

"What about...do you want to meet any of the other students?" Mrs. Cruz asked.

"She's politely telling you to fuck off. Take the hint," I sneered.

"I've never. In all my years. You're a hateful, demon child Emilia, and you deserve those scars. I'm finished with you. Face your troubles on your own from now on."

"How will I ever survive?" I quipped sarcastically as Mrs. Cruz stormed out.

"Your arrogance begets ignorance, little one," Penelope said, which swiftly wiped the proud smile from my face. "Those who trade strategy for spite are destined to win small battles but lose large wars."

It was at that moment that my intrigue for Penelope became respect. Her confident energy was no façade, and it cut through my steel ego like a spoon through pudding. I dared not respond with my trademark snark to a woman who could verbally split me in half. I didn't want to battle Penelope or shut her out like everyone else. I was immediately desperate to impress her.

"You're right. There's no telling what secrets she may have spoken in her perceived safety of English around me. It was worth it to wipe that smug look from her stupid face, but I could've had that moment any time I please."

"I knew I didn't travel all this way for nothing," she said with a pleased smile. "Now tell me something, darling. What did this Ana do to you that warranted such a ruthless retaliation?"

"It's nothing. She said something rude, it pissed me off, and I taught her a lesson."

"Emilia, do you know what your family surname means?" she asked rhetorically. "*Vera* is closely associated with *verus*, which means truth in Latin. It's an ironic name for such a liar. I've read your file, along with monthly reports and updates. You are not the person you show the world."

"You going to dissect me now too? You see the way it worked out for the last pendeja?" I asked with a nervous lump in my throat.

"I'm not going to dissect you. I'm going to reassemble you. I know about all the bullying. I know that you have no friends, and you're all alone. I know why you hide yourself in the library and lose yourself in education. Come. Walk with me, and I'll teach you something about yourself," she offered.

We walked down the dimly lit hallways of the school, passing by the rows of lockers and closed classroom doors. The only sound that could be heard was the click of Penelope's heels, which echoed through the corridor ahead of us. Even when dark and quiet, that was not a place of happiness for me.

"Intelligence isn't a gift, Emilia," she said as she tapped her forefinger against random lockers as we passed them. "It's an isolating curse. Intelligence has made the pair of us awkward guests at the party of society." I had only just met this woman, and there wasn't a person in the world who could possibly understand me more.

"Did you know that the average human has an IQ of 100? That's not the median. It's the average. 70% of people are within 15 IQ points of that unimpressive number. Most of the leftover 30% fall into the knuckle-dragging 85 or lower category. Men have a larger standard deviation in IQ than women. Can you tell me what that means?" she tested.

"There's more male geniuses than female, but there's also more halfwits," I answered, anticipating where she was driving the conversation.

"Indeed. The female genius is less common and often overlooked, especially by lesser men. Even genius men are threatened by a brilliant woman. They fear *me* because my bloody balls are twice the size of theirs without the dead anchor weight of a cock holding me back."

"Are you going to tell me what I scored, or are you going to keep taking the long way round?" I asked pointedly about my IQ test, to which she had no response but a smirk.

We approached the exit, and she held the door open for me without answering my question. Parked outside was a white town car with blackened windows. The rear passenger door was open with a waiting driver standing by. "Ride with me, and I'll teach you something about the world," she offered, holding the door to invite me in. If I wasn't already starstruck, that moment sealed the deal. I was in no position to turn my nose up at the invitation.

"Jorge Newberry airport," Penelope directed to her driver once the two of us were settled into the backseat. He weaved us in and out of the side streets that I knew well but were unfamiliar to me through dark paned windows. It was as though my entire world disappeared the moment I rode off with Penelope.

"These people will never accept women like us. Your disinterest in their sports teams, celebrity gossip, and network television will always be a barrier between you and society. Hate to break it to you child, but things will only become more difficult as you age. I can teach you how to navigate it, though."

"I know this is a sales pitch so you can save the theatrics. Whatever it is you're selling, I'm clearly buying. So cut to the chase. Who are you and what do you want with me?"

"I'm with an organization called the One World Governance. My job is to find gifted youth, bring them into the fold, provide access to accelerated education, and place them into positions fitting of their skills."

"Right. One world. Peace and harmony for the people, and all that jazz. You're offering me a career?"

"I'm offering you access and power." She rolled down her window to view the pedestrians and passing traffic. "Look at them. They're sheep, and they'll follow any wolf who presents as a shepherd. The entire world is an angry mob holding fire, Emilia. All they want is someone to tell them what to burn. Aren't you tired of them holding the flame to you?"

It may have been a coincidental turn of phrase, but it certainly felt personal to me. If Penelope hadn't been so disarming, I may have thrown a childish fit over her attempt to use my facial scars to manipulate me.

The escort drove us through a gated entrance directly onto the tarmac before stopping near a small, single-engine plane with OWG markings. "Have you ever flown private?" she asked, already knowing the answer.

"Never mind private, I've never flown period."

"I want you to come with me to London. Right now. You can stay at my estate in Mayfair. I'll put you into a proper school where you can get book-smart by day and street-smart by night. Heed your directions, and I'll have you on the college campus of your choosing by sixteen and into a career where you have agency by twenty."

"I don't have a passport."

"Don't need one."

"I don't have any clothes."

"I'll fit you with a new wardrobe for a proper young lady."

"But what about my family?"

"If they're third on your list of excuses, how important could they really be?" she stated coldly while exiting the vehicle. She waved to the pilot to start the engines before leaning in through the open window into the back seat. "The car will take you home if that's what you desire, but this will be the last time we meet."

I paused for a moment, mostly for dramatic effect. In anyone else's company, I may have feigned difficulty in the decision to exit the car and leave my parents behind so callously. That was an opportunity that there was no turning away from. My heart was already a malfunctioning soulless organ, and the decision to board that plane gave me a new brand of painless but irreparable damage.

It was three days before I called my parents from London, and another three years before I saw them in person. Every further correspondence featured reiterating why I chose this life, even long after they had come to terms with my decision. I frequently repeated my pros and cons list, not to ease their pain, but to quell any buried regret I had within myself rather than admit it existed.

Life with Penelope was as advertised. I took advanced classes with students who, while being on my intellectual level, were still as mean-spirited and cruel as the bullies I left in Argentina. My living conditions improved tenfold with an entire estate open to me, save for Penelope's locked office. I had all the world history and advanced computing my brain could soak up by day. By night, I had lessons on culture, politics, strategy, and survival direct from Penelope whenever she could make time for me.

I advanced quickly onto a college campus in the United States, where interactions with my peers were more taxing than the classes themselves. The only socially structured events that I enjoyed were with the other OWG youth in studying and think tanks. We tackled hundreds of assigned hypothetical world events, and how each could be used to advance the unification of all nations into one controlling body. Everything from famine, climate change, and world war to an asteroid collision, development of artificial intelligence, and first contact with an alien species.

It wasn't long after graduation that I was recruiting, running my own team, then a department, and then the entire central US division within the OWG. My highly effective digital age manipulation tactics changed the way the OWG conducted subterfuge and propelled me through the ranks to my director position. My long game was to penetrate the education system and gain access to children before nationalistic ideals took hold. My short game was to attack local elections through intense social media campaigns. The combination of the two garnered me notoriety that wasn't limited to the positive variety.

"Ms. Vera? Ms. Vera? Ms. Vera?" the intern beckoned progressively louder to pull me out of my daydreaming. It wasn't until he began waving his arms that I yanked a single headphone down and met him with a dissatisfied gaze. "Uh, don't mean to disturb you ma'am, but she's back. She's been live streaming from the sidewalk for ten minutes."

I transitioned my headphones around my neck and opened the Conspiriousity YouTube channel on my desktop while waving my hand to dismiss my errand boy. I clicked into the live stream and looked in on Alexis X from ten floors above. An attractive woman in her early thirties, who seemed to go out of her way to make herself ugly. Her shoulder-length, brown hair was a FEMA disaster zone in a messy bun or ponytail when it wasn't being matted down by a ball cap. She was of average height and never added any inches with lifts or heels. She had a curvy build that would turn heads if she ever bothered to dress in something besides hoodies, tee shirts, or sweatpants. White trash swag who grew too pretty and smart to remain in the trailer park but could never abandon the roots of her past.

Alexis was more emphatic and bombastic than her previous days of broadcasting from our headquarters. "They're already in your schools. Called it. They've penetrated your local, state, and federal governments. Called it. They don't answer to voters, and they don't rely on your tax dollars. They're more secretive than the CIA, greedy than the IRS, and corrupt than the DEA. The lies the OWG can spin are the masturbatory fantasies of CNN, Fox, and MSNBC. They're worse than the DOD, DHS, NSA, SIS, and KGB all rolled into one evil PB&J sandwich. You watch, the OWG is going to use the crisis in the Pacific to their benefit. That's an official Conspiriousity call."

Alexis and those in her network had us pegged right, and if anyone would take her seriously, she could submerge the organization in hot water. I quite enjoyed her as an adversary, albeit an overmatched one. There was a lot to admire about Alexis. Her passion was enviable. Her persona was free of care of the judgments passed by society. She was tireless in her pursuit of truth, and she was often over the target. Alexis could have been a threat if she wasn't so easily outmaneuvered.

"Intern! Get in here."

"It's Bryan. With a y. I told you last week, remember?" he corrected while hurrying into my office.

"Close the door, Bryan with a y," I instructed. "Strip."

"Excuse me?"

"Strip," I repeated, drawing out enunciation.

"With no music?"

"Settle down, Magic Mike. This isn't Chippendales. Strip to your boxers, tie your shirt around your crotch like a diaper, and wear your socks on your hands."

"I...what?"

"You want to make recruiter? You're going downstairs to ruin the livestream, and when you come back up, I'm going to promote you. Chop chop," I said as I rifled through my drawer to find a black marker as he began to remove his clothes.

"Hold still," I demanded as Bryan awkwardly tied his sleeves around his waist. I pressed the marker to his skin and wrote, "The OWG is Jewish upside down-ism," across his chest and abs.

"What the hell is that supposed to mean? Doesn't even make sense."

"That's the point, genius. Mess up your hair. Now, when you get down there, get right into her business. On camera. If she moves, you follow her. Babble conspiracy theories that are crazy but still sane enough to be true. Bonus points if you get Alexis to engage with you, but in general, I want you to terrorize her."

"I can't believe I'm doing this."

"Shut up. The idiots in the bullpen will idolize you. You'll move into recruiting, and you'll have a catchy nickname. The Talibryan...with a y. Off you go. Don't come back until she's gone."

Regardless of having a hundred other things to work on that afternoon, I spent a full hour watching Alexis do her best to avoid the embarrassment of being linked to a maniac. Bryan chased her up and down the sidewalk while screaming phrases like, "The lizard people chipped you," and "Conspiriousity is CIA propaganda." Alexis hung in there the best she could, but Bryan eventually ran her off the property, across the street, and all the way to her car in the parking garage. If she wanted to battle me, she was going to have to do it from the comfort of her home studio.

I looked forward to more of the parry and joist game with Alexis, but she became an afterthought a few, short days later. I was at home when I received my first call in months from Penelope, and her voice was as excited as I had ever heard.

"Pack your bags, darling. A ticket to Paris is waiting for you at O'Hare. You leave in three hours."

"Pass. I hate flying. I hate customs and I hate crowds. I always end up sitting next to some asshole who tries to show me pictures of their children."

"Emilia, you're coming to Paris," Penelope said firmly. "As a student of history, maybe you'd enjoy seeing some of it made firsthand for a change. Besides, you need a break. Lord knows you've earned it. I worry about you, cooped up in that house of yours. Get out a little. Touch some grass. See..."

"All right already. Enough," I interrupted. "I'll come to Paris, but you're coming to the States next time."

"Wonderful. A car will take you to the embassy upon arrival. Speak nothing of this. I'll explain when you arrive."

I packed my bags, collected my passport, trudged my way through TSA, and boarded that long flight overseas. I used a combination of sleeping, both fake and real, and my headphones to avoid all unwanted advances of conversation from my neighbors. A car was waiting for me as promised, and the closer I got to the embassy, the more I anticipated sorting out Penelope's big secret.

Once stopped, a man approached the car and began removing my bags. "You're late," he hurried as he placed a lanyard over my head and around my neck. "Go inside to the auditorium. Take the stairs on the right to the balcony. Your host is waiting for you there."

The embassy was packed with press and security. Assorted dignitaries, politicians, and members of the media were herding through the large, marble lobby towards the main floor auditorium entrance. I took the stairs as directed until I arrived at a balcony box with a dozen rows of theater seats. The noise of chatter from below was deafening to the point of being disorientating.

I could see Penelope's wavy, blonde pixie cut in the front row, so I made my way to the reserved seat to her left. "What the hell is all this?" I asked with genuine intrigue.

"Ah, Emilia, my dear. You made it. This is General Kelly." She drew my attention to the man to her right. "United States Air Force, and friend to the OWG."

He stood to greet me, and his bulking presence cast a wide shadow. I begrudgingly stood as well to find myself at eye level with his chest, where his assortment of medals and accolades covered his uniform. He took my hand firmly and shook it with an iron grip.

He was a senior, white man whose skin had a withered tan and leathery quality to it. He stood at least 6'4" and was thick, but not necessarily fat. There were noticeable bags under his brown eyes that seemed to have more purpose and focus than other men his age. His head was shaved clean for utility and not vanity. I could smell cigars on him, and I imagined he'd be chewing the soggy end of an expensive import if the venue permitted.

"Ms. Vera, I presume," his grizzled voice bellowed. "You're so young. Ms. Martin guaranteed me her *Argentinian Assassin*. You're not the killer I expected."

"You know a thing or two about killers?" I forcibly removed my hand from his grip.

Penelope looked up at me with a warning in her eyes. "Emilia. Play nice. Don't make enemies for sport."

"I just got off a twelve-hour flight. I haven't showered or changed, and I have no idea why I'm here. This *is* me playing nice."

"Full of piss and vinegar. A killer, as promised," the General quipped to Penelope with a satisfied smile as he returned to his seat.

"Quiet in the auditorium. Please be seated," a voice announced over the PA.

"Showtime." Penelope smirked as the lighting focused on a center-stage podium.

Out marched General Liang, a three-star Chinese naval captain in full uniform. His slight frame nearly disappeared behind the podium as the onlookers raised their phones to capture the moment. He set his military cap on the wooden structure and lowered the microphone into position before taking a composing breath.

"I come before you today as our world stands on the precipice of its third great and horrible war. My countrymen and brothers in arms will attack me as a traitor for my actions today, and I will armor myself in truth. There was no nuclear meltdown in the Pacific. A warhead was deployed for Taiwan, but the actions of a brave submarine captain traded the lives of fifteen hundred Chinese sailors for millions."

"The captain's defiance and valor that day infected me and my crew with newfound virtue. We stared down orders to launch twenty-six targeted strikes against Taiwan and her allies, and we seek neither praise nor recognition for our mutiny. We simply ask that you, the people of the world, also choose peace. Choose diplomacy."

"Here it comes," Penelope whispered with a nudge from her elbow to mine.

"Let it be noted who opened their arms to peace. It wasn't NATO or the UN. It was the One World Governance. Our borders and nationalistic pride have made enemies out of neighbors. We stockpile weapons and hold each other at the threat of certain death. I call upon the nations of Earth to recognize the destruction averted this day. I challenge you officers and military servicemen to lay down your arms and instead, embrace your families. We can welcome a new age of human enlightenment by simply reaching out and taking hold of it."

The General droned on with details about his valiant crew's escape from the Pacific and the brave new world they sought to create through disarmament and peace. The room was hushed outside of an occasional gasp for the better part of an hour. Once he opened things up to questions from the media, Penelope began breaking things down.

"We're calling it New World's Eve. When the ball drops on 2032, every nation will be disarmed and borderless. People will welcome in 2033 with intelligent adults in charge for a change. Their fears of war and turmoil gone forever."

"Four months? Are you outside your damn mind? This could take years."

"Is this going to be a problem?" General Kelly asked ominously.

"No. No problem," Penelope assured. "Emilia is up to the task, *isn't she*?" Penelope asked pointedly towards me.

"Why is this all hanging on me? What did you promise this fossil?"

"We're putting you in charge of North America." Penelope put her hand on my shoulder. "The directors are at your disposal, and I have insights that may prove helpful. If you're not up to the task in the allotted time, they will find someone who is." Her words rang as a warning with the General lurking over her shoulder.

"You're talking about waging war on the federal government, the bureaucrats, politicians, special interest groups, and the military-industrial compound," I said, looking in the General's direction, hoping for a reaction, but his demeanor was steel. "We take the food out of their mouths and it's going to turn into a knife fight. I'm going to have to get dirty on this project."

"Make the power brokers fight the people," Penelope suggested. "Give the moral high ground to the average citizen, and they'll commit treachery without regret in the name of world peace. The politicians who aren't already in our pocket will crumble under the terrible weight of their constituents. Those who cling to their power can be bribed with positions in the new regime."

"Or removed entirely," the General added.

"Yeah. Right." I nodded along. My head was swimming with ideas at that point. Penelope was officially taking me off the leash and she was about to find out what I was capable of. The General asked for a political killer, and regardless of my distrust or distaste for him, he was going to get one. "Call your gopher and have him bring my bags back. I'm taking the next flight home."

Multiple stages of jet lag couldn't keep me from hitting the ground running the following Monday morning. Everything was in place, and manipulating the public was far easier than I had expected. The people were more than happy to pile on anyone who stood in the path of progress. If someone spoke out against the OWG, my bots went into attack mode, and the clumsy citizens followed right along, labeling dissenters "racist, warmonger, boot licker, fascist, antisemite, homophobe, Islamaphobe," and a wide variety of other slanders. Most of the attacks didn't even make contextual sense, but it didn't matter to the fools spouting them when they felt that sweet endorphin rush of social media likes piling up on their comments.

The populace chose the side of peace, and they basked in the glow of their newfound virtue. No amount of politicking or debating was going to change their minds, and to try was to incite public rage. Penelope was right about them. They'd fight any war so long as they felt holy. They were the unhinged idiot majority, and the world would be better off with someone intelligent doing their thinking for them.

The days flew by leading up to New World's Eve as I lost myself in the work. Old systems and hierarchies were falling by the wayside as the cabinet of the new world government was staffed with people from all corners of the Earth. It was a blow to my ego to be left out of those conversations and positions, but I was plenty satisfied keeping my anonymity and privacy. I went content into the new year, knowing that Penelope would never let my efforts go unrewarded.

The fools took to partying in the streets on New World's Eve while I stayed hidden in my home, much as I always had. I opened a bottle of wine as I scanned from one boring broadcast news station to the next. Those who weren't bought and paid for were far too afraid to take any opposition to the future. Their biased and paralyzed coverage drove me back to Conspiriousity to check in on my old pal, Alexis X, who was live-streaming the event of the century.

"I don't even know what to say anymore. Welcome to the new world order, I guess," she said, dejected, from her basement studio. "It doesn't feel right to put a *called it* on this shit show of a situation. I've broadcast with my hair on fire more times than I can count, and this is the first time that I've felt genuinely terrified."

Alexis poured liquor from an unmarked bottle into a plastic, disposable cup, sipping it slowly between taking long puffs from her vape and blowing clouds of smoke into the webcam. "You guys want to see who did this to us? You're not going to believe this. It's almost comical," she said as she tapped on her keyboard and dropped a photo of me onto the screen, which caused my blood pressure to spike. It was an image of me in the OWG parking garage, getting into my car, followed by another of me driving.

"This little hellcat is Emilia Vera. On paper, she's an Argentinian immigrant who's been hooked up with the OWG as far back as I can trace. Under the flesh, however, she might legitimately be the devil. Check her out," she said as she zoomed in on my face. "She's all burned up like some damn Bond villain. You can't make this stuff up. Don't say I didn't warn you when she's the one pulling strings on ESG and digital currency soon. This is exactly the kind of person who would love to hang a social credit score on your neck and cut off your access to banking when you don't play by the rules. I'm telling you, she's bad news. If she was working with the Nazis in 1941, we'd all be speaking German right now. She makes Goebbels look like Willy Wonka."

Alexis poured another drink and turned her baseball cap backward. "All right, let's switch gears here for a minute and read some paid comments from the *Co-conspirators*," she said, referencing her fans who funded her show and paid to be a part of it. I couldn't have possibly cared less what those societal flunkies thought of me, but having my name and likeness in the open was enough to get me involved in the conversation out of fear alone. I typed a message of self-defense, coded in anonymity into the chat, sent the minimum of $25 to get it noticed, and sat back with bated breath.

"Okay, let's see here." Alexis scrolled through the flood of messages to choose from.

"*UnAmericaned* says, 'They can't take our country from us.' Sorry, my friend, but they already have," she read with her own commentary added on.

"*WellHung12in* says, 'Will you go out with me?' I don't know, big boy. Send me a dick pic and I'll get back to you," she laughed. "But seriously guys, for the love of God, don't send me dick pics. It's a joke."

"*Liberty4Life* says, 'That scarred-up bitch is going to come for our guns next.' I hate to say it, man, but you're probably right."

"*Pro-conspirator* says, 'Ending nuclear wars isn't a typical trait of villains.' Fair point, but you might be ignoring some key details."

"Okay, last one. *BulletsandBrainstems* says, 'Why did you blur out Emilia's license plate?' You guys are ruthless!" she laughed. "I appreciate the, ya know, steadfastness to justice and all; but I'm not doing that. Don't worry, she'll get what's coming to her. Nobody fucks with the deep state and gets away clean. Them boys over at Raytheon, Northrup Grumman, Boeing, and Lockheed Martin aren't going to take this lying down. That's an official Conspiriousity *called it.* There will be a reckoning."

Alexis was correct about the inevitable digital currency and social credit scores. She had been on my ass since the very beginning. One of the only outsiders who had a rich understanding of what was happening in the world. Was she right about the supposed deep state and the military-industrial compound as well I wondered?

What had I done? How could I have been so foolish to think myself invincible? Was I in control, or was I just another puppet of the organization who would take the fall when retribution came due?

Chapter 2

The Venn Diagram of Science and Faith
Malik Emmanuel

"Baby? What's the verdict? Should I wear the blue tie?" I shouted toward the bathroom.

"As opposed to what? The other color tie that you don't own?" Lydia chuckled back.

"Be serious. Tie or no?"

"You planning on wearing a tie on the space shuttle one day?" she asked as she entered the bedroom, held the tie to my neck, and then removed it to compare the looks.

"I've got to get the job first." I popped my collar and raised my chin suggestively.

"Lord help me, I married a child." She grinned as she draped one end around my neck and fastened the fashion accessory into place.

I put the sport jacket on and modeled my look in front of Lydia rather than the mirror. "Well? Whatya think?"

"You look like a bald President Obama," she snickered. "Very handsome," she added while straightening the tie with the jacket. "Mmmhmmm. You should let Mama Bear dress you more often. Nail this interview, and I'll undress you when you're done." She winked and gave a quick peck to my lips.

"Ooh, mama. Don't tease me." I playfully grabbed at her hips.

Lydia wiggled away from me and plopped down on the bed to lace up her sneakers. "I'll be back from the One World food drive around noon. Don't have lunch without me. We'll celebrate. No cereal and no syrup for the baby bear's breakfast."

"What about Papa Bear? I don't get no sugar?"

She got up off the bed, pulled a sweatshirt over her head, straightened her hair, and leaned in to give me another kiss. "That's all the sugar you're getting."

"It's all the sugar I need."

"All right, baby. I've got to go. You're going to do great. Good luck. I'll see you in a couple of hours. Love ya bad," she shouted as she rushed out of our bedroom.

"Love ya mad," I replied, as I had a thousand times before. Whether it was the moment after I dropped her off at home following our first date, or her leaving the room after thirteen years of marriage; I missed her the second she was gone.

Every breath was a gift from God, but the air only tasted sweet when I was sharing it with Lydia.

I knocked on consecutive doors as I passed through the hallway on my way to the kitchen. "Marcus? Maisie? I'm making breakfast. Bring your devotions to the table."

I fired up the stovetop and laid some bacon in the skillet. Before the aroma had reached the kid's bedrooms, I felt two little arms wrap around my leg. "Morning Maisie," I said without having to look down to see who was hugging me.

"Hi, Daddy. I want French toast!"

"No sugar this morning, baby. Go sit by your brother."

Marcus sat at the table, eyes barely open, resting his head in one hand. "Good morning, Marcus."

"Mmmm," he groaned.

"I'll make you some cheesy eggs if you read to your sister."

He picked his head up out of his hands and forced his eyes open. "Scrambled?"

"I wouldn't bribe you with over-easy."

Marcus pulled the chair with Maisie in it close to him and opened their children's devotional. I flipped the bacon, stirred the eggs, and listened in as he read the tale of Job to his little sister and concluded with a prayer.

I poured two glasses of milk and placed their breakfast in front of them. "Let's try to be quick, okay? I have that big interview this morning. I need you to keep an eye on Maisie while I'm busy. Can you do that for me?"

Marcus nodded his head in the affirmative and I could sense his mind was elsewhere. "I don't get this chapter of Job. Is this one of those stories that is made up to teach a lesson?"

"You mean a parable. As far as I've been taught, it's a true story. What don't you understand about it?" I was always excited when either of my children would take an active interest in their devotionals.

"Job is a good guy. He loves God and his family. He doesn't hurt anyone. Then God kills all his cows and fields and stuff. His family dies and Job gets really sick."

"I'm not sure if it's quite that bad." I tried to sugarcoat the adult themes the way the children's devotional had.

"I've read the Bible, Dad. That's what it said."

"Are you sure you're only twelve years old?"

"Be serious, Dad. Did God torture Job to prove a point to the devil?"

"It was a test of faith. Job praised God for the many blessings he received in life, and his faithfulness was never shaken when God took those things away. Everyone told Job to curse and forsake God, but he refused. In the end, his blessings were magnified. He had more children, cattle, crops, and riches than before because he maintained his faith."

"Yeah but, his kids. God like, collapsed a house on them. They didn't do nothing to nobody, and they died. Then Job gets new kids? I don't get it."

"We're not meant to understand everything, Marcus. There's a lesson in the story that is important though. Don't take your blessings for granted. Keep your faith strong regardless of what trials life presents you."

"I don't know. I think it's one of those parable things. It can't be a true story."

"You might be right. We can talk about it again later when your sister isn't around." I spent my life choosing faith and rejecting the questions the devil sought to plant in my mind. A single seed of doubt can grow into a tree that casts a dark shadow. I wasn't about to allow those seeds into my life or the minds of my impressionable children.

Marcus took Maisie to their rooms while I set up in the home office. My knee bounced with the anticipation of seeing the call come in from NASA that I had spent my whole life waiting for. I said a silent prayer for composure and acceptance of whatever God's will may be that was interrupted by the sound of the Zoom ring.

"Malik?" the interviewer asked. The beads of sweat that were marching to the front lines of a war on my forehead were stopped dead in their tracks when I saw a friendly black face on my screen. As a black man married to a white woman, I didn't view life through the same racial prism as many others had. Regardless, I felt relief to see someone that I had a skin-deep connection with, no matter how shallow it might be.

"Yes, sir. Thank you for seeing me today, sir."

"My pleasure. Let's get right into it, shall we? I'd like to review some items on your resume, starting with your time in the service. You're surprisingly low on flight hours. Can you elaborate on that please?"

"I assure you sir; my lack of logged flight hours isn't a testament to my skills as a pilot. I can navigate an F-16 Falcon with the best of them. What I can't do, however, is strike defenseless civilian targets. My superiors found me unfit to perform combat duties, so my wings were taken away. It's a principled Christian decision that has delayed my career, but one I've never regretted."

"I see. It says here you still received an honorable discharge in 2016. Mechanical engineering degree from the University of Arkansas in 2020. Then on to Lockheed Martin where you've been employed for twelve years. Aerospace division. Satellite missile defense systems," he read directly from my resume.

"That's correct. I was unfortunately part of the mass layoffs at Lockheed following New World's Eve. There's not much use for missile defense systems with war firmly in our rearview, you know what I mean?"

"That was almost four months ago," he stated with a tone of judgment. "You've been out of work since?"

"Yes, sir. I've passed on other opportunities because NASA is where I want to be. There's nothing I want more than to train to be an astronaut. It's been a dream of mine since childhood to feel zero gravity and look down on Earth from the upper atmosphere. To add my name to the list of Bluford, McNair, Bolden, Jemison, and my personal favorite, Victor Glover."

"Reciting a memorized list of black astronauts won't earn you any brownie points, Mr. Emmanuel."

"Have I said something to offend you?" I asked while shifting my posture.

"Frankly, I'm not buying the principled man of faith act. You're far short of the required flight hours that you claim were stripped from you because of your conscientious objection to war. Yet, once out of the service, you went to work for one of the largest military contractors in the United States. Something doesn't add up."

I took a deep, anxious breath while rubbing my clammy hands together. "I was only ever trying to build a resume for this moment, sir," I said with less respect than before. "The Venn Diagram of war and faith features more overlap than one might think. Actions can be taken to save lives. Not every mission puts the innocent in harm's way. Heck, the missile defense systems that I built helped maintain peace."

"Do you know what the Venn Diagram of faith and science looks like?" he asked while raising his hands into camera view, balling them into fists, and crashing them into each other. "There's no overlap. They're polar opposites. Water and oil."

"I can promise you, sir, my faith won't impact my ability to pilot a spacecraft. Nor will it stifle my passion to pursue my dreams. And if I may speak freely, I find it inappropriate to discuss as a qualifying factor," I said, my voice raised.

"Look, Malik. You've applied nine times. You don't have the required flight hours. You haven't piloted anything in over a decade. You're on the wrong side of forty. You're an unemployed engineer with a history of standing down in the face of a challenge. NASA's available spots for training are limited by our own questions of funding, and we have no guarantees from the OWG that we'll receive continued support. The best I can do is keep your name on file. A day may come when we're looking for good engineers."

"I see," I lamented through pursed lips to hide my disappointment. "I appreciate you seeing me today," I lied and was cut off by the call terminating on his end.

Twenty years of careful preparation undone in five minutes. I had pushed the first block out of a sturdy Jenga tower, and the structure collapsed in on itself. I paced the room, running my hands through my nonexistent hair, wondering how that went so poorly. Could I apply again? Maybe if I spoke to someone else, they would give me a chance. Was I truly too old to enter the program? Did I cost myself this opportunity? The urge to close my laptop and jar it into the drywall like an axe to a tree was overwhelming.

I sat down, unclenched my fists, made prayer hands, and asked for the Holy Spirit to bring me calm. "Show me your will above my own, Lord," I prayed. Every effort to control my breathing and find my center was pointless with the anger so fresh.

I slammed the door behind me before jolting up the stairs, skipping one with each paced jump. The music coming from Maisie's room was pounding loudly from behind her closed door, and it only served to annoy me further. I swung the door open prepared to give my children a tongue-lashing for whatever trouble they were getting into while unsupervised.

There sat my two angels on the floor. A hundred Lego pieces spread out between them as they worked on assembling a project together. "No, Daddy! It's not done," Maisie stood and shouted with her tiny arms spread to hinder my view. I picked her up by the armpits, cradled her against my chest, and instantly felt the pressure release from my shoulders when she naturally hugged me.

"It's a space shuttle, or at least it will be," Marcus explained. "Mom got it for you as a surprise."

"Did she now?" I lowered Maisie to the floor, turned down the volume on the Al Green blaring through the radio, and sat next to my babies. My eyes rolled to look upwards, and I gave a knowing nod to God above. His message was received. "You kids put it together, and I'll help if you need it."

Having my dreams dashed should have made for one of the worst days of my life, and yet somehow, I had never been happier. We laughed and played for the better part of an hour before hearing Lydia's footsteps on the stairs.

"Well, if this isn't the most adorable thing in the world," she said, standing in the doorway. "How did it go? Are we celebrating?"

"How was the food drive?" I asked, changing the subject.

"It was incredible! Turnout of at least a thousand. You were right about the OWG. They're doing some good stuff in the community. There's a lot of new hope on people's faces. Hi baby," Lydia said to Maisie, who was tugging at her shirt. "Who's hungry? Let's get some lunch."

The kids raced down the stairs ahead of us, and Lydia took my hand to hold me back. "You okay?"

"Yeah. I'm actually great. I have everything I could ever want."

"You're a...you know." She smiled and wiped a single tear away from her eye. "I love you," she said through a crying laugh.

"Love me bad or mad?" I joked as I gently touched the side of her face.

"Neither. Both."

"Yeah, I'm pretty great," I quipped sarcastically. "Come on. Let's cut up some hot dogs, throw them in macaroni and cheese, and eat like the royalty that we are."

I went to bed that night at peace with God's will and every intention of finding another job. The work might not put me on the path for a walk on the moon, but it would provide for my family. I woke the next morning not to the sounds of my alarm, but to a cocktail of tornado and police sirens outside. I rolled over to find Lydia's side of the bed cold and empty, and the smell of breakfast wafting into the room.

I rubbed the sleep out of my eyes, tossed on my robe, and found my crew in the kitchen. Lydia worked the stovetop, and the kids sat at the table. "What's with the early morning test of the emergency broadcast signal? Is there a storm blowing in?"

"Oh, sweetie. I was trying to let you sleep in," Lydia lamented while stirring the skillet. "I don't know what's going on out there, but we're having eggs and sausage in here."

"Look, Daddy. I cut myself," Maisie said, holding up her hand and showing me a large bandage on her palm.

"Baby, what did you do? When did this happen?"

She peeled the bandage off to expose no wound underneath, giggled hysterically, and said, "April fools."

"You think you're pretty smart, don't ya?"

"Yes!" Marcus cheered with his face buried in his phone. "School is canceled. Is it okay if I eat breakfast and go back to bed?"

"Hardy-har, funny guy. Your sister beat you to the April fool's punch. You know the rule with phones at the table."

"I'm serious. Look," he said, turning his screen to show the notification on the school website. "It's the comet cancellation."

"Everybody, bring your plates. Breakfast is ready," Lydia announced.

"Babe, what is this? You see the news this morning?"

"It's a comet," Marcus explained with Maisie repeating after him without having a clue what she was talking about.

I filled my plate and rushed into the living room to turn on the TV, and that was all the invitation the kids needed to follow suit. "Oh come on, guys. Not in front of the TV," Lydia shouted.

"Here you can see satellite imagery of the anomaly as it passes by Venus," the newswoman said as they cut to a grainy video of a silver streak cutting through the dark of space. "What do you make of this, Dr. Keith?" she asked the expert on the panel.

"NASA says it's a comet and the OWG scientists claim it's an asteroid. I don't see how either of these explanations can be accurate. The sheer speed alone makes either assumption highly unlikely."

"Can you confirm the accuracy of the trajectory that NASA is reporting?" she asked.

"Our calculations match those that NASA has released. The anomaly is on a direct course for Earth if it holds its current course."

"We'd like to reiterate, please do not panic. We have no official confirmation of what the anomaly is or if it will impact. Please stay in your homes, remain calm, and stay tuned."

"What's going on?" Lydia asked as she bit from a single sausage link on the end of a fork.

"I uh, I don't know," I said, masking my concern for the sake of the children. "They're calling it *the anomaly*, and they think it's headed for Earth."

"Twitter says it's going to be here late tonight," Marcus chimed in.

"Tonight?" I gasped. "That's not possible. They said it was near Venus. That's a hundred and sixty million miles away. It would have to be moving a hundred times faster than a meteor. That can't be right."

The emergency whistle stopped, but there was a constant echo of police and ambulance sirens coming from multiple directions. I peeled back the living room curtains a few inches to find the neighbors on all sides frantically packing up their cars.

I quickly pulled the curtains back and turned off the TV which drew an angry look from Marcus. "Everybody, finish your breakfast. Marcus, when you're done, pack an overnight bag and help Maisie do the same."

"Where are we supposed to go?" Lydia asked with her mouth full and not a care in the world. "We have a doomsday bunker that I don't know about? It's not like we can survive if a meteor comes crashing into Earth."

"That's no meteor. It's something else." I stopped short of expressing my theories for the sake of our children's sanity. "We're going to pack some batteries, flashlights, radio, clothes, food, and the first aid kit. We can hole up at church with our community."

That's exactly what we did, and we weren't alone. The church parking lot was half full by the time we arrived. There were fifty congregation members huddled into small groups in the foyer, with another fifty in the worship hall. "Your kids can go downstairs. There are some adults looking after them in the Sunday school rooms," a patron directed as we entered.

"Our kids are fine, thank you very much," I replied, holding Maisie in my arms while Lydia held Marcus's hand. "Let's set up in one of the pews for now," I said as Lydia led us into the worship hall. We claimed a spot near the back and rested our bags on both sides of us with Maisie and Marcus sitting between us.

It wasn't midday yet, and the sun was pouring through the stained-glass windows. The images of Christ, his disciples, Abraham, and Moses were illuminated in radiant color from the daylight, but they didn't fill the church with the same hope as a Sunday service. Some of the congregation was in prayer while others were quietly sharing theories of the doom hurtling towards us in space. Up front, the projector screen was being lowered as the hum of the organ played familiar hymns. Normally, the screen would be filled with lyrics to guide the voices in singing along, but today it was showcasing a local news broadcast covering the event. There was no volume and some of us read along with the captions at the bottom of the screen.

"We still know frighteningly little about the anomaly. While NASA and OWG scientists can confirm the speed and trajectory, we remain in the dark about its size and point of origin. What we do know, however, is that if the anomaly holds its current course, it will directly impact Earth somewhere in the Atlantic Ocean around 2:15 a.m. EST," the scrolling text read. The screen was filled with images of still shots of the streak of light and videos of rioting and violence in the streets.

"You suppose the dinosaurs would have robbed their local 7-11 if they saw a space rock coming to kill them?" a woman sitting behind us asked her husband.

Marcus popped up on his knees in the pew and turned to engage them. "It's not a meteor. My Dad says it's moving too fast. It's a spaceship," he declared.

"It's the Minimal Falcon," Maisie added, with the *Millennium* getting jumbled up on her young tongue.

"Oh, sweet child, I don't think that's real," the woman replied kindly, trying to not overstep her boundaries.

"The kids are probably right," I said lowly without averting my gaze from the news stream. "It's standard scientific reduction of probabilities."

"That's crazy," the husband replied. "Unless I missed it in the chapter of Genesis, God didn't create any little green men."

"If they exist, then God absolutely did create them," Lydia said confidently, speaking to the couple even though her comforting words were meant for our children. "There's no chapter about God creating plastics or viruses or yogurt either, but they exist all the same. All things spring from the Father." Her faith was as unshakable as the base of a mountain in an earthquake and was the very foundation upon which we had built our family. Most of humanity saw the news that day and reverted to their most primal form. Panic, fear, and chaos consumed them. Their truest colors were exposed with the binds of consequence cut, but not my Lydia. She was authentically her same, beautiful self.

Lydia remained our rock all day as we counted down the hours toward whatever it was that was coming. The afternoon and evening were filled with worship, singing, positive leadership from our pastor, and conspiracy theories from those who were having their faith tested. The sun had long gone down before we received what felt like our thousandth breaking news report, only that time there was something significant worth reporting.

Most of the congregation had settled into the sanctuary when the audio feed was unmuted. "The anomaly has drastically slowed its speed, and we have our first good look at it," the reporter said as a frame-by-frame video played. The object appeared to be blocky in shape with a narrowing tipped nose at one end. It was silver in color and was surrounded by a glassy aura like a calm lake that had a single stone skipping across the surface. It was no shooting star or chunk of space rock. The *anomaly* was something that had been manufactured.

"Who had *first contact* on their 2033 bingo card?" I asked playfully to those sitting near us, and only Lydia was particularly impressed with my sense of humor.

"They waited for us to destroy our nukes before they attacked," someone shouted. If there was a logical and well-rationed response, it wasn't being heard over the increasing chatter amongst us.

"Please, everyone. Quiet. Don't let fear take you," our pastor wisely counseled, to little avail.

Uncertainty had tempered panic all day, but the threat coming into focus had unleashed it. I wasn't about to let that terror grip my children. I sat Maisie on my lap and squished Marcus tightly between myself and Lydia. I put my arm around him and my hand on Lydia's shoulder, which she covered comfortingly with her own. "There is absolutely nothing to be afraid of. We are God's children, and He will never abandon us."

We huddled together tightly for at least an hour as the craft continued its approach with slowing speeds until it finally came to a stop in Earth's outer atmosphere. The news estimated that the ship was the size of a professional football stadium. It was square in shape with the edges and corners rounded into the same smooth surface as the rest of the craft. What could only be assumed as the front quarter came to a shrinking point that ended with a spear-like tip. Judging by man-made designs, the sheer bulk of the hull suggested that it was a freighter or an alien version of an aircraft carrier.

It didn't hover there long before panels on the lower half rolled back. The glassy aura surrounding the craft disappeared momentarily as a much smaller ship emerged and dropped into its own flight toward the surface of the planet. It was cylinder in shape with both ends coming to similar tips like the carrier craft, and the tone of the hull suggested that it was manufactured from the same silver alloy.

The floating tree trunk entered free fall into our atmosphere and piloted its way toward eastern Europe. The glassy aura was far less present and could only be seen momentarily when light from Earth refracted against it. The ship entered British airspace unabated while what little unified military presence we had on the ground mobilized in defense of a strike.

We watched on from our sanctuary with the rest of the world as the log lowered into a hover over London before finally coming to a stop near the OWG headquarters. It settled into place ten feet above the ground and was immediately surrounded by tanks, armed soldiers, and swarming press who delivered the images of our first contact moment.

Panels on the side that were otherwise undetectable separated vertically from each other. There was no steam, bright lights, or a slow-moving ramp like in the movies. Three creatures emerged side by side, which were quickly met by spotlights and gun barrels aimed in their direction. Their bodies and heads were egg-shaped ovals with a short neck connecting the two. They had two eyes that were separated so wide that they were almost on the sides of their heads. They had no apparent nose or ears, but their mouth placement was like that of a humanoid, except for it being lower on a triangular-shaped jaw.

They were dressed in some sort of skintight-powered suit that propelled them effortlessly three feet off the ground. The maneuverability of the suit freed up the use of their three triple-jointed legs. At the end of each limb were four equal-length fingers. If they were to be without their gravity-defying tech, they could stand at least ten feet tall or as low as three feet with all their leg joints bent.

The suits covered everything but their heads, which revealed their yellowish-hue skin tone. They stood there, in front of thousands in person and billions via broadcast, without a single word to say. Their mouths remained closed as they hovered and examined their surroundings. Tensions were rising in the church, and I could only imagine what everyone was feeling who was seeing this firsthand.

After a couple of minutes of a hair-raising standoff, the soldiers began lowering their weapons in unison. Men popped out of the top hatches of tanks and the field reporters on hand silenced their whispered commentary. A brave emissary from the OWG walked forward cautiously before extending his hand as a human greeting. The creature on the far left mirrored the sentiment and our representative took hold of three of the four fingers and gave it a shake. It lowered itself to meet at eye level and leaned its forehead forward while waiting for the emissary to mirror in return in what seemed like their customary greeting.

Before the representative could complete a greeting with all three of them, a female soldier's face appeared on our screen with her hands gripping the lens of the camera. "It's okay! It's going to be okay! Did you feel that? Did everyone feel it? They mean us no harm!" she exclaimed before the camera operator wrestled control away from her. We watched her wipe tears away from her face before the camera was turned back to its intended target.

There was an audible sigh of relief in the church that was like the gasping of the first breath of air after having your head held underwater. The coverage lasted long into the morning hours after our extraterrestrial visitors were whisked away inside the OWG headquarters. Most of the congregation went home, but once Maisie had fallen asleep against my chest and Marcus with his head laid in Lydia's lap; we were planted for the night.

There was no refraining from being glued to the television when we returned home in the morning. The kids had hundreds of questions that I didn't have the answers to, and the media had left us on the edge of our seats. Once a press conference was announced for 1 p.m. that afternoon, I was finally able to pull everyone away. Marcus and Maisie each took a bath, and Lydia and I had a shower. We prepared cold sandwiches for lunch and reconvened on the couch as a family to hear what information was fit to print.

A well-dressed woman took the podium in London to address the hundreds of members of the press. She read her speech directly from the pages in front of her, only looking up at the crowd with brief breaks to give everyone a chance to digest before moving on.

"Citizens of Earth. As you know, we were visited by an alien life form last night. Our new friends are called the Praxi and they hail from their home world Prius."

"They named their planet after a Toyota," I smirked at Lydia who chuckled at my observation.

"Maybe they wanted to call their home world *BMW M series*, but the name wouldn't stick," she bantered back.

"Dad! Shhhh," Marcus demanded.

"Prius is the fifth planet of six in their solar system and is home to over two million life forms. The ambassadors who arrived last night traveled for over two months from the other side of our galaxy. They informed OWG leadership through empathy-based telepathy communication that they had long monitored mankind. It was only once we exhibited a change in our warring ways that they sent their welcoming party."

"We have made a peace accord with the Praxi, and they have agreed to help ensure that we won't backslide as a civilization. The Praxi have achieved gravity-controlling power by combining the power of their sun and their most precious resource, triaxum. Effective immediately, they will begin unloading parts and fuel to construct a *Jump Point* in Earth's orbit. Praxi scientists will teach our engineers to assemble this technology to create a portal between our two planets and link us forever. Once constructed, the Jump Point will expedite travel time to mere days rather than the months that separate us with traditional space travel."

"We will be given access to a limited amount of triaxum and taught how to use it to attain energy independence. This technological advancement will forever change our health and agriculture industries, along with many others. In return, all the Praxi ask for is volunteers to aid in the mining of their rare mineral."

"Don't even think about it," Lydia pointed at me.

"Once supplies are unloaded, the mother ship will return to Praxi to share the good news and prepare the next cargo shipment with parts to finish the Jump Point. In the meantime, we're calling upon any skilled metallurgists and engineers to join us in London to assist in the assembly process. You may apply on the OWG website or follow the link provided on social media."

I had my phone unlocked to research these positions before Lydia could strike me down as the spokeswoman opened the floor to questions from the press. "Lyds, look at this," I forwarded the link to her phone. "They're going to convert an old London naval base as the HQ for operations and assembly. Barracks provided as housing, free of charge."

"Really, Malik?" she asked with a defeated tone. "London? You know I hate flying."

"It would be one trip. We'd stay there for four months and come back when it's done."

"What about Marcus for school?"

"I'll read a million books, Mom. Whatever you want. The aliens are going to be there. We have to go. Please," Marcus begged.

"It's the last few weeks of the school year. We'd be there for the summer. Baby, look at the pay. Did you see the pay? I'll get you a Prius," I teased with a sing-song tone.

"You can keep the Prius. For this kind of money, I'll take the M Series. Black. Convertible."

"Is that a yes or a well-played joke?" I raised an eyebrow.

"Both. I really don't need the car though, babe. I know how bad you want this, and I suppose I can stomach a few months of bad British food and a couple flights."

"I love you bad baby," I exclaimed as I sat up to kiss her forehead.

"I must be mad, because I love you too."

I submitted my resume and had an offered position within a day. A week later, we packed our bags and made the trip to London. The OWG set us up with two rooms in the barracks, which weren't exactly the Hilton, but we were good in tight spaces.

I was assigned to Ring Team 4 with a group of other engineers. Our assignment was to assemble fifteen equal brackets that would be hauled into space to form a two-mile beam which would be connected to the other seventy-eight pieces to form the superstructure.

People on the base had begun referring to the Praxi as *the grays*, a name commonly associated with alien visitors by UFO enthusiasts, even though the Praxi looked nothing like the stereotypical description. We knew that the alien scientists were somewhere in London with us, but they never showed their faces, and this further added to the lore around them that we fabricated. They didn't even have meetings with the construction team leaders to teach us ring assembly. Contact with the Praxi was strictly limited to OWG leadership, and they, in turn, fed instructions to us laborers.

We worked tirelessly on the project without a single section being sent back after inspection. One by one, all our completed brackets were hauled into space, where they were being fit into place. I wanted to get up there so badly, but I wasn't about to complain. In my mind, it would only be a matter of time before humans were constructing new-age flight crafts and selling vacation packages to Prius.

As the days went by, the Jump Point grew larger in the night sky. Months evaporated in a flash, and one day at the end of July, deep space scans picked up a fleet of Praxi craft returning to Earth. There were ambassadors and dignitaries amongst them, but their embassy was strictly off-limits to citizens. It was months after our first contact event, and there wasn't a single person without a high-security clearance who had access to our new friends. We had a million questions, but there was only one that was pressing. Whether religious or secular, everyone wanted an answer on God and our creation. I was steadfast in my faith when Marcus would press me on the subject, and I covertly hoped that the secretive nature surrounding our visitors would hold long enough for me to avoid the answer until I was ready for it.

The first time the Jump Point powered up was quite the spectacle. The region was cleared as the structure channeled the power of our sun. It illuminated the night sky with a gorgeous, glowing, purple hue through every quadrant of connecting beams. It looked like we had a pulsating, neon, grape halo capped on our dusty ball of dirt. When fully charged, the center of the sphere filled with vibrant waves of violet.

Testing followed soon after with unmanned crafts carrying various forms of life back and forth. Two days to Prius and two days back was the travel time. Single-cell organisms, plant life, and animals had all survived their trips with little calibration needed. It eventually came time for a human to make a testing voyage, and even though the Gray scientists assured the OWG of safety, it was difficult to find a volunteer.

Before it came to drawing straws, a brave Indian Air Force pilot named Ranbir Chopra volunteered. He was the storybook image of a prince-charming hero.

Ranbir stood tall at 6'2" and carried himself with an upright confident posture. His styled black hair was wavy from left to right, and it was so dark that you would think he was coloring it if everything else about him wasn't so flawless. His smile was disarming and mischievous, and he used it often in conjunction with his boyish dimples and sharp blue eyes to win over the entire world, women especially. He was fit like a man whose workout regime was all glamour muscles and no core. I fancied myself as attractive, but there's no way the public would have rallied around me the way that they did to Ranbir.

His most charming feature wasn't his appearance though. It was his dog, Amir. A brown and white beagle with floppy ears and pouting eyes who went everywhere with Ranbir. The two of them became folk heroes overnight. Ranbir only had two conditions to accept his role as our test dummy. The first was that he be allowed to be the primary pilot of the craft with his Gray scientist counterpart Gio serving as co-pilot, and the second was that Amir be allowed to fly with them. Ranbir was a man who knew how to play to his audience.

The family and I went to the tarmac the afternoon the three of them boarded their ship and rocketed it off into space. "Just think, Marcus, in two days they're going to be on the other side of the galaxy." I shuttered my eyes from the sun while watching the craft zip out of sight.

'We're going to get our chance too, right?"

"I certainly hope so, my boy," I replied with my arm around him. "Ranbir and Amir will be back in four days. Make sure you give them a warm welcome home without me, okay?"

"Let's just go home, babe," Lydia said. "We don't need to be here when they get back, and you did your job. There's no more sightseeing to do in London, and I think the bloody accent is starting to take hold," she said comically, affecting her best British impersonation. "I'm ready to put my feet back on Arkansas soil."

"Yeah, Daddy. Let's go home," Maisie echoed from her mother's arms.

"One last thing to do, sweetie," I said as I kissed Maisie's forehead. "Daddy is going to go help some farmers make their machines better so that everyone has enough food to eat. I'll be back in a week, and then we can all go home together."

"This is the last thing? You promise?" Lydia asked.

"The last thing. I won't ask for anything else forever. I'll stay home all day if you want. It will be nothing but breakfast in bed, foot massages, and warm bubble baths for you. Promise."

"I'm going to hold you to that," Lydia said with her trademark finger point and a forced smile.

"Look after your mother and sister," I directed to Marcus. "I'll be back in London on Tuesday." I kissed each of them goodbye, told them I loved them, and walked to the hangar to join my team for our work trip into the English countryside.

There's a false sense of security that settles in when things are going your way. It's easy to forget the humbling nature of a powerful storm after experiencing thirty days of sunshine. The metaphorical clouds were rolling in, and God didn't afford me the same luxury as Noah. There would be no ark to carry the faithful to safety once the rain started falling. Leaving my family behind for the sake of one last project was an innocent mistake, and there was no way to foresee that it would be the genesis of God's Job-like tests for me.

Chapter 3

Nerves of Splintered Steel

Alexis X

Late again. Ugh. I tossed my phone into the passenger seat of my rusted-out Pontiac Grand Prix to give parallel parking the old college try. The clock on the dashboard read 6:27, which meant I had exactly three minutes to twist into a parking spot before I was officially thirty minutes late. The first attempt was an epic failure, so I pulled out to give it another go. The dashboard clock flipped over to 6:28 and the front quarter of my shit box of a car was sticking out into traffic. Close enough. I twisted the rear-view mirror down to take one last look at myself, fixed my ponytail, and gave myself an encouraging "ugh." It's beyond me why I continued to date. I had a better chance of executing a flawless parallel park job than turning a one-night stand into a two-day affair.

I ran across the street dodging cross traffic with my phone in hand. I hit play to resume the video I'd been watching while driving as I rushed toward the pizza parlor. I heard someone yell "Miss, your car is going to get hit," to which I shouted back "Just leave a note," as I burst through the door.

6:29 on my phone, and I scanned the room looking for Andrew. There he was, sitting alone with his tie loosened, sports coat over his chair, and an empty beer bottle. "Andrew?" I asked as I introduced myself, "I'm Alexis. Hi!"

"You're thirty minutes late and..."

"Nuh uh uh. Twenty-nine minutes late. Look," I said as I flashed him my phone. 6:30. Fuck! "Okay, fine. Thirty minutes late. I'm so sorry. I hope you didn't do all *this* for me," I waved a finger at his formal attire. "Did you come here straight from work?" I made small talk as I settled into my chair across from him.

"Yeah. I work as a loan officer over at Chase. What do you do?" He graciously bounced the verbal banter back to me even though his posture could be best categorized as annoyed.

"Have you seen this?" I twisted my phone to an angle on the table where we both could watch it. I hit play to continue the video of reporting on Ranbir and Amir returning to Earth. "OWG is moving them from London to a facility in Oxford right now. Crazy son of bitch probably has sixteen types of radiation poisoning from going through that portal. Or worse, he'll get chest burst like Kane while eating horrible hospital food."

Andrew looked confused by my reference before continuing to express his displeasure. "Yeah. I've seen the news. I had thirty minutes to kill."

"Right." I offered a diffusing smile. "Anyways. What do I do? I host a podcast where I dig into government cover-ups, conspiracies, UFOs, and generally anything the legacy media won't touch. Or wouldn't touch. Turns out, when aliens land in broad daylight suddenly it's a story. Those uppity boobs are usually too busy polishing their Pulitzers to cover *real* stories. I'm telling you, they're nothing but propaganda chop shops. They sell the politically or financially viable pieces of information and trash the rest. Anyway, you've been waiting and you're probably hungry. Shall we order?"

An ad popped up on my screen mid-video stream, and I hovered my finger over the five-second countdown button to skip past it, which I mashed at the first opportunity. I navigated away from the video source and opened the notes tab on my phone to add Huggies diapers to my list of boycotted advertisers.

"What's that all about?" he asked.

"I refuse to purchase from any company that places ads in the middle of videos. If you're going to interrupt what I'm doing, you're never going to get my money, ya know? So, I keep a list."

"You're a YouTube streamer, and you don't pay for Premium? You know you can go ad-free, right?"

"Premium is for suckers. You're not a sucker, are you, Andrew? Threatening me with ads that diminish the user experience isn't my idea of good customer service. If they want my money, they gotta earn it. So, what are you thinking? You want to split a pie?"

"I think I'm actually going to go." He collected his coat from the chair.

"Hey, come on, Andrew. Let's get some pizza. I swear I'm not crazy."

"Aaron. My name is Aaron! You can't even get that right. You show up thirty minutes late. You look like you just rolled out of bed. Are you even wearing makeup? I'm *so* not interested."

"Whatever, Andrew. You go." I paused to search for the searing last words of the exchange. "You're not interested? You didn't even get my *Alien* reference! I'm not interested!"

Publicly embarrassed again. What else was new? I should have known better than to venture out of my recording studio cave. As Alexis, I was clumsy, anxious, neurotic, and nerdy. Getting through a day without burning my breakfast or cursing in front of someone's children was worthy of a gold star. As Alexis X, I was assertive, capable, and ambitious. A fierce warrior of truth, draped in the armor of a wireless headset and hot mic. Neither persona existed without the other, and I'd need to merge the super geek with the superhero if I was ever going to be my true self.

I'd been recording daily podcasts for almost ten years when the nuclear warhead exploded. At the time, I was obsessed with the OWG and their positioning in global politics. They made no attempt to hide the fact that they sought to take over the world. They were saying the quiet part out loud, which caused people to be less curious. It's insane to me that a global cabal can meet yearly and publicly declare, "We're going to elevate our young leaders into political offices all over the world," and the citizens respond with, "meh." It was right out there in the open, and the only way people were going to care was if it was scandalous.

I had done three months of digging into the OWG and their Young Leaders before I discovered Emilia Vera. You wouldn't find her on the ballot for a Congressional seat, and she wasn't listed on the OWG's website as a partner. I noticed her in a ten-year-old group photo of a Young Leaders graduate class and found it suspicious that everyone was tagged but Emilia and a slender white woman whom I had seen in other OWG photos. Emilia was some variety of South American. Gorgeous, dark hair falling just below her jawline that paired well with her sun-kissed complexion. Underneath her hair, which held tight to her face, was a scar that covered from her right cheek to chin. Regardless of the scar, she was pretty in the photo, but it was a fabricated brand of beauty. She was the type to pair the appropriate heels, blazer, makeup, and jewelry into a perfect symbiotic partnership of fraud. I doubt she ever had an *Andrew* walk out on her, but they might if they saw who she was instead of who she was pretending to be.

She couldn't have been a day over twenty at the time of the photo, and it didn't appear that the organization was grooming her for political office. This made no sense and was a huge red flag. She was young, polished, and Ivy League-educated. What the hell were they using her for? I tracked her down to the Chicago OWG field office and started tailing her. She left her home by 7 a.m. every morning, and she looked like she had been up since 4. This bitch had a workout, filmed a makeup tutorial, and prepared a healthy breakfast most days before I had thought about coffee. I would camp out in my car every morning down the street with a greasy breakfast sandwich waiting for her pretty ass to come rolling down the driveway.

Emilia never missed a day of work, and that's not hyperbole. She was a machine! She wouldn't even leave the compound for lunch. The rest of her co-workers would stuff their faces downtown on ninety-minute breaks, and Emilia never joined them. Most days she would walk to the parking garage to eat alone in her car. The building would start clearing out around 5 p.m. every day, and I can't remember her ever being out of there before 7.

Once home for the night, that was the last I'd see of her. She would grab packages off her front stoop and wouldn't poke her head out until morning. I tried tracking her online, but Emilia had the intentioned quiet absence from social media like a B-list celebrity in rehab after uttering racial slurs during a DUI arrest. I found Emilia's Facebook by hunting down her parents in Buenos Aires, who had but two pictures of her on their page. Her profile had zero information, no photos, and her parents were her only friends. I'd never seen someone so in need of a good lay, and she didn't even have a dating profile. As far as I could tell, she was completely isolated and cared only for herself.

My first thought was that the OWG had made a breakthrough in AI technology. She had the cold, sociopathic demeanor that you'd expect from an android, but she was entirely too narcissistic to be synthetic. The OWG politicians were dangerous, but they had nothing on Emilia. It was her total lack of political convictions that made her poisonous. Her special project was indoctrinating and recruiting teachers to push ideology that she didn't even seem to believe in herself. She was manipulating the public nonstop, and for the life of me, I couldn't understand why she did it. If her motivation was money, I was going to be supremely disappointed. I hated everything she stood for, and I wanted her to be the monster I had made her out to be in my mind.

All my attention was focused on finding who was working for her, the calls they were making, and the campuses they were visiting. This was the OWG story that could finally wake people up. "Globalist Senator wins dirty election," wasn't a headline that caught people's attention. "Sexy sociopath OWG robot indoctrinates children," would do the trick, however. I was ready to knife fight her in the streets if that's what it took. Unfortunately, I'd never get my chance. The Praxi arrived, and I didn't have a single ounce of energy left over to hunt down my prey.

Aliens! Real-life creatures from outer space. Easily the greatest day of my life. I had big I-told-you-so energy. I was so petty about my validation that I went through my old UFO YouTube videos to reply to people who made negative comments years prior. Should I leave the, "This bitch is crazy," comment from six years ago alone? Yeah, probably. Was I going to? Absolutely not! I was serving crow with a side of, "Suck my lady balls." It took a while, but the victory lap did eventually wear off and I had to get back to business.

From the lead-up to New World's Eve through the arrival of the Grays, I was working non-stop, sometimes filming three episodes per day. Someone had to ask the questions that the media was ignoring. We were calling them the Grays, but they looked nothing like the aliens people claimed to have encountered in the past. None of their craft even resembled the footage captured by Naval pilots and tracking systems. Was that the Praxi all along? Was there something else out there that we didn't know about, and they weren't telling us? I was posing these questions and hundreds more, but nobody seemed to be listening.

The novelty of aliens visiting Earth had worn off for most people. They weren't interested in the wonders of the unknown. They did what they always do. Got caught up in hero-worshiping the hottest new celebrity. Ranbir and his pooch Amir were front-page news, and I can't say that I minded. The man had everything that people adored. Good looks, a great smile, confidence, swagger, and the cutest damn dog you're ever going to see. He had it all. Then he goes and volunteers to become the first human intergalactic traveler.

Normally, my pessimism would have convinced me that Ranbir was going to return with a third arm growing out of his ass because of a black hole miscalibration. It would have made for a great story, but I think we all knew he was going to be fine. Guys who look and smile like that are bulletproof. And wouldn't you know it, he returned safely from a successful mission to space while I was having a crash landing of a first date.

Everything seemed fine and I had no story. It was August 11, 2033, and I was taking my first night off in a long time. The sounds of the original score of the film *Interstellar* were filling my dilapidated two-bedroom rental in Joliet, Illinois while I prepared one of the few home-cooked meals that I can remember. It was a peaceful evening right up until the moment that it wasn't.

My phone started blowing up around 8:30 p.m. One missed message. Then two, three, a missed call, and a voicemail. Then another call. Finally, I angrily answered it. "What? What the heck do you want, Fitzy? You know I'm not recording tonight for the first..." before he cut me off.

"Alex! Turn on the TV," he interrupted. The fright in his voice made it nearly unrecognizable, which was enough to scare the hell out of me.

There it was in big, bold, letters in the chyron. **LONDON DESTROYED**. There were no live feeds from inside the city examining buildings with the windows blown out and tattered bricks holding structures in place. No fires and sirens with emergency workers rushing in to help the wounded. No interior impact zone with the suburbs barely standing on the outskirts. The only footage available was coming from drones flying into the impacted area. There was no way to tell where a hospital, school, or skyscraper had once stood.

The crater was miles wide. It was at its deepest point in the center and became gradually shallower in every direction like a fading ripple from a boulder thrown into a lake. The full extent of the damage was impossible to assess with the sheer amount of dust in the air.

I didn't have a moment to process what was happening and who was doing it to us before the coverage flipped. Next was Moscow. The early images might as well have been from London. The scene was the same. A city with twelve million people. Gone. Nothing but a crater in the ground and a dust cloud blanketing the carnage remained.

Then it was Buenos Aires. Three major commercial metros on different continents in a matter of minutes. This was about the time that I collapsed to the floor having a panic attack that I thought would kill me long before I got cratered like those other poor bastards. I was shaking uncontrollably when the coverage swung over to General Kelly attempting to address the world. "Take shelter and find comfort in prayer. The Praxi and the OWG have betrayed us, but God never will. Love each other and fight li.." was as much as he could muster before the feed decayed into static.

My body went warm as my heart raced at an inhuman pace. Every panic attack feels like certain death, but there are some where you can slowly talk your mind off the ledge. This was not one of those. This was the make-your-peace-with-God variety. My body convulsed like an electrical current was running through me as I pinned my arms to my chest. Every calming thought of controlling my breathing was drowned out by the nightmare that was unfolding. My brain manifested pain in my left arm to further convince me that a non-existent heart attack was about to cripple me. I began yawning uncontrollably, which was one of my subconscious supposed cures for snowballing down Anxiety Mountain.

The next thirty minutes in my mind are as dust-covered as the cities that lay in ruin. Delhi, Shanghai, Washington DC, Tokyo, São Paulo, and Paris. One after another being reported as destroyed. There were over one hundred million feared dead before we had the first footage of our attackers. There were no less than nine Praxi attack vessels, with none of them being larger than a B-52 Bomber. Examining the craft footage on my TV screen was strangely the only thing that pulled me out of my catatonic state.

The Grays appeared to be using three different models of attack ships in their assault. A large, cube-shaped bomber, a saucer-like sphere, and the third looked like the flying pencil that had landed in London months ago. The latter two were shockingly small to be delivering such devastating payloads. They weren't showing up on any tracking systems and there didn't seem to be a counterattack of any kind being launched.

The military reaction was swift, but they might as well have been going at it with swords and shields compared to what we were up against. The only thing our fighter jets were good for was acting as reconnaissance. Their recording systems would occasionally catch a stream of light shooting across the sky that indicated who might be next to get hit.

The attack shifted from leveling cities to surgical strikes. The best footage was coming from people on the ground near a target who were either brave enough to capture the moment or smart enough to understand there was nowhere to run.

The ships attacking the United States were working their way around the east coast. They hit New York City first, and this is where we got our first look at their weapons. One of the pencil-shaped crafts appeared in Manhattan out of thin air. It moved at speeds impossible for the human eye to track and could still stop on a dime. It hovered amongst the skyscrapers for a few moments before firing what can only be described as a gravity cannon that was attached to the belly of the ship. There were no laser beams or bright flashing colors, just a seismic sonic boom explosion of sound. The first target was the OWG embassy. The windows shattered from the sound before the energy wave hit them. The support beams snapped into thousands of pieces. Every particle of steel splintered like Zeus blowing down a matchstick house. The structure was leveled in a second with some adjacent buildings in the blast radius following suit. A dust cloud exploded from beneath the wreckage, mushrooming into the sky.

By the time visibility returned, the craft was gone. An entire city block had toppled over and been driven into the ground where a small crater in the concrete-covered Earth had formed. The people viewing the destruction firsthand couldn't hear the roars of sirens or the screams of their neighbors over the intense ringing in their ears. The sound of the cannon unleashing hell echoed throughout the city four more times before the craft sped off.

It was confirmed that there were two ships hitting the U.S. coastline when Philadelphia and Miami were hit at the same time. It was the same story as in NYC. OWG offices were destroyed along with a few other surgical targets. Energy facilities and cellular towers were the final victims they were scratching off their list before leaving the area. Surgically decimating what they deemed to be their enemy targets and then turning out the lights behind them. As soon as they moved on from an area, the reporting ceased to continue.

The craft were working their way west, and the terror was setting in for every major metro area. Chicago would almost certainly be on their list and could be hit at any minute. I tossed my go bag and my expensive filming equipment into the trunk of my car while my entire neighborhood was doing the same. I sped off towards the I80 on ramps and ran into the log jam of traffic trying to escape the area. Everyone was merging onto I80W to head for a quiet patch of countryside that might survive the night. I stared at the I80E ramp sign that led to Chicago for a few moments while fighting back another wave of panic attacks that should have served as a warning not to do anything foolish.

I don't know what drove me to peel out of line and head towards the danger. It wasn't one of my brighter moments, and I didn't do it out of a sense of journalistic integrity. Someone else could point their phone into the air and capture the impending attack on video. I wasn't equipped to save or help anyone in any impactful way. I think I needed to see it with my own eyes. There was a small part of me that was ready to die after shaking on my living room floor, and I wasn't about to kick the bucket while having a panic attack stuck in traffic with the rest of the dopes.

There was something eerily calming about cruising the multi-lane highway toward death with no one joining me. I rode in the far-left lane so I could see the faces of the thousands of people in their panicked gridlock on the westbound side of the freeway. I kept calm by laughing to myself at the insanity of the moment. If just one viewer of my work could recognize me, it would all be worth it. "Was that the chick from Conspiriousity? Was she...smiling?" The thought of it made me laugh even harder.

My panic attack reduction tactics were pointless when I saw the first car approaching head-on driving down the wrong way on my side of the interstate. Then there was another and another. Eventually, the previously clear horizon was filled with incoming headlights. The closer I got to Chicago, the more desperation I ran into. I had to slow my speed and veer from lane to lane to avoid collisions with the fleeing maniacs who were utilizing the eastbound lanes to escape from harm. The interstate had become too dangerous, so I was stuck with local highways and side streets. "Alexis X died in an auto accident," doesn't have the same ring to it as "Alexis X killed while defiantly filming Gray attack."

The closer I got to downtown, the thicker the traffic became. I ditched my car in gridlock, slung my go bag over my back, and hung my camera around my neck. The OWG building was only six blocks away and there were no dust clouds in sight. I ran up the street to the parking garage where I had stalked Emilia during simpler times. It was far enough from the presumed target to provide a safe vantage point to capture the carnage.

The lower levels of the garage were packed with honking bumper-to-bumper traffic, like a thousand rats abandoning a sinking ship through a single hole in the hull. I took the stairs to the uncovered rooftop and surveyed the doomed OWG building kitty-corner across the street. I checked my phone for updates to find that Charlotte and Pittsburgh had been hit with surgical strikes while I fired up my livestream. I gave a panoramic view of the mania on the streets below to provide setting before turning the camera to show where I was broadcasting from as I narrated the situation.

I had two million subscribers and not even one of them was tuned in. My only audience was the other brave soul who was sitting with her back against the concrete wall. "Don't you ever stop?" she asked, taking an awfully familiar tone for a stranger.

It wasn't until I took a few paces forward that I could make out her face. It was Emilia Vera, and that was the first time I had ever heard her speak. She wasn't nearly as imposing as I had imagined. Her makeup was running and had been smeared on both cheeks. Her hair was tossed, and her heels had been kicked off haphazardly. "You must be loving this," she sneered at me before taking a swig from a bottle that she had been nervously peeling the label from.

"Shouldn't you be running away with your friends?" I asked.

"They're not my friends…" she replied with a softer tone before trailing off with something I couldn't make out.

"You know, if there were ever a time for a death row confession, this might be it," I suggested with a smirk as I flashed my camera at her. "Wouldn't want you to die with a guilty conscience."

"We're not going to die, and my conscience is fine," she stated without a hint of self-awareness. "What? You think I know what's going on?"

"You're right. You're totally innocent in all this. I'm sure it's just a coincidence that Grays are going city to city, obliterating all the One World Gangfuckers outposts."

"Here. Help yourself" she said as she rifled through her purse. She threw her keycard and a USB thumb drive at my feet. "Tenth floor. 2115. Go get your story. Have your big break. Who knows, you might even be able to afford a new hoodie."

Walking the OWG halls with unfettered access was tempting, but I wasn't insane. "You know, when I pictured toppling the OWG, it was more figurative than literal," I said as I sat down a few feet from her. I looked directly at the bottle in her hand and gave her an eyebrow raise with a nod. She sighed as she begrudgingly passed it to me. "I always thought I could save all these people, or at least wake them up," I lamented as I took a swig.

"You can't save them. They don't want it, and they sure as hell don't deserve it. Every one of them is going to get what's coming to them." She stumbled to her feet and collected her heels. "Sheep get slaughtered," she said coldly as she tossed one shoe after another over the ledge onto the gridlocked streets below.

I sat quietly as I held myself back from verbally lashing her. Emilia was every bit the sociopath I thought she was, which made her tear-stained eyes an anomaly. Even with her makeup smeared and her guard down, I couldn't see through to the person behind the cracking mask.

Neither of us spoke for what felt like an eternity as we silently passed her bottle back and forth. Without any conversation to fill the void, my mind was left to wander. London, DC, Tokyo. I felt another panic attack coming on, so I instinctively started humming "Where We're Going," without realizing I was doing it.

"Mmmm hmmm. Mmmm hmmm," Emilia mimicked the melody. "I know that. What is that?"

"Interstellar," I replied as I resumed humming the soothing tones.

"Mmmm hmmm mmm mmm hmmmm," she hummed along, wearing a half-drunk smile.

"I have nasty panic attacks when I get mentally worked up. Music calms me. Turns out, the world ending is a massive trigger for me. Who knew?"

She continued humming while I pulled another swig off the bottle and waved a hand at her like I was Hans Zimmer conducting a one-drunken woman orchestra. I passed the bottle back, but she sat it down on the ledge. "You have panic attacks. I have crippling social anxiety," she said with a sigh of discomfort while purposely avoiding eye contact. I didn't want to interrupt her moment of vulnerability. I kept on humming, less as a cure for my own anxiety at that point, and more to encourage her openness.

"I was perfectly happy to sit here alone, waiting for the end, until you showed up." She paused like a disturbed patient on a therapist's couch who was debating how much of her darkness she was comfortable exposing. "I like being alone. There's no one to impress. No one around to judge you."

"Is it cause of, you know, your scars?" She didn't respond, though I could tell by her frozen demeanor that she heard me plainly. "What happened to you?"

"Don't pretend to care. It's insulting. You think I'm going to spill my guts to you? *Share my trauma*? Maybe have a good cry?"

"Sure, if you'd like to. It might feel good," I playfully mocked.

"I don't hum tunes to stifle the pain."

I understood Emilia at that moment. Prideful. Angry. Isolated. She was scared, and she counted it among the flaws she was unwilling to examine or share. Her entire persona was fraudulent. Her biting attitude was a high wall to hide behind. She lied constantly, and none of the tales she spun for others could compare to the ones she told herself. Continuing that conversation was pointless once she had retreated to the comfort of remoteness.

Again, we sat in silence, and again, the panic crept up in me. I pulled my knees to my chest, closed my eyes, rocked gently back and forth, and tried to recall the lyrics of any song that could bring me calm. Emilia tapped me on the hip with her foot, then kicked me properly when I ignored her. "Hey," she whispered. "Hey!" she repeated louder.

Emilia was down on her haunches. Her hands on the ledge and her eyes were high enough to see over the concrete like a scared kid watching a horror movie between their fingers. I turned my body around, reached up to mimic her pose, and peered out over the ledge beside her.

"Ho-ly shit."

The ship was hovering over the city streets without making a sound. It had taken position a few hundred feet in front of us without ever alerting us to its presence. The craft was disc-shaped with a small bubble on the interior of the sphere that could house no more than five Grays. It couldn't have been more than thirty feet from its lowest point to its highest. The outer rim of the disc appeared to be spinning laps around the perimeter of the craft. It had the same silver alloy features as the other Praxi vessels, but we hadn't seen that particular model until the night of the attack. Its design was more in line with the reporting from UFO sightings over the years.

It took aim with a cannon attached under the thinnest exterior point of the outer rim, and I raised my camera to capture the impending strike. The ship emitted a low electronic hum as it powered up to deliver the blast. A howling came from the west which turned our heads to track an inbound fighter jet. It released a missile as it rocketed overhead in ascension above the city landscape. The direct impact burst into a ball of flames, and my screams of a standing triumphant "Yes!" couldn't be heard over the explosion.

We didn't receive the bad news until the fire subsided and the craft remained fully intact. It had been slightly pushed off its mark, but the rocket blast did little other than leave a black charring on the side of the ship with no visible structural damage done. It hovered back into position and carried on as if nothing had happened. The Praxi didn't bother to pursue the fighter jet, and that was almost more terrifying than the aggressive blows they had been landing across the East Coast. The height of our military capabilities was little more than an annoyance to their level of technology.

The screams of a thousand shattering windows were drowned out by an acoustic boom as the weapon unloaded its horrible power. I was able to capture the moment of impact before being hit with the shockwave reverberating from the destruction. I dropped my camera which hung from my neck and held onto the concrete ledge to avoid being pushed back as my senses went dull. My eyes closed to avoid the dust and my hands quickly covered my ears to protect my drums from exploding.

I couldn't see the crater or the destruction, but I knew it was there. The only thing I could hear besides the intense ringing in my ears was another sound wave of weaponized gravity colliding with its target a few blocks away. It felt like a lifetime before the dust cleared and returned the stolen visibility.

The few operational streetlamps cut through the dissipating aerial debris. Emilia stood beside me, her one-button jacket and blouse coated in the filth that had rained over us. The soot on her face masked her smeared eyeliner. I tried to ask her if she was okay, but I could barely hear my own voice.

Emilia picked up her purse and turned to walk away. I shouted to her, but I don't think she would have acknowledged me even if she could hear. I don't know why she stayed to witness the carnage while everyone else fled, but once her headquarters had been reduced to rubble; she was headed for the exit.

There was a dust cloud mushrooming in the distance from where the Chicago Tribune stood moments earlier. My position for years had been that the mainstream media should be burned to the ground, but this wasn't what I had in mind. I had long hoped to guide the populace to a realization that their trusted news sources had devolved into nothing more than propaganda printing presses. The American people were meant to figuratively dismantle the systems of power and oppression, not watch on in horror as a planetary outsider razed them to the ground.

The streetlights, digital signs, and storefronts went dark as a further echoing boom knocked out the power. The only remaining light came from the headlamps of abandoned cars left idling. I walked down the five flights of stairs and joined the small group of pedestrians who were wandering around aimlessly. There was nowhere to go. Nothing left to run from. No power, no emergency services, and no hope.

I walked up the street towards the disaster zone until I came to the point where the concrete itself was impacted and cracked at the furthest perimeter of the blast radius. The ground was covered in assorted rubble that made steel indistinguishable from wood. Water cascaded into the air from a ruptured water main which I held my face in front of to wash the soot away from my eyes and mouth.

I followed a crowd of looters who were climbing through the blown-out windows of a corner grocery store. They ransacked the place for as much as they could carry, fighting and trampling over each other to get their hands on an amount of food that wouldn't last them a week. The basic instinct of survival caused them to become what humans are at our core. Wild animals who ignore thousands of years of domestication at the first opportunity to go primal.

I pinballed off the looters to avoid getting caught up in the frenzy as best as possible. I made my way to the frozen section and grabbed a tub of ice cream that was melting from the lack of power. I drank the delicious sugary liquid from the tub before squeezing the softening container to force the ice cream to the surface. I bit into it with my front teeth ignoring the freezing pain on my gums.

I knew this same scene was playing out in every city across the world. Hundreds of millions dead. Billions more driven to hysterical violence and chaos. It was a zombie apocalypse triggered by the simple virus of fear.

I couldn't help but cry. I let the tears roll right off my chin into the tub of ice cream as I pondered the fall of mankind. I started adding up all the OWG offices further west. Denver, Salt Lake City, Austin, Vegas, LA, San Francisco, Portland, Seattle. Boise? Did they have an office in Boise? I couldn't remember. For their sake, I hoped they didn't.

I sat there on the floor alone for an hour. I began talking out loud to myself once the tinnitus subsided, verbally running through scenarios of why this happened. What had caused the Grays to turn on us? If they had been planning this all along.

Why their attack was coordinated the way that it was. What the OWG had to do with this.

The more questions I asked myself, the more I needed to know the answers. "Get off your ass and fucking fight, Alexis," I encouraged myself. I picked up my camera and realized that I had never turned off the livestream through my examination of the damage and my mental breakdown. My YouTube broadcast listed *Pro-conspirator* as my lone viewer.

I looked into the camera to address the one person who had stuck with me through the end of the world. "Don't trade your humanity for anything. Keep fighting," before finishing with my trademark sign-off from my late-night broadcasts. "You have to wake the fuck up before you can go to sleep." The cellular service went dead shortly after as I walked back to find my car.

Chicago was in ruins, and the looters had done equal damage as the Grays. I still didn't understand why they hit surgical targets when they had weapons to raze entire cities to the ground. If their plan was to break our spirits rather than wipe us out entirely, it was working to design.

I returned home hoping to piece things together, but the power was out everywhere. It felt weird going to bed when there was so much going on, but my hands were tied, and exhaustion had defeated me. When I woke the next day, the story was the same. I started rationing what food I had on hand and tried not to panic when thinking about the power never coming back. The only thing worse than death would be checking out before knowing the full story.

Another day went by, and things were getting real. Just as I was about to voyage out and scavenge for supplies, I heard my AC power on. I rushed over to the TV to see if anyone was broadcasting. Every station carried the same message banner. "Important updates coming soon. Stay tuned."

I turned on my phone to see if anyone was talking on social media, but cellular service was still down. I often ended podcasts with a message of "Turn off your TV," as a nod to the film *Network*, yet there I was on the edge of my seat, staring into the void, begging for some programming. I knew that whatever news was coming would be horrific and filled with bullshit and spin, but I had to hear it.

Chapter 4

Lust at First Sight

General Kelly

"I can't read the teleprompter with those blasted lights in my face. Turn them off," I barked at the director.

"We need the lights, otherwise the broadcast is going to come off as too Darth Vadar-y," the director calmly responded.

"Lieutenant, open the bay doors. We'll shoot it with natural light," I ordered. I was comfortable being surrounded by a hundred people in a military hangar, but the lights, makeup, and especially the director were thinning my patience.

"Sure, sure. Natural light. Whatever. It's only the most important live broadcast in the history of mankind. Why listen to a professional when you can just wing it? Will someone please talk some sense into this man?" the director stammered.

"Corporal, escort this soft belly off my base, please. You there, you're the cameraman?" I asked the nervous gentleman not taking sides with his head down.

"Yes...yes, sir."

"Give me a simple countdown and keep the shot wide with the service members and aircraft in the backdrop. Don't roll that teleprompter while I'm talking. I'll pause during the paragraph breaks and then you can advance it. Can you do that, son?"

"I can do that, sir."

"Good man. Nice and simple. Count us down when you're ready."

"Oh, okay. Three minutes until we go live."

I paced back and forth nervously knowing that I never wanted to do anything like that ever again. There was a war to plan, and in the future, someone else would handle these duties while I stayed out of the public eye.

"We're live in five, four, three," the cameraman said before holding up two fingers and then one.

"Citizens of Earth. As most of you know, our planet was struck without warning by eleven Praxi attack craft three nights ago. I regret to inform you that Shanghai, London, Washington DC, Paris, Buenos Aires, São Paulo, Delhi, Moscow, and Tokyo have been destroyed. All one hundred and twenty-two other metro areas containing OWG hubs were subsequently attacked over the course of the following thirty-six hours. Our estimated death toll is in the hundreds of millions."

"Though most was out of my control, it is with a heavy heart that I must accept whatever blame falls on my shoulders. Our leaders within the One World Governance made a trade agreement with the Praxi behind closed doors. Our planet would be granted access to the cosmos and its rich variety of resources in exchange for human capital. The Jump Point wasn't constructed as a bridge between worlds. It was built as a trade route for slaves."

"An initial payment of five hundred thousand human lives as slaves was due. Twenty-five thousand more every month to replenish those who were inevitably dying in the mines. The agreed-upon term of the deal was to last one hundred years. Thirty million men, women, and children would work the mines of Triax II to their deaths to collect precious triaxum."

"Once the Jump Point was cleared for human passage, I was ordered to mobilize the World Military and round up citizens for transport. The OWG message was clear. Take the poor. Take the weak. Take the useless dregs of society. Take the Christians, Jews, and Muslims alike; and I refused. Our new world leaders are as much our enemies as the creatures who attacked us. The OWG is crippled beyond repair, and we must not allow those who survived the attack to escape from their culpability. Round up the OWG who remain and turn them over to the World Military."

"The Praxi were removed from their embassy and I barred them from the planet before they attacked. Our lives are not trade goods for those who think they are better than us. We WILL NOT be slaves to a heathen race of technocrats. We will fight. We will be free. We will love each other. And we will put our faith in God again."

"I wish I had acted sooner. That monstrosity in the sky should have been destroyed before those vicious demons could infect our world. If you will follow me now, I swear to every one of you that I will not hesitate again."

"We will not lay down and wait for the Praxi to take as they please. They will rue the day that they failed to destroy us. We will strike back at them, and God will repay tenfold the damage that they have done here."

"I call upon all of you now to do your duty. Our people need medical care, food, and water. Our infrastructure must be rebuilt. And we must assemble the greatest strike force mankind has ever seen if we're going to survive. We need workers to construct ships and weapons, and we need pilots to fly them. We will turn the technology they worship against them. We have deactivated their portal, and when we turn it on again it will be to deliver them a crushing blow the likes of which they have never felt before."

"If you are called to serve in some capacity, you will find the information and locations for projects on every continent following this message."

"Love each other, pray, and fight like your lives depend on it."

"We're clear," the makeshift director announced to a round of applause from the soldiers watching on.

I returned to my office at Edwards Air Force Base to hold meetings with my officers. Their instructions were to organize the volunteers into service groups depending on their skills. The most essential tasks were weapons construction, rebuilding and maintaining the energy grid, and disaster cleanup.

I cleared my large oak desk of clutter to make space for rolling out the local area map with blueprints for our planned expansions. I pulled the string on the cheap, plastic shades and lifted the window to its max height. The fresh breeze blew through, flipping the pages of various documents piled on the filing cabinet. I poured a glass of scotch and set my coaster on one corner of the map to hold it in place. I rested my wooden cigar box on another corner, an ashtray on the third, and a second coaster with an empty scotch glass on the final corner.

"Corporal," I shouted with an unlit cigar between my teeth, "Bring in the prisoner."

Moments later, the Corporal rapped his knuckles against my open door to announce his presence and walked Emilia Vera in by the chains around her wrist and waist. She was fitted in a standard-issue prison orange jumpsuit with sandals. She wore no makeup, but the men had the decency to allow her to keep her hair.

"You may uncuff her, Corporal. Ms. Vera isn't a threat without an internet connection." He rattled the key into the lock around her wrist and unbound the chain. "Thank you, Corporal. Dismissed. You may sit if you'd like," I suggested to Emilia while sparking my butane lighter to put flame to the cigar between my lips.

"What the hell is this? Did our rights go out the window because we're under attack? I'll tell you like I told your goons. I had nothing to do with this. I wasn't privy to whatever deal the OWG worked out. I'm a digital assassin, not a bureaucrat."

"Yes, I know. I've read your file, Ms. Vera. Smear campaigns, social media manipulations, and penetration of propaganda to youth within schools. You were very effective in the lead-up to New World's Eve. It's all very impressive. Especially the reviews from your supervisors. Be a doll and read the highlighted portion out loud," I instructed as I passed the confidential internal review document to her and pointed to the open chair in front of my desk. "Sit," I demanded firmly this time.

She read the first few lines silently to herself before clearing her throat to read them out loud. "Emilia shows great promise with her tireless and sometimes obsessive approach to achieving her goals. She is without a doubt the most brilliant young student I ever had the privilege of guiding. She exhibits the anti-social behaviors of a singularly focused genius. My only concern is that she doesn't adhere to OWG ideals. She is passionless to the cause, and I fear this makes her subject to her own principles, whatever they may be. It is my recommendation that she is not considered for holding even the lowest level of public office. Her talents lie elsewhere, and she will need to be supervised closely, preferably by someone she aims to impress."

I let her sit with that information for a moment as I gauged her reactions, but she seemed to have none. She was every bit as cold and under control as advertised.

"Is that statement accurate? Are you a brilliant, passionless, manipulator or are you not?"

She tossed the review defiantly onto the map rolled out on my desk. "What is this? Did Penelope write that?" she stammered. Perhaps she wasn't as unshakable as I was led to believe. "Do you want an apology? *I'm so sowwy, General Daddy. I've learned my lesson. I'll be good, I pwwwwomise,*" she mocked.

"You can return to your cell if you'd like. The men would be happy to count you among the guilty and give you the same treatment the rest of the OWG is receiving. Or," I said while pouring scotch into the glass on her side of the table, "You can hear my proposal and maybe put your talents to good use for once."

Her shoulders rolled back, and her arms uncrossed as she realized this could be an opportunity instead of an admonishment. "All right. Okay. I'm listening," she responded with a notable change of attitude.

"We are here," I said, pointing to Edwards on the map of southern California. "This right here—" I drew a circle with my finger over a large piece of real estate to the northeast. "—is now also property of the military. Construction is underway to build an energy facility. The white coats claim we can power the entire continent with triaxum from a single location. That's not why you're here, though. I want you to oversee the installation of a new network from this same property. Our grid is smashed, but most of the fiber optics remain in place..."

"And you want to get people online again," she correctly interrupted.

"That's right. If the OWG coup of the world taught us anything, it's the value of a direct line to the people, and we need their undying loyalty now more than ever. I want you to design it, build it, and run it for me."

"If you want to do it right, you're going to need the largest server farm on the planet," she said, standing over the map and taking her first sip of scotch. "You could HQ telecommunications, social media, and traditional broadcasting into one compound if you had the manpower to construct it."

"Manpower is not a problem."

"You'd need thousands of men to build it, and double to program and staff it."

"They're already breaking ground, Ms. Vera. All they need is someone with a vision to point and demand. You'd have carpe diem over the entire production, and you can CEO it once operational."

"I can have *carpe diem* over it? Jesus, no wonder you need me," she condescended.

"I don't appreciate your blasphemy, and you're in no position to make judgments," my tone warned. "I understand that you're not a religious person, and that's fine. We all find God on our time. I will not tolerate the disrespect though, and that goes hand in hand with the platform. You weren't a believer of the cause with the OWG, and you don't need to be one now either. However, it's my belief that the only way we're going to survive as a species is if our people find God again. If you can execute that vision, we can forget all about your past."

"I can do that," she responded without apology. "Aren't you kind of ignoring the elephant in the room though? We're under attack and outmatched. Sure, the Praxi can't get through the Jump Point with the power off, but they could be here in two months' time to finish us off if they take the long way around. Keeping the lights on and rebooting social media isn't going to win the war."

"You're absolutely right. Military heroes win wars. They inspire greatness in others, and who's more inspirational right now than Captain Ranbir Chopra?"

"That's clever, but we don't even know if he's alive. He touched down in London hours before the attack. Even if he's out there somewhere, it would be nearly impossible to verify and find him."

"I don't need to find him. He's already here. He came across the pond with military personnel this morning. My men are debriefing him right now. He's your final task as my Minister of Propaganda."

"You're joking, right? *Minister Of Propaganda*? You're not much of a history scholar, are you?"

"You can take whatever title you'd like. A spade is a spade, so let's not pretend otherwise." I pulled a file from my top drawer and slid it across the map to her. "Enclosed are the mission details. You've got ninety minutes to review them and clean yourself up before you meet the captain. I expect you to brief him, bring him on board, and annex him as a tool of the regime. I want him controlled, Ms. Vera. Do we have an understanding?"

"I'll figure him out. Now, get me out of this jumpsuit."

"Corporal! See to it that Ms. Vera finds the showers and her personal possessions and prepare a temporary workspace for her."

"Yes, sir. Follow me, ma'am. We'll get you sorted out."

I wasn't fooled by Emilia playing nice. I knew she was toxic from the moment I met her. A conceited, self-involved, ungodly little monster. I didn't trust her, but I did trust her ambitious nature. "Bait the hook with power," was the advice

I received, and I was convinced that if I hadn't made her such a tempting offer, she would have returned to her cell to spite me.

I was comfortable letting Emilia think she had total control over the situation. I needed her to be at her manipulative best and singularly focused on the task at hand. There was concern that she had been given too much responsibility without enough clock to deliver, but I had been reliably informed that the girl would rise to the challenge.

I retired to the security office and excused the soldiers on duty so I could watch in private as the future young leaders met each other. As much distaste as I had for Emilia, I was excited to watch her work. I relit my cigar, put my feet on the desk, and slowly sipped my scotch while waiting for my killer to show up on the video feed and join the captain in the interrogation room.

When she finally walked in, she looked like an entirely different person. Her hair was styled with a part down the middle, snuggling close to both sides of her face. She had done her makeup and dressed herself in the blue blouse, black skirt, pantyhose, and heels she had been apprehended in. She carried the file I had given her and a yellow legal pad.

"Ranbir Chopra?" she asked as the door closed behind her and she took a seat across from him at the stainless-steel table. The room had a cold feel to it with lowlights and all steel furniture, but Emilia brought warmth to it with her confident body language and the genuine smile of a practiced liar.

"Chop," he responded.

"Chop? You self-glossed a nickname, and the best you could come up with was *Chop*? Like the salad?"

"Nah. More like a karate thing. Chop," he replied as he swung an arm in a striking fashion.

Emilia laughed with a "pfft," like a short burst of air her lungs were too full to contain. If she was laughing to shine him on, I couldn't tell. "You're the guy we sent into space? Out of billions of people, we chose you?"

"I wasn't chosen. I volunteered," he said as he tapped the table with two fingers as if to make a point.

"Well, you're certifiable, that's for sure. Maybe you'd like to volunteer for something equally stupid again."

"I'm brave, not stupid," he continued to correct her.

"Bravery and stupidity are rarely mutually exclusive," she said as she opened the file and pulled her chair tight to the table.

"What's your name?" he asked while mirroring her posture. As predicted, he was hitting on her.

"Emilia Vera. Not Veritas, or Big V, or anything quite as catchy as Chop."

"You're not military?"

"You're awfully cocky for a guy who's being detained, don't you think?"

"I'm not sweating that. Military detainees don't get visits from pretty girls in skirts unless they're meeting their attorney." Emilia cocked her head to the side and didn't say a word. "You're not my attorney, right?"

"You're in street clothes and we're not talking through bars, genius."

"Well, if you're not my attorney, and you're not military; then who are you? I already told the MPs everything I know about the Grays, but if this is like some seductive interrogation tactic, then I totally know more than I led on, and you should try to mine me for the info."

"You certainly didn't lose your sex drive in the Jump Point, did you?" Emilia playfully flirted back. Under different circumstances, I imagined she would have verbally destroyed him by now.

"No, ma'am. Docs checked me out. Everything's in working order."

"How about your sense of adventure? Is that intact?"

"All right. Enough already. What is this? What do you want?"

"I come with a mission. *The* mission. The kind that makes bottles pop and panties drop if you make it home."

"I'm listening," he said as he leaned his elbows forward on the table.

Emilia thumbed through the pages in the file even though she had memorized the information. "In thirty days, we're going to reactivate the Jump Point. A small strike force fleet will travel to Prius to deploy hundreds of the same gravity wave bombs that obliterated our cities. The plan is to catch them off guard, destroy every major metropolitan on their planet, and bring the boys back home."

"You're joking," he laughed. "That's a suicide mission. The Praxi have a docking station near the portal on their end. There could be dozens of ships in there. They could have targeted gravity missiles or God knows what else aimed at us the moment we appear."

"Nobody said it would be easy, but if you don't want to go; that's fine. You can cower at home and wait for death to come to your doorstep, and it will. You'll find no comfort in the extra weeks of life you cowardly stole away when the regret sets in at the end."

Chop smiled at her, raised an eyebrow, and effected a cartoonish Scottish accent. "Would you be willing to trade all the days, from this day to that? For one chance, *just one chance!*" he recited from memory. "Are you manipulating me with *Braveheart*? I mean, your version was a little more grim, but that's the *Braveheart* speech."

Emilia's shoulders rolled forward, but she didn't allow getting caught in plagiarism to throw her off. "Did you know the actual battle of Sterling was fought over a bridge? The overconfident English marched their northern army over the wooden crossing but were outmaneuvered by the Scots. Once a portion of the

English forces reached the other side, the Scots attacked. The Brits were caught off guard and the bridge collapsed beneath them, trapping those who had crossed. Some fell to the sword, most drowned, and only the British archers escaped with their lives."

"So, we're the triumphant Scots in this scenario?"

"And you're William Wallace." She paused for effect. "I'm not asking you to join the fleet. I'm asking you to lead them. You're the only pilot who has flown their craft. The only person who's been on the other side. There's no one more qualified."

Emilia closed her file, rose out of her chair, and walked seductively to the other side of the table until she was behind Ranbir. She massaged his shoulders and leaned down with her mouth near his ear. "I'll make you into the greatest hero mankind has ever known. Headline news. The cover of 'Time.' Posters, action figures, and commercials. The people will worship you as the man who saved Earth. The annals of history will never forget you," she whispered temptingly into his ear.

I extinguished my cigar and returned care of the security systems to the guards. Emilia had the captain primed to be thrust into the role he was cast to play. I picked up Amir from the kennels as a good-faith gesture and made my way to the interrogation room. I entered to find the pair of them huddled over the table examining documents. "I brought a friend," I announced from behind them.

Amir pushed out of my grasp, ran to Ranbir, and leaped into his open arms. "Hey buddy! How are you? Yeah, that's my good boy," Ranbir said, affecting a baby-talk tone as Amir spazzed happily.

"I see you're reviewing mission details. I'll take that as a good sign."

"You asked for a captain. I delivered," Emilia boasted.

"Very good, Ms. Vera. I'd like to show the captain around. You have other duties to tend to, yes?"

"We're busy here. Later," Emilia snapped. Judging by her tone and disapproving eyes, she was tempering her sass in the presence of the captain.

"Ms. Vera, I wasn't asking."

She stared me down like a predator working out which angle to attack from. She closed her mouth, and her tongue ran across her teeth behind her lip. "Fine. Fifteen minutes. We have a lot to do," she compromised. "We'll talk again soon," she assured Ranbir while touching his arm and heading for the door.

I knew I was going to need Emilia to control the captain, but I hadn't fully anticipated needing the captain to control her.

"Where the hell did you find her?"

"She's reformed OWG," I said, leaving the implications unspoken.

"Oh," he nodded. "That tracks."

"You like her, don't you? You might be the first." My disgust for the girl was more than I was willing to hide. "Even with the..?" I said while casually rubbing my cheek in reference to her scar.

"That's pretty rude," he replied with a disgusted tone. "She's interesting. Loads of confidence. Intelligent. That's sexy."

"Careful. She's your boss now," I said playfully, hoping to keep things smooth between us. Twenty minutes with Emilia, and I had already lost the captain to her. "Come. You need to see what we're working on," I invited.

We walked through the office complex and onto the tarmac where F-16s were being towed away to create space. "R and D is on the other side of the base," I pointed to the north while shielding my eyes from the sun. "The lab rats are using what little triaxum we have on hand to replicate the gravity bombs. They're being designed like torpedoes that we will drop from the upper atmosphere. This is the hangar where you'll be spending most of your time," I said as we walked through the giant open doors. Inside sat two Praxi cargo ships with a litany of workers preparing them for battle. "Look familiar?"

"*This* is our attack ships? They don't even have weapon systems."

"We're making the best of it, captain. We confiscated twelve of these cargo ships, along with seven of the smaller crafts. Everything will be outfitted with weapons by the time you launch, not that you'll need it. The heavy cruisers will deliver the payloads and the one manned fighters will fly in support. We have more than enough pilots, but I need you to train them."

"I don't know, General. I might be a little out over my skis here. I can train your pilots to fly them well enough, but I'm not sure I'm the man to lead this mission."

"Ms. Vera was more convincing, wasn't she? Take heart, son. You're going to do great. Those godless bastards will never see you coming, and you won't be alone. Come, meet your commanders," I invited. "Risa! Kai! Front and center," my command echoed through the hangar.

My two most trusted pilots hopped out of one of the cruisers and approached with the negative attitude I had instructed them to lose. "I'm not flying this clunky boat," Risa shouted in my direction. "I want my fighter, as promised," she complained.

"*Risa*," my tone warned as my eyes drew her attention to Captain Chopra. Her appearance was disheveled as always. Her uniform was halfway unbuttoned with a pack of cigarettes poking up from the chest pocket and her cleavage exposed. Her multicolored pink and purple hair spiked in all directions in a coordinated mess. A tiny firecracker of a woman who became more potent with every explosion. If she wasn't so useful, I'd never allow her in my company.

Kai followed closely behind, and he was more tempered in every way. He wore his uniform appropriately and studied his surroundings before opening his mouth. He was calculating in all the ways that Risa was not, but that's not to say that his tongue wasn't equally sharp. He stood only a few inches taller than Risa, and though he was slight of frame, he was not a man to be underestimated. His ambition made him dangerous, and his unassuming appearance masked his snake nature.

"Captain Chopra, meet Risa and Kai. My Zeroes," I introduced. Neither extended the captain a hand nor offered a greeting.

"Zeroes, sir?" the captain asked.

"The most deadly and ruthless pilots to ever fly combat missions," Kai explained without emotion. "Samurai of the sky."

"Just like Pearl Harbor, we're going to surprise our enemy. It's only fitting that the two strike teams be led by Japanese fighters. Kai will command Titan Group with the single-man fighters and Risa will command Arrow Group with the heavy bombers. Won't you, Risa?" I reinforced, to which her only answer was to spit at the ground.

"Seems you have things under control," the captain said. "Not sure what you need me for."

"Me neither," Kai added without hesitation.

"There's much work to be done, and our people need a hero to inspire their labor and embolden their faith," I explained. "Come now, let's not keep Ms. Vera waiting." The less time spent with my zeroes; the better.

I led the captain to the offices with Amir trotting a few steps behind. It hadn't been fifteen minutes, and Emilia had already seized control of project operations. Her voice echoed through the hallways, and I stopped Ranbir short of entering the room she was barking orders from so we could hear her management style without her being alerted to our presence.

"I. Don't. Care. Unload the shit off the trucks. Push it off the back onto the highway for all I care. I want those trucks in Silicon Valley by 9 p.m."

"And who's going to load them? We don't know shit about servers or transporting them," a soldier pushed back with a tone he'd never dare use with me.

"Take fifty of your jarhead buddies. Unplug the big boxes and secure them in the trailer. Are you military boys really that dumb? *The few and the proud* isn't supposed to refer to your active brain cells."

"Cute, but that's Marines. I'm Air Force."

"And what's your catchy slogan that lures nineteen-year-old burnouts into the service?"

"Aim high, fly-fight-win," he responded proudly.

"Great. Aim your ass towards those semi-trailers and fly them up to San Fran."

"Who the hell do you think you are? We don't take orders from you."

"Well, you do now, Private Pile of Shit."

I looked to Ranbir to make sure he had heard enough to remove the shine off his affection for Emilia. Had we waited any longer things could have gotten sloppy. "That's quite enough Ms. Vera. You know, you'll catch more bees with honey."

"No offense General, but I don't take advice from people who get their wisdom out of a cracker. And I don't want bees. I want those trucks loaded with servers."

"Staff Sergeant. Round up any men without assignment. Take the trucks north and bring Ms. Vera her servers. Find me in the morning when you return, and I'll treat the men to breakfast."

"Yes, sir."

"See." I tried to make my point to Emilia, but she had already shifted her attention to Ranbir. Her posture and attitude changed the minute he entered the room, and it became apparent that it wasn't an act she was putting on to manipulate him.

"Did you see the sights?" she asked him with a jarringly softer tone than she had been using moments earlier. "Come and bring Amir. I want to take some promotional photos for posters and TV spots. Everyone needs to know that you're involved as soon as possible."

Emilia led the captain away, and he followed her the same way Amir followed behind him. These were supposed to be our future leaders, and they left me with little hope for the next generation. The entire lot of them were faithless and heretical. I wouldn't entertain the company of any of them if I wasn't forced. They would serve their purpose for the time being, and I wouldn't hesitate to dispatch with any of them if they failed to play their role. Mankind would find their faith again, whether they liked it or not.

Chapter 5

Love at Last Sight

Ranbir Chopra

I sat on my bunk with a notepad, recounting my journey to Prius, wishing I hadn't dug a hole for myself. I told the world a single white lie, and the next thing I knew I was married to it. All I ever wanted was to be a hero pilot. To live up to my family's legacy. A suicide mission was never part of the plan.

It was too late to come clean about my lack of military experience. The mission might have fallen apart if everyone discovered I was a fraud. Worst of all, Emilia wouldn't want anything to do with me. Even if those things weren't true, I was enjoying the attention and prestige too much to turn back, regardless of the danger.

I buried the truth beneath my ego and pretended to be what everyone needed me to be. The lie stood as a barrier between myself and everyone else, and it had to be protected at all costs even if it meant carrying an uncomfortable pit of anxiety in my belly forever.

There were two knocks before Emilia walked through the door uninvited into my tight quarters. "Good, you're awake," she said as I swung my legs over the top bunk and hung them off the bed. She put her white-tipped fingernail on the top of my notepad to tilt it down and placed a sheet of paper over the top of it. "Today's itinerary."

"9 a.m. flight training. Noon lunch. 1 p.m. strike team selections. 3 p.m. flight training. 6 p.m. interview taping," I read aloud.

"You feeling good? Let me hear what you've got so far," Emilia prompted.

"Honestly, there's not much to tell. I can't fill an hour with the story, and I don't want to get put on the spot with a bunch of questions."

"Relax," she said with a smile as she shimmied her way between my legs and put her hands on my knees. "We'll approve every question beforehand, and I'll see to it that they're softballs. It's not a live broadcast. We can edit it however we want in post. Now come on, let me hear it."

I cleared my throat and speed-read through the story that took me an hour to write. "I met the Gray scientist, Gio, in London while preparing for the mission to Prius. I'm one of the few humans alive who has communicated extensively with our enemy. Their words aren't words at all. It's feelings and raw information.

Talking to Gio was like having curated data downloaded into my brain. It will take me a month to pass on the flight knowledge Gio taught me in five seconds."

"Can I stop you for a minute?" Emilia interrupted. "You're saying its name too often. Don't humanize them. We need people inspired to labor towards their defeat, not see them as living creatures with names."

"I'm going to have to cut all of this then," I sighed.

"It's okay. Keep going. I want to hear the muddier truth before I tidy it into a shiny lie."

"I learned a lot from my new friend," I continued. "He trained and taught me all about Prius customs. We spent our time in the Jump Point exchanging stories and quirks about our different cultures. I learned that he had a daughter waiting for him on an outer colony where the Praxi grow the future members of their society. His mission to Earth had earned him the privilege of adding a member to his family, which is the highest honor. I dropped him off at the spaceport, and we shared a desire to see each other again one day."

"I truly believed Gio was my friend. He took a special liking to Amir and handled him with great care. We had a deep emotional connection; the likes of which humans require years to build. I felt what he was feeling, and he understood my emotions in ways I've struggled to express to anyone else. He was earnest and decent and unintentionally hilarious."

"If Gio had any knowledge of what his people were planning, he must have been in perfect emotional control and a master of deceit. No one was more shocked than I when they brutally attacked us. I saw the wake of disaster firsthand in London where I lost many friends and acquaintances. These were decent, hardworking, peaceful people; and the Praxi buried their unrecognizable bodies under a million tons of wreckage."

A lump formed in my throat as I recalled witnessing the gaping hole in the Earth that had claimed so many lives. I swallowed hard and placed the notepad in my lap to try to compose myself.

Emilia was quiet in the face of my empathy boiling up. She had an answer for everything, but complex human emotions evaded her. "Is that all true?" she asked. "The daughter, and the friendship, and the connection?"

I nodded yes to avoid my voice cracking if I spoke.

"It's good, okay? It's good," she reassured clumsily. "The storytelling is a little wooden though. People need to see your personality. Your smile. Your charisma. None of that is in here," she said as she grabbed the notepad. "You can show some emotion, but I need to clean a lot of this up."

"It's the truth though, and it matters."

"You're right. It matters to you. It won't matter to them out there. You're going to have to get comfortable lacing your truth with some lies. You need to tell them whatever story inspires, but you will never lie to me. I should be the one and only person who sees you unfiltered. Understood?"

If she only knew. Emilia presented the perfect opportunity for me to give her the full truth. I should have shared the lie that made me into a hero, but I didn't want to see the disappointment in her eyes. "Permission to hit the showers, boss?" I asked, choosing to slip into the comfort of light banter over facing the deceit I was propagating.

"Permission granted, soldier," she played along. "I'm working off base today, but I'll be back before the interview. I'll get you sorted out before you step into the ring. Keep your head in the game until then."

I took a shower, dressed in the provided Air Force uniform, and carried on living the lie. I led ninety minutes of classroom discussions with the General's selected pilots covering the Praxi control panels and instruments. Afterwards, each pilot took a turn in the cockpit of the small fighters performing maneuvers and getting accustomed to the craft's capabilities while I sat in as co-pilot. The rate they became comfortable bending the ship to their will was surprising. Both Kai and Risa were masters at the controls and weren't shy about showcasing their superior abilities while continually condescending and undermining my authority. With their level of experience, they barely needed my guidance, and they wanted me to know it.

While in the air, I instructed a trainee to fly us over the compound that Emilia was constructing in the region. It looked more like a city sprouting out of the ground than a budding server farm. Concrete was poured in multiple locations, spread out by miles across the fenced-off construction zone. From the sky above, the thousands of workers labored in unison like an ant farm being led by their warrior queen who demanded excellence.

Emilia had mobilized an army of workers and inspired them with the hope of rallying behind a just cause. They acted as though the war was won and we were rebuilding a sturdy base for our new civilization. I wondered if any of them considered how trivial their efforts would be in the high likelihood that our attack on Prius would fail. They'd wait with bated breath for their heroes to return home through the violet curtain. Instead, they'd be met with shock and defeat when a host of Praxi attack craft arrived to finish off humanity in a final soul-crushing strike.

Those not buried under rubble would be turned into slaves. The history of Earth would be forgotten and rewritten by the victors. It would be as though we'd never existed, and the only thing standing between our species and total erasure was the crew that I was assembling. The tip of the spear needed to be sharper than any time in human history, especially when they were being led into battle by a fraudulent captain.

We took a break for lunch and most of the personnel grouped in the mess hall. I filled my tray and sought out a quiet place in the hangar where I knew no one would ask me any pressing questions about my non-existent time as an IAF fighter pilot. The less I had to explain myself, the better the odds my secret would stay hidden.

The hangar was empty except for the two cargo ships stationed there, and the one soldier decorating the hull of my transport with paint. I recognized him from the flight we shared from the UK to the States days earlier. He was a short, bald, black man wearing standard-issued military fatigues. He knelt to dip his brush in a can of white paint, and I could see he had already written "The L," but was yet to finish the name he was painting.

"Hmhmmm." I cleared my throat to announce my presence, which received no reaction. "Hey there, friend. That's my ship you're marking."

"She needed a name with some soul, so I figured I'd give her one," he responded without turning around or interrupting his task.

I walked up to him and jumped into the open side paneling of the craft to sit a few feet from him. It gave him pause when he noticed who he was talking to, but it didn't dissuade him from going to work on the lowercase *y* after the uppercase *L*.

"I saw you board this very ship and rocket off to the cosmos a week ago," he said with a neutered southern drawl.

"You're American, or whatever we're calling people from this part of the world now. I haven't really figured out this business of no more countries. What were you doing in London?" I asked as I took a bite from my sandwich.

"Chasing the dream," he answered solemnly.

"Yeah? Didn't find it, did you?"

"No. No, I did not," he spoke slowly. "There was only a nightmare."

"A lot of that going around. I'm Ranbir. Friends call me Chop," I said, leaning towards him and extending my hand.

"Malik," he responded in kind as he turned his body to me, shook my hand firmly, and looked me in the eyes for the first time. His hand was warm, but his gaze was cold and vacant. He had the look of a man whose final death row pardon had been rejected.

"Nice to meet you, Malik. What outfit you with?"

"Air Force, but that was twenty years ago," he said as he returned to his work, painting a *d* after the *The Ly*.

"You're a pilot? Why aren't you with the rest of them?"

"Age. Experience. Psychological stability. Pick a reason."

"You know, we're selecting co-pilots and bomb technicians this afternoon, right? Plenty of opportunities to get in the fight if that's something that interests you."

"Oh, I know. I'm taking the ride to Prius on my baby here. Even if I have to stowaway," he said as he moved on to painting an *i*.

"Is that right? I could use a good co-pilot, but I don't want to fly with anyone who doesn't have some skin in the game," I challenged him, trying to draw a reaction.

"Chop, with all due respect, *all* my skin is in the game."

"Yeah. I was kind of getting that vibe."

He painted *a* to finish the name and stepped back to admire his work. "The *Lydia*," I announced as his jaw clenched with his lips pulled tight. "Was she in London?" I asked, taking special care with a soft tone. He made a fist and held it tight against his closed mouth, nodding his head as he swallowed hard. "I'm sorry to hear that."

He wiped a tear from both cheeks while clearing his throat to try to squeeze out a few words without breaking down. "They took her away from me. They took my Marcus. They took my Maisie." He paused to bite down hard on his upper lip.

I jumped off the panel I was sitting on and approached him. I put my right hand on his shoulder and squeezed tight. "Fly with me. Fly with me, and we'll take the *Lydia* to their doorstep together."

He nodded again, this time with resolute rage in his eyes. It was in that moment that things became real for me. Malik's pain and anger was visceral and infectious. It was the closest thing I had felt to a moving emotional resonance since my time with Gio. We couldn't bring Lydia, Marcus, Maisie, or the millions of others back, but we could deliver their retribution. I didn't care that I had no combat leadership experience or that the mission was suicidal when I witnessed the anguish he was experiencing. Emilia had talked me into the attack, but it was Malik who gave me the heart and purpose to carry it out.

"Get yourself some lunch, and I'll keep your seat warm. The others will be here soon, and we'll assemble the rest of our team," I instructed.

1 p.m. approached, and dozens of airmen, soldiers, and volunteers began filing into the hangar to secure their place on the strike team. Everyone congregated into groups making small talk until Kai, Risa, and the other pilots joined us.

"Yo! Everyone. Bring it in tight," I shouted. I climbed into the back of the open cargo hull to get an elevated position to address them from, and they huddled shoulder to shoulder in front of me. "I know everyone's clamoring for their chance to get some payback, but we're keeping this crew small. We have twelve of these heavies," I said as I banged my fist on the side wall, "and we need twelve co-pilots. Flight and weapons systems experience is preferred, but obviously the tech is more than a little foreign. Any former American rednecks in the lot of you who spent your summers on the farm firing gravity cannons at watermelons and tin cans?" I asked, which received less laughs than I hoped.

"Don't petition me for a spot in the cockpit. I want our pilots selecting the men and women who they're going into battle with. The same goes for the bomb techs. I need twelve demolition experts to operate the targeting and drop systems on board the heavies. For those of you doing the math at home, that's thirty-six crew, plus the seven pilots flying small fighter escorts. We're carrying three hundred and sixty total gravity bombs, and we're going to drop every last one on their asses. The scoreboard in this fight is uneven right now, but we're going to put some freaking runs on the board!"

The reaction from my audience was less than inspired. I didn't know what to say to sell those people my fraudulent package as their military leader, and my ineptitude was showing.

"Cool speech, dipshit," Risa mocked. "*Today, we celebrate our Independence Day,*" she continued, which drew laughs and shrunk my confidence further.

"Have a seat, poster boy. The adults will take it from here," Kai added, further undercutting my authority.

Those without a spot secured on the mission made their case to Risa, Kai, and the other pilots, which took their attention off me. Malik wandered back into the hangar carrying a bucket of red paint, and he went out of his way to make eye contact with me. I think he needed the reassurance that I hadn't been shining him on with the co-pilot position so I could escape our awkward emotional moment. I gave him a nod that told him our connection was legit, and he returned to his art project to add red outlining to his Lydia graffiti.

The spots were filling up fast with most of the pilots selecting their team members from those they were friendly with. A mad scramble of musical chairs took shape among those desperate to serve who didn't yet have a spot on the team. I had intentionally kept my distance from the soldiers at Edwards during the free time that Emilia allowed me to have, which led to having no friends or anyone I could trust. The pairing with Malik happened naturally, and he was the ideal co-pilot who had bigger fish to fry than worrying about me.

I was happy to hang back and not get involved in the commotion. I decided to casually hide out in the back of the cargo hull and hoped that the General would later notice the bomb technician vacancy on my team and fill it himself. Unfortunately, that was not a luxury I was afforded.

I raised the rear ramp of the cargo hull a quarter of the way to dissuade anyone from approaching me as I pretended to labor on something I wouldn't be able to explain if anyone asked. I'd have to close the ramp all the way, lock the door, and weld it shut if I was going to keep Maya out though.

Her knuckles appeared first as she jumped to grip the edge of the platform, followed by the spikes of her brown faux hawk hair as she pulled herself up and swung her legs into my hiding place. Maya was in her mid-thirties with punk edge style that made her appear younger. She wore a tattered retro "Guns N' Roses" tee shirt with the sleeves and midriff cut off to expose her defined biceps and abs. There were various tattoos covering her arms, but the one that stood out the most read "Dishonorably Discharged." She had more piercings in both ears than I could count, along with a small hoop through her right nostril. There was another hoop in her right eyebrow, and she wore a white bandana tied across her forehead high enough to not cover the piercing.

"Ranbir Chopra," she said with the inflection of an acquainted enemy who was surprised to see me. Her accent slanted American even though she presented like a Latina guerilla freedom fighter.

"I'm sorry, do we know each other?"

"I know you, but I suppose you get a lot of that. You're Mr. Popular. Big hero boy with the posters, and TV commercials, and custom-made uniform." Her approach was aggressive and confrontational which had me on my heels immediately.

"If you're looking for a role on the mission, you should see one of the pilots," I said, hoping to pass her off to someone else.

"I talked to those boys. They didn't seem terribly interested in my brand. You know how these things go. It's all background checks and presentation of experience if you want to land these exclusive combat roles. Or maybe you don't actually know." She forced eye contact and wore a slick smile. "What's the matter, *Chop*? Am I throwing you off?"

"Who the hell are you?" I asked, matching her combative energy.

"Maya Fontaine. Mexican by birth. U.S. Marine by trade," she said without extending a customary handshake or salute.

"You know those things don't exist anymore, right? And even if they did, you're no Marine."

"And you're no pilot. So what?"

Her blunt accusation was disorientating to the point where I had no response. I couldn't weasel my way out of such a direct and confident cornering. I bit my upper lip and averted my gaze while trying to process a way out of the situation. "I don't know what the hell you're talking about," was the best I could muster.

"No? Let's see if I can jog your memory. Viraj and Jayna Chopra. *The Baby Bomber*. Ring a bell? I was in Peshawar seven years ago doing a little merc work when I first heard their story. My crew sacked up with some IAF boys in the region and I learned all about their folk heroes during a night of drinking. They spoke of a pair of married aces who dominated the skies over Pakistan in 2002. As the legend goes, Jayna flew six successful combat missions while hiding her pregnancy from her superiors. When her deceit was uncovered, she was awarded medals rather than a court martial. It's quite the tale, and I imagine it was a lot for you to live up to."

My stomach knotted a dozen times over like a shoelace that would need to be cut off because it would never untie. Not only was my secret out, but it was in the most personal way possible. "Who else knows?" I asked, hoping to contain the situation.

"I don't know. Maybe nobody. Maybe everybody," she taunted. "You're like seventy feet tall, man. How could they not know that you're not a pilot? I doubt you're the only one burying your secret, and now I'm part of the inner circle too. Lucky for you, my silence can be purchased for the one-time low fee of the final spot on the team."

"Do you know anything about demolition? Bomb tech? Handling the pressure of a war zone?"

"Bitch, do you?" she snapped back. "Don't get it twisted. When the shit goes down, you're going to need me there to make sure things don't go tits up."

"I can handle myself. I served too. Maybe not as the pilot I advertised myself to be, but I was a helicopter gunnery in the army."

"For what? Two minutes before they gave your lazy ass the boot? This isn't a debate. You're stuck with me, or I'll tell your little girlfriend and everyone else about your stolen valor."

"I really don't understand you people. Why would you even want this?" I asked frustratingly with my voice raising.

"I don't see you backing out of the mission," she rightfully challenged.

"I don't have a choice like the rest of you maniacs. You do realize we're launching toward certain death, right?"

"You only die once," Maya smirked a lunatic's swaggered smile. She turned her back and walked to the edge of the raised ramp with me blackmailed into submission. "Have a nice day, *captain*. I'll see you in training." She jumped off the edge to the hangar floor below and disappeared into the crowd.

I exhaled deeply as soon as she was gone. The situation was plenty complicated before a mercenary had my balls in her death grip. Worse yet, her read on me was perfect. The only combat missions I had ever flown were in my mother's womb. Growing up in the shadow of living legends made my small accomplishments feel like giant failures in comparison. Who could have blamed me for exaggerating my experience as a pilot? My parents' deceit earned them medals and prestige when they should have received punishment. My lie may have been more selfish and less good-intentioned, but it's not as though anyone else was volunteering to fly with Gio through the purple curtain in space. I thought I had finally done something to live up to the family name, but I was having serious doubts over how much pride my parents would feel if they could witness how far I was taking the deception and the lives I was putting at risk.

I made my way to the briefing hall to lead the second round of classroom flight training and found Malik and Maya loitering in the hallway alone. "You two found each other. Good. Let's get started," I said with my hand on Malik's shoulder and my gaze averted from Maya.

I entered the room to join the rest of the team that had gathered, and Kai slid behind me to block the doorway. "Strike team only," he announced. Kai raised his open palm to deny entry, and Maya intentionally bumped her shoulder into his as she pushed past.

"They're on the team," I explained.

"No, they're not," Risa snapped.

"Yes. They. Are," I stated with authority. "Malik is my co-pilot and Maya is my bomb tech."

"He's a weepy old man and she's a merc. They're a liability." Risa scoffed.

"And what are your qualifications, besides looking like poorly drawn anime characters?" Maya joked.

Kai studied Maya like a snake preparing to strike, and then thinking better of it, turned his attention towards Malik. "Pops let his family die, and now you expect us to trust him with our lives?"

Malik calmly took a seat at an empty table, and any anger he could rightfully display seemed to transfer to Maya. "This ain't over," she promised Kai before finding her place next to Malik. She briefly studied him with a caring glance but was sure not to let her eyes linger.

Everyone else took their places and I began the instruction. I had doubts about my flight crew, but the worry washed away as I witnessed their attentiveness to the task at hand. Malik asked pointed and intelligent questions about the mission and Maya jotted down studious notes like a student getting her doctorate in gravity weapons. When the briefing was finished, Malik joined the engineers in prepping the cockpits for human pilots and Maya left with the science team to study the inner workings of the ordinance she was responsible for. Everyone else was decorated and experienced, yet it was my wounded warrior and punk rock mercenary who were the most dialed in. They were a perfect fit for me, and an even purer pairing for each other.

Malik and Maya became inseparable. They shared a space in the barracks, trained together, and rarely ate a meal apart. The three of us were a team, but the two of them were genuinely bonded in a way that my lie wouldn't permit.

The final piece of business on my schedule for the day was the recorded interview. The filming team set up a conference room with lowlights, two leisure chairs, and a backdrop of the *Hero Chop* artwork Emilia was plastering everywhere. I nervously sat in front of a mirror as the hair and makeup team went to work on me. Rather than watch my improving reflection, my eyes were fixed on the door I could see behind me in the mirror as I waited for Emilia to walk through it. Every time it opened with someone else coming or going, my heart skipped a beat with growing anxiousness.

I was unable to hide my smile when the door opened and Emilia finally walked through it. She saw me looking at her and we both shared the same rolling of the corner of our mouths upwards into a flirtatious smile as our eyes met.

"Hi," she said as she plopped down in the chair next to me, leaned back as far as it tilted until she was no longer visible in the mirror, and kicked her feet up onto my lap.

"I spied on you today," I said with a boyish grin.

"I know. We saw you boys up there showing off. It was a nice touch for morale."

"I can't believe how big the compound is," I said as the hairdresser turned my cheeks and forced me to look forward.

"When it's finished, I'll be able to plug the entire planet into one network. I'm calling it *Connect Earth*. Whatya think?"

"It's good," I said, hiding my worry that her work might be for nothing.

"We're going to start repurposing old phones and manufacturing new ones that will tie everyone together. A total consolidation of telecommunications and social media into one provider."

"That's great. I know you're excited, and I'm happy for you; but I go on in ten minutes here. I need an Emilia pep talk."

"Right. I got you," she said, sitting up and reaching into her purse. She presented my notes from earlier that morning, folded into four parts. She opened them and held the paper in front of me to read. The only edits she made were crossing out "Gio" and writing in emotionally neutral pronouns in place of his name. At the bottom of the page, she had scribbled "Be yourself," and signed it with the imprint of her lipstick marking a kiss on the paper.

"Are you sure?" I asked, surprised that she hadn't rewritten the entire document.

"Yeah, I thought about it today. You should tell your story as is. People connect with raw emotion and truth. It's binding. That said, I need that smile," she said as she tore up the notes and discarded them on the floor. "Wing it. Let your personality guide you, and I'll be right there with you if you get into a pinch," she said sweetly before her tone shifted sharply when the hairdresser moved to stand between us. "Do you mind?" Emilia condescended as she yanked the comb out of her hand and tossed it across the room. "Fetch," she said, like commanding a trained dog.

I stood to straighten my uniform and center my refined fly-boy act. Emilia stood face to face with me and ran her hands over my shoulders to round me into shape. Her heels lifted ever so slightly off the ground as she stood on her tippy toes, and I thought she might lean forward to bite my lower lip. "Hmmhmm," she awkwardly cleared her throat. "Remember. Authentic personality. You're going to do great," she said as she turned me towards the door and slapped my ass encouragingly.

Emilia was correct. Outside of restarting a couple of answers, or recording multiple takes, the interview went perfectly. I navigated through the questions with equal parts charm and emotion, looking over to Emilia to find her smile any time I needed an extra boost.

I wrapped up, thanked the crew for their hard work, and was prepared to return to my bunk so I could rest before another day of being happily micro-managed. I thought Emilia had retired for the night, but she was waiting outside for me.

"I thought you went back to your quarters," I said playfully, pointing out how she was loitering around.

"And I thought you might like to come with me." The insinuation was plain. I would have continued the flirty dance with Emilia until launch day without being presumptuous enough to make a move, but Emilia played things forward. I knew it was foolish to get further attached to her considering the circumstances. However, every decision I'd ever made was influenced by a ballot of three organs: brains, heart, and cock. The votes were counted, and my rational mind had been overruled by the other two members of bodily parliament decision-making. It was comforting to have my heart on board with the two-thirds majority seeing as how in situations like this, the cock usually pulls rank, gives an additional vote to both its hanging balls, and overrules the heart and mind on a 3-2 count.

We walked to the officer's building where she was stationed with a proper space to call her temporary home. It wasn't anything special, but she seemed to have made herself comfortable enough. There was a small living area with a couch, TV, and end table covered in books. The kitchen was connected, and there was a single bedroom with a bathroom attached. It was difficult to picture a woman such as herself living in a cramped and modest situation, but she seemed to be making the best of it.

I paced anxiously around her living room, casually thumbing through her copy of *The Art of War* which had handwritten notes in the boundaries and a copious amount of highlighted passages. "You have my permission to sit," she said, keeping up her mischievous approach in her role as my superior officer.

She filled two wine glasses, placed one on the end table next to the right side of the couch, and motioned for me to scoot to the left while handing me my drink. Whether by force of habit or a subconscious nature, she would always find a way to position herself so that her facial blemishes were turned away. "Cheers," she said as she clinked her glass to mine.

"I want you to stay with me," she said without framing her desire as an order.

"I kind of assumed that's what we were doing here," I said, referencing the inevitable sex that I thought was on the menu.

"No. Well, I mean yes, but that's not what I'm talking about. I want you to pack your things, bring Amir, and stay with me until launch day."

"Are you sure that's such a good idea?"

Her pause made it obvious that even amongst all her confidence in our success, she held concern under the surface.

"You can either stay here with me until the mission, or I'm going with you," she presented earnestly and sipped her wine.

"Are you outside your mind?" I asked with my tone bordering on insulting. "You're not going," I said with finality.

"I'll do whatever the hell I please," she stated defiantly before composing herself with a deep breath and looking me square in the eyes. "I know you feel this spark as well. You can either join me in fanning it into open flame or I'm riding along on the mission. One way or another, you're going to have the max on the line when it's crunch time."

I hadn't anticipated her bordering on insanity, but her logic made a lot of sense. My mind had warned me not to become too fond of Emilia for the purpose of avoiding the conflict of additional heartache. She was forcing me to either commit to an attachment to her that made failure less of an option, or she was going to literally put her life into my hands.

I placed my palm on her knee and was surprised by the amount of recoil and apparent discomfort she experienced. Emilia had affectionately touched me multiple times, which made her reaction to my physical reciprocation seem odd. It was as though she hadn't experienced human contact initiated by anyone else in years, if ever. I watched her chest rise and fall with greater acceleration as I witnessed her under stress for the first time.

She moved my hand from her knee, slid her ass toward the opposite end of the couch, and laid her head into my lap. Her subconscious had either failed her, or she was intentionally exposing me to the scarred side of her face. Her hair pushed back behind her ear, and I ever so gently dragged my fingers across her arm and towards her hand which she turned upwards and welcomed mine into her grasp.

The feeling was similar to the first time Amir allowed me to embrace him. He was a frightened and damaged pup the day I picked him up from the rescue. His body language communicated the mistreatment he experienced from mankind and his distrust in letting anyone get close enough to hurt him again. To see the same reaction from Emilia was jarring. It opened my eyes to the level of performance art she carried out in her presentation to the world. Seeing this layer of her personality caused a pit in my stomach as if I was sharing in her pain, which was the moment I knew this was no common infatuation.

No words needed to be spoken as she lay there in my lap. Emilia's moment of vulnerability, no matter how subtle, was her way of binding to me. She had invited me behind the wall she used to keep everyone else out, and I was honored to be the one to experience the individual behind the icy exterior. Even so, I couldn't bring myself to share my own guarded secret. I promised myself at that moment that if I made it home, I would come clean and tell her the truth.

I woke up the next morning with my arm around Emilia's waist as she spooned against me on the couch. Nothing remotely sexual had transpired, yet the night before was somehow the most quietly intimate I had ever experienced.

We approached the final two weeks leading up to launch day in the spirit that we had captured that evening. It wasn't as though she was withholding sex from me, but more so like we had intentionally abstained for reasons we weren't comfortable examining.

By day, I would follow her planned itinerary and prepare for battle while she would sow the seeds of her growing media conglomerate in the desert nearby. By night, we would enjoy each other's company over dinner, in deep conversation, sharing stories, and cuddling on the couch or in bed. We had but a single DVD copy of *The Breakfast Club*, which we watched repeatedly without complaint. On occasion, I would kiss her neck softly, but she would stop my hand any time I touched her face. Aside from some casual sexual frustration, I respected her boundaries and cherished what time we had together. She fertilized an iron resolve in me to go to Prius, destroy our enemies, and take whatever measures were needed to get home to her. I knew Emilia was working me when I first met her, and if our continued relationship was part of a 4D chess manipulation to inspire me to victory; she had designed and executed it flawlessly.

An underrated element of our time together was the lack of digital distractions. There wasn't a single moment where one of us was isolated from the other by tweeting, uploading pictures of our dinner to Instagram, or tweaking our relationship status on Facebook. There were political shifts happening in the world with massive implications for our future, but there was no 24/7 news stream to feed the dreary bulletins into our living room TV. It was only in the absence of the outside world that we were able to form the type of connection humans were capable of but had forgotten. It was a brief moment in time when mankind returned to its roots of authentic communication, yet every day the construction team brought Connect Earth another step closer to ending it.

The dreaded morning to say goodbye arrived sooner than either of us hoped. We woke up extra early, took our morning showers, and came together around the small round wooden table in our compact kitchen. I unloaded multiple boxes of cereals from the cupboard and fitted both of our places with an oversized bowl and spoon.

"You're really serious about this?" she asked.

"Yes! I can't believe you've never mixed cereals. It's our last meal together. We're doing this."

I filled my bowl with a mixture of Trix and Lucky Charms before coating the sugary concoction in milk and stirring it together with my spoon. My smile was childish as I did everything in my power to hold onto the lighthearted relationship we'd built and ignore the doom rising on the horizon.

"Okay, Cinnamon Toast Crunch. Good first choice," I narrated as she filled half her bowl. "Frosted Flakes? Okay, okay. I shouldn't have doubted you. Kid's a natural." Emilia rolled her eyes and shook her head at me with a grin she couldn't hide. She dipped her spoon into the bowl and took the first bite of her creation. "Well?" I asked.

"You win. It's incredible," she conceded with her mouth full and a streak of milk running down her chin.

"See! I told you."

"I'm going to have to run an extra five miles today, but it's totally worth it."

"It's all about the mixtures too. There are no hard and fast rules to this racket, but you're playing a very dangerous game if you start mixing Honey Nut Cheerios with Fruity Pebbles."

I wanted to keep the mood light so I could trap and bottle the positive energy between us and take it with me for later. Even while pigging out on cereal like a stoned teenager, Emilia couldn't help but bring me back to reality.

"It's great, but it's not our last meal together," she stated as a matter of fact.

"It's grrrrrreat," I nervously imitated Tony The Tiger as a humorous self-defense mechanism from the dread I was dodging.

"Ranbir. Stop. Be serious," she demanded. "You're coming back. Say it."

"I'm coming back," I repeated less convincingly than she had.

She sighed deeply and dropped her spoon into the bowl. "Don't go," she whispered like the first bubbles of emotional lava from a volcano that was struggling to control its eruption.

"Em, you know I can't do that. I can't...they need me." Of all the commands she'd given me in our month together, the one I wanted to follow the most was the only one I had no choice but to disobey.

"I know. I just...I mean...who's going to watch *The Breakfast Club* with me tonight?" A single tear formed in her eye, and she blinked to execute it like a prison guard unwilling to let it escape.

I got up from my seat so I could put my hands on her shoulders from behind, and Emilia didn't shrink away from my massage. "I'm coming back," I said more confidently.

I cleared the table while Emilia retired to the bathroom to begin her hour-long process of makeup application. "I'll see you down there," I shouted as I left our quarters and made my way to the tarmac for the sendoff ceremony.

The sun was bright that morning, but the air was cool. Our nineteen attack ships were staged on the runaway as the co-pilots conducted their final walk-throughs and checklists. Crowds of onlookers snapped photographs and offered their well wishes to the service members.

The forty-three of us posed for a group photo, and General Kelly brought forth an assortment of priests, pastors, imams, and holy leaders to pray over our procession. He was supremely confident that morning and his message to us was simple. "If God be for you, who can stand against you?"

Once we had finished our promotional obligations, I sought out my flight team. All the other pilots and crew members dressed in the uniforms provided. Malik bucked the trend by squeezing into a dated US Air Force jumpsuit, and Maya went even further off course. She wore a backward-fitted ball cap that read "Demo Dawgs", a white tank top with a camo military vest, camo pants, and combat boots. She was the only member of the team who carried a visible sidearm.

Maya and Malik stood upright and confident but stunk of liquor. "You good?" I asked Malik while slapping his arm.

"He's fine," Maya answered for him.

"I wasn't asking you."

"Nah, Chop. I'm good. We're good," Malik reassured.

"All right then. Let's..." I said when Malik nodded his head to draw my attention to the north.

Emilia walked the tarmac with Amir traipsing behind her and the sun acting like a spotlight that followed the main character on stage. She had traded in her pajamas for a light blue open blouse and pant combo, with a white designer half shirt underneath. She exposed just enough of her cleavage and midriff to scream her sex appeal while still maintaining a chic modesty. She lifted her oversized sunglasses to rest on top of her head once she walked in the shade of the attack ships.

"Hot dayum, Egg Shells. Work it, girl," Maya commented as the sea of people parted for Emilia, and my team graciously slunk away to give us privacy.

Amir ran ahead to me, and I knelt so he could jump into my arms and lick my cheek. "Hey buddy. You ready to go on another trip?" I asked in my puppy dog voice.

"You sure you don't want me to look after him while you're gone?" Emilia asked with a leading tone.

"No. We do everything together, don't we?" I said, rubbing my nose against Amir's.

"Good. I was hoping you'd say that."

We stared silently at each other for a minute, neither knowing what to say or how much to leave unsaid. Emilia stepped closer to me and awkwardly put her hands on my chest. I ran my hand across the side of her neck and my thumb across her chin. I couldn't leave without knowing the taste of her kiss.

I tilted her head towards mine, leaned forward, and closed my eyes to invite the moment we had actively avoided. Instead of my lips meeting hers, they crashed into her two raised fingers.

She pulled me closer to her and left an imprint of lipstick as she kissed my cheek. "You're going to want it so bad that you'd do unspeakable things to get it," she whispered with a dark eroticism that sent a chill up my spine.

"Emilia, I..." was all I could respond before she reinforced her fingers against my lips.

"Listen to me," she ordered which drew a hypnotized nod of compliance from me. She looked me dead in the eyes as serious as ever and enunciated every word. "You. Do *not*. Have. My. Permission. To die."

"Yes ma'am. Understood," I responded like the soldier I was pretending to be.

"Go," was her final order, and I did as I was told.

I rejoined Malik and Maya as we made our way to the *Lydia*. Neither had anyone there to send them off, which was a stark reminder of the hurt and loss that traveled with us. They boarded the craft through the side panel of the cargo hull, and I let Amir run off and follow them before taking one final look back at Emilia. She didn't raise a hand to wave goodbye or shout an "I love you," that she'd regret if left unsaid. She had done everything in her power to ensure that my focus was singular and purposeful, and she had nothing left to give.

I stepped onto the ship and watched Emilia disappear as the panels folded shut between us. It was only once I had lost sight of her that I knew I had fallen in love. The entire world hung in the balance, yet my number one priority was saving the most unique soul among them all.

Chapter 6

It Wasn't Supposed to be Like This

Maya Fontaine

I sat in the captain's chair with Malik beside me in his co-pilot position as we waited for Chop to join us on deck. The engineers had done an acceptable job of preparing the instruments for human hands, but it was Malik who made the cockpit feel like home.

He replaced the Praxi seating pods with flight chairs ripped out of F-16s and welded them into place on swiveling mechanisms. The touchscreen control panel rested at a 45-degree angle and concave around both sides of the pilot seats. Above the controls was a digital viewing screen that delivered a visual read-out of whatever direction we chose to look. Overhead and centered was a rear-view mirror that Malik stole from a Humvee and secured into place. It was a small detail that served no utility besides pulling the space-aged bridge into a familiar symmetry.

Behind the frontal controls was my targeting station equipped with digital mapping and energy sensors. The entirety of the bridge was roughly the size of a fifteen-passenger van except the ceilings were twelve feet high, rounded off into a bubble, and equipped with speakers Malik had mounted at my request.

I started my playlist titled, "God'll Sort Em' Out," which filled the cabin with the opening drum beat and harmonica of Led Zeppelin's, "When The Levee Breaks," while Malik switched on the control panel and fired up the gravity drive. Chop peeled back the Semper Fi flag I had hung as a curtain between the bridge and cargo hold and gave me a dirty look when he saw me in his seat. I had no reason to antagonize him at that point, but I did it anyway.

"Excuse me. We're leaving so...get up," he ordered without having the balls to make it a proper command from a superior officer.

I got out of his seat and stood face to chest with him. "Look at me," I imitated with my best African accent and used two curling fingers to draw his attention, "I'm the captain now."

He stared down at me, and once I knew there was some fear behind his eyes, I let him off the hook. "I'm messing with you, bro. Chill. Do your thing," I said as I took my place at the targeting station.

Chop and Malik donned their headsets and opened communications with the fleet. "Arrow group. Titan group. Mount up," Chop said as he pulled the single-handle navigator towards his belly and engaged the gravity thrusters.

The display screen showed the clouds ahead which we shot through in an instant. We moved at incredible speeds beyond any human fighter craft and didn't feel so much as a single tickle when making the precise maneuvers.

We broke through into the outer atmosphere with the fleet in tow behind us. I watched Malik's knuckles go white as he gripped the armrest and his ass raised out of the seat when the darkness of space enveloped us. "It wasn't supposed to be like this," he muttered to himself. His mouth hung agape, and he swiped quickly at his cheek to catch a falling tear. "Why did it have to be like this?"

We were two beers deep one night after training when Malik confessed what this moment would mean to him. How under different circumstances, the soul of his younger self would see his dreams become reality while looking back at Earth from above. It wasn't until we were six beers deep that I discovered the awful truth of a man who'd lost everything in the pursuit of his ambitions. Even on our vengeful mission, he harbored a deep guilt for himself for daring to see his boyhood fantasy come true along the way. Blame and regret would inevitably turn to rage, and it was my personal duty to see his manifesting anger point where it belonged.

The fleet navigated towards the Jump Point where we pulled to a stop. Chop got on the radio to give the signal, and Malik switched on the gravity cannons and straightened up in his seat. "What are you doing?" Chop asked.

"Hypothetically, there could be Grays on the other side waiting for us to turn it on. If they think they're going to bum rush me, they've got another thing coming," Malik replied as he aimed the cannon towards the portal.

"That's...actually brilliant," Chop said with surprise. "Edwards control. This is Arrow 1, in position. Plug in the Christmas lights," he radioed.

The interior of the sphere came to life with a purple wave that rolled across the surface in a single ripple. Malik's hand slowly ungripped the cannon control as we breathed a collective sigh of relief when an ambush didn't appear out of thin air.

"Arrow 1, proceeding. Arrow group. Titan group. Lock on to our signal," Chop commanded as he pressed the navigator forward and flew into the lavender ocean. On the other side was nothing. No far-off stars or reflective light from our sun. The reverse side of the Jump Point looked like a white sheet hung out on a clothesline on the darkest night ever. "All right gang. Maximum speed on my mark. Three, two, one, mark," Chop guided as he fired the gravity thrusters to full and the fleet of ships shot forward in unison.

"That's it? It's just...dark?" I asked, disappointed.

"You watch too many movies," Malik said as he switched off the overhead display and rotated his chair around to face me. Chop hung his headset and followed suit. We were sitting in a triangle, but nobody had anything to say.

I was more comfortable when it was just me and Malik getting through training together on our own. We didn't have much in common with the buttoned-up officer's club, so we sequestered ourselves as a pair. Seeing as how he was clueless; I didn't count Chop among the Boy Scouts who were indifferent to our existence, but I disliked him all the same. Marines don't ask much of civilians. We only have one rule: don't pretend to be one of us, and Chop was in violation. Forgiveness for this slight wouldn't be given freely but could be earned.

No one was eager to make conversation until finally, Chop broke the silence. "You guys come here often?" he asked sarcastically.

"It's my first time. Got the tickets on Trivago," Malik played along. "They were having a 50% off I've-got-a-score-to-settle sale."

"You cheap ass," I jabbed.

"I hope you booked it round trip and not one way," Chop added ominously.

Amir scurried under the curtain, ran by me, and placed his paws on Malik's knee. "A one-way ticket would have been fine, but you had to bring this little guy along," he said as he patted his lap as an invitation. "Somebody has to get you home. Yes, they do," he inflected his puppy dog voice and cracked a rare smile.

I hated that Malik had cozied up to his death wish. He was a genuinely good man whose pure heart had been smashed into a million pieces. It may have taken him a lifetime to reassemble it, but I was committed to seeing that he had found the time beyond his pain to put the pieces back together. The world needed people like Malik, and if saving him was the only good thing I ever did, it would have made up for all the bad.

I knew how much the presentation I had planned was going to hurt him, and I waffled on whether to go through with it or not. Taking justice for myself and others as a way of processing my own pain had never truly healed me, but it was the only thing I knew. My best hope for Malik was to draw his grief to the surface, force him to face it, forgive himself, and focus his rage externally rather than internally.

"Hey. Can I show you something?" I asked Malik as I pinched his knee.

He let Amir carefully down from his lap, stood up, and said, "Sure."

Chop looked at me like he was expecting an invitation to join, but I avoided eye contact to deny him. I held the makeshift curtain to the side to let Malik pass, and Chop tried to follow. I raised my hand to stop him and dropped the flag between Malik and myself. "Look bro, I know you want to be a part of the team, but this isn't for you," I explained calmly to our good-intentioned captain. "Give us a little time, okay?"

"Yeah. Okay. I get it," he nodded and sat down.

I peeled the curtain back again and joined Malik in the wide-open cargo hold. "Come on, it's over here," I said as I led him to the storage of the thirty gravity bombs. Each of them was secured tightly with mechanical clamps against the wall, and I drew Malik's attention to the first one. "This is Gabriela," I said as I tapped the bomb with her name marking it in red paint. "Gabriela was a fifty-two-year-old mother of four and grandmother of one. She lived in Buenos Aires with her husband Javier. They enjoyed doing crossword puzzles together over their morning coffee. Gabriela died a month ago, and her body has never been recovered."

Malik ran his hand over his head uncomfortably and audibly groaned at the loss that connected with his own.

"This is Mikhail," I said, moving on to the next bomb marked with a victim's name. "Mikhail was a seventeen-year-old boy from Moscow. He had just learned to drive, and he was saving up to buy a used car. He was very much looking forward to using his new wheels to take a young lady out on a date. Mikhail died a month ago, and his body has never been recovered."

"Please," Malik stuttered. "Please don't." His eyes welled up with tears as his breathing became erratic. I almost stopped as his pain rose to the surface and presented itself in a visceral fashion.

"This is Maisie, and this is Marcus," I said through tears of my own as I highlighted their names marking the bombs assigned to them. "Marcus was a bright boy with an inquisitive mind. He was as sound of a role model for his younger sister as one could hope for. Maisie was an innocent little girl who had nothing but love in her heart. She was the..." I paused as my lip quivered and my nose ran. I wiped the snot away and summoned the strength to continue. "She was the apple of her father's eye. They died one month ago, and their bodies have never been recovered."

Malik fell to his knees in a full-body weep that released weeks of pent-up pain and sadness. He sobbed uncontrollably with his hands over his eyes, gasping for breath between his deep wailings. I stood over him, rubbing the back of his head gently. I gave him time to let it all out and pour his tears like a river flowing to join the ocean of everyone else's.

"We don't go simply to honor Gabriela, Mikhail, Marcus, Maisie, and all the others. We go to avenge them. Stand up, Malik," I encouraged. I hugged him and my vest pulled snug as his hands vice-gripped around my backstraps. "You're charged with purpose, Malik. Justice has selected you, and not just for your family, but for *all* the families. We represent them and they demand that you know your enemy."

He released me from his bear hug and found the chest of his uniform stained with a mixture of my tears and nasal leakage. "Sorry," I said with a trembling half-cry and half-laugh at the mess I'd left behind. "Tell anybody about that, and I'll kill you," I joked.

"You're a good friend, Maya. Your secrets are safe with me," he paused. "You think I could be alone for a little bit?" he asked as he examined the names of the other twenty-six bombs.

"Sure. We'll be on the bridge whenever you want to join us."

I grabbed my duffle bag off my cot and returned to my station. "Everything good?" Chop asked.

"Yeah. With a little mood shift, I think we're going to be peachy," I said as I scrolled through my playlist to find something to change gears. I skipped ahead to Stabbing Westward's "Save Yourself" and removed my kit from the duffle bag.

"What the hell are you doing?" Chop asked as I unknotted the small, twisted-up corner of a sandwich bag.

"Coke. You want some?" I asked while pouring a small mound on the smooth face of the energy sensors and cutting out a line. "I brought plenty," I continued with the tooter to my nose and a strong inhale vacuuming up the powder. "Oof," I groaned with my thumb plugging my nostril closed from the outside.

"Jesus Christ, Maya."

"What? You going to throw me in the brig? Rat me out?"

"You know I'm not, but it might be a decent idea to keep your head in the game when you're flying a billion miles an hour through a murder hole in space."

"Bro, you're so uptight. There's two days to kill. You can park the act for a bit. Egg Shells ain't around to put you under the microscope."

The flag rolled back, and Malik joined us with a new composure. We shared a glance, and though his eyes were red, he had the look of a man with purpose. "There's my dawg," I said, raising my fist for him to bump.

"What is this *Egg Shells* thing?" Chop asked, which received a chuckle from Malik.

I went back into my kit and put a pre-rolled joint to my lips. "You want to tell him, or should I?" I asked Malik through the corner of my mouth while flicking the spark wheel and putting flame to paper.

"It's your girl, Emilia," Malik explained. "That's what the troops call her, 'cause you know." He paused with an embarrassed smile. "She's scary."

Chop didn't take an immediate defense of Emilia, but his cheeks turning blush gave him away. "What's the story with you two, anyway?" I asked as I exhaled a plume of smoke.

Malik leaned over to grab the strap of my bag, pulled out a bottle of whiskey, and sipped straight from the source. "She's his publicist," he joked.

"She's not my publicist."

"Come on, Chop. Spill it." I teased as I tried to pass him the joint. "Hit it. Don't make me smoke alone," I pleaded, and he turned his nose up at the offer. "I tell ya what, scars or not, I'd fuck that girl in half," I said, intentionally crossing the line to get a rise out of Chop and causing Malik to spit up whiskey at the same time.

"Maya!" Malik gasped like a father surprisingly amused at his child's potty mouth.

"Gimme that," Chop grinned and shook his head as I passed him the joint. He hit it twice and slipped into a coughing fit after exhaling a cloud that coated the ceiling. He passed the joint towards Malik who waved it off. Before Chop could apply any peer pressure, I reached forward and claimed my goodie.

"She is hot, right?" Chop asked rhetorically with a buzz kicking in.

"Like the surface of the sun. Details. We want details," I encouraged.

"Nothing happened," Chop smirked.

"What a gentleman. Good for you, man," Malik said.

'Don't encourage him," I teased, slapping Malik's knee. "Chivalry is dead. Don't you dare revive that bitch now. I want my deets."

"I'm serious. Nothing happened." Chop motioned for Malik to pass him the whiskey, and I knew there was far more to this story.

"Earth's last mission and I get stuck with a couple of prudes. Go figure," I bemoaned.

Chop took a swig, wiped his mouth, and said "She's like, the most interesting person I've ever met. Honestly, and God, she'd kill me if she could hear me, but I think she might be a virgin."

"Get the fuck outta here," I said, dismissing the idea.

"In this day and age, that's pretty incredible if true," Malik added.

"I don't think it's like a *saving myself for marriage* type situation," Chop elaborated. "I've been trying to hit it for weeks, but she's stonewalling me," he said, which set off my bullshit detector. Chop was putting on a show; saying the things he thought were expected of him as a soldier sharing pillow talk stories. He was into Emilia in the most respectful of ways, and he'd never be in this conversation if not for the buzz inspiring him to mimic who he thought he was supposed to be. "I think she might be, uhh, I don't know, damaged?" he concluded.

"B-F-D," I said as I cut out another line of coke for myself. "Everybody's damaged."

"What about you? What's your story?" Chop asked.

"Good luck with that," Malik interjected. "Maya is a bank vault."

"Oh, bullshit. I've told you plenty."

"Well, now you can tell me too," Chop begged. "What else are we going to do to fill the time? How about that?" he asked, pointing to my arm. "There has to be a story behind *Dishonorably Discharged*."

"All right. You boys want to get real? Fine. I'll tell you the story, but only if you hit this blow with me," I stated my terms to Chop.

"I'll do it if you will," Chop said to Malik.

"No thanks. My imagination can fill the gaps," Malik said.

"He doesn't have to," I excused Malik from the obligation, "but you do," I said to Chop.

"Ugh. Fine. *Chop* me out a line," he said, making his pun intentional.

"Wow, dude. That was so bad," I said with a laugh that was more at him than with him.

Malik, however, thought it was the funniest thing he'd ever heard. He laughed so hard that he couldn't squeeze out a verbal response until he had composed himself. "Oh, man. That was elite," he chuckled. As lame as the joke was, it brought me delight to see Malik happy.

"All right son, hit it," I said, handing Chop the tooter. He launched into snorting the exceptionally huge line I laid out for him and pulled back with a cough and groan before he could get to the end. "Pussy," I said as I pushed him back towards his captain's chair with my foot, licked my finger to dab up what he left unfinished, and rubbed it on my gums.

"Go. Let's hear it," Chop said as he sniffled the last of the dust into his system.

"I was eight months into my first deployment with the Marines," I said with all the gravitas and speed of a coke-fueled storyteller. "Fresh out of boot camp and ready to kick the world's ass. Instead of getting a proper battle, we were the cleanup crew in a series of shit-hole towns two hundred miles outside of Mogadishu. There were these Zeets, or Zips, or whatever the hell they named themselves. Freedom fighters in their own minds, pirates and terrorists to everyone else."

I paused to light a cigarette and add dramatic suspense. "Anyways, we were in pursuit but had orders not to engage. Civilian casualties and all that bad PR bullshit. The officers always think they've got it all figured out, but they weren't seeing what we were seeing on the ground. These pirates were ruthless. They'd roll into a village, kill the men, rape the women, take anything of value, and move on. We wasted so much time avoiding collateral damage that we inevitably became responsible for some of the carnage."

"We did finally catch up to them though. We entered a village under raid at dusk, and the sun had already set on the hopes of those poor people. There were bodies of men and even children everywhere. Too fresh for the stink to set in. I can still see this kid. Couldn't have been more than three years old. He had a terrible wound from his neck to his chest, and he was just screaming and screaming. Bloody murder screaming," I emphasized as I recalled the horror.

"Some of the pirates were killed in the ensuing firefight, and others surrendered to capture. I kicked into a hut during the engagement and found Toes. I don't know his real name, but he was wearing sandals, and he had the nastiest damn toes I'd ever seen. I'm talking corns, warts, and toenails like a velociraptor. His dirty, torn pants were around his ankles as he stood between the legs of a teenage girl. Toes had gone through the trouble of binding her hands so she couldn't put up a proper fight no matter how hard she kicked or squirmed."

"You shot him?" Malik interrupted with intrigue.

"No. He was unarmed. I shouted at him, which of course, he didn't understand. He wouldn't get off her, so I yanked him to the ground and subdued him. He was disgusting. His breath. His body odor. I mean, the guy stunk like an unwashed asshole. I felt filthy being anywhere near him, and this poor girl had to endure the worst of him."

"Toes was taken into custody with five of the other pieces of shit. I stayed behind, untied the girl, and tried to comfort her in any way I could, but there's no language you can speak to erase the unspeakable. The damage was done."

"The other Marines were quite proud of themselves. They stayed up late, drinking and celebrating their supposed victory. I was in my bunk alone, and all I could think about was the screaming child and that poor girl. It was so triggering. I couldn't help but think back to.,.," I paused to decide how much of myself I was comfortable exposing, and I lit another cigarette. If I had known our death was a certainty, I might have shared my actual personal trauma with the team.

"Anyways, I couldn't sleep, and it was really pissing me off that Toes and his pals were resting comfortably in the care of the US Marine Corp. They'd have hot meals and medical care would be provided if necessary. A real plush situation for scumbags who didn't deserve to take another breath. Meanwhile, the girl that Toes defiled would never get her chance to see him bleed because I followed protocol. I had caught him in the act, and all I had to do was pull the trigger, make up some bullshit story to cover for it; and the prick would be in a body bag." I took a final long drag that burned my cigarette to the filter, swiped it against my pants to extinguish it, and exhaled the smoke through my nose. "Better late than never was my assessment."

"So, I walked my way into the holding area, drew my sidearm on the guard, forced my way into the cells, and murdered Toes' five pals in front of him. I waited long enough for him to experience hope that I had come to my senses and that I'd spare him. Then I put two in his belly. He begged for mercy, but justice was the only item on the menu. I watched him squirm and bleed out on the floor, tore off a patch of his shirt as a souvenir, and disappeared into the desert night on my own. I've been on the run ever since, and I was pretty sure I'd never be allowed to serve again. *Dishonorably Discharged.*"

Chop slowly rubbed his hands together and Malik swallowed hard as my story came to its conclusion. It was an uncomfortable moment between the three of us, and neither of them spoke any commentary nor asked any questions even though I knew they had some. I was indifferent to sharing the intimate look into my life. The only shame or regret I harbored for the things I'd done was the isolation they'd caused in my life from those who didn't agree with my methods.

It was quiet on the bridge except for the music for some time after that. We passed the bottle between the three of us for the better part of thirty minutes before I decided to break the ice and lighten the mood.

"Hey. What's the one thing you can do sober in a combat zone that you can't do when you're wasted?" I asked as the setup to my joke.

"I don't know," Malik said.

"Me neither. I never tried it." Their laughter brought us back and opened the conversation again which lasted deep into the night thanks to being fueled by drugs and alcohol.

We went a little too hard that night and ended up paying the price in the morning. Malik got sick from the drinking, and Chop complained of a headache the entire next day. I brought enough party favors to go full-on *Fear And Loathing In Las Jump Point*, but I stashed my kit for the day. While it would be a waste of some perfectly good drugs, I held out hope that we'd have something to celebrate on the way home.

We lounged about all day. Sometimes in solitary on our cots and other times in groups of two. Later in the evening after we had dinner together, we broke down the battle plan one last time to make sure that we had our shit together. We were ten hours from our destination when we went to bed on the second night, and we woke two hours before go time.

We had a lively breakfast before Chop and Malik took their stations and locked in. I loaded the first ten bombs into the launch tube and took special care to ensure that *Maisie* and *Marcus* stayed on the shelf. I hoped for an element of final justice for Malik by dropping his babies as our last two pieces of ordinance to close out the attack.

I joined them on the bridge and took my seat at the targeting station. Malik had my phone, and he was scrolling through the songs to find something to play. "It's on here, right?" he asked.

"You know I got you, bro. Keep looking," I replied.

"I got it. Thank you." He handed it back to me.

Malik's choice was Al Green's "Let's Stay Together," and I risked a little extra volume to encourage him to sing along even though Chop gave me the look of a disapproving father.

"Good morning, Arrow Group. Titan Group," Chop broadcast through the radio. "Jump point exit ahead. Switch to manual and stick to the plan. Five minutes to target."

"Try not to screw this up," Risa's voice came over the airwaves.

The white dot on our visual display was growing larger by the second as we sped towards it. Chop switched off the radio, folded his hands, and prayed the Meditation On Lord Shiva in Hindi softly to himself. "You suppose prayers are heard in a black hole?" he asked.

"God couldn't hear mine from the kitchen table. I doubt he's listening now," Malik replied coldly as he powered up the gravity cannons and pulled his targeting controls close to his lap.

I did a triple check of my energy sensors and targeting computer. The moment was upon us, and we were less collectively anxious than I had anticipated.

"Sixty seconds. Slow to exit speed. Everyone, on point!" Chop announced louder than before. He reached over and grabbed Malik's shoulder and waited for their eyes to meet. "For Lydia," was all he said.

"For Emilia," Malik responded in kind.

"For Marcus and Maisie," I added.

"Five, four, three, two, one," Chop counted us down before we blasted through to the other side. There wasn't a ship in sight waiting for us. Only the spaceport to our left and the planet surface below.

"Go go go!" Chop yelled with no composure. He banked sharply to the left towards the giant silver sphere of a space station that was reflecting the purple light of the Jump Point as the other heavies navigated their way into position over their assigned continents from space.

Malik gripped the cannon targeting tightly as Chop slowed to an attack speed. "Malik? Malik?!" I shouted as he hesitated to fire. "Fire! Malik, fire!" I yelled.

He took aim and squeezed the trigger as he let out a primal "Ahhh!" The gravity wave only became visible by the damage it caused impacting the side of the spaceport.

"We're coming back around, Malik. Hit it again," Chop instructed.

Once more, Malik unleashed a wave at the damaged structure, this time cracking through the hull and inevitably applying the pressures of the vacuum of space. Before we could make our third pass, the crack splintered like glass in an unpredictable spiderweb pattern. The station split into two, and Malik's next targeted wave decimated the exposed ships on the interior, crushing them like empty beer cans against the foreheads of drunken frat boys.

"Arrow 2. Bombs away," Risa announced over the radio as the first drop took place on the other side of the planet. Excited hollering filled the airwaves followed by Kai informing "They're not ready for us. No surface weapon engagement."

"Go Chop. Go!" I encouraged as he meandered in space examining the wreckage of the port. We were close enough to witness dozens of lifeless Praxi bodies floating frozen in space among the destruction.

"Right. Right. Uhhh, Arrow 1. Heading in," he announced as he navigated towards our assigned continent with one of our pencil craft fighters covering our backs.

"That's it. Slow it down," I instructed as I read the energy sensors and aligned the targeting. "Right there. Stop," I said as the targeting computer locked on. "Suck on this!" I shouted as the first of our thirty bombs deployed to the surface below. It moved so fast we could barely see it disappear through the upper atmosphere. The cloud cover was heavy over our target, but they pushed away in all directions five seconds after detonation. The destruction on the surface below was an instant circular indentation where a city stood moments earlier.

"Ahhhh. Fu...fuck," Chop stuttered in pain as he ripped his communicator off and gripped his forehead.

"Hey. Hey!" Malik said as he shook Chop by the shoulder.

I moved on to the next largest energy reading on the continent that was targetable from our position and released the second payload. "Bu-bye," I said with a sing-song tone.

Chop's eyes rolled in his head momentarily, but he maintained consciousness. We didn't have time for whatever he was dealing with, and I continued scratching targets off the surface one by one until the firing tube was empty of the first ten shells.

"Get him sorted out," I barked as I ran into the cargo hull and loaded the next ten bombs into the tube, again leaving *Marcus* and *Maisie* secured in their place on the wall.

By the time I returned, Amir had curled up in the seat he felt I had warmed for him. He stared at me with puppy dog eyes that were oblivious to the tensions around him. "Get. Get!" I shooed him away. Chop had his headset on again, moved us into position over the next continent, and seemed to have regained the limited amount of composure he had to begin with. "Titan group: move to the surface," he commanded as Kai and the one-man fighters dropped into the atmosphere to seek out more targets and check for defenses.

I locked onto ten more energy signatures and systematically wiped them from existence one by one without so much as a hint of resistance. "Where the hell are their fighters?" I asked, almost disappointed that we weren't getting any combat up close and personal.

"Destroyed in the spaceport," Malik answered logically. "Go load the rest, Maya," he ordered. I ran into the cargo hold for the final time, loading the bombs with *Marcus* and *Maisie* at the very end.

Again, Amir had claimed my vacated spot as if it was rightfully his. "All right, buddy, we'll compromise," I said as I let him sit in my lap. We were preparing for what felt like the leisurely final stage of our assault when some excitement came over the radio. "Titan 5. Bogeys! Multiple bogeys. Continent 5."

"The other way," Malik instructed as Chop pulled back from the planet and navigated in the wrong direction.

The first of three Praxi pencil fighters shot out of the atmosphere to our right and buzzed overhead at a speed that made it impossible to target. Chop tried to swing around, but by the time we were in position to pursue, the craft was out of sight.

"Where the hell'd he go?" Chop panicked. The ship popped back up on the visuals and had one of Titan group on its tail.

"Arrow 1," I announced taking command. "You see us, Titan 5? Herd him in our direction."

"I've got this, Maya," Chop stammered.

"Do you?" I challenged. "Ready on those cannons, Malik. Hit that prick as they fly by."

The enemy craft was on top of us before we knew it, and again, Chop failed to maneuver and follow a line of sight to set up Malik's shot.

"God dammit, Chop!" I shouted.

"Titan 1. In pursuit of two more bogeys headed for the atmosphere. Check that. Make that one bogey," Kai calmly relayed his ace kill.

"The Jump Point. They're going for the Jump Point!" Malik shouted as he pointed at the monitoring screen. "Go Chop! Go."

We zipped around to the other side of the planet and sped toward the portal structure. "Line us up so we're facing across the surface," Malik instructed. "That's it. Right there. Right there. Keep it steady," Malik calmly ordered as he gripped the cannon controls. "Come on, you suckers. Come to Daddy."

The first of the two pencils still in the air was fast approaching without anyone in Titan group in pursuit. "There he is," I said, needlessly pointing it out.

Malik didn't wait for the craft to catch us off guard. He held the trigger down and pulsated a constant energy wave across the surface, and our enemy took the bait. The ship rocketed through Malik's fire and shriveled into compact, mangled wreckage that disappeared as it passed through the Jump Point and into the dark of the black hole. "Boom! I got you!" he celebrated.

"Titan 4. One more bogey. In pursuit and headed your way."

"Arrow 6. Moving into position."

We were setting up a perfect shot of two gravity beams side by side, covering a larger area of the surface ensuring there would be no escape, but the enemy was on us too fast. Arrow 6 was pacing towards the portal when the pencil craft slammed into its hull. There was an initial explosion on impact, but it was nothing compared to the eruption of the triggered gravity ordinance from inside Arrow 6.

The ship exploded into tiny pieces of shrapnel that went careening into space in every direction. The wave expanded fast and nearly pushed us into the physical rim of the portal housing.

It happened so quickly that we collectively sat in shock trying to process what we had seen. In one second there were two ships, and in the next, they were reduced to particles and spread like ashes across the sea of space.

"Umm. Uh, Titan group. Sound off," Chop radioed.

"Titan 1. No bogeys."

"Titan 2. No bogeys."

"All right. Okay." Chop hyperventilated as he struggled to stay on task at the first moment that things didn't go perfectly.

"The rest of the targets? Let's go, Chop. There are still energy signatures down there. Move your ass!" I barked.

We dropped back into targeting range with the rest of Arrow group and scratched every city center off the planet. I scrolled through the sensors, looking for any signs of life or power on the surface, but there was nothing remaining. "I've got four of these babies left, and nowhere to put them," I announced.

"Arrow group. Move to the surface for a closer look," Chop instructed.

I wish we hadn't gone down there. I had seen enough carnage for ten lifetimes, and the destruction on the surface put everything into terrible perspective. The craters left on the planet were at least a hundred miles wide. The wreckage would pile to the sky if it hadn't been driven deep into the sod below.

"Oh my God," Chop lamented as we hovered over the quiet surface below. The Praxi had built their civilization with condensed city centers meant to preserve enormous boroughs of wildlife across all five continents of the planet. Their attempts to sustain their environment had made their people perfect targets for elimination. The scattered craters were surrounded by thick areas of jungle, forest, and bodies of water where the other various life forms of Prius thrived.

"Let's drop the last of them into the thick stuff," Malik suggested.

"No. I uh, I think we're done," Chop replied as he ran two fingers across his forehead and his thumb across his temple. The other pilots over the radio were jubilant about the successful attack, but we didn't share in their excitement. Malik was the only one who had anything resembling a blood lust remaining.

"They could be hiding down there in the bush," Malik stated his case again.

"It's over, Malik. Justice had its fill today," I said with a shakable confidence in the principles I lived by. I didn't expose how dirty I felt because I knew that win was important for Malik, and I didn't want to sour the moment for him.

"Arrow group. Titan group. Stow the remaining ordinance. Circle up, we're going home," Chop announced.

We pulled away from the surface and grouped by the Jump Point before starting our two-day journey to return triumphantly to Earth. I doubted anyone back home was holding their breath waiting for us, and they would rightly feel saved by a miracle. How were we supposed to reconcile what felt like genocide when met with the excitement of our people?

We hit the maximum thrusters on cruise control, and the first thing I did was get back into my kit, but not because I wanted to party.

"You guys didn't feel him, did you? Chop asked.

"Who?" Malik asked.

"It was Gio. I heard his cries. I felt his pain, and it's...it's in me. He was down there somewhere, and I'm absolutely certain he was innocent. I think we killed him," Chop said with confusion and lifeless eyes.

"They got what they deserved," Malik stood on conviction.

"Bro, honestly, I don't really want to think about it," I added.

When we set out on that mission, Malik said, "It wasn't supposed to be like this." I couldn't help but feel like we ended up on that same sentiment for the journey home.

Chapter 7

Kiss of Death

Emilia Vera

It was midday when the blaring air raid sirens brought Edwards to attention. The ominous whistle was like a bedside alarm that had been triple-checked but still wouldn't allow for peaceful slumber. It was as though I had been anxiously lying awake for four days, afraid that if I went to sleep the alarm would either never sound or would fail to wake me.

The officers poured out of their quarters prepared to celebrate victory or die in a counterattack. General Kelly was out front of the building in his Jeep, and the men piled into the seats and hung off the edges to hitch a ride to the tarmac.

I opened the passenger side door and stared down at the young soldier in my seat until he sheepishly forced his way into the cramped rear bench. "Smile, Ms. Vera. Things are exactly as I promised they would be," the General boasted arrogantly.

We drove up the landing strip where hundreds of soldiers had gathered to welcome the victors home. Our attack fleet shot through the cloud cover above and landed side by side where they had sat four days earlier. I did a physical count of the converted cargo ships to find that one of them had not returned and panickily scanned the hulls searching for the *Lydia* insignia of the only craft that mattered to me.

The relief I felt when I spotted Ranbir's ship was short-lived. The other flight crews raised their fists and joined in the jubilant shouting as they met their welcoming party with handshakes and hugs. There was no such excitement from Ranbir and his crew. Their shoulders were slumped, and their heads tilted forward as if they were weighed down with shame.

I had envisioned myself out of character when daring to dream of this moment. I would run into Ranbir's open arms, he would kiss me, and I'd transform into a different person who could experience love and happiness. Instead, I muscled through the crowd to get to him, and while he smiled when he saw me; there was darkness behind his eyes. I rubbed his arms awkwardly, waiting for him to make the first move, and he hugged me tight without saying a word.

When we released, I put my hand to his neck and then his cheek, physically begging him to kiss me. He was supposed to manhandle and devour me when our lips met for the first time in fiery passion. Life, however, proved once again that fairy tales are propaganda sold to little girls to keep our hopes alive and souls intact. I had lost both long ago, if I ever had them to begin with. I wasn't surprised to have my zeal stripped away from me, but it was disappointing, nonetheless.

My hand curled around the back of his neck, and I pulled his mouth to mine. The kiss didn't last long enough for our lips to part or tongues to meet. The pressure of our lips together was barely enough for me to mark him as my property with smeared and coated gloss.

"The cameras are watching. Smile," I instructed as I forced his hand into mine and our fingers to interlock.

"Can we please get out of here?" he asked softly.

"Yeah. Yeah, sure," I replied, masking my disappointment at the subversion of my expectations.

I led Ranbir by his hand away from the crowd with Amir in tow at his feet and poked my head into General Kelly's Jeep to find that he had left the keys in the ignition. "He needs the cardio anyways," I suggested as I took over the driver's seat.

"Ms. Vera! Hey, Ms. Vera!" the General barked as I commandeered his vehicle. I sped off in the opposite direction, stuck my left hand out the window, and raised my middle finger without looking back.

"What the hell is the matter with you?" I chastised as soon as we were alone. "Everyone's watching you out there, and you're pouting like somebody kicked your dog." Truth be told, I couldn't care less about public perception. I wasn't even mad at Ranbir so much as myself for daring to believe that I could have anything resembling a positive emotional experience or storybook first kiss.

"We completely wiped them out," he answered with a blank expression.

"Yeah? And?"

"They had no planetary defenses. No engaging aircraft. They didn't even put up a fight. The few ships that cleared the surface made a mad scramble to escape without firing a single shot."

"That was the plan, right?" I asked, completely overlooking the weeks we'd spent expecting defeat now that victory had been delivered.

"Gio was down there somewhere. I felt him. I can *still* feel him."

I parked the Jeep, leaving the keys in the ignition, and we went inside. Amir ran off to find his toys, but Ranbir didn't share the same excitement to be home. He threw his bag on the floor and slumped onto the couch. "I think we did something terrible, Emilia."

"You saved billions of lives, including mine."

"I don't know. Something's not right," he said, running his hands through his hair. "What happened up there wasn't war. It was slaughter."

"What if they didn't fight back because their forces were already on their way to Earth?" It was a terrible suggestion that would mean we were living on borrowed time, but I was willing to entertain any possibility that could bring the old Ranbir back to the surface. "Maybe they tried to use the Jump Point, couldn't get through, and decided to take the long way round?"

"I guess it's possible," he conceded without showing much interest in my theory.

I sat next to him and had to turn his cheek with my hand to induce eye contact. "Hey. You did what you had to do, and whatever you're going through right now; we'll face it together." It sounded good coming out of my mouth but felt unnatural. Consoling him was like following a recipe for dealing with complex human emotions, and I was missing all the key ingredients. If Ranbir had come home with PTSD, I was not equipped to deal with it.

"I need some time to figure this out, and I don't want to do any of the publicity stuff."

"That's okay," I lied. "Take a week for yourself. Get your head right before we get back to work."

"You're not listening, Em. I don't want to do any of it. Ever. And I want to get the hell off this base."

Those were sentiments I could understand. Our motives were different, but we wanted the same things. I lived life trying to create space between myself and everyone else. It was a chore going to work every day knowing that I'd be forced into interactions I wanted nothing to do with. Ranbir was the only person I'd allowed into my life, and I could wrap my head around him needing the same buffer from everyone else. I set out to provide that for him, while also putting him to work towards my other goals.

"Let's move. Immediately. I can't stand it here either and I want to be closer to the Connect Earth compound. I'll buy a house and we'll get away from everything," I suggested.

"That sounds incredible," he said, exhibiting the first signs of the pre-mission Ranbir.

"You can take some time, but you are going to have to fulfill your obligations, you understand me? Those people out there need you," I said, which wiped the blossoming smile from his face. "I need you," I reinforced with the proper motivation.

We set out to make the best of things with our part in the war seemingly coming to an end. I purchased a quaint three-bedroom ranch home at the end of a quiet cul-de-sac less than ten minutes from CE, and we started a new life together. I said and did the things I thought a nurturing partner would. I taught Ranbir how to present the version of himself the world needed to see. His charm was natural, and even though his pain and damage remained; the more time he spent wearing a mask the better he became at it.

I kept him as distracted with public appearances as possible. Every minute he spent pretending to be who I wanted him to be was another where he wasn't forming new conspiracy theories or getting bogged down in depression. When he'd start to come off the rails, I'd employ my latest uncomfortable method of controlling him.

I'd learned a lot of lessons from Penelope over the years, and the only one I'd never implemented was sex as a weapon. She'd once said, "The greatest wars ever won had their most pivotal battles fought in a bedroom." I understood the concept but was never willing to compromise myself in that manner until Ranbir.

He demonstrated signs of healing, and anytime he backslid into depression I fed him a steady diet of home-cooked meals and passionate sex as the cure. That's the beauty of the simplicity of men. Their tolerance for physical, mental, and psychological pain is directly proportional to how often their bellies are filled and their balls are emptied.

This was a powerful emotional period for me, even though I kept it bottled up and private. It was too embarrassing to confess that I had given Ranbir my virginity and doing so would have surrendered control over the merging of business and pleasure. I had fallen in love with him in my own twisted way, and I was terrified of speaking it into an open existence.

Six weeks went by with my energy split between nurturing our relationship and working feverishly towards the launch of Connect Earth. In the meantime, the only news we had on the war front was that the World Military had located the triaxum mines on Triax II, one solar system away from Prius. The reports said our soldiers killed the Grays they encountered and seized control over production. This was thought to be the final blow for the Praxi, and General Kelly was turning his attention to his pursuits on Earth. I was set to have a meeting with him the morning before Connect Earth went live to discuss his ambitions.

I was applying my makeup when Ranbir joined me in the bathroom. "What are you doing taking a shower this early?" I asked as he warmed the water and disrobed.

"I thought maybe I could sit in on your meeting with the General," he replied as he closed the shower curtain behind himself.

"Of all the days, Ranbir, this one might be the worst. We have a lot to cover today." While that was the truth, the only person trying harder than me to keep the two of them apart had been the General himself.

"He's been ducking me, and the only way he's going to hear me out is if it's on your time," Ranbir raised his voice over the noise of the high-pressure wash.

"Are you going to antagonize him?"

Ranbir peeled the curtain back to stick his head out and look at me in the mirror. "Are you?" he grinned.

"I'm being serious. If I let you come, you're not bringing any of the crazy talk. You've left that stuff in the past, remember?" I reinforced as I had a dozen times before.

"Speaking of leaving things in the past, I've been meaning to talk to you about your plans. Connect Earth doesn't have to be OWG 2.0, you know?"

I wiped the spreading steam cloud from the mirror even though I was examining my soul rather than my physical appearance. I'd spent two months designing CE to be my personal digital joystick of control over the populace, but perhaps I didn't need that power to fill the gaping hole inside of me anymore. Maybe I could do something so positive that the next time I'd wipe the steam away to see my reflection, I wouldn't hate the person staring back at me.

Ranbir's concern for my indulging in the dark habits of my past was different from my care of his depression in motive only. I wanted Ranbir to ignore his trauma and distrust of the events on Prius for my own selfish reasons, while his interest in seeing me change for the better was genuine and pure. I might have been incapable of changing my abrasive personality, but I could potentially learn to love the way he did and be better for it.

"You should come today," I said as an invitation to a partner rather than permission to a subordinate. Ranbir had faith that I could change, and I set out to prove that he would see he was right.

We made the drive to Edwards and marched into the General's office. He sat behind his desk, a cigar burning in the ashtray, and his hands fumbling with his new Connect Earth phone.

"You brought a friend," the General said with annoyance.

"It's good to see you again, sir. You're a hard man to get a hold of," Ranbir said as he took a seat.

"Winning wars is busy work, my boy," the General replied while turning his phone front to back. "First order of business, how do you turn this blasted thing on?"

"My God, give me that," I condescended as I reached across the desk and snatched the phone out of his hand. "You see this button? The one marked 'power.' This turns it on," I said with a thick patronizing tone. The swooping CE logo coming alive on the screen gave me butterflies in my stomach. "I'm not going to hold your hand through this process,' I said as I tried to pass it back to him.

"My people will help me sort it out. The last thing I need from you is the administrative passcode."

"Ha! Administrative controls? Over *my* baby. That's fucking adorable," I mocked.

"Who else has the codes, Ms. Vera?"

'Well, there's me...and also me. Oh, and I almost forgot. Me. That pretty much covers it."

"Someone else needs to have those codes, Ms. Vera. What happens if you experience a tragedy? Connect Earth would be useless."

"Why? Are you planning something?" Ranbir asked, making his suspicions obvious.

"Connect Earth is mine, and that includes the succession plan," I stated firmly. "I'll find someone I trust to carry out my vision for the platform, and I'll whisper them the administrative codes on my deathbed and not a moment before. Satisfied?"

I knew what I was doing from the moment I designed the system. Centralized power of that magnitude would draw the attention of people with greed equal to my own and locking everyone out was one of my insurance plans. It was no secret that the World Military was calling the shots, but if they wanted control over the people; they were stuck playing ball with me. I couldn't be removed or eliminated without loss of administrative access to the platform.

The last thing I wanted was to see my creation destroyed, but I was prepared for every eventuality. I even embedded a virus I aptly named Armageddon Protocol into every line of code and software in the event I was ever backed into a corner. All it would take was a few keystrokes, and I could reverse the flow of power from the triaxum generators, frying the entire system from the inside. This would of course be a last resort, but it was available if necessary. I wanted CE to live on forever, but only in the hands of someone I trusted.

General Kelly sighed with the dismay of a novice chess player who wasn't equipped to put his master in checkmate. "Very well, Ms. Vera. The World Military still expects your compliance in aiding the war effort, however."

"State your requests," I said, which caused Ranbir to lean forward with interest.

"This war won't be over until every last one of those godless Gray demons is dead, and we can't hunt their other outposts without triaxum. The mines need workers, Ms. Vera, and it's not an environment fit for a volunteer."

"*State your requests,*" I repeated.

"We're going to empty the world's prisons. Those with life sentences will be deported to Prius, and those with shorter sentences will be given an option. Either deport with the lifers or work the mines for a year to earn their rehabilitation back into a faithful society."

"What?" Ranbir interjected with a laugh at the ridiculousness of the idea. "You can't do that."

The General ignored him and continued his request. "We need you to use Connect Earth to *soften the blow* with the public. Convince them of the merits of purging our society of the sinners while advancing the war efforts at the same time."

"Anything else?" I asked.

"I want you to monitor traffic on the platform and report back on individuals speaking out against the state. I also expect you to hold up your end of the bargain concerning incentivizing citizens to embrace their religion to the point where they'll pressure their faithless friends and neighbors to do the same."

"Yeah, I'm not doing that," I informed the General and looked to Ranbir for his approval of the new me in action. "I can help you with the war efforts, the prisoners, and the mining; but I'm done manipulating freedom of thought away from the citizens. They've been through enough without having you jam religion down their throats." I might have been more amenable or tempted to be my old terrible self if the General's request wasn't so uninteresting and boring to me.

"That will not do, Ms. Vera. Where is my *Argentinian Assassin*? Don't forget, I had you in chains not long ago. I let you go under the assumption that we'd be partners."

I reached across the desk, lifted his simmering cigar out of the ashtray, puffed it twice, and extinguished it. "And how's that working out for you?" I taunted.

"Concerning the war effort," Ranbir piggybacked off my control of the situation, "I was curious why you never debriefed with me following the assault."

"You ran away like a wounded doe. I only have time for *real* soldiers," the General sneered.

"Oooh, burn," Ranbir quipped sarcastically. "I'm also curious why you made no efforts to defend against the next wave of attacks. Did it never occur to you that the whole of the Praxi forces may have ventured on the two-month journey to get here because the Jump Point was shut down?"

"There's no fleet coming, *boy*," he insulted.

"How could you possibly know that?"

"I know many things," the General replied with insinuation.

Ranbir paused as he worked out how hard he was going to push. I could get away with whatever I pleased where the General was concerned, but Ranbir didn't have that same armor. I hoped he would understand his lack of leverage, but his strategic thinking went out the window as soon as his theories and anger took hold. "What *actually* happened on Prius?" he pressed. "You knew when you sent us up there that it would be a slaughter. You never would've sent your marketable poster boy on a suicide mission, would you? You can't inspire everyone to work to the bone remaking the world without my smile."

"Your smile might be even more effective if you were dead," the General replied coldly. "Now, get the hell out of my office with these innuendos before this becomes a conversation about how you got on that mission in the first place."

Ranbir stormed out and the General held me with the type of stare I was familiar with, but not accustomed to being on the receiving end of. "Secure your property and check your priorities, Ms. Vera," he warned.

I joined Ranbir in the car and waited until we were off the base before I laced into him. "What the hell were you doing in there?"

"I was right all along, and you wouldn't hear it. The man is hiding something."

"No shit. He's not the only one," I said, staring over at Ranbir with intent rather than the road. He looked away from me and took the wheel to keep the car from veering into traffic. "Well? Do you have something to share with me?"

"Like what?" he played stupid, momentarily taking his eyes off the road to look at me.

"You tell me. Does he have some dirt on you?"

"Will you please just watch the road," he begged.

"No. Screw you," I snapped as I pressed harder on the accelerator and released the wheel entirely. "What aren't you telling me?"

"Nothing! I swear," he proclaimed as he took the wheel with both hands.

I reached down, unbuckled my seatbelt, and threw it over my shoulder. "Swear on my life," I said as I increased the speed further.

"Em. Em! Red light! Slow down!" he panicked as we blasted through cross traffic in the intersection. "Jesus Christ! I swear! I swear on your life! I have no idea what he was talking about. He's trying to play us against each other."

I took my foot off the gas and swiped his hands away from the wheel with disgust to regain control. I wanted so badly to believe him, but I had tasted so many lies on my tongue that I recognized the sounds of others when they reached my ears.

Neither of us spoke again until I had parked the car in the garage, and I took a deep composing breath before I started. "I want to make sure you're crystal clear, Ranbir. Kelly threatened to kill you today, and I suspect the only reason you're still breathing is because I won't allow it."

"I don't need your protection," he stated like a petulant spoiled child.

"You idiot. Do you have any idea the kind of people you're dealing with or how to navigate this world? If there's a buried grand conspiracy, the last thing you want to do is pick up a shovel."

"So, what am I supposed to do?" he asked with dejection.

"Let it go," I offered with as much care as I could. "Please. For me. Just let it go. I'm trying really hard to be a better version of myself, and I can't do it without you."

"I'll try," was the best he could offer.

It was supposed to be a huge night for me, but I couldn't have cared less when Connect Earth went live. I had been emotionally compromised. When everyday people have relationship problems, the issues can be worked out in therapy. When I have them, someone might die. The pit in my stomach and the uncomfortable silence in my home was a reminder of why I avoided relationships in the first place.

Three days went by, and every moment I spent at the CE compound was shrouded in worry that Ranbir would be doing something foolish while left unattended. We were gaining tens of millions of users every day, and great success meant nothing if I was unhappy when I went home. I had to trust that if I remained true to being a better person, over time Ranbir would let the past lie.

I cooked dinner that night and Ranbir was doing the dishes per our arrangement when there were three knocks at the door. The sound of knuckles rapping was foreign and felt ominous. I peered through the peephole like a sniper through a scope, ready to eliminate whoever dared seek me out. When I saw who it was, I couldn't unfasten the series of locks and deadbolts fast enough.

"Penelope Martin. In the flesh," I laughed with cheerful excitement to see my only friend. "I thought you were dead."

"My enemies wish it so, and I continue to defy them," she announced with Broadway regality. "You look wonderful, darling."

"I can't believe you're here. Where have you been? What did you do after the OWG?" my tongue raced.

"Patience, Emilia," she said with a Cheshire grin. "Take my coat," she continued as she peeled it off her shoulders.

Ranbir stuck his head out of the kitchen to see what the fuss was about. "Do we have company?" he asked surprised.

"Oh my. You're co-habituating," Penelope said with veiled judgment.

"Penelope Martin, meet Ranbir Chopra," I introduced.

"Ah. The savior of Earth," Penelope said as she struck a pose with her fists to her hips mimicking Ranbir's propaganda posters.

"And that makes you the Lady Penelope," Ranbir replied, turning on the charm that had been missing for days. "You're pressed with a difficult task if you're going to live up to everything Emilia has made you out to be."

"She was a brilliant yet insolent child when I met her, and it seems you've accomplished the one thing I could not. You've turned the brat into a lady," she congratulated.

"Let's have a whiskey and see how ladylike I become," I said, inviting them into the kitchen. "How did you find us?"

"He's easy to find. You, not so much. I see your work everywhere though. Connect Earth, my God, Emilia. It's brilliant. Look at this," she said as she slid her CE phone onto the table, "you've even got me carrying around this bloody contraption. You're probably tracking my whereabouts and listening in on my phone calls."

I poured three glasses and left the bottle on the table. Hearing praise from Penelope was the nectar of the gods to me, and I hoped she wouldn't judge me for turning over a new leaf. "I'm taking a different approach this time around. No more surveillance and manipulation for me. Let people do and think whatever they want."

"Yes, I've heard," she revealed as she sipped her whiskey. "I went to Edwards Airfield looking for you, and I wound up in the company of the stuffy General Kelly. He's a boring and unintelligent man, but his ambitions have never been higher."

"What did he say?" Ranbir perked up.

"He's shipping the prison population off to the deserted planet, and he doesn't intend to stop there. The man hasn't experienced an erection in twenty years, but he was full throttle when he mentioned enacting articles of the religious state."

"He can't do that!" Ranbir started in while shooting me I-told-you-so eyes. "We haven't even elected a governing body yet."

"The World Military is in control now, and I'm afraid they're being led by a theocratic zealot," Penelope lamented.

The last thing I wanted was a triggered Ranbir rant in front of my idol, and Penelope was pushing all the right buttons to send him over the edge. "The General's hands are cuffed, and I'm holding the key. He can make whatever moves he wants, but I'll always have final say over the opinions of the people."

Ranbir looked at the clock and got up from the table. "Stay here. There's something you ladies need to hear," he said as he hustled towards the basement.

Penelope took another sip and sighed when she put her glass down. "He wants me to work for him."

"Now, that's rich. Are you looking for work? Why didn't you just ask me?"

"Pride, I suppose. You think you'd have something in your digital empire for this old crow to do?"

"Absolutely! I'm surrounded by people who hate me that I can't trust. The developers and programmers are less than pleased that every tweak and update must go through me. I could really use a friend," I said earnestly.

"Okay, check this out," Ranbir said as he plugged in an old boom box on the counter. "After the blackout, most of the airwaves went dead. Resistance networks started popping up on the radio, and they have some very interesting theories."

"Ranbir," I said with warning in my eyes, "Penelope doesn't want to hear any of this."

"Quite the contrary, darling. I'm intrigued," she said.

"This girl does a radio show every night at 8 p.m. She's all over the General's ass. It's like she has every piece of the puzzle, but she doesn't know where they fit," he said as he flipped the radio on.

"If you're hearing this, it's because you're curious. Curious why the advanced, galaxy-hopping aliens would give a shit if we had nuclear weapons or not before they attempted to enslave us. Curious why the Praxi didn't wipe us out when they first attacked. Curious why they left their door open by not shutting down the Jump Point on their end. Curious how they could allow themselves to be killed by a fleet of converted U-Haul trucks dropping bombs from space. Curious how we seized control of their mining planet with almost no resistance. You're asking the right questions, and if we work together, we can..." the voice said before I pulled the cord from the wall.

"I think she sent a message to me on CE today," Ranbir said as he unlocked his phone and navigated towards her profile. I didn't need to see the name or the picture to know who it was. My personal, demented gravitational pull had a way of gripping hold of the few people I allowed inside my circle and trapping them in my life forever. "Alexis X" Ranbir announced. "Her profile is still pending verification, but I'm pretty sure this is the radio girl. Check it out, she sent these maps and an official timeline of the attack on Earth," he rambled since Penelope was willing to listen. "She wants to meet."

"That's about enough crazy for one night," I said holding back the fury boiling inside of me. "Why don't you come see me at the compound tomorrow at 8 a.m.? I'll get you a security badge, and an office, and we'll find something for you to work on," I said to Penelope as I held up her coat.

"That sounds wonderful darling. I'm itching to get back in the game. It's lovely meeting you, Ranbir, savior of Earth. Do be careful where your curiosity takes you," she winked.

I couldn't get her out of the house fast enough. "Good night," I said as I closed the door behind her and watched her walk to her car through the peephole.

"Alexis X? Of all the people. Have you been talking to her behind my back?" I ask with paranoia talking hold.

"Not really," he replied sheepishly.

"*Not really* means yes, you prick."

"It was one message, and it's not like that. I don't even know this girl. It's strictly business. I love you."

"Don't use that tired sentiment as a shield. I told you, *specifically*, to leave this shit alone. Not only do you ignore me when I'm trying to do what's best for you, but you embarrass me in front of the only fucking person on the planet I care to impress!"

"I love you," he repeated with purpose as if to draw a confession from a subject.

"Stop saying that!"

"Why? Because you can't say it back?" he pressed.

"No, because I *don't* say that."

"I noticed," he sneered to mask how much my inability to openly state my love hurt him. "The least you could say is that you're sorry."

"Yeah well, I don't say that either."

"Were you ever not working me? Was this ever real for you?" Ranbir's buried concerns rose to the surface.

"Don't turn this shit around on me! This is about you! I changed who I am at a fundamental core level. For you! All I asked in return was that you leave well enough alone. That's literally all you have to do for us to be happy together."

"You didn't commit genocide, Emilia! I did! You either don't want to see it, or your heart is so cold and dead on the inside that you can't understand what I'm going through."

"Oh boo-hoo. Poor soldier killed some aliens and now he's *a sad wittle boy*. Grow up."

"I was used by this regime, and I deserve to know what happened."

"The truth has never set anyone free, Ranbir. Stop trying to be the first."

"You know what, I'm done. You said we were going to do this together, but you have zero interest in the truth if it threatens what you want. I'm taking this meeting with Alexis X tomorrow."

"If you do this to me, I won't protect you," I warned with futility.

"Like I give a shit," he barked as he stormed towards the bedroom.

"Whoa. Where do you think you're going?"

"To bed. This conversation is pointless, and I can't stand the sight of you anymore tonight."

"Like hell you are! You're not sleeping in *my* bed!" I shouted as I chased him down the hallway and pulled him into the living room by the back of his shirt.

"Fine, Emilia. That's fine. I'm leaving in the morning, and don't expect me to come back. You can crawl back into your hole of loneliness for all I care."

I wasn't myself by that point. The old Emilia would have never let Ranbir get the last word in, but she also would never be in the position to get hurt in the first place. The new Emilia wanted to cry but her tear ducts were dammed by ego and pride. I wanted to both hurt him and apologize for the first time in my life simultaneously. My emotional confusion drove me to do neither.

I went to my bedroom and closed the door gently behind me rather than instinctively slamming it. Finding love for me was like discovering a rare flower in the wild, but the moment I plucked it as my own, it withered and rotted in my hand. I could only watch others enjoy it from a distance while never attaining it for myself.

I kicked the sheets all night like a drug addict sweating out the last few drops of affection. You can't appreciate the perks of being a sociopath until you live a few days as a normie. The lack of care for anything or anyone makes the bed softer and blankets warmer.

Empathy builds a theater in your mind, and bedtime is the world premiere of the film "Today: The Stupid Shit You Said and The Things You Wish You Could Take Back." The genre of the film is never buddy cop or romantic comedy. It's always a drama, and it features a repeating loop of your blunders and things that are hurting you until the screaming in your mind subsides to an audible level that rolls the credits and allows for sleep. I pre-ordered my tickets for this show the first time Ranbir made me smile. I allowed him to pass through the barricades into my life hoping that nights like this would never come. I had no idea that when I'd be forced to strap in and watch the highlight reel of my relationship pain it would be the 6-hour director's cut edition.

I tried not to cry when I stood in front of him with my heart breaking, and now that I was alone, I couldn't force a single tear to the surface. It had taken me months to learn how to love. It only took me a few hours to remember how to hate.

I tossed and turned until the sun crept through the windows and forced me to realize that I wouldn't be able to sleep. I climbed out of bed with the intent of sneaking out before Ranbir woke, but I discovered that he was gone but left all his things including Amir. He'd be back, and so long as he didn't do anything rash, I could still choose to pursue an apology if that's what I wanted.

I got ready for the day and made my way to my office at CE where Penelope was waiting outside my door.

"Good morning, boss," she smiled.

"Eh," I grunted as I opened the door with my security badge and plopped down into my executive chair. I powered up my terminal and wasted no time logging in with my administrative password.

Penelope sat across from me, anxiously tapping her nails on my desk. "Are you going to tell me what's bothering you?" she asked.

I helped myself into Ranbir's CE account without answering her. I scanned through his messages to find his communications with Alexis hoping to discover something scandalous enough to further fuel my rage. Alexis had shared some documents with him, and there were only a few messages back and forth, the last of which was setting an 11 AM meeting in LA. I checked in on his GPS tracking and found him traveling on the interstate toward his date.

"This stupid son of a bitch," I said under my breath.

"Boy troubles?" Penelope asked.

"He's on his way to meet the radio girl, no thanks to you. God knows what kind of trouble she's going to get him into. He's not in a positive mental state."

"Well, don't let him get there," Penelope suggested.

"He's hours away already, and I doubt he's going to be taking my calls."

"You have everything you need to get him off the streets, and you don't even need to leave your office."

"Would you cut the cryptic shit? If you've got a good idea, let's hear it."

"You're already in his account. Post something.," she suggested. "Strong enough to get him picked up by the authorities, but not bad enough to do any real damage."

"I don't know. He won't know that I'm spying on him, but he'll definitely know it was me if he gets locked up for a post he didn't write."

"Emilia Vera, when did you lose your edge? Did this man break you?" Penelope pulled out her phone and opened the Connect Earth log-in screen. "Here, I'll do it for you. What's the admin passcode? I'll post from his account, you can blame me, and I'll add Ranbir to the long list of men who hate me."

"It's fine. I've got it," I assured as I began typing a post from Ranbir's account.

"I can't live with this pain any longer. If I can't get my meds, I'm going to hurt myself or someone else. Do not test me. I'm armed," I typed out, wondering if I had gone too far or not far enough.

Penelope walked around to my side of the desk and stood over my shoulder to inspect the damage I was about to inflict. "That should do the trick," she approved.

I closed my eyes, took a deep breath, and hit send. I had done things a hundred times worse and had never wanted to take one of them back until now. I didn't have a choice though. He would be better locked up than getting entangled in real danger.

I watched his GPS tracker until he stopped ten miles short of his destination, paused briefly, and started heading in the opposite direction. I assumed he had either changed his mind or was in the custody of law enforcement. The crisis was averted, but I'd still have to deal with his blowback when confronted with what I'd done to him.

I filled the next few hours getting Penelope set up at CE, making some introductions, working on some programming, and taking an extended lunch. I left my phone behind so I could clear my head with no distractions, and by the time I returned to my office, I had multiple notifications. Ranbir was under arrest and was being held at Edwards. Penelope was looking for me and left a message that she had gone ahead to iron things out until I got there.

I hustled to the airfield and into the Military Police building hoping that I'd either take him home that afternoon or he'd only have to spend a single night locked up. Penelope was waiting for me, nervously pacing the prisoner intake lobby.

"What?" I asked with concern.

"Oh darling, it's better if you see for yourself," she said. "Come," she led me down the hallway towards an interrogation room. We entered to find General Kelly, some MPs, and a monitor on the table next to some files. The wall was mirrored glass, and on the other side was Ranbir chained to a steel table alone, much the same as the first time we met.

"This is a little overkill, don't you think?" I asked the General.

"There's no overkill for treason, Ms. Vera."

"Treason? You can't be serious."

"He was in possession of some very suspicious and illegal documents when we picked him up this morning, and he's making some very bold statements and threats against the state. I wanted to show you something and confer with you before charging him officially. Sit," he pointed to the chair in front of the monitor.

Penelope put her hand on my shoulder as the General played back a video. It was a recording from inside the bridge of Ranbir's attack ship. He and his two partners were sitting in a triangle passing a bottle between the three of them. Ranbir said "Honestly, and God, she'd kill me if she could hear me, but I think she might be a virgin."

I swallowed hard as my heart started to pound with a cocktail of anger and embarrassment rushing through me. I was exposed and humiliated in front of everyone watching with the man who revealed my secret sitting on the other side of the mirror.

"Get the fuck outta here," Maya said.

"In this day and age, that's pretty incredible if true," Malik commented on my virginity.

"I don't think it's like a *saving myself for marriage* type of situation," Ranbir's voice continued on the recording. "I've been trying to hit it for weeks, but she's stonewalling me. I think she might be, uh I don't know, damaged," he concluded as the video feed cut off.

I thought I might throw up, and the presentation wasn't even over. The General flipped open the file on the table with Ranbir's entire history. His medicals, education, prior arrests, and limited military experience laid out for me to consume. "He lied, Ms. Vera. He's no pilot. He fabricated his entire story to take the test run to Prius and kept up the lie to lead the mission. He put everything and everyone in jeopardy for his selfish pursuits."

I could have dealt with having my heart broken privately. I would have hated myself for letting my guard down, but at least I could heal in the solace of isolation. Instead, my humiliation was laid out for all to see. There was no wall I could raise to keep Penelope and General Kelly from witnessing me weakened and wounded. My entire persona crashed down around me revealing the sheltered and scared little girl who had her virginity stripped away. I was manipulated, lied to, and damaged.

"I'm sorry, darling," Penelope whispered as she massaged my shoulder. "Let her speak to him," she ordered to the guard who dimmed the lights to remove the one-way mirror feature between us and activated the audio linking our rooms.

"*You*. You evil bitch. How could you?" he sneered at me as he tugged on his restraints. "I swear to God, if I ever get out of here, I'm going to kill you. I never loved you. I..."

"That's quite enough," Penelope said as the guard raised the lights and removed the audio.

I couldn't believe that was the same man I had been willing to change myself for. I wanted to kill him for what he was putting me through. I would have shot him if I could, followed by murdering Penelope, General Kelly, the MPs, and anyone else who had witnessed me crushed. Once the secret of my humiliation was buried, I'd take my own life with my legacy intact rather than face another day.

The hate in his eyes was palpable, but it was nothing in comparison to the hate in my heart. The world was going to feel my rage. My pain would be a social contagion that would infect every last person on Earth. They'd wish the Praxi had mercifully killed them quickly by the time I was finished turning this world upside down. I became Hurricane Emilia. A category 5 storm whose winds would topple homes and uproot trees. Whose rains would drown anyone who dared to find happiness in my presence. The eye of my storm would punish everyone by forcing them to share in my pain.

"Will you testify at his trial?" the General asked.

"Trial? No," I said with no expression. "The only trials we're having will take place in the court of public opinion, and I intend to testify on all of them. Enact your articles of the Religious State, General. We'll enforce them with CE. As for Chop, you can do with him as you please," I said with frigid malcontent.

I pushed the chair under the table, but couldn't leave without getting the last word in. He had left me speechless the night before when personal confusion had frozen me. I wasn't the old Emilia or the new Emilia. I was becoming something much worse and inhuman.

I adjusted the lights so that Ranbir could see me and flipped the switch to activate the audio. I stared at him until he made eye contact and intended to look through him until he was forced to uncomfortably look away, but he never averted his hateful gaze. I took two steps towards the barrier between us and slowly said "Ranbir, you have my permission to die," before pressing my lips to the glass and leaving the red glossy stain of my kiss behind for him.

Chapter 8

A Captive Audience

Alexis X

"I can't breathe in this damn thing," I complained with a cloth sack over my head. "Where the hell is Fitz?" I questioned into the darkness.

The covering was removed, revealing a dimly lit concrete basement with the small windows blacked out with construction paper. The air was dense and musky, and it stunk of spilled alcohol and sweat. In the corner sat a table covered in broadcasting equipment.

"This is Fitz's bar," I chastised the couple who picked me for that secret rendezvous. "I've been here like a hundred times, you dopes."

"Hey there, Alex," Fitz welcomed as he walked down the stairs.

"I like what you've done to the place. What's the second rule of Fight Club?"

"*Come on, Lou. We really like this place,*" he quoted the movie back to me without missing a beat. "It's good to see you, Alex. When you went dark, we all kind of figured you got...*" he said as he made a noose around the neck gesture. He approached and pulled the chain on the dangling light fixture from the ceiling.

"Wow," I exclaimed as I saw him dressed in a full Muslim tunic robe and ghutra headscarf. "You're really committed to the part, Fitzy."

"It's Faariz now. The only way to walk freely and avoid the MPs is to hide in plain sight. Fitting in with a religion is the golden ticket. That's a lesson you should have learned," he lectured. "You double-checked for her CE phone, yes?" he asked his pathetic henchmen.

"I ditched it months ago. It's probably washed up somewhere along the Atlantic coast by now."

"That was clever, but coming here was not. The reward for your capture is approaching a tempting number. You're on North America's top ten list."

"Oh shit. I'm a star climbing the charts," I joked. "What's a girl got to do to get to #1?"

"It's five thousand notes, Alex, and they've added a two hundred social credit score boost as an extra incentive," Fitz cautioned.

"Well, lucky for me, a good upstanding Muslim citizen such as yourself already has a perfect credit score."

"They'll find my price point eventually."

"Hold out for a couple days, and I'll have that reward up to a million. Make sure you collect the notes fast though. If I pull this off, there won't be anyone left to pay for my capture."

"Because you're smart, I presume you're not going to tell me what you're planning," Fitz said as he curled his finger for me to follow him to his makeshift broadcast table and work center. He unplugged a USB cable connected to a small square drive from his computer and dangled it by the cord in front of me. "As promised," he said, tempting me with the device I requested.

"How about a demo?"

"Sure," he said as he unlocked his CE phone to reveal his profile, which he'd given a Muslim makeover to. "It's really simple. Plug and play." He pressed the USB connector into his phone, the screen glitched out, and a black and white countdown timer popped up reading "23:59:59," rolling backward towards zero. "It won't affect the network, but it will lock down the phone to the point where it feels like a real virus." He unplugged the USB and showed me how the countdown timer remained on the screen. "See. It's planted and will keep counting down even after disconnection. Whatever you're going to do, you've got twenty-four hours until time ticks off and the phone goes back to normal."

"That's perfect." I reached for the cord, and he swung it away from me.

"Nuh, uh uh. Cough it up," he demanded payment for the trade.

I went into my bag and pulled out a VHS copy of *The Thing* in its cardboard sleeve, and we swapped items at the same time.

"This is John Carpenter's signature?" he pointed to the scribbling on the case.

"Sure is," I lied.

"Oh, Mama. What a find," he said with a nerd's grin.

"Fair trade, my friend. Now, which of your two bozos is going to give me a ride back to my car?"

"That's it? Just like that? No foreplay? No cuddling? You stick it in ole Fitzy, and kick me out of bed when you're done?"

"Turn on Connect Earth News tomorrow if you want to get your nut. That's the best sexual experience I can offer," I promised cryptically and turned to leave.

"Alexis," Fitz said as I walked up the stairs, "Don't get yourself killed now, all right?" I nodded back in compliance with his request even though I knew the odds were stacked against me.

I had no choice but to act. Months earlier, I had waited at a café to meet Captain Chopra. I was convinced that he was the link to breaking the story wide open and stopping the World Military before they took control of Earth. He never showed up for our appointment, and that was the last anyone had seen of him even though Connect Earth continued to use his likeness and account to push their message of hate for the Praxi and love for religion. The only new promotional films released featured Amir without Ranbir.

He was likely dead, and I knew that I would join him if I didn't go underground. I took my radio show off the air, abandoned my home, threw my phone in the ocean, and disappeared. I counseled everyone in my network to do the same, and many of those who ignored my advice were locked up under any number of different pretenses. It was only a matter of time before the Military Police caught up with me as well. If arrested, I'd be lucky if I was shipped off to Prius with the rest of the prisoners. Emilia Vera would probably have me shot in the streets as a warning to anyone else who dared think for themselves.

She had to be stopped and was also the only person who could help me. Connect Earth could be the best thing to happen to mankind, but in Emilia's hands it was the worst. She was causing people to turn on each other and spread hate. Citizens were ratting out their friends and neighbors for thought crimes and slights against the state so they could receive the social credit crumbs from Emilia's table. People were aligning themselves with a religion to avoid a loss of access to banking or other privileges. She had turned our world into a dystopian hell, the likes of which even I had never dared to predict. We were better off when the OWG was in charge.

I would have killed her if I thought it would have made a difference. The best hope I had was to do something crazy and try to wake her up like she was a first-time Conspiriousity listener. I had procured my device from Fitz to trick Emilia into acquiescence, and I went down my checklist of everything else I needed. Xanax, roadmap, recording devices, cold cut sandwiches, bottled water, Trolli Gummy Worms, a snub nose .38 caliber pistol, and more Xanax.

I camped out in my car up the street from her home and waited until the sun began to rise on a Sunday morning before I pulled into Emilia's driveway. It was the only day of the week that Emilia didn't work, and I hoped nobody would count her as missing for twenty-four hours. I had rehearsed how this was going to go a hundred times, yet I couldn't make it to her door before things went sideways. I ran up the sidewalk, saw the three concrete steps leading to her porch, and thought to myself, "Superheroes don't take the stairs."

I tried to leap the steps in a single bound, but I panicked when I reached my launch point and attempted to bail out midjump. My left foot caught the second step, and I went careening headfirst into the base of Emilia's front door. I rolled around in pain and embarrassment for a minute, fully ready to pick myself up and take my trip and fall as a cosmic sign that this was a bad idea.

"What in the blue hell are you doing?" she asked as the door creaked open. Either I had a concussion, or that wasn't the Emilia I remembered. Her hair was greasy and matted, she wore glasses and no makeup and was dressed in grey sweatpants and a Linkin Park concert tee shirt that was three sizes too big for her.

"You look like trampled shit," I groaned as I rotated my shoulder blade to make sure everything was working properly and checked my forehead for blood.

"What did the pot say to the kettle?" she replied like a Jeopardy contestant.

I crawled across the threshold near her feet, and she tried to close the door on my abs to pin me into place. I reached into my jacket pocket, pulled the gun, and pointed it up at her.

"Seriously?" she asked with more irritation than fear. "You screw up my whole life, and now you're going to end it too? Whatever," she plopped down on her couch.

Her home was nothing like I imagined. There were blankets and pillows on the couch, with a coffee table in front covered in empty beer bottles, ice cream containers, candy wrappers, and stained silverware. The carpet was dirty, and the place stunk of cigarette smoke.

"*I* screwed up *your* life?" I questioned as I picked myself up off the floor and closed the front door. "You really have no perspective, do you?"

"Spare me the sermon." She lit a cigarette. "If you came here to kill me, get on with it."

"Lucky for you, I have no plans to shoot you. Wouldn't want the authorities to find your body looking like a junkie overdose."

"Well, then what the hell do you want?"

"Answers. I want answers. And Aspirin," I massaged my head.

"I don't have any."

"Who doesn't have aspirin? You do experience physical pain, yes?"

"Answers, you twat. I don't have answers."

"Hey puppy!" I exclaimed as Amir ran to my feet and begged to be picked up, which I obliged. "Where's your daddy? Did mommy do something terrible to him?"

"Whatever they did to him, they'll do it to you too."

"*They*? You are *they*! Now, give me your phone," I demanded as I set Amir down.

"Ha. Do your worst," she laughed as she threw it at my feet. "You'll get nowhere without the admin passcode, and I'll die a million times over before I give it to the likes of you."

"We'll see," I replied as I kneeled, unslung my bag from my back, and fished out the device. Emilia leaned forward with a visible gulp and watched as I plugged in the USB and prayed. The home screen glitched, and the countdown timer took over. I unplugged it and tossed the phone back to her. "23:59:59, 23:59:58, 23:59:57," the clock rolled by.

"What is this?" she asked with panic.

"That is what is commonly referred to as a doomsday device. For all your genius, you should have really been more careful when you designed Connect Earth. Telecommunications, media, GPS, and broadcasting; all directly connected to the biggest power source on the planet. When that countdown hits zero, an electromagnetic current is going to blow back from your generators and fry every circuit board and server on the Connect Earth compound," I lied.

"How the hell did you know? Did Ranbir know? Did he tell you?" she interrogated, which caught me off guard. The doomsday device bit was a ruse, but it appeared luck was on my side. Not only was my threat possible, but it was more realistic to Emilia's design than I could have imagined.

"It doesn't matter. What does matter is that you help me get what I want before that timer hits zero. I'm going to put this away now," I said shaking the gun and placing it in my backpack. "Get yourself cleaned up. We're going for a ride, and I can't have you looking like a meth head. It's six hours there and six hours back, plus however long it takes me to find what I'm looking for, so you best move your ass."

Emilia picked herself up off the couch and I followed her to the bedroom. "Go! Get in the shower," I demanded as I rifled through her closet searching for something to wear so I could look the part of her professional sidekick. Her assortment of blazers, blouses, pantsuits, camisoles, jackets, pants, and dresses was overwhelming. I tried on a few different outfits before deciding on a light blue double-breasted blazer with white pants and admired myself in the mirror from multiple angles.

"You look like a common ghetto whore who's trying to upgrade her prowl to Wall Street," she judged from the bathroom.

"Hush. I look good."

"You're wearing sneakers," she shouted back. "Pick some heels like a grown-up."

I followed her advice and tried on a pair, taking them for a spin around the house even though they were a size too big while she freshened up. I looked over her wide assortment of books but was far more interested in her impressive collection of vintage DVDs. Once I knew she was a film fan, I had to know what disc was currently in the player. I turned it on, hit the eject button, and the tray exposed that *The Breakfast Club* was the last movie she had watched.

I stumbled in her heels into the kitchen and found the sink overloaded with dirty dishes and the table covered in boxes of cereal. I helped myself to a handful of Cap'n Crunch and rejoined her in the bedroom where she was matching jewelry with her navy pantsuit.

"I don't care about your earrings. Get your military ID, grab some food for Amir, and let's get a move on," I hastened.

"You know, you could look this good too if you put in a little effort every once in a while."

"Come on," I dragged her by the arm into the living room. She tried to collect her phone, but I slapped her wrist. "Ah ah ah, leave it. You get me back here in under twenty-four hours, and I'll give you the code to shut it down."

I pushed her out of the house and down the driveway. She made her way towards the passenger side door of my rusted-out Grand Prix, and I hip-checked her to the side. "You're driving," I said as I slung my bag into the back seat and took my spot with Amir on my lap. "Take the 15 east and keep it under the speed limit."

As we departed the San Bernardino valley, the Connect Earth compound loomed large in the distance. I had a lecture planned for Emilia about the similarities between Nazi Germany and her role in the dissemination of wartime propaganda, but I decided not to waste my breath. She knew exactly what she was doing, and the only way to force her to own what she'd become was to expose her to irrefutable evidence of the truth. If I could dull the razor's edge of her personality, Emilia had the access and know-how to legitimately save mankind.

I washed down a Xanax, opened a bottle of water for Emilia, and offered her a pill as a peace treaty. "Wanna get weird?"

Emilia snatched the pill from my palm and threw it back without asking what it was. "Can we get some music going in here or something?" she asked as she turned the knob on the radio. She scanned from station to station, being met with nothing but the sound of dead static air.

"There's no broadcasts anymore. You either put them out of business or you had them arrested, remember?" I wasn't trying to antagonize her. It was a simple fact that every horrible thing that had gone wrong with the world was partially her fault.

"Ugh. You kidnapped me. The least you could do is offer some entertainment. Perform the latest episode of your little talk show. *Constapationality* or whatever."

"You mock me, but I've been right more times than I've been wrong. I was right about the OWG when everyone else was cheering them on," I listed as my first accomplishment.

"That's because *everyone else* is an idiot. Spotting the OWG as a Trojan horse doesn't make you Nostradamus."

"I was right about you," I said cautiously, not wanting to alienate her from the conversation.

Emilia's back straightened and mouth closed as her hands gripped tight around the steering wheel. She didn't have a snappy comeback, nor did she attempt to defend herself. "Yeah. You *called it*, all right," she said, dropping one of my show catchphrases. "You had me pegged from the beginning."

"So, you do watch my show!" I grinned proudly.

"Settle down. I've seen it a couple times."

"God, I miss it," I lamented.

"You don't have to. I'm a captive audience of one over here, and I've got nowhere else to be." She was practically begging to hear what I had to say, and I hoped that if I led that horse to water, she would drink when it came time for it.

"All right, all right. You win," I said as I placed Amir in her lap and pulled my bag into mine. I removed a manilla folder and sorted through the treasure trove of photos and documents. "Take a look at this," I instructed as I passed her a full-page photo which she pinned against the steering wheel so she could study it. "What do you see?"

"It's an attack site. A big hole in the ground where a Praxi bomb went off. So what?"

"Now look at this one," I said trading photos with her.

"It's another attack site, except it's filled with rubble. Wait. What?" she questioned.

"Exactly! W-T-F. Why is the first photo a big empty hole and the crater in the second one is full of collapsed buildings, homes, trees, and cars? This one," I said pointing to the second photo of the crater filled with rubble, "is Moscow. The first photo is also in Russia, but the longitude and latitude don't match a city, which is why there's no debris left behind."

"What was the target? A missile defense system or something?"

"Kapustin Yar," I said with a mysterious tone.

"Is that supposed to mean something to me?"

"It's Kapustin Yar!" I repeated, annoyed with her cluelessness. "Russia's version of Area 51. Home to their most protected UFO secrets and dark projects. Now look at this," I said gathering two similar photographs. "Same thing. Two big craters in China, only one of them is filled with debris. The crater that's full is Shanghai. The one that's empty is Lop Nur..." I said, leaving room for her to follow along and narrate the blanks.

"China's version of Area 51?" she asked.

"You're good at this game. What do you suppose this one is?" I asked as I held up an aerial photo of a deserted but intact military base.

"Area 51, but it's still standing? Why would the Praxi hit the Chinese and Russian top-secret bases, but not Area 51?"

"Good question! I should have had you on Conspiriousity as a guest."

"Wait. Is that where we're going?" Emilia asked with concern. "This is stupid. You're going to get yourself arrested or worse. You think we're going to waltz in there and the commanding officer is going to give us a guided tour of military secrets?"

"There's nobody home. The timeline is a little murky, but they cleared out either days before or days after the attack on Earth. The place is a ghost town except for Military Security, and you're going to get us passed them."

Emilia didn't follow up with another question because she was quietly working things out on her own. Her fingers tapped nervously at the wheel as she stared over the precipice into the abyss of truth below. I would push her over the edge, if necessary, but I really wanted her to jump on her own.

"Care to venture a guess as to who was the commanding officer stationed at Area 51 for the last seven years?" I asked rhetorically. Emilia didn't need to guess. She knew exactly who it was. "Think about it. *General Jesus* takes command of Area 51. He has access to fifty years of UFO coverups. He inspects crashed Praxi ships and God knows what else collected over the years. He touches them with his own hands. Can you imagine his crisis of faith? Maybe he snaps. Just loses his shit. The presence of alien life millions of years older than ours destroys the religious foundation he built his existence on. He's got all these ships, and a science team with a rudimentary understanding of their technology, but no triaxum to fuel any of it..."

"Until the Grays show up," Emilia interrupted.

"Until the Grays show up. Right," I echoed and intentionally halted my theory hoping that Emilia would pick up where I left off.

"The OWG plays nice and constructs the Jump Point. The military get their hands on a shit load of triaxum. And then..." she paused.

"And then Ranbir and Amir," I scratched the head of the puppy in her lap, "flew to Prius to make sure it was safe for human passage. Now the military knows they can send a strike force team through safely, and all they needed was something to unify the world in support for General Kelly's holy war. The Gulf of Tonkin times a million. The greatest false flag in history."

"It's a good story. Very entertaining, and it's a shame you're not still on the air. I bet this episode would kill with your audience."

"It's not a story. It's the truth. Gummy worm?" I asked as I ripped open the bag of sugary treats with my teeth.

Emilia fished out a few worms for herself and proceeded to tear a giant hole in my theory. "There's one big problem," she said with her mouth full. "General Kelly is a moron. He once confused carte blanche with carpe diem. He owns Velcro shoes. Is he evil? Maybe. Evil genius though? No. Any other entertaining theories?"

"You don't believe me?"

Emilia didn't answer immediately, and it wasn't because she was chewing through a mouth full of gummy worms. Both her hands clenched to the wheel and her gaze averted away from me as she stared forward blankly. I had opened her mind to a plethora of possibilities, and it seemed she was working out the implications as they pertained to her own life and choices.

"You don't *want* to believe me," I amended the question into a statement.

Again, Emilia didn't reply, and I could understand why. If I was right, it would mean that she had done unspeakable things under the pretense of a lie. She sheltered herself away from judgment and prided herself on having manipulative control over every situation. To consider that she had been played by someone as doltish as General Kelly had to sting. I wouldn't want to face up to responsibility if I were her either. I knew something terrible had happened to Captain Chopra and I feared that she was personally responsible.

We rode quietly for some time, only speaking when I gave her directions to our destination. We ate the sandwiches I packed for lunch, and I fed Amir from my hand. My anxiety rose the longer we sat in silence, so I popped another Xanax and hummed to myself until the meds kicked in.

"Are you trolling me?" she asked with her voice cracking from the dryness of the desert and not speaking for so long.

"Hmm? I don't follow."

"The song you're humming. That's 'Somewhere I Belong' by Linkin Park."

"Oh. Yeah, I guess it is. It must have been subconscious. Why? Are you actually a fan? I figured your pajama tee was a leftover from an ex-boyfriend or something."

"I like them," she replied plainly, burying her fandom as if she wasn't willing to let me in on even the most basic personal details of her life.

"Oh my God! I have CDs in the back!" I exclaimed as I leaned over the seat and brushed aside empty Burger King bags and random trash to find my case. "Boom. Third page. *Meteora*. You want to jam out?"

"It's fine. Whatever," she replied.

I inserted the disc and turned the volume halfway up. My head bobbed with the opening guitar riffs of "Don't Stay," and I pumped my fist in unison with the record scratch effect that kickstarts the song. Emilia cracked a smile watching me get into it, and her fingers tapped the top of the steering wheel with the baseline. I sang along while holding up Amir to my face as if he was a microphone. Emilia didn't join me, but she did mouth the lyrics to herself.

"You know, I could be convinced that you're kind of cool if you'd let your hair down once in a while," I suggested as the track rolled over to "Somewhere I Belong."

"I'm not cool, and neither are you," she laughed as I continued singing along and botching the high notes with no regard for being judged. I speed-pumped my fist with the guitar and smashed the air drums along to the song's percussion.

"Come on! It's just us here. I won't tell anyone that you had fun while kidnapped," I encouraged as the album rolled into "Lying From You." I turned the volume up a bit louder and played Amir like he was my guitar while tossing my hair back and forth. Emilia bobbed along, her palm tapping the wheel with the baseline.

I rapped along with Mike's opening verse, turning in my seat to face Emilia, and spitting the lyrics into an invisible microphone. I arrived at the bridge of the song and extended the mic to have Emilia sing Chester's part, but she wasn't ready for it.

Emilia joined in through the first chorus, and even though she was rolling her shoulders with the beat, she wasn't putting her back into it. "I'm coming back to you after the second verse, and you better belt that chorus out this time," I said playfully. Again, I rapped Mike's part, and Emilia turned the volume louder, forcing me to really bark out the lyrics if I wanted to be heard.

She mouthed along with me, her whole body swaying with the music now. Her hands slapped harder against the wheel as she hit the drumbeats with her fist instead of her palm. I reached the pre-chorus, rapping along and again extending the mic to her, and she nailed the bridge in perfect harmony with my smile encouraging her. I hit the last line leading up to her part, and I couldn't believe what I saw.

"Lying! My Way! From You!" she belted out ferociously, holding the 'you' lyric in a primal scream.

"No. No turning back now," I rapped under Emilia who had seized control of the song at that point.

"I wanna be pushed aside, so let me go!" she matched Chester's vocal anger.

"No, no turning back now," I echoed.

"Let me take back my life, I'd rather be all alone!" She held the drawn-out notes at full pitch as her fists punched the ceiling.

"No turning back now." I kept up my part while being in awe of her transformation.

"Anywhere on my own, 'cause I can see!'

"No. No turning back now."

"The very worst part of you. The very worst part of you, is me!" she screamed, no longer trying to mimic the correct pitch, instead letting all her frustration flow naturally as she internalized the lyrics. She banged her head so hard that her hair moved, and I realized she wore a wig. I could see scars starting above her temple and up into her scalp, and Emilia didn't bother to straighten herself out.

The chorus came around for one final pass, and this time it was Emilia encouraging me to join her. We screamed it out together, but I couldn't hit the notes or match Emilia's emotional performance. We concluded the song together, and Emilia quickly swiped a tear away from her eye and adjusted her hair back into position.

The irony of the lyrics wasn't lost on either of us, though we didn't bother verbally acknowledging it. Emilia felt the words in the soul that I wasn't aware she remained in possession of. She was dodging the awful truth of the villains she was in league with and had become herself, yet I maintained hope that if she saw concrete evidence; she could reverse course and help me take them down.

We finished the album, occasionally singing along, but nothing like what happened when Emilia went primal. When it was over, I turned the music off and gave her the final directions towards the base. It was time to get on point.

"It's a couple of miles up this road. There will be a barricade with guards stationed at the entrance. I don't want to draw any attention, so no funny business. We're a pair of attractive, young, professional ladies. We should be able to charm our way in."

"I've got it," Emilia said confidently. "You're my assistant, and assistants don't speak. You play your part, keep your mouth shut, and I'll get us past them," she said as we sped up the gravel road with desert on all sides of us.

We pulled to a stop once we reached the barricade, and Emilia lowered her window to address the two soldiers who approached from their small station. We must have looked so ridiculous rolling up to them in my dumpster on wheels dressed like we were headed for Capitol Hill.

"This is a restricted area, ladies. The highway is back that way," the guard said with a flirty tone. It was a perfect opportunity for Emilia to use some playful charisma to get us through the only checkpoint.

She passed her military ID badge to him and said, "General Kelly's business. Raise the barricade," with no charm whatsoever.

"Emilia Vera? What are you doing way out here? I'll have to verify this. Just a..." the guard said before being interrupted.

"No. Not one moment. Not even half a moment. I just drove six hours through the desert, and if you don't open that gate right now, *I'll find you*. I'll out you as a Praxi supporter so fast..." she threatened which sent him hustling for the gate controls. "That's a good boy. I want you to stand right there and wait for me, because when I come back, I'll have even less patience than I do right now. Understood?" she asked without waiting for his response.

She pulled the car forward as the barricade rose and looked at me with an authentic smile. "See. I charmed my way in."

"Anyone ever tell you that you're one scary bitch?"

"Not to my face," she smirked as we raced towards the meat of the base. "Think he'll move?" she laughed. We drove a mile or two inwards before reaching the campus of buildings I was seeking.

The bulk of the buildings were aligned in a horseshoe fashion a few miles inside the gated perimeter. There was a limited number of barracks, an assortment of administrative buildings, and eight large hangars with the doors down, some of which backed up to the mountains. The sun beat down hard on the large concrete causeway that separated all the structures.

"All right. This is your show now," Emilia stated, searching for direction.

"Pull up over there." I pointed to the nearest administrative building. "We need to check all the hangars, but I want to see if they left a paper trail first."

Emilia parked the car, and I looked at her nervously when I opened my door, and she wasn't prepared to follow. 'What? It's hot! I'm not getting out unless I have to. I'm not going anywhere," she assured me.

I closed the door behind me and was relieved when I didn't hear the engine roar and rocks kick up from the tires spinning as she left me behind. The front door was locked, but I circumvented it with a fist-sized rock through the window. I cleared the jagged glass away and reached through to unfasten the deadbolt and gain access.

There was a collection of filing cabinets with the drawers pulled out and emptied. I inspected them one by one to find none of the materials I was hoping for. There were papers all over the floor, and none of them revealed anything more interesting than personal information on soldiers once stationed at the base.

I left the building empty-handed and walked towards the small outpost connected to the first hangar. "Come on." I waved to Emilia to move the car along with the search. I broke the window and helped myself inside again where I found a desk covered in discarded coffee cups and an electrical panel on the wall adjacent to the connected hangar. The walk-in door that connected the buildings was locked and had no windows to break out. I flipped all the switches on the wall, but the airstrip lights didn't illuminate, and the hangar doors didn't budge.

"Hey! There's no power," I shouted to Emilia. She rolled her eyes, left the car with the air conditioning on for Amir, and joined me in the station. I watched her eyes trace the wiring up the walls, across the ceiling, and into the back of the building. I followed her around the corner, and she fumbled around in the dark for a bit before opening an electrical panel door and flipping all the breakers on.

The creaking, industrial moan of the hangar doors peeling up sent a surge of excitement through me. I ran through the front door to find open access to the first hangar and some of the runway lights switched on. The interior walls were covered in four tiers of racking that maxed out at the forty-foot-high ceiling. On the racks were various boxes and skid packs that had been left behind.

I raised the cardboard lid of the first crate to find various small firearms. Look at this. They left guns behind, and ammo," I proclaimed as I moved on to the next box.

"So, what? Check this thing out!" Emilia said as she climbed into the back of a militarized Humvee and rotated the 50-caliber mounted rifle from side to side. "It even has the chain ammo thing loaded up."

The Humvee wasn't the only vehicle parked inside the hangar. There were four Jeeps left behind and a tank with the treads broken off. I continued rifling through the various assortment of military items in the boxes, and Emilia checked the casings on the wall. "The keys are still here too. We should take it for a spin and fire off a few rounds before we leave."

"I love your excitement and that you're getting into the spirit of the moment, but I could really use your help to search these boxes if we're going to make it back to your house before the timer expires," I warned.

We sorted through box after box, frustratingly discarding the unhelpful contents on the floor. I found the keys for the forklift and started pulling down the skids from the higher racks, but they didn't reveal any more secrets than the ones below.

I raised the forks to the third level to grab the next skid pack, and had to back up, raise, and lower the forks over and over trying to get them to line up. "Get off of there," Emilia barked at me and slid in front of the controls. She backed up, whipped around, and came at the racking system from the side. She inserted the forks under the bottom of the steel housing and pulled the lever to raise the racks off the ground. "You should probably move," she said as the bolts broke free from the ground. She dropped the forks, backed up twenty feet, and rammed forward causing the whole racking system to collapse in on itself. The boxes from the top row splintered open and spewed their contents into a mountain of trash spread across the concrete floor.

We kicked through the items to search for anything of value, but it was more of the same. "We've been at this for an hour. Let's move on," Emilia suggested while I continued searching. She ran ahead to the next hangar and had the power restored and doors open by the time I gave up on the first one.

Besides a helicopter that was torn apart, the scene was much of the same. A few abandoned vehicles and some boxes were left behind. Emilia again tore down the racking structure, but not because we held any hope that there'd be important military secrets hidden in them. She did it because it was fun. I wasn't sharing in her enjoyment of the moment seeing as we were coming up empty-handed.

"There's nothing here," Emilia said as she kicked a box of ammunition across the floor.

"Yes, there is!" I shouted back. "They left all this stuff behind. That's proof too. They don't need any of the small arms or other bullshit because they've got access to the Praxi tech."

"You're connecting dots that don't exist. Look, Alexis, I think you're all right. I can help you," she offered, completely out of character.

"You can help me search the other six hangars is what you can do."

"I'm serious. I can get you a new identity, and a CE phone to match. I'll set you up with enough notes to get you by and a plush social credit score to keep you off the radar. You can start over."

"I don't want your fucking notes or your social credit. I'm not going to participate in the hellscape you've built for us, I'm going to burn it down!"

"Sure you are. Just know, that when we finish up here and find nothing, the offer still stands."

"You don't want to find anything here! Admit it."

"So what if I don't! You're right about me. I want your insane conspiracy theory to be wrong."

"Why? Why are you so afraid to face the truth?"

"Because I sent Ranbir to his death! Okay? He believed some form of the same lunacy as you, and I fucking crucified him for it! Is that a good reason enough for you?"

"He's dead? You're sure?" I asked, softening my tone.

"I don't know. Probably," she said dejectedly and sat on a pile of trash on the floor. "They probably tortured him and buried him in a shallow grave in the desert. If we find whatever it is you're hoping for, it means I turned on the only person who ever loved me for nothing. For a lie."

"Come on. Get up," I encouraged. "There's six more to go, and it's too damn hot for all this arguing. We'll search the other hangars, and when we come up empty, I'll take you up on your offer. It's more generous than a kidnap victim needs to be."

"Fine. That's fine," she coldly agreed to my terms.

We spent the next four hours going hangar to hangar, repeating the same process we'd already been through twice. The sun dropped behind the mountains, and we used the runway lights to illuminate the remainder of our search. We were both covered in filth and our clothes were soaked in sweat as we came to the final two hangars at the edge of the base.

I entered the adjoining station going through the motions of switching on the breakers, but the controls didn't set off the lights or raise the hangar doors. I ran out onto the tarmac and yelled, "this is it! This is the one," before tripping in my heels and falling with my right arm taking the brunt of the concrete impact.

"Ow!" I groaned as I rolled over onto my back and felt the blood running from elbow to wrist.

"Jesus Christ, girl," Emilia said as she helped me to my feet. "Maybe you should have stuck with the sneakers after all."

"This is the one. Whatever we're looking for is in there," I explained as I smeared the blood from my arm onto my already filthy clothes.

"Well, what are you waiting for? Open it."

"That's the thing. It won't open. There's no power."

Emilia looked at me confused, as if I had gone delirious. "What am I missing?"

"It's movie rules, don't you see? We searched all day, and the last two hangars won't open. We have to break into them. By movie rules, that means there's something good in there."

"Right. Movie rules." She laughed.

I inspected around the heavy steel door for other controls, and then around both sides of the building for another way in. "Son of a bitch! How do we get in there?"

"Oh. Oh!" she exclaimed. "I've got a good idea. Stay here," she said with a mischievous grin as she ran back in the direction we came from.

I waited for five minutes and was starting to get worried until I saw headlights pointed in my direction and heard the angry RPMs of a Humvee rumbling towards me. Emilia had managed to get into first gear but hadn't mastered shifting into second, and she was pushing it to its max. She pulled to a stop thirty feet in front of the door and dipped under to gopher through the gunnery station to man the fifty-caliber rifle.

"Do you know what you're doing?"

"Nope, but movie rules say I don't need to," she replied as she fumbled with the trigger, and nothing happened.

"Pull the lever back to engage," I coached.

Emilia yanked the shaft back and mimicked the clicking noise it made once locked into position. "Oh hell yeah. This feels good," she said, pulling the trigger again with nothing happening.

"The safety. Turn the safety off. I thought you were some kind of genius?"

"I've never shot a gun before," she said as she clicked the safety.

"A fifty-caliber rifle seems like a good place to start," I said sarcastically, and barely got the words out before Emilia started unloading rounds into the door, completely uncontrolled.

"Whoa! This thing kicks like a bitch!"

"Slow down! Short, controlled bursts. Hit the same spot repeatedly until it breaks."

Emilia fired again, this time ripping off rounds in bursts of five. She peppered an area three feet high, ripping through the structure, and covering the ground with torn shrapnel until the weapon was out of ammunition. "This thing is incredible!"

"That's great, but I don't think I can fit through there without getting torn to shit," I shouted back as I inspected the hole she cut in the door. I kicked at the edges where it was the weakest, but I was completely ineffective in heels.

I ran back to the Humvee, fully prepared to do whatever it took to smash through the door. "I'm gonna ram it," I said as I nodded for her to get out. She ducked through the gunner's hole and dropped into the driver's seat. I opened the driver's door, but she wouldn't budge. "Get out, Emilia. I saw you drive. You can't even get into second gear."

She slid over the console into the passenger's side and buckled her seat belt. "I'm serious, Emilia. You should get out. I can handle this," I said as I took over the driver's position.

"No way. Movie rules suggest we have to do this together."

"You're really leaning into that, aren't you?" I said with a smile as I buckled up and put the Humvee into first gear. "All right, here we go," I said as I released the clutch and hammered down on the gas. I shifted gears and got the speed over thirty miles per hour before we smashed headfirst into the ruptured door. The steel bent out in every direction around the bumper, and the front wheels pushed through the hole before the Humvee got hung up halfway through.

My face smashed into the steering wheel, leaving me dazed, my nose broken, and my mouth filled with the warm acidic taste of blood. "Ugh," I groaned in pain as I attempted to shake off the near-unconscious state. "These things don't have air bags? That would have been nice to know," I said, noticing the empty passenger seat.

"Alexis! Climb through the top," Emilia directed, whose silhouette stood out amidst the dust and smoke ahead of me. I flipped the high beams on to pour light into the hangar, muscled my way through the gunner's nest, and slid down the cracked windshield into her arms.

I tried to spit out a mouthful of blood, but a good portion of it leaked off my lip and onto Emilia's borrowed blazer. "Sorry about all...this. You might be able to salvage it if you've got something that pairs well with blood stains," I joked as I scanned over the beaten mess the day had made of me.

Emilia touched under my chin and forced my gaze upward. I peered through the dark with my eyes adjusting to what the headlights didn't illuminate and saw my prize. There sat two of the pencil crafts partially covered in blue tarps. "Ho-ly shit!" I exclaimed.

I yanked the coverings off and ran my hand across the cool steely surface as if I were trying to caress secrets out of the material. On the lower surface of both crafts was bracketing that held gravity cannons at one time, but they had been removed.

I walked around both crafts examining them with Emilia speechlessly in tow behind me. It was darker on the other side, but we didn't need much light to make out the saucer craft parked with one of its circular outer edges resting on the ground. "Look, Emilia," I said as I felt the charred surface area. "We saw this one the night we first met! This is the prick that hit Chicago. Check out the burns and the impact point. This is where that missile hit it, remember?" I asked with childish excitement, but she didn't respond. "I have to document all of this."

I unlocked the side door to get out, ran back to the car, and drove myself back. I grabbed my camera, attached the portable light, and went to work. As I was walking back through the door to start my recording, Emilia was walking out. "Where you going?" I asked, but she brushed past me towards the car and sat in the passenger's seat with Amir in her lap.

I filmed for almost an hour as I captured all five of the crafts that were hidden stationery out of sight. I knew there was more in the next hangar but had no time to document them. When I wasn't recording the ships from every angle possible, I was pointing the camera at myself, narrating my theory in action, and recounting the events of the day that led to my discovery. I could barely contain my excitement as I filmed the downfall of our oppressors and prepared myself to break the biggest news story in history. All I had to do was get Emilia back to her phone and upload the proof. The world would see the truth, and I would be cemented as a guerilla journalist legend.

"We've got these bastards now," I said as I leaned over the backseat and stashed my recording equipment. "Hey. You still with me?" I asked Emilia, but she stared ahead blankly, petting Amir. A dog can comfort you out of any depression, but he didn't seem to be doing much good for Emilia. "I need you to pull it together and keep our cover for the guards on the way out. Can you do that?"

No response. With a single hill left to climb, my partner in crime had turned into a zombie. I was going to have to talk our way off the base. I snatched her military ID, composed myself with some deep breathing and Xanax, and drove towards the exit.

I pulled the car to a stop at the barricade, and a different guard had taken over on shift. "You're Emilia Vera?" he asked with a suspicious look. "Were you in a brawl?"

"She's Ms. Vera. I'm her assistant. It's been a long day, and we're ready to complete the General's business if you could lift the gate there."

Emilia opened her door, placed Amir in her seat, and walked around to my side of the car. I thought she was going to give him the business to get us clear, but instead, she pulled the handle on my door.

"Alexis. Get out of the car," she said with an odd calm, her cheeks stained with running mascara.

"What...what are you doing?" I asked as my panic meter shot up to a thousand.

"Get. Out. Of. The car," she directed with more force.

"No no no no no." I quickly reached into the backseat, grabbed my camera, removed the tiny memory card, and swallowed it while Emilia reached across my lap to pull the keys from the ignition.

"Get out of the fucking car!" she pressed again, this time sticking my own gun in my face.

"Emilia!" my voice cracked as I screamed at her. "You saw what I saw. You know what they've done! Don't do this," I begged.

"I can't change the past. The dead are already buried," she said as her hands shook.

"At least give me the keys! Give me a fighting chance!" My pleas fell on deaf ears. She had made up her mind an hour earlier, and there was nothing I could say to change that. I got out of the car, and she took two steps back as I approached her.

"Don't. Don't test me," she warned.

"What the hell is all this about?" the guard questioned as he drew his weapon but didn't point it.

"Get Edwards on the phone. Inform them that there's been a breach," Emilia directed.

"I trusted you!" I yelled as I lunged forward and heard the clicking of the trigger and the snap of the hammer. Emilia looked at the gun surprised that it hadn't gone off, then put it under her own chin and pulled the trigger over and over and over.

She dropped to her knees, discarding the unloaded gun in the desert sand, and sobbed uncontrollably. Before I could process the darkness of Emilia's suicide attempt, my face was met with the butt of the soldier's rifle, and I joined Emilia on the ground. I slipped out of consciousness, and the only thing that registered was the whirling of helicopter blades.

***

I opened my eyes, unable to shelter them from the bright lights above because my hands were chained to the legs of a chair. The walls were white, which made my situation more disorientating. Next to me was Emilia, chained to a chair of her own, and in front of us was a two-way mirror that showed my reflection. My forehead was red and had a sizeable welt. My nose was crooked to the right, broken in at least one spot. Both of my eyes were swollen to the point that they were almost shut. Dried blood caked over my mouth, on my chin, and down my neck.

Emilia was filthy and sweaty, but she didn't have a mark on her. "You somehow look worse than I do," I quipped, surrendering myself to that horrible situation immediately, and using humor to deal with it.

"Keep your mouth shut, and maybe I can get us out of this," she counseled.

"You know, I think I'm going to pass, *pal*. You lost me with the whole murder-suicide thing."

The General entered the room and paced the floor in front of us with Emilia's phone in hand. "Care to explain this?" he asked as he flashed me the timer. "00:19:58. 00:19:57," the timer ticked away.

"It doesn't do anything," I laughed, which earned me the back of his hand across my face. "Ow! For fuck's sake. It's a ruse!"

"She's lying," Emilia piped in. "When the countdown is over, an electromagnetic charge is going to blow back and fry the Connect Earth servers. She has a password to stop it."

I widened my mouth with my teeth together and examined myself in the mirror again. "Are my gums bleeding now?"

"Stop screwing around, and shut it down," Emilia begged.

"How are you the two idiots who ruined the world?" I asked with a laugh. "It's fake! I had a hacker design the software so I could trick Bitchenstein over here to get me into Area 51. Oh, and by the way, you've got a hell of a collection of vintage spaceships locked away. You should really show them off," I said before getting slapped again.

"If it does nothing, then you won't mind shutting it down, will you, Ms...?"

"X is fine. Ms. X. Or Triple Lex. I always thought that sounded cool, but I don't want to be one of those people who forces a nickname, ya know?"

"Ms. X? What's her name?" the bewildered General asked Emilia.

"I don't know. She's one of those fringe society people. What does it matter?" Emilia barked in a frustrated tone.

"Fine! Ms. X. If there's a code to shut this down, I'm going to give you one chance to hand it over nicely," the General explained in a vaguely threatening manner.

"*X gonna give it to ya uh. She gonna give it to ya. X gonna give it to ya uh. She gonna give it to ya,*" I rapped at the crotchety old prick. "Come on, General. You know DMX, right?" I was rescinded to my fate at that point, so the least I could do is go down being a smart ass.

"You're going to force me to do something terrible, Ms. X," he warned.

"All right, all right, all right. I've reached my allotment of pain for one day. All Emilia has to do is enter the admin passcode, and she can navigate away from the program. Not that it matters, because as I've said, nothing is going to happen."

"Ms. Vera. Let's put this ugliness behind us. The CE password please," he requested gently.

"She's seen things now, bub. We got a look behind your curtain, and you've been a *naughty* General. She's—" was as far as I got with my antagonizing before my head whiplashed from the back of his hand again.

"The passcode, Ms. Vera."

I watched Emilia mentally work out the situation. Weighing whether I was telling the truth about the virus and whether she could negotiate her way out of that pickle. "Release me, and I'll stop it," she bargained.

"No, I don't think I will. I've had enough of your games, Ms. Vera. Your condescending attitude. Your potty mouth and blasphemy. You're going to give me your system passcode, or I'm going to let that timer expire. You can kiss your precious Connect Earth goodbye."

"Fine. Let it fry," she said coldly.

"That's a bluff," I laughed at the idea of her being willing to watch her powerful platform burn.

"Last chance, Ms. Vera. The passcode or I'm going to get a pair of plyers and start removing things."

"That's...not a bluff," I continued narrating.

Emilia stared up at him with steely resolve. "Off you go. Let's find out if your God allows for torture," she taunted.

"Very well," the General said as he tossed the phone to the floor and left the room. "00:09:23. 00:09:22."

"For Christ's sake, Emilia. Is this really worth it?"

"I've lost everything else. Connect Earth is all I have left, and he can't have it. It's only nine minutes of torture, the system will melt down, and he'll have no further use for either of us."

"For the millionth time, nothing is going to happen! The clock is going to hit zero, CE will survive, and he's going to keep right on torturing you."

"Shut up, *Triple Lex*. You lie! I don't know how you did it, but you found my Armageddon Protocol."

"*Armageddon protocol*?" I asked with a laugh. "You know what, go ahead. Get an industrial pedicure from this prick. Don't say I didn't warn you."

The General returned with a pair of plyers in hand as promised and knelt in front of Emilia removing her heels. Without warning, he angled the grip of his tool against the nail of her big toe and cringed as he yanked it off.

Emilia's face went red as she clenched her jaw and shook from the great pain but wouldn't give him the satisfaction of crying out. "The passcode, Ms. Vera. Two minutes and nine toes to go," he announced as he gripped onto the next toenail and pulled it off, a good deal of flesh coming with it.

I was horrified to the point that I hadn't noticed the door open, and a second party entered the room. A posh thin blonde woman stood over the General's shoulder and announced her presence with a 9mm pressed against the back of his head. "That's quite enough, General." She didn't bother giving him time to heed the warning. Before he could react to being caught off guard, the woman pulled the trigger and sprayed the General's brains all over Emilia. His body flopped to the floor without so much as a twitch and his blood pooled up at our feet.

"Penelope!" Emilia exclaimed as she spit the liquid cocktail of blood and brains away from her mouth.

Penelope? Who the hell is Penelope?

Chapter 9

Paint by Numbers

Penelope Martin

No matter what the canvas, it's always shocking to see a man's brains painted all over it. Whether it be a wall, floor, or in this case, a helpless young woman tied to a chair. There's often so much more human tissue than you'd expect. You can see the art in the randomness of the spray pattern if one is so inclined. The way chunks of the frontal, parietal, and temporal lobes cling to the surface, with the combination of brain fluid and blood running away in thinning streaks to the lowest points makes the splatter work in an abstract fashion.

I'd known the General for the better part of three decades, and I expected his brains to paint a much smaller portrait. I suppose pressing the gun directly against his stalky brainstem was my final gift to him. Whoever had to mop up the messy legacy he left behind on the floor would admire the sheer mass of his soupy intellect. They'd certainly count him as more scholarly on volume alone than I ever did.

He was a simpleton, which made his ascension to a high-ranking government position exponentially more infuriating. I'd spent my entire career watching men like him fall ass backward into power. Accumulating titles, access, and wealth with a second-nature effort akin to remembering to breathe. There was nothing particularly exceptional about any of them, and they ensured to never be over-shadowed by their subordinates or successors by appointing even less exceptional men to all available positions around them.

As a woman, I was never afforded the same opportunities as my male counterparts. There were no handouts or free lunches. No one was going to serve me my tea. If I wanted it, I was going to have to turn up the heat and boil my damn own water.

I had to fight and claw my way through British SIS. I had made it into Mi5 before the age of 30 with my sights set on Mi6. Everyone hears Mi6 and thinks the bureau is full of dashing James Bond agents with their lovely but ditzy Moneypennys on the side. The dichotomy was accurate, except for the bit about the agents being as formidable as the famous Bond.

They were men who did what they were told. Effective field agents who played by the rules as they waited for the accolades and promotions to fall into their laps.

None of them with goals as grandiose as my own, not that they could handle the responsibility.

I found the perfect home for my aspirations in a decade-long mission to penetrate the One World Government. I slipped amongst their ranks which gave me an inside look at how they sought to subvert national governments. It was interesting and thought-provoking, but it was in the young people that I connected to that I found my future network.

I was able to recruit brilliant children from all over the world. I got to them before they could be corrupted by nationalism or their regional politics. Some of the kids would never be smart enough to do anything but the bidding of the OWG. Others found their way onto my shortlist of usefulness. Then there were students like Emilia.

She had the most beautiful mind I had ever encountered. She retained information with a photographic recall. If I gave her a three-chapter reading assignment, she would finish the entire book. I would reference the specific segments that I felt were important, and she could paraphrase them back to me, sometimes even with page numbers.

There were other students who were as brilliant as Emilia, but none of them had what made her unique. Her intellect made her cold, and her scars made her hateful. I encouraged her to separate herself from those she felt superior to as I groomed her to follow in my footsteps.

I didn't want her mingling with classmates who would slow her down, or dating boys who would distract her. Those lucky enough to be in her orbit were either steppingstones or irrelevant. I taught Emilia the lessons her parents never could and prepared her for the harsh realities that awaited every ambitious young woman in global politics. I assumed the role of her mother, father, only friend, mentor, teacher, and priest. I directed all the lesson plans that would equip her for the changing world of the twenty-first century. She became as gifted with computer programming as she was with retaining world history. Of all the things I'd done, she was my greatest achievement.

The higher she climbed, the more I pulled away. I let her get out into the world and put some wind beneath her. The more distant I became, the more obsessively she set out to impress me. We held a shared adoration and respect for each other. Love is a funny word to be thrown around in the ruthless circles we traveled in, but it was the best way to describe our bond.

If it had been anyone else strapped to that chair, I would have let General Kelly remove as many body parts as his heart desired. Not Emilia though. Not ever. I put that gun to his head and relieved him of his obligation to life without hesitation.

"We have to get you out of here, darling," I said as I frantically shook the chains binding her hands.

"The keys. Check his pockets," Emilia blurted out as we kept an eye on the countdown. 00:01:12, 00:01:11, 00:01:10...

I rifled through his pockets and came up empty-handed before flipping him over and patting down the front of his uniform. "They're not here. The tosser doesn't have them!" I said as I grabbed the phone and scrolled away from the ticker to the CE admin login. "Put the administrative password in," I instructed as I held the phone near her right hand.

"I can't see the buttons!" Emilia shrieked as she struggled against the cuffs.

"Emilia. Give me the password. Hurry."

"Don't do it Emilia! Nothing is going to happen," her beaten kidnapper implored.

"15 seconds Emilia! Don't be foolish, child."

"G78-80P-HHW-N9M" Emilia recited slowly as I punched the numbers and letters in to gain access to administrative control of the system. I closed out the countdown simulator with two seconds remaining and tucked her phone into my purse. I pulled out my own to punch in the twelve-digit code for verification, and I took control of the entire Connect Earth system.

I shook my head at my former protégé and gave her a sigh like a disapproving mother. "Oh, Emilia. I really expected more of you. How did you let yourself get kidnapped by this bumbling fool?" The confused look she gave me was equally disappointing as seeing her chained and beaten.

"You know, for a while there I thought maybe you knew. I always chose my words carefully around you. I assumed you'd figure things out if I ever slipped up on a single detail, but you never did quite sort things out for yourself, did you?"

"You bitch!" Emilia howled at me with a rage that would break her chains if it could manifest physically.

"Sshhh sshhh, now. I have to pay you a compliment darling. Connect Earth is muah." I mimicked a chef's kiss. "Hijacking the fiber optics of all the previous providers and claiming them for yourself was a nice touch. Pairing every digital communication service all into one was the icing on top. The thing I should have seen coming was your sheltered paranoia consolidating the power into your hands, and your hands only. I must say, that was a puzzle I hadn't solved until Tweedle Dee here took you on a guided tour of our indiscretions."

I had kept so many secrets for so long. It felt great to release them out into the open for a change. Having your life's work come to fruition is nothing without an audience to share it with.

"You were working with this filth?" Emilia insulted as she nodded her head towards the corpse at her feet.

"Working *with*? Heavens no. I don't work *with* anyone. Do you really think so little of me? He was an asset. A particularly high-value asset, but an asset all the same."

"Why help him at all?"

"Goodness child. If I must spell out every step of my twenty years of planning, it will make me a villain by default."

"She's got a point, Emilia. Movie rules," her bloody accomplice jested.

"Seeing as how you have no cards left to play, radio girl, I'm curious; was the countdown truly a fraud?"

"The two of you are really incredible, you know that?" she replied with blood running down her chin. "Your steady diet of lies erased your memory of the taste of truth. Or maybe it's fear that blinds you. It's always so easy to imagine the monster under the bed as being real, isn't it?"

"That's poetic, but you didn't answer my question," I pressed.

"No! Of course it wasn't real! Look at me, for Christ's sake. Do I strike you as someone who's capable of crippling your precious network?"

"I can help you run it," Emilia interjected with a change of tone.

"Oh? Is that right, darling? You're going to teach me the ins and outs of your system? Be my loyal number two?"

"It's a complicated platform, and I already have the leadership experience of guiding the developer team."

"Mmmm. Ha. Oh, Emilia. I could never trust you. And you never should have trusted me, but here we are. That's why I'm the mentor, and you were the protégé. If I were to free you, you'd never stop working to steal your baby back."

"I'm serious," she pleaded. "I'd rather you have it than see it destroyed. Haven't I proven that much?"

"This is a rather pathetic display, child. I do have one last compliment to pay you though. None of this would have been possible without you, and I'm not referencing the OWG or Connect Earth. I may have organized the minutia of details, but you're the genesis of the plan. The next time you're looking for someone to blame, I suggest you think back to your college days and look inward."

Emilia averted her gaze from me and towards the floor in defeat. It wasn't going to take her a lifetime in isolation to put the pieces of the puzzle together. She was already fitting them into place and shouldering the weight of what her brilliance had wrought.

"That's my girl. Always so clever. Now then, this is where we part ways. I'm not going to apologize because women like us don't say sorry, do we? Consider the gift of life I let you keep as the best amends I can offer because I still love you in our twisted way," I said as I lightly tapped on her nose with one finger. "Besides,

I only paint with the brains of men, and yours are too beautiful to spill in this world anyway. Guards!"

Two guards entered the room and began unshackling the cuffs and bonds on both of their hands and feet. "Easy now. Careful with them. These ladies have been through a lot."

Emilia lunged forward but was held back by the guard gripping her under her armpits. She did get close enough to spit in my face before sneering some colorful insults that don't bear repeating.

"Understandable, but not very polite," I said as I grabbed a clean corner of her dress to wipe the spit from my face. "Sometimes, there's only one way to teach a lady some manners. Put them on a transport with male prisoners," I directed to the guards who hauled them away.

I had played puppeteer to the world for as long as I could remember to earn that moment. I almost didn't know what to do with myself once there were no more men to climb over to get to the top. Emilia didn't respect the power when she had it, and that was a mistake I wasn't going to make. I wouldn't be tricked out of it, nor would I be manipulated. If anyone was going to take it from me, they'd need to paint my brains in abstract art on the floor. It was time for the One World Governance to become the One *Woman* Governance I designed it to be.

Chapter 10

Hell on Earth

Malik Emmanuel

"Chris. Another one," I requested as I tapped the rim of my empty scotch glass. I opened the CE Notes app to pay, and the barkeep delayed my order and gave me a concerned look.

"Maybe you should slow down, Emmanuel," he counseled as he withheld the bottle and payment scanner.

"Is there a speed limit I don't know about?" I asked as I snatched the digital device out of his hand, ran it over my UPC code to transfer the funds, and attempted to take the bottle.

He begrudgingly poured the drink and tried to talk me into behaving myself. "Just be cool, man. Your last outburst in here got our credit score docked."

"Ooooooo," I howled with a buzzed ominous tone. "Not the almighty social credit score," I mocked.

The bar had become my home away from home. It was a small, dimly lit establishment that played good music, but that's not why it was my favorite. It was located just miles from Edwards which brought in a lot of soldiers and sometimes officers. My time spent there was meant to escape the quiet torture of being home alone while offering me opportunities to connect with the people who could get me back on a mission hunting down Praxi outposts. Unfortunately, I struggled to accomplish either of these goals so long as my CE phone sat in front of me.

I closed the payment app and navigated back to the Connections platform to find a host of notifications waiting for me. There were no new 'likes' on any of my angry comments, but I was receiving several responses from those who counted themselves as righteous. The current exchange I was wrapped up in had been consuming my life for the past two days as I volleyed public messages back and forth with a woman from my old congregation in Arkansas.

When I knew her, she was an intelligent and caring person. The kind who would make polite conversation in passing at the grocery store or would bring a casserole to a family who had lost a loved one. That is not who she was anymore.

Connect Earth had changed her. She was no longer part of the Christian church. She was a member of an ideological cult whose every action was emboldened by the magnitude of positive responses online from the vocal majority that shared her beliefs.

Our exchange had started innocently enough, but quickly devolved into something hateful when the status of my profile came into question. I listed "none" under my religious affiliations tab, and I didn't partake in glamorizing my bio with Christian flags or a customizable black Jesus emoji. I lost my faith on the same day the rest of the world found theirs, and I stubbornly thumbed my nose at the self-righteous. I wouldn't be counseled on matters of religion by people who thought "The King James Version," was a basketball term or those whose hair was still wet from being baptized.

With every message sent back and forth, more members of the cult piled on. I was no longer arguing with one person. I was facing down an army who openly discussed the merits of internment, forced conversion, and a segregated society. I sipped my scotch, and nearly spit it out when I read the most recent reply. "Would a second holocaust of atheists be such a bad idea?"

The disgusting proposal had over three thousand likes in under ten minutes and was drawing even more negative attention towards myself. I drown the bubbling rage inside me with the last of my drink and let the aggressive slamming of the glass against the bar top serve as my request for another.

Chris returned with the bottle without adding commentary and ran the scanner over my payment app. "Sorry, Malik, I can't serve you," he said.

"You can't or you won't?"

"I can't. It says your social score dropped below 650. You've been cut off."

I reached across the bar to grab his wrist as he tried to walk away. "Pour. The. Drink," I demanded.

I felt a hand on both of my shoulders, and another on my knee that forced my butt back into my seat. Kai sat on the stool next to me and held me in place, while Risa and another cohort wrangled control of me from behind. "Are we going to have a problem again, Emmanuel?" Kai asked.

"Only if you don't take your hands off of me," I warned, even though I was outnumbered.

"You just don't learn, do you? You know, if you really want to join your family, we'd be happy to oblige," he taunted as I struggled to break free from their grip.

I turned my head to stare him down and curse him out, but before I could give Kai a verbal lashing, I watched his face collide with the wood finish and two teeth go careening across the bar top as his stool was kicked out from underneath him and he collapsed to the ground.

There stood Maya, my only friend in the world, and she seemed to be in a sporty mood.

"The little dyke bitch knocked my teeth out!" Kai cried from the ground as he held his bleeding mouth. The accosters released my shoulders and turned their attention to Maya, but she had her 9mm sidearm drawn before the violence could escalate.

"Dyke? Oooo. An oldie but a goodie," Maya said as she pressed the barrel to his temple and restricted him from getting back on his feet. "Go ahead, Risa. You wanna step to me? I'll put your homie in the dirt," she warned.

"Let's find out how tough you really are," Risa suggested. "Ditch the gun, and we can have a fair fight."

"Like the one I walked up on?" Maya snapped without missing a beat. She holstered her gun and stepped forward until she was nose-to-nose with Risa.

"Not in here!" Chris begged from behind the bar.

I reached down to offer Kai a hand, and he promptly swatted me away. "Keep your pity," he snarled with a toothless whistling speech impediment.

"Come on, *Dragon Ball*. Let's go outside," Maya challenged Risa with a wink.

"Risa. Leave her," Kai warned as the wiser half of their duo.

"Another time," Risa promised while helping Kai to his feet.

Maya smiled back confidently, collected Kai's teeth from the bar top, & secured them in her chest pocket. "It's a date," Maya replied playfully and wrapped her arm around my shoulder. "Let's roll out. I've got something for you," she said as we turned our back on our antagonists.

Once outside, I slapped Maya's bare upper arm. "Appreciate you."

"Don't mention it. Kicking a stool out from underneath an asshole was a bucket list item," she grinned.

"Come on. Let's get a drink somewhere else," I suggested.

'I've got something better for you. A job."

"What kind of job?"

"You're going to come work with me."

"For real? What happened to your pilot? The commercial aviator guy," I asked.

"We had a uh, slight difference in *principles and values*."

"So, he didn't like all the coke?"

"Or the weed. Apparently, they didn't do a lot of blow on the Southwest flights he used to pilot. He quit two days ago, and I thought this was a good chance to get you out of bed."

"I'd rather wait for a spot on the deep space military missions, but I suppose this would get my foot back in the door."

"Good, because I already signed you up. Our first flight is 8 a.m. tomorrow morning, so get your ass home and get some rest."

"Yes ma'am," I replied.

I was genuinely excited to get off Earth. The environment was growing more toxic by the day, and as much as I hated my Connect Earth phone, I couldn't put the darn thing down. I looked forward to entering the Jump Point and losing access to the network for a few days.

I arrived at the hangar the following morning to find Maya hard at work, and she was wearing a gray World Military jumpsuit to my surprise. Buses were pulling up to unload hundreds of inmates for transport, and I walked around the cargo ship to find the *Lydia* marked on the side. Maya raised her gaze from her clipboard to make eye contact with me, and we shared a smile.

"What's with the modifications?" I asked as I ran my hand over the creases and panels in the lower quadrant of the cargo hull.

"Drop hatch. The floors roll back, the gravity field opens, and *bye bye* prisoners," she explained. "We don't have to land to drop off the cargo. Will you help them with the restraints please?"

I acquired keys from the transport guards and started to unlock the wrists of hundreds of women who were chained together while armed escorts stood watch. I eventually gave the key to the last woman I unlocked and had them pass it around between themselves to get free.

Maya stood on the rear ramp and started shuttling the prisoners into the cargo hold. "Listen up, ladies! I'm Commander Fontaine. We're going to take the *Lydia* on a little two-day pleasure cruise to Prius. There are rations for when you want to eat, pillows for when you want to sleep, and buckets for when you need to shit. You can get your running water out of one of the three faucets. There's no assigned seating and no shackles. If you make a mess of my ship, I will not hesitate to drop your ass from twenty feet. The last thing you want to do when starting a new life on an alien planet without healthcare is break an ankle or rupture a spleen; so, pick up after yourselves. Once these doors close, it will be the last you see of me, but rest assured I will be watching."

Maya loved this. While the prison transport might not have been a military mission, she had taken a liking to referring to herself as Commander and barking orders. Outside of the attack on Prius, this was the closest she'd been to being back in the service since she'd gunned down Toes and fled the Marines.

"How many are there?" I asked.

"Seven hundred and fifty per trip."

"That's a little tight. They must be standing wall to wall. It's kind of inhumane, don't you think?"

"Two hundred thousand lifers in the old United States region alone, Malik. We bus the west coast, and there's another that flies off the east coast. These gravity drives are hard to come by with the World Military putting all the assets into search and destroy missions. We're low priority. Don't feel sorry for these scum. They made their bed, and at least they're not getting a bullet."

I tried to do the math in my head for how many trips it would take to move all the human cargo. We were going to be in this process of cruelly transporting these people for years, and that wasn't even counting all the political prisoners that were being locked up every day.

We loaded our passengers, closed the ramp, and used the officers' quarters entrance near the front of the ship to access the bridge. The frontmost area of the cargo hold had been sealed off from the prisoner's area, with a mess hall and two bedrooms installed; each with its own bathroom and a shower. There was a single locked door between us and our cargo, and the bridge was equipped with monitors to keep an eye on them.

"You're on the right." Maya pointed out my bedroom. "Oh, hold on one second. This one used to be mine. Let me tidy it up for you," she said as she pulled the bed sheets down to the floor to conceal something underneath.

"What are you hiding?" I asked as I lifted her bedsheet curtain and found a pair of gravity bombs. "Maya!" I exclaimed.

"Sorry sorry sorry. I'll move them," she said as she fished them out from under the bed and revealed that they were labeled "Marcus" and "Maisie."

"Are these?"

"Yeah, shit man. I'm sorry. We ran out of targets, and I didn't want to give 'em back to the WM, so I stole them," she explained. "It's totally safe though. I think. I removed the trigger housing, so they should be fine."

"It's okay. You can leave them there." It was strangely comforting to sleep above a pair of gravity warheads. Seeing the names of my children made my quarters feel more like home than what I was leaving behind on Earth.

"Shall we?" Maya asked as she led me to the bridge and pointed to the pilot's chair. "It's all yours now."

Piloting the craft was no problem without the stress of war affecting every decision and we left Earth's upper atmosphere and entered the Jump Point with no fanfare at all.

"A thousand notes each way, my man," Maya bragged. "There's not an easier job on Earth," she said as she unloaded her kit and sparked up a joint.

"Notes don't do you much good when the WM restricts your spending."

"Yeah, about that. You've got to give that shit a rest, bro. You can't bring that negative energy onto the base. These guys don't play. Mark your CE profile with any religion you'd like, stop picking fights, and keep your head down. It's worked for me," she said as she reached down her neckline and pulled out a chain with a cross on it.

"Seriously? They got to you too?"

"It's no big deal. I'm repping Catholic, and I even reconnected with my folks."

"You realize you're being indoctrinated, right?"

"Bitch, please," she said as she dabbed a small pile of cocaine onto the space between her thumb and index finger. "Bless me, Father, for I'm about to sin," she quipped as she snorted it up.

"I don't know what's worse. Someone who's radicalized or someone who pretends to be and goes along those who are."

"You're one to talk," she snapped with a tone she rarely used with me. "You watch that Connect Earth News trash every night. All they ever talk about is hunting down and killing the Grays before they hit us again as if we didn't already slaughter billions. They've got your head all fucked up."

"You don't support the war effort to finish them off? If those Marines offered you a chance to get your stripes back and go on the offensive; you wouldn't take it?" I aggressively questioned her dedication to the cause.

"Nah man. I'm done," she answered while exhaling a cloud of smoke. "I don't like a fight where I can't tell right from wrong."

"Oh, so you think we were wrong? Is that it?"

"Malik, I don't want to do this with you again, bro."

"Just say it. We didn't take justice for my family. We did something terrible. I know that's what you think."

"I'm not the only one. Chop saw it too."

"Chop? Right. Real reliable source there. Guy hasn't answered my calls or responded to a single message in a month."

"I don't know what that's supposed to prove, but whatever. You're ruining my high. I don't want to talk about this," Maya said as she abandoned her post and retired to her quarters.

She was the only person left in the world that I cared about, and I couldn't get through fifteen minutes of flight time without pushing her away. Religion and the war were topics we were going to have to learn to avoid if our relationship was going to flourish. I was never going to convince her of the merits of continuing the attack on the Praxi, and I was wholly unwilling to consider that I didn't know my enemy.

In the past, I would turn to prayer in a quiet moment of frustration. I'd ask God for the strength to carry on and I would instantly feel relief. I didn't possess the faith of Job though. If God was real, and He took everything from me as a test; I hated Him for it. I felt silly even entertaining the idea that there was a God. How could there be? Why would He create mankind and the Praxi only for us to destroy one another? What kind of sick ant farm was He running?

I had believed in fairy tales well into my adult life because I had learned the stories as an impressionable child. Religion was just another machine of control.

A mythical way to convince people to act in opposition to our ugly human nature. I didn't need the threat of Hell to manipulate me into being a decent human being. I did it my whole life even though God was a lie, and I wasn't going to stop now that my mind was opened to the truth. I did, however, require some outlet for positive energy, and I certainly wasn't going to find it on Earth with my CE phone in my hand.

Maya and I didn't speak again until the next day, and once we did it was as though our disagreement had never taken place. We played cards, had some laughs, and shared stories. Our bond was too strong to be bruised by a minor disagreement.

We took our places as we exited the portal to make our drop. All the wreckage of the spaceport I destroyed had long since been cleaned up. From a distance, you never would have known that a great war had unfolded there only months earlier.

"Continent 2," Maya directed. "That's where I've been dropping the ladies."

"Any particular reason?"

"General Kelly doesn't want them *getting their hump on* in exile. If the generations continue to die out on the planet surface, we can maintain this place as a criminal depot indefinitely. Plus, as a personal note, I don't think these ladies want to intermingle with the types of men we're dropping down there anyway. They're better off being kept separate," she explained.

I navigated the ship around to the dark side of the planet, and we zoomed over the continent looking for a good spot to drop.

"You can put them anywhere, so long as it's not too close to another colony. It's better if we spread them out in my opinion. Hurry up and pick a spot though. Schedule allows for thirty minutes on this end, and I want to show you something before we leave," she said.

"We should find a spot with access to fresh water, right?" I asked.

"Who cares," Maya responded coldly.

"I mean, why drop them in a desert if you can put them near the ocean? Give them a fighting chance."

"They don't deserve you," Maya complimented before switching on the intercom and giving a landing warning to our passengers. "We're making our final descent into Continent 2, where the weather on the ground is a brisk fifty-eight degrees. Please stow away your tray tables and deactivate any electronic devices you have at this time. Thank you for flying Jump Point Airlines and enjoy lovely Prius".

I picked a spot along the coastline, lowered the ship to a few feet above the beach, and rolled back the cargo floor causing the hundreds of women to fall to the sand below. They piled up on top of each other so much that I had to raise the ship higher to clear them all out.

"What a mess," I commented. "Let's land next time. Let them exit with some dignity."

"We don't land, and we don't linger. Now come on. Take elevation and go to Continent 5. You've got to see this colony," Maya directed.

We swooped around to the other side of the planet. There was hardly any cloud cover that day, and I flew low enough that our shadow could be seen on the ground below. The planet was rich with beauty and vegetation if you could avoid the pits of destruction that we had left in our wake when we bombed their cities. The forests, jungles, and bodies of water appeared untouched by industry or pollution. The plant life grew wild and provided more than enough food and shelter for the various indigenous lifeforms and prisoners alike.

"It's down that way. You see that lake? It's on the south side," she directed. "Slow down. Easy. Check them out. This is the first crew I dropped here."

The colony below had made incredible progress. There were huts constructed against the tree line, and an irrigation funnel being dug from the lake leading up towards their encampment. The men below appeared to be busy working on any number of different projects. There were at least twenty of them in the shallow end of the water, and I presumed that they were trying to gather food for their tribe.

A group on the beachhead waved their arms and shouted at us, though we couldn't hear what they were saying. One of them picked up a stick and wrote *nets* in big letters in the sand.

"They've been here maybe a month, and they're miles ahead of any of the other drops," Maya narrated.

"We could help them. You know, drop them supplies and stuff," I suggested.

"Why? They're criminals on vacation. There's not one of them that would trade this for the cell they left behind. We've done enough for them."

"I want to bring them some stuff. Nothing crazy, just the basics. Is that okay?" I asked for her blessing.

"Do whatever you want, man. Don't let the supervisors see you loading it and don't involve me in it." Maya didn't agree with my act of goodwill, but she didn't stand in my way either. If there was one thing she understood, it was action taken to help someone even if others disagreed and there could be consequences.

Adopting a colony on Prius was better than anything I had back on Earth. The next time we returned, I dropped them a care package including fishing nets, an axe, two hatchets, and some matches. Four days later we were back again, and the men had written *hooks* in the sand like an item added to a shopping list.

I brought them essentials and fulfilled their requests on every trip. Over the course of the next month, I outfitted them with fishing equipment, spear tips for hunting, tarps, cutlery, cooking utensils, rope, a water filter, a first aid kit, and other health care essentials. The only items Maya wouldn't let me drop were a compass and a map of the continent. She was adamant about keeping the colonies separate from one another.

I stuffed a duffle bag full of these essential starter items to give to every new load of prisoners we deposited. The more I saw our planted colonies grow and thrive, the more I envied them. I would leave them in exile without the amenities of our *civilized* society, yet I was the one who was miserable when I was allowed to return to those supposed luxuries.

Our prisoners were living freely in their new world. Free from oppressive governments. Free from digital manipulations. Free from soul-crushing jobs and spirit-destroying stress. Their only cares were making shelter and finding food like the cavemen of old. If life on Prius was Heaven, then by contrast, life on Earth was Hell.

At home, I'd respond like Pavlov's dog every time my Connections notifications would buzz and fan the flames of my anger. I'd tune into CEN to watch the latest news praising our great military in their hunt for the Grays across the galaxy and stoke my coals of hatred. When I was able to avoid either of these inputs of stress, the silence summoned tears for my babies and mourning for my wife.

My only happiness came in three-second bursts from the disorientation of waking from sleep. In the fog of slumber, my confused mind would forget everything I'd lost, and it wasn't until reaching into Lydia's cold side of the bed that I would be reminded. I started sleeping with a heating pad under the covers to extend those three seconds into five, but the pain awaited me at the end of my vegetative state regardless.

Road trips off the planet were my only escape. Maya and I started doing triple shifts where we'd spend twelve straight days going back and forth before taking a break, and I would have done it nonstop if I could. It was virtually stress-free, and it wasn't until we'd been on the job for a couple of months before we had our first dust-up.

We were hanging out in the mess hall with a spirited game of Monopoly laid out across the table. "I'll give you $500 for New York Avenue," I offered.

"Absolutely not. Roll the dice."

"$600," I increased the bid.

"No, bro. Stop. You always kill me with them orange ones."

"That's because you always roll for doubles to get out of jail," I explained.

"I'm not paying that $50 bullshit fee. My little top hat did his time. He's earned his parole."

"What do you want to watch after we make the drop?" I asked.

"What I want to watch is you rolling them damn dice and landing on Pennsylvania Avenue. Now stop stalling and come to Mama."

I picked up the dice, rolled a seven, and Maya grunted in excitement. She picked up my race car and counted out each move on the board until I landed on her property.

"Pennsylvania Avenue. Three houses. $1000. Pay up, sucka. That's the most money I've ever made while locked up," she celebrated by dancing her top hat piece in jail.

"You win," I conceded. "Spare me the embarrassment of mortgaging everything. It's probably about time to get on station anyways."

"We're not finished. Don't you dare pack it up," she grinned. "We'll make the drop and then we're playing this out. *Imma bleed you. Real quiet. Leave ya here. Got that?*" she gloated with an accent and a movie quote that I couldn't place. Maya had spent months getting her butt kicked by me in every game from poker to checkers, and she relished any chance she had to win a matchup.

We took our stations on the bridge and went over our final checklist as we made our approach to the Jump Point exit. Maya switched on the monitoring to get one final glance at our particularly rowdy crew of male prisoners and put her feet up on the digital dashboard.

"Dropping to approach speed," I announced. "Any other expected traffic to watch for?"

"There's a hauler on its way back from Triax II with a load of the good stuff heading home, but they're not set to pass through here for three hours. Skies are clear."

"Copy that. Fifteen minutes on approach."

Maya pulled her feet down and sat up to get a closer look at the monitor. "I think these boys might be entertaining us with one last fight," she said gleefully.

"They wouldn't be fighting if they knew how much their lives were about to improve."

"Hold up," Maya said as she gripped the sides of the monitor. "Are those women in there?"

I leaned over in my seat to examine the scene and it seemed that Maya was correct. "What the heck? How did they get on this transport? Were they on the manifest?"

"How the hell should I know?"

"It's your job to know."

'There's seven hundred and fifty of them. It's not like I lift everyone's skirts and run a genitals check. It's never been a problem before."

The situation continued to escalate as a group of three male prisoners accosted the two women while everyone else stood around and watched. Those who would dare to defend the women were outnumbered by their more violent counterparts.

"Maya...hey," I said as I watched her hands turn to fists. One of the attackers ripped open the front of the orange jumpsuit of one of the women, and Maya sprang out of her seat towards her bedroom. "Maya! We'll be in Prius air space in ten minutes. On the ground in fifteen."

Maya reappeared out of her quarters, slapping a clip into a pistol and sparking the end of a taser. "Unlock the hatch door," she commanded.

"What are you doing with a gun on board?" I exclaimed.

"They're like twenty feet inside the cargo bay. Unlock the fucking hatch!"

"I can't do that, Maya. They could take the ship!"

She approached me with the taser extended and buzzing; and backed me away from my station. She gained access to the controls and hit the override on the locks. "Either lock the door behind me, or put the ship on auto, get your taser, and help me!"

She ran off the bridge, passed our quarters, through the mess hall, and swung open the only door between us and hundreds of prisoners who would happily see us dead. 'Shit!" I groaned as I put the ship on auto and armed myself with a taser.

By the time I stood in the doorway, Maya was already carving her way through the crowd, zapping anyone who stood too close. The sea of bodies parted for her, and she fired her gun in the air twice which caused a series of ricochets inside the compartment. "Move! Move! I will shoot you in the face!" she warned those around her.

A few prisoners stood too close to the doorway for comfort, so I zapped a couple of them to herd them away and dissuade the others from trying anything stupid. My uniform dampened with sweat under my armpits, and my hand shook as I gripped the taser with an iron fist.

The crowd cleared to the perimeter on all sides, and Maya was left in a show-down with the three would-be rapists. One of the girls had her jumpsuit ripped down to her waistline leaving her torso and chest exposed. The other was filthy. The orange of her smock was covered in smeared brown stains of feces.

"Put the gun down, little girl. You don't have enough bullets for all of us," one of the sweaty pigs sneered at Maya.

"You gonna rape her? Go on. Put your hands on her again," Maya taunted as she escalated a situation that didn't need it.

"Her? She's covered in shit. She smells like a fucking sewer. She ain't getting this cock until she's been cleaned up," he said as he groped himself. "This one though, she's pretty if you can look past the damage. I fancy 'em a little bruised. You can share this cock with her if you'd like. I've got more than enough to go around."

"You sure?" Maya asked as she pointed her pistol at his groin and fired. He instantly dropped to the ground, rolling around on his back as he grasped at what was left of his physical manhood. The orange of his jumpsuit turned dark as he gushed blood, and the gasps from the onlookers were drowned out by his pained screams.

The next accoster quickly grabbed the beaten girl and pulled her back against his chest as a human shield. He hid his head and body behind hers while threatening, "Go back to your office before something terrible happens to you. This girl is m---," before being interrupted by more gunfire from Maya.

He joined his friend on the ground as the blood poured from his foot. "First time holding a human shield? You gotta be mindful of your feet, homie." Maya was putting on quite the show, and she had struck the fear of God into her audience. I was so accustomed to the carefree and fun version that I had forgotten what a badass she was.

"What about you, amigo? Any tricks up your sleeve? Anything snappy to say?" she asked the last man standing.

"You think you're so tough with that uniform and gun. It won't make any difference. These two belong to us now, and I'll think of your pretty face when I'm having a go at them later tonight."

Maya shrugged her shoulders in disappointment as though she would have let him off the hook if he could act right. She hit him twice with the taser to drop him to the floor, spun her pistol backward, and offered the handle to the girl with her uniform ripped open. "Want to show him how you feel about his plans?" Maya offered.

The girl didn't take the gun, instead choosing to pull her tattered clothing over herself as much as possible. Before Maya could extend the same offer, the woman covered in feces snatched the gun from Maya's hand and put the barrel to the incapacitated man's head. "Apologize, and I'll only wound you," was her bargain.

"I'm sorry," he pleaded as he continued to shake from being tased. "I'm so sorry. It wasn't my idea. Please don't kill me."

"Not good enough," she replied before squeezing off a round into his forehead. His body lurched forward toward her feet, and she put her heel to his shoulder and pushed his discarded body toward the other two wounded jerks. She rolled the trigger guard on her forefinger until the gun was turned upside down and offered it back to Maya.

"Come on. We'll get you sorted out," she helped the wounded woman with the other limping behind.

"Get back," I warned the prisoners lurking around the doorway to make space for Maya's rescued victims. Once through the doorway, I closed it behind the four of us, locked it, and let out a sigh of relief.

"What's your name?" Maya asked the woman with the pulverized face.

"Alexis," she replied.

"I'm Maya. This is Malik," she introduced. "What about you?" she asked the other woman who limped into my bathroom. I could hear the running water of the sink, but no verbal response.

"What happened to you two?" I asked.

"Well, let's see. We raided a secret military facility, exposed the greatest government coverup in history, endured torture at the hands of none other than General Kelly himself, and saw him murdered by the woman who took over the world," Alexis said.

"Is that all?" Maya quipped.

"That about covers it."

The other woman came out of the bathroom with her face washed even though her clothes were still soaked in fecal matter. "Hey, Maya! It's Eggshells," I exclaimed.

"What the hell? What are you doing here?" Why are you covered in crap?" Maya questioned.

"There's a reason my clothes are still on and hers are torn to shreds," Emilia explained.

"Gross, but effective," Maya commented.

"Where's Chop?" I asked.

"Yeah, Emilia. Where's Chop?" Alexis added aggressively.

"You have to take us back." Emilia avoided the question.

"Oh, hell no. Do *not* take her back there. This maniac tried to kill me and screwed everything up."

"You guys need to hear this," Emilia pleaded. "We've all been played. The Grays never hit Earth. The whole thing was a false flag. They're not our enemy."

"You lie!" I shouted. "You and that damn Connect Earth. Freaking poison! The Grays took my family, and you're not going to trample over their graves with your bull shit," I barked, unwilling to hear what she had to say. I turned my back on them, returned to the bridge to find the ship idling in Prius airspace, and used manual controls to navigate towards our drop zone.

I hovered into position and prepared to unload the human cargo. "Throw them in the back!" I shouted to Maya.

She walked onto the bridge and purposely kept some distance between me and Emilia. "We can't drop them with this crew, Malik," she counseled gently to avoid my ire. "Alexis is hurt pretty bad, and she's going to need some medical attention. Make this drop and we'll unload these gals at the fisherman's village on five. They've got the supplies to tend to their wounds."

I rolled the floor back, dropping the prisoners from a greater height than usual, and sealed the lower hatch without speaking. I pulled the ship back above the clouds and sped off towards Continent 5.

"Take these. Just in case," Maya equipped both women with our issued tasers. "I think there's some good people down there, but this is an all-male colony."

"Get them off my ship," I hastened.

Maya led them back to the cargo hold and sealed them behind the door. "All good," she shouted up to me, and even though my rage was pounding, I took special care to drop them from a safe distance above the ground. I checked the time to make sure we were on schedule and accelerated towards the Jump Point to head home.

Maya returned to the bridge, sliding over her armrest into her co-pilot seat.

"Don't," I said preemptively to dissuade Maya from speaking her mind.

"I don't have to. You're already thinking it."

Maya was right. There wasn't a logical explanation for what Emilia was doing on a prison transport, but I wasn't interested in examining things logically. It was difficult avoiding the question while traveling with Maya who needed no convincing, but it was much easier when we returned home.

The social pressure to join the fight against the Praxi had risen to religious levels. I couldn't pick up my phone or turn on the news without being inundated with hate. Everywhere I looked was blanketed with ads to enlist with the World Military, find a career in weapons and flight systems manufacturing, or join the mining outposts on Triax II. The messaging connected perfectly with our kill-or-be-killed violent human nature. The WM was handing out social credit score boosts like candy on Halloween to everyone supporting the cause. Those who dared to have a contrary opinion were shouted down online, docked socially and financially, and would sometimes be arrested or flat-out disappear.

I didn't require positive or negative reinforcement to fuel my hate. I was determined to join the deep space search and destroy missions, and I wasn't about to be deterred by the pleas of a lying stowaway.

Chapter 11

The Penitent

Emilia Vera

I waited nervously for the floors to drop out and make me a permanent resident of Prius. If I had been more studious with my relationships on Earth, I might have made enough of a connection with Maya and Malik to earn their attention for more than two minutes. I suppose being saved by them was more than I deserved.

Maya Angelou once said, "Hope for the best, be prepared for the worst. Life is shocking, but you must never appear to be shocked." I didn't have much hope, but I was presuming the worst and was unwilling to show the prisoners awaiting us even an ounce of shock or fear.

"You know how to use that thing?" I asked Alexis and tapped my taser against hers.

"I don't think so," she replied before sticking the wand into my ribs and firing a bolt of electricity through my body that left me limp and prone on the floor. "Never mind. I figured it out."

I rolled away from her to avoid being zapped again and hadn't done two bodily rotations before the ship discarded us onto the planet's surface. The grass was yellow and thick but didn't offer enough padding to soften the blow. I gasped for breath with the wind knocked out of me, and a dozen men ran in our direction before I could compose myself.

"Hey, fellas," Alexis waved nervously.

The men were disheveled and confused. Their hair, nails, and beards grew long. Their orange jumpsuits were in varying states of disrepair and filth. They looked like we should be able to smell them, but I could not.

"Are you two lost?" one of the men asked.

"Is this not Philadelphia?" Alexis asked, using humor to keep things light. "See, I knew I got on the wrong flight."

"You shouldn't be here," another man added.

"We were told with some confidence that there were decent people down here, and we'd find access to medical care," I said.

"We've got a good thing going here. They're going to ruin everything," the first man said, completely ignoring the question I was posing.

"We can't send them away, at least not until we've patched them up."

"Come with us," one of the men reached out for my arm, and I engaged the taser to warn him with the shocking tone. "Okay, okay. I don't mean you any harm. We have supplies, food, and fresh water, if you'll follow us."

They led us through the grove and a garden where every man tending to it stopped to stare as we passed by. The village itself was a series of huts made from planks and heavy shrubbery pressed against the tree line a few hundred yards from a sprawling lake. They had constructed workspaces for cleaning fish, and they maintained a continuous firepit for cooking. A clothesline was attached between two posts, and naked men went about their business as their orange smocks dangled to dry. The closer we got to the encampment, the more men dropped what they were doing and gathered around in an ominous crowd.

"You guys have like a cool, gay, Amish village vibe going here. Just a bunch of dudes. Doing dude stuff. Bro-ing out," Alexis kept up her humorous defense mechanism.

"Shut up, Alexis," I cautioned, knowing how quickly the situation could become untenable. 'What's the deal, here? You boys going to be able to keep it in your pants, or is this going to get super rapey? Cause I have to say, I've had my fill of that shit for the day."

"No one's going to harm you. It would be nice if you would drop your weapons and fill us in on what exactly you're doing here though," an older man said calmly.

"Sit down, grandpa," an ogre of a man ordered as he pulled his elder to the ground by the back of his shirt. "Women. Real live women. I'm Max, and I'm the guy who decides how pleasurable or painful your time will be with us." He stood remarkably tall for a man of east Asian descent, with multiple braids in his overgrown beard, and a three-inch scar trailing from his right eye down his cheek.

"Stop it. You're frightening them," the elder complained.

"I'm not scared of this neanderthal," I stated confidently.

"Uh, for the record, I am," Alexis chimed in.

"Look at us. We're twins," he said as he ran his forefinger across his scar. "I think we were meant to be together."

"You touch me, and I'll remove the pieces of you that set us apart," I threatened.

"Ooh. You're fiery. How about you ditch the shock stick, get cleaned up, and we'll get better acquainted?"

"We should breed them!" one of the men shouted, joining Max's disposition.

"*Breed them*?" Alexis echoed with concern.

"The rest of you can share the piece of bruised fruit, but this little strawberry is all mine," Max taunted as he licked his lips.

"Your move, big boy. You can take what you want, but if I zap you first, I'm not going to stop until you're unconscious," I warned. "Once you're out cold, I'm going to pick up a rock and cave in your melon fucking skull."

He lunged towards me, and I pressed the taser against his belly, which did little other than piss him off. He grabbed my hand and squeezed it until I dropped the wand. I tried to knee him in the groin, but I came up short and hit his thigh instead. He overpowered me, spun me around, and bear-hugged me back against his chest to subdue me.

I squirmed and kicked to no avail, but before he could carry me off, one of the other men interceded by jumping on Max's back and weighing the three of us to the ground. I broke free from his grip as the two men wrestled, and I rushed to pick up my taser. Both Alexis and I kicked and thrashed at Max until the fight was in our favor, and once our hero was clear of him, we held our tasers against his chest and hip until he passed out.

I knew I was going to have to make an example out of him if we were going to survive that environment, so I quickly foraged around in the grass until I found a softball-sized rock. I rolled Max onto his back, straddled his chest, and raised both hands above my head to smash his face. The hero grabbed my forearms to stop me, and we made eye contact for the first time.

"Emilia?" he asked as he released me and staggered back.

I dropped the rock and my jaw at the same time. "Ranbir?"

"Ho-ly shit!" Alexis exclaimed.

His hair had grown long and his beard wild, but he was the same man I thought I had sent to his death. He stared at me in shock with nothing to say. I was relieved to see him alive but also horrified that I had to face him.

"Hi *sweetie*," I chipped away at the ice between us.

"This is Emilia? *The* Emilia?" the elder man asked.

"Oh, look at that. You're famous," Alexis jested.

"She can't stay here. She's a spy," the elder accused.

"Yeah genius. I'm a spy. I flew halfway across the galaxy so I could embed with your fishing village and gain vital intel on who has the ugliest beard. You're an early front-runner, but fingers crossed. Who the hell is this guy? Who's in charge?" I condescended.

"Nobody is in charge. We don't do that here," Ranbir informed me.

"She'll try to take charge if you let her stay," Alexis warned. "She'll lie, cheat, and steal. She'll screw you over if you give her half a chance. I'm not saying you should kill her, but it would be a huge mistake to trust her."

"Thanks *friend*," my eyes cut a hole in Alexis.

"I'm not your friend. You made that painfully clear."

The situation was slipping out of my control. "Ranbir, you have to hear this. You were right. You knew something was off, and I wouldn't listen. It's so much worse than you could have possibly known."

"Oh, that's great. Did you hear that everybody? I was right. How vindicating. What do I win?" he asked sarcastically. The shock of seeing me was wearing off and his anger was settling in.

He stormed off, and I followed closely behind as I was afraid to lose him. "Where are you going? Will you talk to me, please?" I begged.

"I'm going to give you some food, and then you're leaving," he said.

"Where the hell am I supposed to go?"

"Anywhere but here. You're not welcome."

"Ranbir, come on," I said as I dared to touch his upper arm. He pulled away from me angrily and folded some fruits and vegetables in heavy foliage as a sack. "We can work this out, right?"

"I told you if I ever saw you again, I'd kill you. Consider this mercy," he said as he stuffed the pack of food aggressively into my gut. "Leave."

"Where is this coming from? You're no saint either. You lied to me! You humiliated me!" I wanted to say more, but every word I spoke drove him further away.

"What about me?" Alexis asked as she tailed along with our drama. "Am I going to be like, safe here or what?"

"You're welcome here. I'll look after you, and everyone else will adapt. You'll see. We'll get you all patched up, and you'll be good as new in no time," Ranbir promised.

"Come on, *Triple Lex*. You're not going to trust a bunch of criminals, are you?" I asked, desperate not to be alone, which was a new sentiment for me. "One more adventure. Whatya say?"

"No thanks. I'll take my chances with the boys," she replied dismissively.

"Fine. That's fine. You stay. I don't need you anyway. I don't need any of you."

"Great. Go. Bye," Ranbir said coldly while refusing to look at me. He motioned for Alexis to follow him, and as they turned their backs on me, everyone else lost interest as well.

My survival instinct was screaming for humility, but I couldn't hear it over the sound of my deafening ego. I held my care package of food under my arm and stomped out of the village while the men returned to what they were doing. All I ever wanted was to be ignored like I didn't exist, and it was the worst feeling ever once I finally achieved my goal.

I walked north of the village, following the shoreline of the lake until nightfall. I made camp inside the tree line to seek reprieve from the cool open-air breeze and

I struggled to start a fire. I nearly froze as I slept covered in branches and leaves that offered little comfort.

I returned to walking the next morning, and sometime after midday, I reached the northernmost point of the lake. I had eaten half my food and decided to try my hand at gathering some fish. My skin was warmed from hours of sun exposure before I managed to get a grip on a blue double-tailed swimmer in the shallow end.

One fish was plenty for dinner, but I failed to build a fire for the second night in a row. By the time my stomach was growling, I was left with no choice but to dip into my dwindling food supply and construct what little shelter I could manage before the cold blew in.

If I couldn't learn to start a fire, I was either going to freeze or starve to death when the seasons inevitably changed for the worst. The next day, I took to scourging through the shrubbery for anything matching what Ranbir had packed for me, but the only thing I could find was nickel-sized blackberries. I plucked as many as I could carry and folded them into a large leaf for safekeeping. I invested the rest of the daylight into building up a stronger enclosure to sleep in.

I was warm. Too warm, and it wasn't because I was sunburnt. I woke in the middle of the night with a horrible fever and my stomach in painful knots. I crawled from my leafy enclosure across the forest floor, evacuating the poison berries through vomiting and diarrhea with no hope for comfort or sleep.

I was sick, exhausted, and completely useless on the fourth day. Without the energy to focus on a task, my mind wandered into the dark territories that I was intentionally avoiding. Blame, responsibility, and self-hatred took hold. I faced the fact that I was incapable of creating anything good. For all my training and studying, I couldn't do something as simple as building a proper shelter. It was as though my destructive nature forboded my hands from fostering or protecting life, my own included. Even fire, with all its capabilities for carnage, evaded me because I'd build it to aid sustenance.

The wild had defeated me. I was going to die there, and much sooner than I anticipated. My only chance for survival was if I humbled myself, owned up to the scope of the terrible things I'd done, and asked for forgiveness.

Ranbir's exile was my fault. Alexis' capture was my fault. Connect Earth, all the damage it did while in my control, and all the future damage under Penelope's control was my fault. Millions of people had died, including my own parents because of me. A peaceful alien race had been pushed towards extinction, and I was just as guilty as those who had delivered them death.

In the face of such things, it wasn't a matter of swallowing my pride. I came to the horrible realization that I didn't deserve to live. To ask for forgiveness from those I had wronged was another slight against them. The only thing I could offer the universe was a quiet act of contrition in suicide.

I wasn't going to lay around my pathetic encampment and wait for starvation to take me. There were cratered cities out there somewhere, and looking upon them seemed a fitting final punishment for myself. I set out into the forest and felt unworthy of the beauty I saw there. The plants and trees were alive in vibrant shades of yellow and orange, and they grew so high and thick that they became my sky. There were creatures chirping above, and I imagined their songs were warnings to the other wildlife of the evil that walked amongst them. If I were to die before reaching the outer edges of the forest, I imagined my decaying body would poison the soil and rot out every living thing from the ground up.

I survived the depressing three-day walk through the bush by drinking rainwater collected off leaves and gambling my health on berries and fruits I discovered. There was a clearing on the other side and the first sign of civilization in the form of a paved landing pad and an abandoned outpost station at the edge of the preserve. The land in the distance was flat, cleared of trees, and covered in fields that hung low and dying without their caretakers. If the Praxi once grew food there, a city center couldn't be too far off.

I set out across the fields in hopes that I'd live long enough to see the destruction I had caused. Once there, I'd lay my body amongst the wreckage as the final victim of my hubris. I'd speak my apology in death that my tongue would never utter in life.

By the first night of trudging through the fields, I realized the universe recognized my desire for penance and was going to take its pound of flesh from me. The sun beat down hard by day, and by night the insects traded their vegetarian diet for one of picking the meat from my bones.

I lost count of the days, the fruit I carried for the journey was long gone, and the only water I drank was when it fell from the sky into my open mouth. My skin was covered in sores from the bugs, boils from the sun, and scratches from the abrasive dead crops. I was malnourished, dehydrated, and would die long before I would find a Praxi cratered city to call my tombstone.

I trudged on even though my wounded toes had become infected and swollen. I was almost ready to surrender when a faint flicker of reflective sunlight in the distance promised hope. There were buildings in the clearing, and the will of human endurance to survive battled against my penitential suicide pact.

I pushed forward to the edge of the fields to find a Praxi factory farm I assumed was used to harvest the crops at one time. There were three square, metallic structures, and the sun was blinding as it reflected off the surfaces. The ground between the buildings was a pad of similar alloys with a crease down the middle as if it was meant to open to an underground enclosure.

I dared to fantasize that the buildings were filled with a mass of food and that the space beneath the surface was a habitable resource offering clean water and shelter from the elements. If I could gain access, I would have a place to hide, rehydrate, and heal. I could journey back to the village and guide them through the fields. The crops could be regrown, and this place could serve as a peace offering to a thriving community that might forgive me. Setting out through the forest was my version of a suicidal jump from the top of a skyscraper. A decision that couldn't be undone and would allow ample time during the fall to reflect on the reasons that made me leap towards death in the first place. I hadn't anticipated regretting my decision mid-fall as the ground raced towards me.

Each of the buildings had eight-foot-high panels with creases for doors and attached to the side was a touch screen which would almost certainly open them. There was no power, so I took to prying at the door, but I was far too weak to make it budge. I moved on to the second building to again find a door with no power and myself with no strength to open it. I walked around the perimeter, searching for any way in, and I felt myself start to panic.

I could barely stand. I hadn't had anything to eat or drink in days. My knees were weak, my body had evacuated every last drop of sweat, and my head fell faint. I was on the doorstep of the death my body had promised the universe, even though my human instinct to survive was fighting back. There was one last door to try, and I knew it was a tease. Discovering the chance for life and atonement was the final twist of karma's knife in my back.

I turned blame outward as I lumbered across the alloy pad between buildings. This wasn't my fault at all. The General's crisis of faith had killed millions. The extremism of militants wiped out the Praxi. Penelope's lust for power paved the twisted road that led us here. Both Ranbir and Alexis had made foolish choices, and the warnings I gave them removed my responsibility for their outcomes. I had been played, abused, and neglected. I would scream and curse them with rage if my dying breath could muster the volume.

I approached the final door, and I didn't need to check the controls for power. I knew it was inoperable like the others. I pried my fingers into the gap between the door segments in a pointless waste of the last ounce of my energy. I had been ready for death for years, and it was only on the precipice that I no longer desired it.

I slammed my fists against the electrical panel in anger and then turned them against the door. I pounded like a drowning swimmer trapped under a sheet of ice, each strike softening as life slipped away. I caught a glimpse of my reflection in the glimmering metal, and I took a final truthful look at myself. I pulled the filthy wig from my head, exposing the ripple of scarring I hid from the world and the patchy growth of my real hair beneath. My eyes were tired, my lips chapped, and every flaw was exposed with no foundation to cover them.

The random rapping of the balls of my fists turned into targeted blows with knuckle forward into the face I saw staring back at me. Each punch landed harder than the last as the blood sprayed from my knuckles onto the ugliness I was shown. I cocked back to shoulder length to deliver blow after blow into my reflection. "Ahhh! God damn me!" I screamed as I wailed away at the mirror that told no lies.

My knees buckled beneath me, I dropped to the ground, and my shoulder came to rest against the door. I smeared the blood from my broken knuckles over the surface to avoid spending my final seconds staring at myself. I hoped that over time, Ranbir and Alexis would venture out far enough to discover my body. That somehow looking upon my sad decay they'd know my final moments were spent in a desire for forgiveness. Ranbir would feel that I loved him in my own demented way. Alexis would understand that I admired her, and would know I had wrongly hated seeing the similarities between us.

My breathing became shallow, my heartbeat slowed, and my eyes fluttered before they closed for the last time. My spirit relinquished its grip on mortal life, and I slipped away.

Chapter 12

Everything is Nothing

Ranbir Chopra

L osing everything sounds like a horrifying prospect until it happens to you. As prisoners on Prius, we were more enlightened about the pursuit of happiness than anyone back home. We had no access to Connect Earth, Xbox, Starbucks, or J Crew. We didn't subscribe to a dozen streaming services or consume network programming. Our success wasn't measured by the size of our homes, boats, or televisions; and we didn't post pictures of our steak dinners or vacations to Prague to showcase our prosperity to others. Our hours were filled with simple survival rather than a corporate ladder climb to nowhere. We had nothing, and in that emptiness, we discovered that we had everything.

The only amenities I was truly missing were a soft bed, air conditioning, and women; and I could learn to live without two of the three. I thought about Emilia all the time, and it was difficult to maintain semi-irrational hate while experiencing the most bliss I'd felt since falling in love with her. Seeing Emilia show up in my village of all places should have been the best thing ever, but her presence brought all the anger back. I couldn't forgive Emilia's betrayal any more than I could expect her to change, and I didn't blame her for harboring her own animosity towards me.

I screwed up and would have gladly apologized for deceiving her, but I knew deep down she would never reciprocate without discovering a crippling amount of humility herself. When I sent her away, I presumed that isolation would either kill her or soften her will to the point where we might find reconciliation. There was a 25% chance Emilia would return, and in the meantime, I focused on ensuring that Alexis would be safe and wouldn't disrupt our utopia.

I didn't watch Emilia walk away because I didn't want her to look back and catch me pining after her. "Let's get you something else to wear," I suggested to Alexis. "I'm Chop by the way; in case you hadn't pieced the conspiracy together on your own."

"Yeah, I cracked that case," she replied while following me to our makeshift clothesline.

"Apologies for the lack of selection. I hope you're comfortable in orange," I said while she stripped out of her torn uniform. "All right then. Just getting right down to it, huh?" I said as I averted my gaze from her naked body.

"Everyone else is looking. You might as well too," she said flirtatiously before picking the smallest clean smock she could find and dressing herself quickly. "You sure this isn't going to be a toxic environment for me?"

"There's probably going to be drama at some point if you plan on letting your *business* hang out in the open."

"I can handle myself," she said confidently. "I'm used to having a hundred horny men make passes at me, though they're usually on the other end of a firewall."

"Well, there's no internet connection here. The most sexual excitement we've had is a bush that vaguely resembles a tight butt in bicycle shorts."

"Is that part of the tour?" she asked suggestively.

"Right. A tour. Let me give you the lay of the land. I work down there," I said pointing to the water line. "We limit ourselves to a hundred fish per day, and we clean them over here," I said leading her to the tables we'd constructed.

"They're beautiful and unique, but my god they stink!" she held her nose.

"Don't worry. You don't have to work with fish, but you will have to pick a job. There's the fisherman, cooks, lumberjacks, builders, farmers, and hunters, though that last group is struggling. There are these pig-warthog things in the forest, and we're trying to catch them rather than kill them. It's a process," I explained.

"How the hell did you guys build all of this?" she asked while inspecting our huts.

"Honestly, it's the *Lydia*. Things were getting dire around here before they started dropping us supplies. We write requests in the sand, and our angel from above drops it. Speaking of which, you look like you've seen some action. If you want to take some rest, I can bring the Doc in for you," I suggested while lifting the foliage curtain to my hut.

"Can I sleep in here?" she asked with her head poked inside to audit the tiny living space with two beds.

"You may if you'd like. We haven't built enough enclosures for everyone, so we're sharing space for the time being. You can like...sleep with me if you want. Or not. No pressure. You can sleep outside by one of the fires as well."

"I'll stick with you if that's all right," she replied.

"Of course. That's my bunk there if you want to make yourself comfortable, and I'll go find the Doc."

Our medical care wasn't top-of-the-line, but it was enough to get Alexis back on her feet. She looked a little rough her first week in camp, but as her bruises faded her beauty showed through. She turned heads everywhere she went, and her boyish playful attitude disarmed the men around her.

Alexis chose gardening as her profession, and she was often heard singing and laughing with her colleagues. Working the soil went from the least requested job to our most. Her presence inspired the village, and as our muse, she was as valuable as any care package the angel Lydia dropped from the heavens.

It didn't take Alexis long to realize the perks of Prius. There were no government coverups that required her attention. No lying politicians or deceitful media for her to battle. The social, financial, and political stresses of Earth didn't transfer to our supposed prison. We were discarded from a society that we wouldn't return to even if we had the option.

Everyone had their own reason to love our new life. For most of the men, it was as simple as no longer staring through bars and locked doors for twenty-three hours a day. If they had food in their bellies and a soft place to rest, their lives were improved exponentially over what they left behind. For Alexis, Prius was an escape from stress. Our carefree lifestyle unfurled the choking grip of panic's hands around her throat. For me, imprisonment was freedom from living a lie. I had spent so much time hiding behind a deceitful barrier that I had forgotten who I was, and I didn't need to pretend to be anyone's hero anymore.

The only time Alexis and I spent apart was when I had my feet in the water, and she had her hands in the soil. We ate our meals together, played games, and exchanged stories; with our only rule being no Emilia talk. I gave Alexis my bed, and I took to sleeping on the ground next to her every night. Our roommate eventually moved out into a hut of his own, and that left the two of us with private escalating sexual tension that had been growing from the moment she arrived and attached herself to my hip.

I counseled Alexis to exercise caution concerning romantic entanglements, but she wasn't interested in my advice. She had taken a liking to me for whatever reason and wasn't shy about expressing her intentions. Maybe it was the amount of time we were spending together or the fact that I was the former lover of her enemy. Or perhaps I smelled less like a dirty sock than the other suitors. Either way, she was making advances even though my core interest was to simply look out for her safety. I didn't do anything to lead her on, but she was undeterred nonetheless.

One night a few weeks after her arrival, I was sitting around the fire before retiring to our bungalow. I pulled back the curtain that served as our door and found that she had pushed our beds together. "Redecorating?" I asked as I stood in the doorway.

"Does that make you nervous?" she asked as she patted the leafy coverings next to her.

"Come on, Alexis. What are you doing?"

"Oh my God. Captain Chopra, hero of Earth. You *are* nervous" she quipped.

"I'm not the captain of anything, and I'm the hero of even less," I said as I dropped the drapery behind me.

"I'm going to be perfectly frank with you, Chop. Whether tonight or a year from now; we're gonna smash. You know it. I know it. Everybody out there knows it."

"We're going to *smash*?" I repeated back to her with a chuckle. "You are epically bad at this."

"Dating was never my strong suit. And besides, I may be one of only two women on the continent. I don't exactly have to check a lot of boxes to win this season of *The Bachelor: Prison Paradise*. Come sit," she invited.

Alexis was right. The two of us hooking up felt inevitable, even though I was enjoying our casually flirty platonic relationship. I sat next to her, and she placed a leg over mine immediately and cradled closer to me. Even though Alexis was a bumbling romantic, I couldn't deny that the slightest bit of human contact sent electricity up my spine.

"You know, we were supposed to have our first date sharing coffee and conspiracy theories, but you stood me up," she said playfully as her finger traced circles over my knee.

"Is that what this is? Our first date?" I asked, stalling the unavoidable.

"Good lord, I've never seen someone work so hard to *not* get laid. Are you going to touch me, or do I have to do all the driving?" she asked as she pulled her leg from mine, stood up, and nearly fell over as she climbed into my lap facing me. She pressed her lips against mine while her hand crept up the back of my neck and her fingernails clawed through my hair. This should have been a no-brainer, but something wasn't right. My hands remained at my side as the tiniest bits of flame between our lips failed to ignite into a roaring fire. My brain, heart, and cock were in a judicial conference once again, though this time it was my heart carrying overruling votes.

Alexis pulled back and held my chin in her hand to examine me. She tilted her head to the side and rolled her eyes. "You poor bastard," she stated bluntly.

"What?" I asked.

"You're still in love with her, aren't you?"

"Who?" I played dumb as I ignored my feelings that were ruining the moment.

"*What? Who? Bleh,*" she sportingly mimicked my voice. "*Who?* Beyonce," she mocked. "Who else? Emilia, you dope. You love her."

"I do not. She's so far in my past that I don't even remember her," I lied unconvincingly.

Alexis pushed herself up by my shoulders and sat on the grassy floor near my feet. "You're either a shit liar, or you're out of practice. I knew it too. You couldn't even look at her when you sent her away."

"I'm over her. I'm serious," I said more to convince myself than Alexis.

"Oh my god, look at you. If you had a notebook, you'd doodle hearts and her name all over it," she teased.

"Don't be ridiculous," I avoided eye contact.

"I bet you could make her a mix tape playlist right now, couldn't you?" she continued, clearly enjoying this more than I was. "She's an awful human being, but I don't know what she could have possibly done to make you so callous while you're still in love with her."

"You'd be surprised. She's worse than you think."

"I doubt it. No offense, but I'm pretty sure I witnessed her darkest moments. If our *first date* is going to be the variety where one party talks about their ex the whole time, then you better spill it. Give me the juicy details."

"She was playing me from the start," I sighed. "She used me, set me up, had me arrested, and got me deported."

"She ever stuff a gun in your face and pull the trigger?" Alexis asked.

"Might as well have. General Kelly could have had me killed, and that's hardly the worst of it."

"Well?" she said, raising her hands to encourage me to continue.

My lips tightened to avoid quivering and I rubbed my hands together anxiously. I swallowed hard to compose myself before speaking and cleared my throat. "She killed my dog," I said plainly to skirt the pain.

"Wait. What? Your dog?"

"Yeah," I replied fighting back tears.

"Amir? The cute, little, brown beagle with the button nose?"

I clenched my jaw and nodded my head a responsive yes.

"No she didn't. She's a bitch, not a monster," Alexis said which raised my eyebrows in doubt. "Okay, maybe she's slightly monstrous. She's one-quarter monster. Whatever. Where did you get this idea?"

"They were holding me for treason, and Penelope said Emilia had gone off the deep end. Penelope tried to stop her, but Emilia ran over Amir in the driveway to get back at me. She..."

"Penelope? The pixie cut British broad?"

"Yeah. She's Emilia's only friend."

"Dude, that is *not* her friend. Jesus, men, and your terrible communication skills. Penelope set this whole thing up. She played Emilia and she clearly played you too."

"How do you know? She had a picture of Amir's crumpled body."

"She faked that shit. I promise you, Amir is fine. The little sweetheart sat on my lap for a six-hour car ride the day before we were deported. I think Penelope is SIS. Former British intelligence and she is way off on her own. She popped Kelly and stole CE right out from under Emilia. She's running shit on Earth, and God knows what she's up to. She said this whole thing was Emilia's idea or fault or something."

I stood up and paced back and forth in our tiny compartment. My stomach went into knots and my mouth dried with the stale taste of defeat. "Shit. What have I done? I mumbled to myself before storming out. Alexis followed closely behind as I tip-toed through our sleeping village. I pulled a shirt off the clothes-line, tied it into a sack, and packed it full of enough food to sustain myself for a few days.

"Have you considered that even if she's alive, she might not want to be found?" Alexis counseled.

"She's too proud to die, and I'm going to bring her back. I never should have sent her away in the first place."

"Pretty heroic for a guy who claims he's no hero," she smirked while tying up a shirt of her own. "What? You think I'm going to sit around here while you go off on an adventure? Emilia tried to kill me. I want to see the look on her face when I show up to save her."

"That'll show her," I replied with a laugh.

We left immediately and began trekking north along the lake. Alexis carried a torch, I hauled the supplies, and we both shouted for Emilia every few minutes. It was optimistic to think she was within ten miles of our camp after she'd been gone for weeks, but she couldn't have wandered too far.

We kept an eye out for tracks, fruit peelings, and any remnants of fires in the hopes that we'd get some sign that we were on the right path. We walked until the morning sun was reflecting off the water before picking a spot in the brush to get some sleep.

We napped for a few hours, prepared a light breakfast, and continued marching north. As we walked, Alexis expanded her entertainment skill tree from singing to include movie reenactments. She performed *The Lord Of The Rings* for me, inflecting her own renditions of each character's voice. Her Gimli impersonation was particularly inspired, and she leaned into it harder when she realized she could summon a positive reaction from her audience.

The longer we walked, the more concerned I became about Emilia's safety. Every time I called out her name without hearing a response made it more likely that she was dead than alive. I hadn't even begun to process the terror I had unleashed on Prius and adding Emilia's name to that list was enough to ruin my utopian happiness.

The dusk sun was painting the landscape in burnt orange when we reached the northernmost point of the lake where we discovered a poorly constructed shelter. I tore through the leaves and branches, partially excited to find our first sign of Emilia, but also terrified to uncover her body.

"Emilia!" I yelled over and over, each time my volume pushed my voice to a further panicked scream.

"Why wouldn't she stay here?" Alexis asked. "There's fresh water, access to fish and fruit, and she was building a hut."

"What if something dragged her off? We don't know what else is out there."

"This is Emilia we're talking about. If anything tried to eat her, she'd probably condescend and curse until the creature slinked away in a mid-life crisis." Alexis continued to keep things light, but the grip of fear had clenched me.

"She wouldn't go into the forest, right? Maybe around to the other side of the lake? Em!" I shouted again.

"Let's stay here tonight, just in case she comes back. If she doesn't, we'll walk to the other side tomorrow and find her there, okay?" Alexis calmed me.

We camped in Emilia's sad abode, she didn't show up overnight, and we didn't find her on the east side of the lake either. There wasn't a footprint or extinguished firepit anywhere. She was gone, and I bore the responsibility for whatever had happened to her. We poked around deeper into the woods for two more days before we surrendered, though neither of us verbally admitted defeat as we walked south towards our home.

There were no more songs, film reenactments, or playful banter. Alexis was respectfully quiet even though she had no reason to mourn Emilia. I shouldn't have given in to grief, but I didn't dare entertain the idea of hope. To maintain optimism that Emilia would one day resurface would ruin every day that she failed to.

My heart broke for a second time, splintering into quarters instead of halves. I shared the blame for the first break with Emilia, but the further fragmentation was of my own making. My mind wandered in thoughts of self-flagellation as we approached our village, and I made plans to isolate myself from the others by moving my lodging onto the beach. I had no interest in human contract to raise my spirits, and I wouldn't sour the colony's joy with my sorrow.

"Ninety-eight million," I mumbled after hours of silence.

"Bottles of beer on the wall?" Alexis joked.

"Ninety-eight million lives. That's the estimated death toll from the attack on Earth. The media rounded up to one hundred million for optics, but it was ninety-eight. The attack lasted thirty-six hours."

"It was horrible, but I don't see your point. We can't do shit about it now."

"Do you know how many Grays lived here before I paid them a visit?"

"Chop. Don't do this to yourself," Alexis begged.

"Six billion? Twenty billion? I don't even know. I was too busy polishing my lie to ask," I lamented as I picked up a rock and skipped it across the surface of the water. "It only took us twenty-seven minutes to wipe them out, and I could have stopped it. Gio cried out for me with a pain so visceral that I nearly lost consciousness, and I was still undeterred. I didn't listen to him, and I wouldn't listen to Emilia."

Alexis had no response besides a poor attempt to skip a rock of her own. She raised a hand above her brow to shield her eyes from the midday sun as she focused on a glimmering light in the distance. "What the hell is that?" she asked.

I glossed over her attempts to change the subject. "Did you know Oppenheimer quoted Hindu scripture after creating the atomic bomb? *Now I am become Death, the destroyer of worlds.* The irony isn't lost on me."

"Seriously, Chop. Look," Alexis pressed.

I raised my low-hanging gaze to see sunlight reflecting off a metallic surface in the distance. There was something above the beach, and most of our neighbors were gathered to inspect it. I continued walking in that direction when Alexis grabbed my sleeve to stop me.

"That's a ship, and it ain't the *Lydia*." She pointed.

"So what?" I said with dejection as I attempted to slither out of her grasp.

"*So what*? Our track record with ominous spaceships isn't exactly inspiring," she warned.

"Honestly, I don't care anymore. If it's the WM, I hope they drop a bomb on us. If it's the Grays, I hope they take their revenge. God knows they've earned it," I said as I yanked my sleeve out of her hand and plodded ahead.

"Chop, let's think about this," she begged. "Chop!"

I came to Prius with an optimism that losing everything was a net gain, and that the unplugged paradise could erase the psychological turmoil of taking billions of lives. I didn't foresee billion plus one being the blow that would topple my fragile mental house of cards. It was better to join Gio and Emilia in death than carry the weight of their loss in life. If there was danger ahead, I welcomed it if it meant an end to my torture.

Chapter 13

Scars and Souvenirs

Emilia Vera

Were my eyes open? I was blinking but I couldn't see a thing. I laid prone, with my back and head propped up, and the surface beneath me was cool to the touch. There were fastens around my waist and forehead holding me in place. I ran my hands over my abs to discover that I was naked and coated in a warm slime. Was this purgatory? The waiting room to Hell?

"Hey. Hey! Where am I?" my question echoed into the darkness.

Moments later, a door cracked open with no sound, and firelight pierced through the darkness and softly lit the room. I was trapped in a small space, surrounded by tables covered in various tools and devices. "Who's there?" I asked as my eyes adjusted to the light.

My pupils focused to find a Gray standing on two legs and using its third to carry a lantern. "Oh shit," I gasped and squirmed against my restraints until I freed a single hand. It approached me with its legs bent at two joints, and as I balled a wounded fist to strike it, I felt my fingers uncurl and a calming rush of euphoria shot through my body.

"Don't be afraid, Emilia Lynn Vera of Earth. I mean you no harm," its words spoke into my mind. It wasn't so much that I was hearing verbal communication, but that I was sent a foreign message that my human brain translated into a language I could process. It was less of a voice to be heard than an emotional connection to be experienced.

"What is this? What's happening to me?"

"You were badly damaged by exposure, malnourishment, and abrasions. You're burned, and your hands are broken. I'm going to heal you." The words felt like spoon-fed chicken soup from a nurturing mother who would trade places with their sick child if it was possible.

"How about you turn on some lights? The darkness is unsettling."

"The gel regenerates better in the dark, and I'm afraid I couldn't bring you light even if I wanted to. Our power is limited and must be conserved."

'So, what, you're like a doctor?" I asked with total calm even though my situation was horrifying. "What do I call you?"

"I understand the science of many things, but I'm a botanist by trade. My name is Gio."

"Gio? Ranbir's Gio?!"

"I'm Ranbir's Gio," he repeated back as his mouth curled upwards in a physical representation of the childlike joy he emanated mentally.

"He's here! On Prius!"

"Yes, I know. I've felt him, but we're forbidden from communicating with the Earthlings."

"You're talking to me, aren't you?"

"I've made a bargain for your life, and the conditions require communication." Gio couldn't hide the negative connotations. His intents were pure, but those of his peers were not.

"We could go see him together. He thinks..." I trailed off as a rush of Gio's emotional pain swallowed me up before I could finish the sentence. A lump formed in my throat and my eyes welled up with tears. "He thinks he murdered you," I choked out.

"You're in great distress, Emilia Vera, and my emoting is not beneficial. You must rest," he said as he sorted through some items on the table. "I'm administering a sedative and will return to check on you in a few days."

I felt a small pinch in my hip as Gio poked me. "A few?" was all I could muster before I passed out.

I woke occasionally, still in the dark, literally and figuratively. I knew Gio had saved me and that I owed him my life, but I had a haunting feeling that the debt would be costly. I couldn't maintain consciousness long enough to piece things together or attempt to make an escape plan.

Once the drugs wore off, I felt my eyelids pulled back and opened to see Gio standing over me. The room was again illuminated with firelight, but I had been moved into an upright position and dressed in a black cloth robe. The slimy gel had been removed from my skin, and I was no longer experiencing the painful burns from the sun.

"You're on the mend, Emilia Vera," Gio's voice comforted in my mind.

"I feel great," I replied graciously as I ran my hands against each other to find them no longer broken and bloodied. I pulled the sleeves back to find my arms in their healthy unburnt state. "This is incredible," I said as I looked to my bare feet to find my toes wrapped and pain-free.

"Your body will do the rest," he encouraged.

I ran a hand over my forehead to find my wig missing, and I froze when my palm grazed over where the scarring should be on my skull. "What happened? What did you do?" I asked frantically as I felt my cheek to find it smooth and soft. "The scars! They're gone!" I exclaimed as my fingers retraced every centimeter where the hideous markings had once resided.

"I healed you," he said as though the outcome was intended.

"No. I don't know," I stammered as I continued rubbing the cells that had been reformed. "You shouldn't have done that," I charged as I felt strangely naked without the mask that had separated me from the world.

"It was not my intention to harm you." Gio's regret was so authentic and palpable that it improved my own confused attitude.

"Can I...can I see it?' I asked, certain that I'd look upon a gross discoloration that would make me more monstrous than I was before.

"Come," he beckoned me from my seat to stand in front of a metallic cabinet. He held the lantern near eye level, and I nervously peered into my reflection.

It was as though I had never been burned. There was no differentiating between the new skin and the old in color or texture. I saw in the mirrored metal the woman that I was supposed to have grown into. "I don't believe this," I said in awe.

"It's real," Gio comforted. "Your cells have healed, but I'm afraid hair won't grow through the repair," he said as he balanced on one foot and handed me my wig.

I fitted the hair over my head with a resolve to make my grotesque inner soul match my renewed outer beauty. I had been physically reborn, and the rest of the world would never recognize it unless I put in the work to fix the rest of me.

"Gio, I don't know what to say. How can I ever make it up to you?" I asked.

"Your joy is my joy," he expressed with a shared happiness. "However, now that you are on the mend, you do have a purpose to fulfill."

"Right. The catch. I'm not in any position to say no, am I?"

"There are questions that need answering for the survival of my people. We've gone underground, and we must escape Prius before we're found. My daughter awaits me on Vocury with the other newly manufactured, and I fear that if we don't leave soon, I may never meet her." There was no mistaking the distress in his emoting. Gio was in pain, and it was my duty to see it alleviated.

He led me out of the room, through a tunneled hallway lit only by his lantern, and into an open bay. The ceiling above was transparent and filled the workspace with natural sunlight pouring in. There were a dozen Grays laboring around a small circular craft with a flat-edged rim and a bubble in the center. Sparks hit the ground below as pieces were being fitted and welded into place which gave the air an industrial smokey smell.

"You guys are really back in the stone age here," I commented.

A Gray approached on all three legs, and I sensed the threat before it spoke. "Your judgments won't be tolerated, human. You killed our people, destroyed our triaxum reserves, and marooned us underground. You'd be lying dead on the surface if not for the compassion of our weaker links."

"Did you save me so you could lecture me, or are you going to state your request?" I asked defiantly.

"What are the military capabilities of the transports that bring your people here?" it asked.

"I have no idea. Why?"

"Are they armored? Are they equipped with weapons? How many soldiers on board, and how much triaxum are they carrying?" The questions were laced with so much malice that it poisoned my response.

"How the fuck should I know?"

"Lies won't avail you, human. Answer the questions before I lose my patience."

I looked at Gio, but I could no more feel his emotional support than hear his voice. He had nothing comforting to add other than his presence as a friend.

"There's two people on board, and to the best of my knowledge, the ships aren't made for battle. Are you planning to attack them?" my voice raised.

"You bring war here and dare to question our response? We should have let your species destroy itself before it polluted the rest of the galaxy. We won't be falling for your peaceful entrapments again."

I knew this was the wrong way to go about things, but I couldn't blame them. Their rage and distrust were more than warranted. I wanted to argue on behalf of humanity, but my culpability in the Gray's predicament was too overwhelming to hide.

"What did you do, Emilia?" Gio asked with sadness as he sensed my guilt.

My conscience was exposed, and even though they couldn't read my mind, I felt compelled to share the truth Penelope had jarred loose regardless. It might not set me free, but it could save someone else. "This is all my fault, and I didn't intend for any of it. I was just a student doing exercises," I explained.

"What exercises?" the leader asked.

"It was a college workshop. A think tank for solving our world's problems. I did so many of them that it was second nature. We were charged with sorting the puzzle of how to convince intelligent life to contact Earth." I looked away, especially from Gio, unable to make eye contact as I bared the secret guilt Penelope gave me as a parting gift. "I believed demilitarization would convince a peaceful alien race that we could change. My proposal was that it could take thousands of years to put wars behind us and that we'd kill ourselves with advancing weapons before we'd achieve world peace. The idea was to use a controlled nuclear incident to expedite the process. Small enough to not trigger global war, but big enough to effect change." I dared to look up and face their reactions, but a physical read couldn't compare to sharing their emotions.

"Get this vile creature out of my sight," the leader demanded.

"I didn't know! Hell, I didn't even remember for the longest time," I shouted as two Grays lifted me up under my armpits to drag me away. "Gio! You have to believe me. I can get you fuel without violence," I promised as payment for my wrongdoing. "Dammit, put me down!" I thrashed against their grip.

They tossed me back into my room and locked me away in darkness. It was a relief to have the truth out in the open, but it would have been wiser to tip-toe around that revelation. I counted myself as lucky to be imprisoned and not executed considering how I was the architect of their genocide.

My hands were healed, but they remained metaphorically dripping with blood. More would soon be spilled, and I had to do everything in my power to stop it. My plan was simple and stupid. Find something with a jagged edge, hold it to the throat of the next Gray to open the door, and force my hostage to fly me out of there. If refused, I was ready to take a Praxi crash course and pilot the ship myself. It was a plan so poorly concocted that Alexis would be proud.

I rooted around in the dark until I found a medical tool with a sharp edge and waited for hours for someone's neck to hold the weapon against. The more time that went by, the deeper my concern grew that I would be too late. The Praxi may have already shot Malik and Maya from the sky and left me to starve.

I was dozing off when I heard the locking mechanisms quietly release, and I sprang into action as candlelight entered the room. I grabbed the first rubbery leg that came through the door, and before I could issue my threats, I realized it was Gio.

"Gio? Why'd it have to be you?" I asked rhetorically as I dropped my weapon.

"Were you going to stab me?" he asked.

"I don't think so, but I'm not exactly sure what I'm doing at this point. I must get out here."

"Desperation breeds volatile action," he said as he took my hand.

"Wait a minute. You sneaky devil. Are you breaking me out?" I asked cheerfully.

"Can I trust you?" he asked point blank.

I bit my upper lip, considered an attempt at burying all emotion to construct a lie that would get by him, but decided to stick with the truth. "No," I answered earnestly. "In fact, those who know me best would strongly advise against it. I haven't earned trust. I want to get back to Earth above all else for my own selfish reasons. But if you can truly feel me, you'll know that I don't want to see anyone else get hurt because of my actions. You can trust that," I petitioned.

"If I free you, can you acquire triaxum from your people without violence?"

"Alone? No. They want nothing to do with me. I need your help, Gio. Is that ship in the bay ready to fly?"

"The others will not be pleased," he warned.

"Yeah well, I've got something of a history of pissing people off. Whatya say? Want to take me for a ride?"

"You humans are so mischievous," he grinned as his hand gripped tighter around mine.

"You have no idea. Come on. Lead the way." I encouraged.

There was no light in the hallway besides the candle that Gio carried. The others rested while we crept quietly into the bay which was only visible by the faint light of stars above. Gio opened a hatch on the lower bowl of the craft, helped me inside, and then crawled in behind me. The space was small and there was only a single seat for the pilot which was surrounded by controls. He powered up the gravity core and punched in commands to open the ceiling doors above as I sat on the floor next to him.

The noise of the massive door panels opening brought the underground station to attention. I got on my haunches to look through the transparent viewing slot and flipped the bird to the Gray leader as he ran into the bay.

Gio carefully navigated us out of the underground encampment and shot us off into the night sky. I looked back to see the three metallic buildings below where I had been waiting for the worms days earlier and was overcome with gratitude that I had no proper experience in expressing.

"Why did you save me?" I asked.

"Would you like me to return you?" he joked.

"That's not what I mean, smart ass. When I was starving outside your compound. Why did you help me?"

"Because I hadn't felt so much confusion, pain, guilt, and self-hate since the day my people were wiped out. Humans, for all your faults, have a deeper connection to your emotions than even us Praxi. I couldn't let you end in that darkness, void of the one thing that binds us together."

"You're about to say something really cheesy, aren't you?" I interrupted.

He smiled and put his hand on my head. "Love, Emilia Vera. If you want to save your world, make it smaller and fill it with love," he explained. It was so simple. The answer to everything was the antithesis of my life's greatest accomplishments. Go figure.

"Ranbir is close," Gio said with a smile.

"Don't let him feel you," I instructed. "They're not going to be happy to see me, and I don't want to spoil the surprise. He's going to shit kittens when you show up," I laughed.

Fill the world with love. Easier said than done, considering the mess I'd made. Gio could enlist Ranbir's assistance easily enough, but I wasn't expecting many allies in my pursuit of extinguishing the fire I started on Earth.

"It's right up there," I pointed as we approached the village marked by dim firelight.

Gio flew in a low circle over the encampment before hovering in place over the beach. "He's not here, but he's close," Gio informed.

"It's fine. The men will be waking soon, and we can get started if you can control them. We'll deal with Ranbir whenever he returns."

"I can navigate the humans and implore their help, but I'd rather make a big entrance when my friend is here," Gio said.

"You little drama queen," I smirked. "You're more theatrical than I would have guessed, but I suppose it makes sense for a being who feeds on emotions."

The prisoners noticed us immediately as the sun rose. They gathered beneath the ship for hours, occasionally throwing rocks that bounced off the gravity field. I paid them no attention, instead choosing to capitalize on my time with Gio. He educated me on Praxi history, culture, and their outer colonies. When Gio wasn't answering my rapid-fire questions, he was rightfully verbose concerning their breeding practices and his deep emotional connection to the daughter he hadn't met. His love was tangible and intensely moving. There was a little girl out there somewhere who needed her father and uniting them would be a greater achievement than saving Earth.

"He's coming!" Gio announced after hours of conversation. He sat up from his pilot's chair and took position over the lower hatch.

I peered over the transparent edge to see Ranbir pushing through the crowd and Alexis remaining cautiously distant. I nervously rubbed my palms together before grazing a hand over my chin and cheek, surprised that my inner rot hadn't re-manifested my scars.

Gio opened the hatch, held the ledge with one hand, and dropped to the sand below onto two legs. The crowd gasped, and all but Ranbir took multiple steps back. I moved to sit over the hatch to get a closer look and eavesdrop without revealing myself.

"Gio?" Ranbir asked. "You're alive! It's really you!"

Gio extended a hand to Ranbir as the customary human greeting, but Ranbir pulled him close and hugged him. I wasn't privy to whatever Gio was saying, but the tears in Ranbir's eyes filled the conversational gaps. They broke their embrace, lightly pressed their foreheads together, and Ranbir laughed out the most joyous sound I'd ever heard.

"How is this possible? Where did you come from? Alexis! It's Gio!" he announced as Alexis charged through the crowd.

"Ho-ly shit." Alexis hung on the syllables longer than usual. "You're real. A real live alien," she said with amazement as she ran her hand over one of his appendices. "It's okay if I touch you? I just...you have no idea how long," she stammered. Her hands covered her mouth as she laughed in place of finding the appropriate words. "You're real!" she exclaimed again. "I tried telling everyone for years."

"I wouldn't be here if it wasn't for my new friend," Gio projected to everyone. He took a few steps back and looked up as if he was queuing me dramatically into the scene. I dangled my feet through the hole and dropped into Gio's grasp who softly lowered me to the ground.

"Hey, gang," I said nervously.

Ranbir sharpened his stare as if he was trying to make sense of a mirage. "Emilia?" he questioned while slowly approaching me.

I raised a hand to temper any aggression. "Ranbir, I can explain. We..." I said before he interrupted me in a tight embrace. I released a pressured sigh and closed my eyes to meditate in search of an emotional experience like communicating with Gio.

"You're alive! And your face! My god, your scars! What happened?" he asked jubilantly. "I looked everywhere for you."

"I died," I said plainly, "and Gio brought me back."

"Alexis, she's alive!"

"Hooray," Alexis said sarcastically. "And look at that. She had a makeover. Karma in action."

"Gio needs fuel." I glossed over Alexis' contempt.

"I know. He told me. I presume you've got a plan," Ranbir said while continuing to examine my reformed cells.

"I think so, but that's not all. I'm going back to Earth," I announced.

"Oh no. Nuh-uh. You are not going back there. I won't let you," Alexis barked.

"Why? Why go back?" Ranbir asked with confusion. "This place is incredible. We can start over here, Emilia. I'm serious. We'll work through our shit and make the best of Prius, I promise."

"I'm asking for help, not permission. Gio gets his fuel and I hitch a ride home. You can stay here if you'd like," I paused to swallow my pride, "but I could really use a hand."

"Chop, don't," Alexis warned. "You should know better by now. What about you, Gio? You trust her?"

"Emilia is my friend," Gio replied with a childlike smile.

"Oh, Christ. Even the alien is on her side. You know what? Whatever. I haven't had a panic attack since I got here, and I'm not starting now."

"Hey, Alexis," I said before she could storm off. "You might have given up, but I haven't." I reached inside my cloak and fished the memory card out of my bra that I had been carrying for weeks. "This belongs to you." I flicked the device to her.

The memory card slipped through Alexis' fingers, and she picked it up like a diamond out of the sand. "Bullshit," she murmured to herself.

"Look familiar?" I asked.

"Did you? Oh my God, Emilia. Gross," she replied.

"Yes. Yes, I did. I sifted through a bucket of shit to find the hope you flushed away."

"What's that?" Ranbir asked.

"A souvenir from Area 51. That's a second chance for all of us." I paused to step closer to Ranbir and injected whispery temptation into my tone. "If you want me, you're going to have to chase me across the galaxy and save our planet. Some *real* hero shit," I teased as I ran the back of my palm against his face.

"That's not actually going to work, right?" Alexis asked frustratingly.

"Eh. It's kind of working." Ranbir shrugged his shoulders to excuse his male weakness.

"Ugh," Alexis sighed. "Oh God. We're all gonna die because you got a hard-on."

"What about the rest of you boys?" I shouted to the crowd who was still lingering about. "Who wants to take a ride and get into a fight?" No one spoke up, and most of them lost interest once pressed with the decision of abandoning peaceful paradise for war.

"Nobody?" Ranbir questioned the men as they turned their backs on us.

"We don't need them," I reassured.

Ranbir, Alexis, Gio, and I spent the rest of the daylight preparing to lure the *Lydia* to the surface. Once everything was in place, we built a private fire for the four of us, and Ranbir cooked a fish for dinner. We had eaten, Ranbir sat on a log, and I rested huddled on the grass between his legs.

We sat around the fire under the stars and Alexis spent the better part of two hours asking Gio pointed questions about the galaxy and the other civilizations that existed. He explained how many jump points were out there and the other worlds within our reach if we could tame humanity.

"I don't think we're meant to," Ranbir interrupted.

"Of course we are," Alexis said greedily. "There's so much out there to explore. I want to see it all."

"Sure. I get that, and it would be fine if you traversed the galaxy alone," Ranbir explained. "All of mankind though? We can't. Let's face it, we're poison. We're not ready."

The three of us looked to Gio to refute Ranbir's dark perspective of humanity, but he couldn't lie to us. "I'm sorry. It's not an inditement of any of you as individuals, but Chop is right. Humanity in its current state will bring war to every peaceful creature in the galaxy. My people will never be safe, and we'll be forced to arm ourselves for the battles your people will bring us."

"We can change, right?" Alexis asked. "We could bring a lot of good to the world with a partnership. Look at Emilia for example. One of the million ways we could heal our people."

"It's skin deep," I said coldly. "Real change comes from the inside and it could take our species thousands of years."

"Oh, come on," Alexis pressed. "You can't tell me that you don't feel better without those scars. I'm not saying I trust you by any means, but you're paying it forward with Gio, aren't you?"

"He deserves it. I didn't, much like the rest of mankind."

"Don't say that," Ranbir comforted. "No matter what you've done, there was no justice in your disfigurement."

I sat quietly, tempted to open myself, yet uncomfortable lowering the draw bridge to my castle of self-hate. I took a deep breath and exhaled slowly with my eyes closed. I turned my head back to look up at Ranbir and rubbed my hand against his knee. "You never asked me. Not once. That's when I knew you were special."

"Will you share your story with us?" Gio asked. "I would like to know."

"Same," Alexis chimed in.

"You don't have to," Ranbir said. "I never asked because it's not important."

"You're sweet, but it's okay," I said as I composed myself. "I've never," I paused to take another deep breath. "I've been asked a hundred times about the scars, but I've never told anyone. I've thought of a dozen juicy lies that would be useful as emotional manipulation. Stories about how I was burned doing something brave that would make people think highly of me. Tales of someone torching me horrifically that would evoke pity. It was the only lie I couldn't bring myself to speak convincingly."

Ranbir massaged my shoulders and kissed the top of my head for support. I leaned back further into his embrace to find the strength to continue. "I was ten years old, living in a shitty shanty in an even shittier neighborhood. My family didn't have any money, and I was awkward, you know? Just a geeky kid with no friends who only wanted to fit in."

"There was a group of older kids, and they'd play soccer in the alley near my home. I'd walk by them after school, and they'd say the most terrible things to me. It was a cruelty contest for who could hurl the most hurtful insult. I don't know if they meant it or if they each participated because they didn't want the bullying turned in their direction. Either way, it was traumatizing as a lonely child."

No one interrupted me, but the hair on my arms stood on end as Gio empathized with me. "I started taking the long way round to avoid them. It was an extra five-minute walk through a rough neighborhood, but it was better than trying to pass by those kids without breaking down into tears every day. This went on for a couple of months, and I started adding up all the extra time I was cost by not facing my fear."

"One day, I summoned the courage to walk down that alley again. There were a dozen kids kicking the ball around, and they were using whatever random trash and items they could find to mark their goal lines. I marched right into their field of play and demanded a place on one of the teams. I thought if I showed some confidence I could get in on the game, you know? Better to show that I could handle myself as part of the crew than hang my head and absorb the abuse. They told me to get lost and flung many of the same tired insults."

"I was unmoved and determined. That was my moment, and I was going to seize it. I chased down the boy with the ball and kicked it ahead to myself towards the goalie. On one side of him was a stack of pallets, and on the other was a rusted steel barrel filled with burning trash and a tire that the homeless were using to keep warm. I wound back and kicked that ball with every ounce of power I could muster, but it wasn't enough to roll by the goalie. He picked up the ball, booted it to the other end of the alley, and then threw me to the concrete. 'Too weak, loser,' he laughed as I nursed my bleeding elbow."

"I took my shot, literally and figuratively, and they rejected me. I wanted to hurt them the way they hurt me. Not one of them stood up for me, and I wanted to punish them for their cruelty," I said as I wiped a tear from my eye. "I picked myself up, stepped off into the boundaries, and waited for that asshole goalie to turn his attention back to the game. Once he forgot I was there, I charged that burning barrel with the seething rage of rejection and spilled the fire in his direction. I wanted to light him up and I didn't care if it killed him. In my mind, he deserved to die, and his friends deserved the trauma of watching him burn. Unfortunately for me, I hit the barrel so hard that I toppled over it," I said as I slowly pulled my wig down my forehead. "A piece of burning rubber seared to my head," I said while running a hand over my hairless scalp, "and another stuck to my cheek."

"One night in the hospital was all my family could afford, and major surgery was out of the question. By the time I was older and had enough money for reconstruction, I no longer wanted it. I grew fond of my scars. They were a convenient excuse to shut myself off from the world."

We sat quietly as the others processed my story. I watched Alexis casually try to wipe her eyes without me noticing, and I turned away as soon as she looked in my direction. "Phew," I exhaled loudly to break the silence. "Feels good to have it out there. Anybody else have a dark childhood secret they'd like to share?" I asked in jest.

"You're going to be all right, Emilia Vera of Earth," Gio consoled. "You're not alone anymore. Heal your world with that energy, remember?"

"Make it smaller and fill it with love," I recited Gio's wisdom. Maybe I wasn't the worst woman for the job after all. My attempts to hurt others had always boomeranged around to hit me. Perhaps if I started exerting positive energy for once, it would circle back to me as well.

Chapter 14

Last Call for Earth

Malik Emmanuel

"One last drink for one last drop?" I suggested by dangling a scotch glass in front of Maya before plopping into my pilot's chair.

"I doubt whoever they replace you with will support my habits, so I better take advantage while I still can."

"It's not too late to come with me."

"Three months is too long to be away from home, but you better look me up every time you're back," Maya warned.

It killed me to lie to her, but Maya didn't understand my position. If she knew I had no intention of ever returning to Earth she would have tried to stop me, and I didn't want to spoil the mood of our final days together. In a week's time, I would board a military cruiser, set out for Triax II, and dedicate the rest of my life to hunting down the Grays. The noxious environment of my former home would be firmly in my past and I would take a final revenge on those who ruined my life.

We exited the Jump Point, found a vibrant piece of Prius, and dropped our passengers like we had twenty times before. I pulled the *Lydia* back to low orbit and navigated around to the sunny side of the planet to take a concluding look at my favorite colony before closing that chapter of my life.

"I'm taking a nap," Maya announced after downing her drink. "Wake me when you're ready to finish that game."

"Baltic and Mediterranean Ave aren't going to save you," I shouted playfully toward her quarters.

I lowered the ship into the atmosphere and descended through the clouds so I could admire the beauty below. As I cruised over the Prius splendor, I noticed an anomaly shining in the distance from the colony ahead. I increased speed to discover a small circular silver craft parked in the sand. Written next to it was text outlined in branches and rocks. "SOS Gray Prisoner-Chop."

"Maya! Look at this!" I shouted.

"Did number five finish that irrigation system?"

"No. There's a ship and a message!"

Maya returned to the bridge and examined the curious scene through the viewer. "What the hell?"

"Could Chop be down there?" I asked.

"No way. It's a trick. Look." Maya pointed to the screen. "That's Egg Shells right there. She's probably trying to lure us to the surface so they can hijack us."

"That ship isn't WM. They must have captured it," I reasoned. "If they have a ship, they don't need ours." I bolted into Maya's quarters, armed myself with her sidearm, and raced into the cargo hold.

"Let the WM deal with them," Maya ordered while hustling behind me.

"We've got to check this out. If they have a prisoner, it could lead us to other Grays. Go back to the bridge, and take off if anything funky happens," I instructed as I lowered the rear ramp.

"God dammit," Maya grumbled as she sprinted to the controls.

I pushed my back against the interior wall and observed the crowd of vagrants who were waiting for action. "Don't try it!" I shouted and fired a single round into the air.

"Malik?" a familiar voice questioned.

"Chop? Is that really you?" I asked with my eyes sharpening on the bearded man who resembled my friend.

"It's really me, buddy. Been here all along. You can relax. Come on out. I've got to show you something."

I kept my firearm pointed towards the crowd while checking my corners coming down the ramp. "Everybody, back up, please. Close the ramp, Maya!"

I took a few steps closer, and it became evident that the familiar voice did indeed belong to my former captain. "It's really you! What the heck are you doing here?"

"Surviving, thanks to you. I should have known it was you up there all along. I don't think we would have made it if not for your supply drops."

"Looks like I should have added some razors and shaving cream to the packs," I cautiously lowered my gun and maintained distance between myself and the colonists. "You got my attention. What's the story?"

"It's better if you hear it from the source. Follow me. He's up here," Chop said before leading me through the village and into the tree line. "We caught one, and he claims that there's thousands more on the planet. Right here," he said while pulling back the coverings to a tent. I ducked my head underneath, and there sat a Gray with Alexis.

"Why isn't it restrained?" I nervously tapped my finger on the trigger. "You. Move," I directed to Alexis who had placed herself as a barrier between us. "Move!" I repeated as I pointed my gun in her face.

"Okay, okay, okay," she said as she slid to the side with her hands up. "Be cool. Everybody, be cool."

"I am not your enemy," the treacherous creature spoke directly into my mind. "Shut up. Shut up. Shut up!" I said as I took another step forward with each word until I had the barrel pressed firmly against its forehead. "Get out of my head. You're a liar! You lied to us," I seethed as I tried to ignore sharing in its harmless emotions.

"Malik. This is Gio. He's my friend," Chop said as he calmly put his hand on my shoulder from behind. "Come on, man. Put the gun down and hear him out. He just wants to get to his daughter."

"His daughter?" I asked as I pressed the barrel forward hard enough to budge the creature's head backwards. "I'll never get to see my little girl again. Why should you?"

"Please. I'm devastated by your loss. I'm sorry, but I'm not responsible, nor is my kind. Your people have deceived you. My family is out there somewhere, and you alone have the power to unite us." My finger twitched over the trigger and my hand began to shake. My angry instincts clashed against the shared painful bond of hearing Gio's voice.

"No. No. You killed them," I stated as a fact I was coming to know as a lie.

"Easy buddy. Easy," Chop comforted as he placed his hand over mine and slowly tried to take control of the gun. I softened my grip, dropped it to the floor, and Emilia quickly picked it up.

My anger was ricocheting inside of me, and rather than place it on those responsible, it remained bouncing inward. I sobbed and dropped to my knees as my sorrow came rushing back. I wanted to confess how my selfish desire to get to space put my family in harm's way, but it didn't need to be spoken. Gio could feel it, and the experience of him sharing in my pain washed the bloody guilt from my hands. I covered my eyes in shame as I wept for my loss. I was isolated in darkness for months, and it was only my supposed enemy who could bring me back to the light.

I felt a hand on my shoulder, then another on my head. Two more hands gripped my own, held on tight, and uncovered my face. I opened my eyes to see Emilia and had to blink the tears away to make sense of her face being healed. "He helped me too," she comforted. "We're going to make this right."

"I need a minute alone."

"Of course," Alexis chimed in as she ushered everyone out of the tent.

"I'd like to stay with you, if that's all right?" Gio asked. I nodded my head yes, and he sat across from me. "You don't have to hurt alone," he consoled.

"I'm sorry. I'm so, so sorry. I didn't know."

"I will share this burden with you. Be free of this pain."

Communicating with Gio was pure understanding. His words weren't really words at all. They were truth, dripping with raw emotion. There was no manipulation, passive aggressiveness, or hidden agenda. Of all the things the Praxi could teach us, connecting in that manner was the most valuable. I craved to apply his soul centering wisdom to every psychological issue plaguing me. "And what of my faith? Can you feel that loss as well?" I asked, hungry for relief.

"My people turned from deity-based faith tens of thousands of years ago. We set aside our idols in favor of worshiping science. We create future generations in a lab, and we think this makes us gods. For all our advancements, we're no closer to answering the biggest questions of the universe."

"It's oddly comforting knowing that you're just as lost as we are," I replied with a sad laugh.

"If you're seeking the answers of faith, do not ask anyone else the question. Ask yourself," he said wisely. "Do *you* believe in God? Whether or not anyone else does is irrelevant. If you should rediscover your faith, never let anyone take it from you. Live it unshakably."

I took a deep breath and wiped my eyes for a final time. "You're really good at this, you know that?" His only response was a goofy smile and an extension of joy. "What can I do to help you?" I asked as I stood and offered Gio my hand.

We walked back towards the beach, and he shared his plans to take two of our triaxum cartridges back to his people, get safely off world, send for help, and meet his daughter. The five of us approached the *Lydia*, and I banged on the rear ramp to signal for Maya to let us in.

The rear entrance was lowered to expose Maya standing guard in the cargo hold. "What the shit is this? What's with the tripod?"

"It's okay, Maya. He's a friend. I was wrong about everything. The Grays never hit us. It was the WM," I confessed.

"I fucking knew it," she said as she marched down the ramp. Gio and I walked by her, but she stopped Ranbir before he could step on board. "Where the hell do you think you're going?"

"It's good to see you too, Maya," Chop replied.

She grabbed the collar of Chop's shirt, slid one leg behind his, and slammed him to the ramp. "Did you know?" she mounted and aggressively questioned him.

"Whoa, whoa, whoa," Alexis panicked.

'It's okay, Gio. Go get your fuel," I said as I hustled back towards the rear. "Easy Maya. Easy."

"Fuck that. Answers or teeth. I'm taking one of them!"

"I didn't know," Chop said quickly with his hands held up to de-escalate. "They planned the whole thing and used us like props."

"What were you doing on that mission, Chop? You were either in on it, or you deliberately put all our lives at risk. Which one?" she asked, and when Chop didn't immediately answer, she punched him in the mouth. "Which one?!"

Emilia calmly walked up the ramp behind Maya and put my gun to the back of her head. "Maya?" she said to get her attention, "I like you. You've got spirit, but so help me God, if you don't get off him, I'm going to relieve you of that admirable vigor."

"Don't, Em," Chop pleaded. He turned his head to the side, spit blood, and looked back to Maya. "You were right about me. I didn't know what I was doing, and I put your lives at risk. It should have been you in command."

"He didn't know," Alexis added with open palms shaking with hysteria and rapid breathing.

"Everybody, just cool out," I said smoothly with a hand on Emilia's shoulder. "We can figure this out."

Maya spun herself off Chop and stood to face Emilia who refused to lower her gun. "You gonna shoot me, Egg Shells?" Maya taunted.

"Stop it! All of you!" Gio's voice commanded with a gut punching rage that sucked the air out of us. "How can you expect to heal your world if you can't heal yourselves? I've put the lives of my people in your hands, and we're depending on you. Make peace, or we're doomed."

Emilia lowered the gun and turned the handle to Maya. "Ranbir's not your enemy. You know that, right?" she asked before relinquishing her grip.

"Mhmm," was all Maya could muster as a response with Gio's emotional resonance restricting her access to anger.

"We need a ride back to Earth, and if you have any interest in knocking the teeth out of the people who deserve it, you're welcome to join in. We've got the proof to expose the truth, and all we need is a plan, and some muscle if you can spare it," Emilia said.

"Oohrah," Maya replied, and Emilia slapped her hands on Maya's shoulders encouragingly.

"This is where I leave you, my friends," Gio said with sadness. "If you are successful, I'm afraid we won't be meeting again."

I shook Gio's hand and forced eye contact like I was searching for one final moment of inspiration for my floundering faith. "Find your little girl, and don't ever let her go," I said.

"Remember to ask yourself and not others, Malik Emmanuel. Your faith will honor your family."

Alexis approached him, and before she could ask for a hug, Gio balanced on one leg and held her close with his others. "I can't fight a war. I can barely get through a day without crippling anxiety. Take me with you," she begged.

"I cannot," Gio lamented. "You have a part to play, and your friends will need you before the end. Find your strength in the face of adversity, Alexis X."

"Safe travels, Tripod," Maya said, trying to cover up the way her brief exchange with Gio touched her. "For those of you interested, this is the last call for Earth," she announced before walking away.

"I'd ask you to come with us if I wasn't afraid you might say yes," Chop said as he stepped up and pressed his forehead to Gio's. "Save your people, and we'll do everything in our power to make sure you live in peace."

I couldn't hear how Gio responded to Ranbir. Whatever he had to say was private between the two of them. Their bond was intensely personal and signaled the type of connection the rest of us would have to forge if we were going to survive.

"And what of you, Emilia Vera of Earth? What final farewell would you offer a friend?" Gio asked.

"I don't know. I've never had a friend," Emilia replied, which caused my heart to ache with familiar pain.

'Well, you do now. Five to be exact. Show them love, Emilia, and they will love you back."

"Tell the others," Emilia paused to swallow hard. "Tell them that even the worst of mankind could change. Don't give up on us," she said as she hugged him.

"Never," Gio promised before walking down the ramp with the hum of the gravity drive serving as his farewell hymn. I engaged the controls to seal the hull, and as Gio disappeared, I felt a hollowed emptiness in the space he vacated. The others must have felt it as well, and I tasked myself with filling the role of empathetic caregiver for my damaged crew.

"Come on. Let's get the three of you squared away." I led them through the cargo hold to the ship's main quarters. "We have two showers and plenty of hot water. You can help yourselves to any clothes that will fit."

"We could, uh, double up," Chop suggested to Emilia.

"I can't remember my last hot shower. If you think I'm sharing the next one, you're sadly mistaken. You go ahead. I'll shower after Alexis on the lady's side."

"Aw, you're sweet. We're like, totally even now," Alexis added sarcastically.

I outfitted them with towels and sent Chop and Alexis to the showers. "You hungry?" I asked Emilia. "I could reheat some leftover wings if you're interested," I offered.

"Microwaved wings sound incredible."

Emilia followed me to the mess hall, and I slid the Monopoly board to the edge of the table to clear some space before going to work on preparing a hot plate.

"Ranbir spoke very highly of you. I wasn't expecting all this though," she said.

"It's just wings," I smirked over my shoulder.

"That's not what I mean. You don't have to put yourself in harm's way. I'll understand if you don't get involved when we get home. I can make my own way to CE from Edwards."

I placed the plate of wings in front of her and snatched one for myself. "You don't know how to deal with having friends, do you?" I asked with my mouth full.

"My judgment in that department leaves something to be desired. I've only ever had one, and she turned out to be a British spy who was working me as an asset," she said between bites and smearing sauce on her cheeks. "I don't really like people. Never have," she confessed quietly.

"Then what are you doing this for? Why risk everything going back to Earth?"

"I don't know," she lied unconvincingly. "Why are you getting involved?"

"Can you handle the truth?" I asked rhetorically. "This might sting, but I'd rather die trying to change the world you created than live another day in it."

"Maybe that's my reason too," she said while picking every morsel of meat from a bone.

"It's going to take all five of us to make that a reality," I attempted to channel my inner Gio. "There's tension amongst us, and I need your help holding this crew together."

"Managing complex human emotions isn't my game. Ranbir is a better choice. Or Alexis. Hell, even Maya."

"That's why it needs to be you. If the others see you making an effort, they'll follow suit."

"Any suggestions on how I do that?" Emilia asked earnestly.

"An apology or two seems a good place to start."

"Any *other* suggestions?"

"Humility. Kindness. Selflessness. Or maybe start with the easy stuff. Don't point a gun at anyone. And definitely don't look at anyone like you're staring at me now," I suggested with a nervous smile. "Just some food for thought," I said with two taps on the table. I reached the limit on how far I could push Emilia. Rather than press her further, I left her in solitude to sort out what it means to support her friends.

Maya was the next stop on my tour of unity. I walked by the ship's quarters where the showers were running, and Alexis was singing off key. On the bridge, Maya was tilted back in the pilot's chair with her feet up on the control panel, and a black Demo Dawgs ball cap pulled down over her eyes.

"You brainstorming or sleeping?" I asked while tilting her hat up. Her eyes were closed, but she cocked one open and pulled the bill back into place.

"I've got some ideas. I'll pitch them to our guests, but I'm thinking it might be better if I go off on my own for this one," she replied.

"They need you, Maya," I pleaded with hope that she wouldn't fall into old, isolated habits.

"That's the problem. They need me more than I need them. What skills do any of them bring to the table?" she asked while holding her prone leisure position.

"Alexis can..."

"Basket case. She'll shrink and panic at the first sign of violence."

"Chop has..."

"No experience. He's a fraud. Liability in combat. He'll let you down. You'll see."

"Yeah, but Emilia..."

"You think you can trust her? I don't."

"What about me, Maya? I need you too. What's my deficiency?"

She paused to choose her words carefully, but still refused to lift the bill of her cap. "I love you like a brother, but you're not cut out for this. Things are going to get loud and messy, and I can do it better quiet and clean."

"So, what, you're going to take on the entire World Military by yourself? You think the others are going to sit on the sidelines?"

"I won't stand in their way if they want to get themselves killed. Hell, maybe they'll get lucky and scratch a few names off my list in the process."

An act of God might've been required to bring Maya on board, but before hypocritically turning to the big guy, I figured I'd give honesty a try. "There's something I haven't told you," I prompted. "The WM mission I joined was deep space. They're setting up a colony with direct access to triaxum to cut out the trips back and forth to Earth. I was never coming back."

Maya raised her seat and yanked her cap upward. "You lied to me?"

"I did, and I'm sorry. I was running away and thought you wouldn't understand. You understand perfectly though, don't you?"

"At least I didn't lie."

"I know, and I regret it. You're the only family I've got, and I need you with me."

Maya tilted her seat back and returned her hat to an eye obstructing position. "We'll see. If Chop tries to take command; I'm out."

I closed my eyes to squeeze in a nap before our passengers finished cleaning themselves up. The only sound in the cockpit came from Maya snoring and the echoes of Alexis singing. I tried to match Maya's level of comfortability flying into a warzone, but I had too many mental threads to pull on. In the past I had found peace in prayer, but the thought of trying to talk to God was hypocritical. I had faced down the question of God's existence, and the answer I found in my darkest moments was not an easy one to come back from.

I wanted to believe that I evolved from a single celled organism. That life on Earth was the product of a hospitable environment, that we weren't special, and there was no plan. I knew in my soul that wasn't the truth though. My faith was never gone, I had merely allowed the horrors of war to mangle it. God was an absolute truth in my life, and I had emphatically proclaimed that I hated Him.

I knew I would be forgiven if I could find the humility to ask for it. I began the words of a prayer with "*Heavenly Father,*" and I could go no further without having a meltdown. This wasn't the time or place, and these ruptured people the Lord had put in my path needed me to be their glue. I simply asked, "*Give me the strength,*" while letting the rest of my thoughts and emotions speak my message.

I slept for a few minutes before waking to the sound of Maya snickering. I opened my eyes and tilted my head back to see Chop standing behind us. He had shaved his scraggly beard and was wearing my vintage Star Wars tee shirt. The sleeves barely covered his biceps, and his belly button protruded uncovered.

"Did you get fat on Prius?" I asked.

"Now this is the look they should have plastered on the recruiting ads," Maya added.

"Hardy-har, smartass. I'm not the one who shops off the children's clearance rack."

"That's a men's medium, thank you very much. Be thankful you don't smell like roadkill anymore."

"I'm not going to lie. That felt amazing. Them military boys didn't spare any expense on those shower heads."

"Now imagine what they've invested in destroying their enemies," Maya brought us back to reality. She got out of the pilot's seat and gave Chop a glare that told him his old spot was off limits. "Come on, boys. Let's figure this shit out." I looked at Chop and we shrugged our shoulders as we followed Maya towards the mess hall. She knocked twice on the door to her quarters where Alexis was getting ready. "Team meeting, doll. Move your ass," she ordered, seizing the moment to be our commander.

Emilia was in the shower, but Maya wasn't interested in waiting for the women. She started reorganizing Monopoly pieces to make the board reflect a map of the airbase. "This is the north hangar," she said, placing a hotel on Marvin's Gardens, "and this is the south hangar," she illustrated with a hotel on Mediterranean Ave. "Free parking is the airstrip, and these are the barracks." She set houses on B&O and Reading Railroads. "There's administrative buildings over here by Jail, but this is what matters most," she said while placing the wheelbarrow on St. Charles Place. "Triaxum storage. We blow this, and those pricks won't have fuel for the war machine."

"What about the Jump Point? *That's* our main target," Chop interrupted.

"Would you please slow your roll? I got this."

"*You got this*? It's a giant portal in space. If you have a plan for that, I'd love to hear it."

"Yeah, I do, you prick. Sit your ass down, and I'll enlighten you." She pointed to a chair before leaving the room.

"Ease up, man. I think I know where she's going with this," I said as we waited on Maya, who returned carrying one of her souvenirs from our first mission. She placed *Marcus* carefully into Chop's lap and smirked at his discomfort.

"I got another one too. I can melt down the cores to make the bombs go live. It might take a day or two for them to explode, but they should be more than enough to tear the Jump Point a new asshole. I say we leave them floating inside the wormhole out of sight. Plant them on opposite ends near the structure and wait for the fireworks."

"That's...not bad, Maya," Chop said as he gently moved the bomb from his lap to the floor and slid it under the table. "They'll never see it coming if they don't know the bombs are there. They could catch or kill us, and it wouldn't make any difference," Chop said as he realized Maya's well processed plan.

"What about the debris?" Alexis asked, eavesdropping from the doorway.

"She's right. Massive portions of the structure could get pulled into the atmosphere. The gravity wave should hypothetically push the debris towards Earth," I cautioned.

"Okay, fine. So, we don't destroy it? Then what?" Maya asked while raising her hands palm up.

"We have to destroy it," Chop added emphatically. "Mankind needs to be trapped on Earth until we figure ourselves out. This is all for nothing if the reach of our civilization isn't contained. The Praxi will never be safe, nor will anyone else who might be out there."

"What if we plant the bombs against the structure on Earth's side?" I suggested. "If the blast wave is between Earth and the portal, it should push the debris away from us. It's still going to be a disaster up there, but at least it won't put innocent people in harm's way," I said as I physically illustrated the moving parts using Monopoly pieces.

"That might work if we had a way to fasten the bombs into place," Maya said. "This is why I wanted to leave them inside the wormhole. Nobody will know what we've done, and there's no duct tape required."

"We could get started at Edwards, and then fly the bombs up there later," Chop added.

"You think you're Iron Man now?" Maya mocked. "You going to carry the bombs through the wormhole like a hero?"

"Ooh. Good call," Alexis perked up. "We're like the Avengers, except Malik is Iron Man and Ranbir is Captain America," Alexis assigned.

"Captain America? Bitch, please," Maya scoffed.

"I'm Black Widow, and that makes you..." Alexis pointed to Maya.

"If you say Hawkeye, I'm going to slap you."

"Right. The Hulk. That tracks."

"Who's leftover for Emilia? Thor?" I played along.

"Actually, I'm afraid she's more of a Loki, and we should address that before she joins us," Alexis cautioned. "Sorry, Chop. I know what she means to you, but you've got her twisted. I'm not buying this whole *new lease on life* act. If she gets a chance to take control of CE, none of the rest of this is going to matter. We'll wish we still had the Jump Point to escape through if she seizes power."

"I think she's legitimately trying to do the right thing," I spoke with confidence that my message had gotten through to Emilia.

"That woman doesn't know the difference between right and wrong. *That's* the problem. When push comes to shove, I don't think she has it in her to terminate her digital baby. She'll try to save CE under the pretense of using it to un-fuck the world. She'll convince herself and the rest of you along with her that she's doing the right thing."

"She saved Gio, and she got all of us to this point," Chop made his case for Emilia's humanity.

"Did you or did you not attempt to convince her to take a shower with you an hour ago?" Alexis asked.

"I may have," Chop replied sheepishly with a grin that was hard to conceal.

"And it's been how long since you've been laid?" Maya asked, seeing the direction Alexis was steering. "Pumping one out on Prius doesn't count," she comically pointed her forefinger at Chop.

"It's been a while, okay?"

"And Emilia was the last person you slept with, yes?" Alexis kept up the pressure.

"What's your point?"

"Seriously? You're compromised, dude," Alexis stated.

"Fine, fine, fine. You're right. Malik agrees with me though. She's not the same Emilia."

"I don't know how you guys get used to these things," Emilia announced her presence while tugging at her tight-fitting uniform. "Fatigues aren't part of my style repertoire."

We collectively went silent for a moment while Emilia poured herself a cup of coffee and joined us in standing around the table. "Well? Here we are. Any bright ideas?" she asked.

"The Jump Point, the triaxum, the memory card, and Connect Earth. Preferably in that order, but I'd settle for any plan that doesn't end with us taking a dirt nap," Chop said.

"That's backwards," Emilia said between sips of coffee. "There's only five of us. We need to get to CE first. If we can get the message out there, we won't have to fight alone. Some of the military will stand down and others will stand with us."

Alexis made eye contact with the rest of us one by one with an *I told you so* look. Emilia's position didn't necessarily mean that Alexis was right about her, but it did raise our suspicions.

"The triaxum is right there on the base," Maya said while tapping the wheelbarrow. "If we leave without destroying it, and then go make a bunch of noise at CE; we ain't getting back on. You don't know these jarheads like we do. They don't take their orders from social media."

"Remind me again why we want to destroy the most valuable resource in the galaxy? Its applications are endless. We can use the triaxum for good if we can sway the public with the truth. All we have to do..." Emilia said before I finished her sentence.

"Is get control of Connect Earth? And what if that fails? What about Gio and the rest of the Praxi?"

"You think blowing up some fuel depot is going to save them? Here, watch," Emilia said as she swatted the Monopoly pieces off the board and inserted mock explosion sound effects. "We just blew up all the triaxum. There are thousands of soldiers coming after the five of us. Now what? Any of you geniuses have an answer for that? We end up dead, the truth stays buried, and the next shipment arrives from the mines undoing everything we accomplished."

Alexis was being oddly silent as her warning about Emilia appeared to become valid. She took a few steps back from the rest of us with her hands twitching slightly and her face going pale.

I should have remained calm, but the heat of the moment was consuming me. There was no way we were going to survive. "This is impossible! We can't win. We should turn around and go back to Prius. You guys had it good there, and so could we."

"You coward, Malik," Chop said sharply. "You're going to fold that easy? Let's hear Emilia out."

"First intelligent thing any of you has said," Emilia stated arrogantly.

Our voices rose as we talked over each other. We became defensive, angry, argumentative, and progressively more aggressive as Alexis slinked down onto the floor with her knees pulled up tightly against her chest.

"I'm no coward. I'm not afraid to die, but I'm not going to seek it out either," I said.

"That's exactly what you're doing if we hit the base before CE," Chop continued, backing Emilia.

Maya gripped Chop's collar and tried to shake some sense into him. "Pull your head out of your ass. This evil little twat is working us."

"Don't put your hands on me!"

Alexis had begun rocking herself slowly back and forth as if the waves from her panicked heaving chest were putting her into motion. "I can't breathe. I can't breathe," she said softly between rapid gasps for air. She was unheard and unnoticed as we tore each other apart.

"Who the hell put you in charge anyway?" Maya questioned with her grip tightening.

"We must get the truth out *and* keep humanity trapped on Earth! How the hell can you not see that?" Chop struggled to get free.

"What good will that do if we can't unseat the corrupt?!" I shouted.

Alexis began humming to herself, and then she followed the familiar melody with soft singing between heavy breaths. "*Today is gonna be the day that they're gonna throw it back to you.*" It was Emilia of all people who was the first to take notice of her, and she immediately removed herself while the rest of us continued bickering.

"Hey. Are you okay?" Emilia asked while crouching in front of Alexis.

"*And by now, you should've somehow realized what you gotta do,*" Alexis responded in song with her eyes squinted shut and hands trembling.

"I should kick your ass, you know that? Smack the stupid right out of you," Maya threatened.

"Big tough merc Maya. Go ahead. See what happens."

"*And I don't believe that anybody feels the way I do about you now,*" Alexis continued while I quickly grabbed Maya's arms before she could cock back and throw a punch.

"You guys, stop," Emilia said forcibly but with controlled volume. She put one hand on each of Alexis' shoulders, rubbed them gently, and swayed with her back and forth. "*And backbeat, the word is on the street that the fire in your heart is out,*" she sang calmly to Alexis.

"*And all the roads we have to walk are winding,*" Emilia and Alexis linked on the bridge of the song. "That's it. We're fine. You're fine. Just breathe," Emilia encouraged.

Seeing Emilia come to her aid was more than I could have hoped to inspire. If the most damaged amongst us could find compassion for her supposed rival, there would be nothing that could stop us. I wouldn't need to be the glue if we came together as one cohesive unit.

Our egos crashed against each other as we fought over the minutiae of how to save the world. The answer was right there in front of us, but we had been too stubborn and self-absorbed to see it. The only thing that could save humanity was humanity. Our humanity. It was all around us, and God had used me as his vessel to bring it into the light.

I lessened my bear hug on Maya as she ceased to fight against me. Her fists unclenched and Chop released his grip on her uniform as our attention was drawn to Emilia's sympathetic gesture. I knew the song well, and I seized the moment to sing the next line before Emilia and Alexis arrived at it. "*And all the lights that lead us there are blinding.*" Alexis was still rocking back and forth with her eyes closed, but Emilia looked over her shoulder at me with a hopeful gaze.

"*There are many things that I would like to say to you, but I don't know how,*" the three of us sang in unison as I fully released Maya and joined Emilia on the floor. Alexis tilted her head away from her chest which pushed in and out with deep slow breaths as we lightly caressed her.

"There you go. Deep breaths. Nothing can hurt you," Emilia continued to console as though she was learning to comfort someone for the first time.

"*Because maybe,*" Chop launched into the chorus and held the *maybe* humorlessly long.

"*You're gonna be the one that saves me,*" Emilia and I joined in with the three of us losing the pitch of the drawn-out *me* and occasionally splicing in loving laughter.

"*And after all. You're my Wonderwall,*" Alexis sang on her own before returning to her breathing exercise.

Chop, Emilia, and I took it from there. We passionately launched into the second verse which is a word-for-word repeat from the first. I looked up to Maya, desperately wanting her to join us in that human moment, but the electricity of the experience hadn't yet shocked her ego into restraint.

Alexis finally opened her eyes once she had her breathing under control and sang along with the rest of us. Emilia smiled at her through the lyrics, rubbed the back of her head, and then awkwardly moved her hand over Chop's. We sang "*There are many things that I would like to say to you, but I don't know how,*" and Emilia's emotion was almost as palpable as one of the Praxi. The moment was a charged electron hanging in the air that could make your hair stand on edge if you would but reach out and touch it.

It was our second time through the chorus when we all finally came together as one. The four of us sang "*I said maybe,*" all now holding the note as long as Chop had, and then Maya broke in with the echoing background vocals of, "*Said maybe.*"

Alexis cheered as Maya completed our quintet and brought the song to life. I couldn't help myself but to have an emotional release that was equal parts laughing and crying. *"You're gonna be the one that saves me,"* we sang in unison with Maya again covering the, *"that saves me,"* echo.

By the time the song had ended, four of us were on the floor and Maya was standing over my shoulder. We waited patiently in silence for Alexis to claim control over her breathing before Maya offered her hand to help Chop to his feet. They shared a look that was something of a treaty before helping the rest of us off the floor.

"You good?" I asked Alexis to which she nodded her head before taking a seat at the table. "We cool?" I asked everyone else. "Good, because we're stuck with each other. Now, let's get something to eat, and figure this out like friends. *Wonderwall* isn't going to work on those boys back home."

Chapter 15

Don't do Anything Stupid

Ranbir Chopra

"Here we go, chumps," Maya announced as the *Lydia* pushed through the Jump Point into the outer atmosphere of Earth. "Fifteen minutes until touchdown."

Emilia and I were lying in Malik's bed, and she attempted to wiggle away as the danger was upon us. I wrapped my arm around her waist and held her spooned against me. "Please," I whispered. "A few more minutes."

She relaxed her muscles, nestled back against me tightly, and interlocked her hands with mine. She was a different Emilia, yet everything remained familiar. From the smell of her hair to the pace of her breathing and the softness of her skin. I had forgotten how comforting it was to be alone with her. "No one will ever know you the way I do," I said as I kissed the back of her neck.

"That's what I'm afraid of," she replied. "No matter what happens, I'll be a villain. If we fail, Penelope will spin the truth, and we'll be labeled as terrorists and traitors. If we're successful, it won't make any difference for me. The rest of you will be lauded as heroes, and I'll still be the freak who poured kerosine on the fire that consumed the world. You'd be wise to distance yourself from me."

"The lines between heroes and villains aren't that simple, and I know a thing or two on the subject. I've murdered more innocent souls than anyone in history, and mankind labeled me their hero. You could bring them back from societal collapse and save the galaxy from the poisonous nature of humanity in the process; and they might still call you a villain. Perception is not reality, Emilia, and there's no such thing as heroes and villains."

"Don't ruin my self-loathing. I'm trying to feel like shit for a minute, and your attempts at being insightfully poetic aren't appreciated," Emilia jested.

"I'm not patronizing you; I swear. I think those labels are broad and aren't necessarily applicable to individuals. The World Military is a villain, but does that make the men and women who wear their uniforms evil? People are far more complicated than the systems of power we're forced to adapt to."

"It's a nice sentiment, even if it's incorrect and naïve," she said while twisting to face me. "Our actions write the truths of inner character, and the book on me isn't particularly flattering."

"You saved Gio. You gave the Praxi a fighting chance. None of us would be here if it wasn't for you, and the book isn't written on you yet. You can be whoever you want to be."

"It's not enough," she repined. "People will hate me regardless."

I released her hands and ran the back side of my palm against her repaired cheek. "Not everyone," I said while holding her gaze. "I love you. You hear me? I'm in love with you." I emphasized every word. "I loved you a month after I met you. I loved you when you showed me the smile you hid from everyone else, when you stage managed me, and when you slept quietly next to me. I've loved you in a wormhole and on two different planets. And I'm going to love you when we come out on the other side of this thing."

"Uhhhmm," Alexis interrupted. "You kids lying in bed all day or are you going to come out and play?" she asked from the doorway.

"All right, all right. We're up, mom," Emilia said sarcastically as she rolled off the side of the bed. She straightened her military fatigues that we wore uniformly, looked back to me, and mouthed the words, "I love you too."

Malik navigated the ship into the hangar while the rest of us made our way into the cargo hold. "Sit tight and stay out of sight. We'll be right back," Maya instructed. "That means you, Chop. No hero shit."

"Wouldn't dream of it," I responded with a coy smile.

"All right, let's check in and get ourselves another load," Malik said as he lowered the cargo ramp. It was around midnight, and that sector of the base was quiet except for the bus loads of prisoners waiting for the next ferry to Prius. Maya gave the drivers a wave and pointed them towards the hangar before disappearing into the adjacent building.

"I hope they're as rowdy a bunch as the crew we flew with," Alexis said to Emilia.

"I still can't believe Maya," Emilia replied. "Remember the look on those prick's faces when she came marching in guns blazing?"

"*You gotta be mindful of your feet, homie,*" Alexis recounted Maya's badassery as they laughed together. "We've seen some wild shit, haven't we?"

"We're just getting started," I said, hoping for my own heroic moment that would be recounted with awe. It wouldn't even matter if I was dead so long as my family name lived on the lips of the living.

"Look at this place," Alexis marveled as we stared out the back of the *Lydia*. "The OWG is gone in name only. This is exactly what they wanted. I tried to warn people, but my platform was too small, I was too afraid of the big stage, and no one would listen."

"They're going to listen today," Emilia said as she flashed the memory card full of evidence.

Malik returned to the ship and Maya ordered the guards to line the prisoners in rows. "They didn't suspect a thing. Give it a few minutes, and the guards will disperse with the buses. This is going to work," Malik said before returning to the hangar to assist with prisoner processing. They pretended to load the first few hundred shackled men into the ship, and once the coast was clear, we came out of hiding and shooed the prisoners to the back of the hangar.

"Okay, Ranbir. You're up. *Go inspire.*" Emilia winked at me. The smart play would've been to follow her deceitful talking points about the horrors awaiting those men on Prius, and how the best chance for survival was to stand and fight. I knew what it was like to follow a lie into battle though, and as much as we needed these men, they deserved the right to choose. I rubbed my palms together anxiously as I recalled how poorly received my first speech was in that very hangar months earlier.

"Listen up, everybody!" I shouted to gather the prisoners round. "I wish I had the speech I'm supposed to recite written down. I've always wanted to sigh, tear up some paper, and go off script," I paused to glance at Emilia, expecting a disapproving glare, but her watch was neutral. "Show of hands, how many of you know who I am?" At least half of the men raised their hands, and the others wore a confused look. "You there," I pointed to a man in the front, "Who am I?"

"You're Captain Ranbir Chopra," he answered.

"Wrong. Anybody else? How about you?" I pointed to another.

"You led the attack on Prius. You're a war hero," he answered.

"Wrong again. I'm a nobody. I'm not a soldier. I'm not even a pilot. I lied to everyone, and boy, did I ever think I was slick. I was so obsessed with being famous that I didn't realize I was being used. I did terrible things because I was too incurious to see the truth. And what is that truth?" I paused for dramatic effect. "The OWG and World Military played us. The Praxi were never our enemy. You're the first people on Earth to hear this, and there's no one more equipped to understand. I've stood where you are. A prisoner of an oppressive regime who has lied to obtain power and killed to sustain it. You know the feeling of their boot on your neck. My friends and I are in possession of evidence that can remove that boot from the throats of billions, but we cannot do it alone. I'm humbly asking you to fight. Not for us, and not for yourselves; but for your friends, family, and those who have lost their lives. This is our one and only chance, and I'm not afraid to die in the pursuit of saving our world. I'm going to pass out these keys now, and the moment you unchain yourselves, you are free men to make your own choices. You can hide here if you'd like, but I promise you, you'll be locked up again if we fail. Should you choose to stand and fight, remember what your enemy thinks of you. You're disposable to them. Show them the same respect and introduce them to the fear they're accustomed to spreading," I said while tossing the cuff keys to the nearest prisoner.

Both Em and Alexis gave an approving nod as they shared a glance. "Inspiring, right?" Emilia joked to Alexis.

"Oh, yeah. Inspiring as shit. That whole *take the boot off your necks* bit was money."

"*Introduce them to fear*," Emilia imitated.

"I liked the two of you better when you hated each other," I responded play-fully to their ribbing. "Sorry, I went my own way with that. It felt right."

"You did great," Emilia assured. "Let's just hope it worked."

"Ships ready to go," Malik said as he and Maya approached. "Coordinates plugged in, and the autopilot is set. My babies are strapped into the cockpit. The ship should hover near the Jump Point's outer structure."

"Marcus and Maisie are about to go nuclear on that ass," Maya said as she slapped Malik's shoulder.

Malik walked around the hull of the ship to the point where he had written *Lydia* when I first met him. The soft hum of the gravity drive filled the hangar as the ship powered up and rose off the ground. He traced his finger across the L-y-d-i-a insignia and said something softly to himself that we couldn't hear. It could have been a prayer, one final word to his wife before she flew off, or a bit of both.

The *Lydia* exited the hangar on its own, rose into the night sky, and disap-peared into the darkness. As far as everyone on the base was concerned, things were running tight and on schedule.

"Whatya say, Maya? Let's go get our ride," I proposed, anxiously anticipating getting back into the pilot's seat of an alien fighter.

"Are we sure?" Emilia asked. "The element of surprise is single use only," she cautioned.

"Stick to the plan. When we fly by, open the hangar doors and let the prisoners out. Stay hidden and don't get caught up in the commotion. We'll be right back to pick you up once we dust the triaxum depot," Maya ordered.

Emilia begrudgingly nodded her head in acceptance of the agreed upon plan and gave me a reassuring look with her lips pursed. Her eyes said plenty, but I could tell that she wanted to say more.

We used the side door and walked calmly so as not to draw any attention to ourselves. Maya inserted her security badge to gain access to the next bay so we could travel indoors without any eyeballs on us.

"They're refitting all the old equipment with Praxi tech. This arsenal would be out of control right now if the bulk of resources weren't going to deep space warfare," she said as we walked by rows upon rows of tanks, Humvees, jeeps, helicopters, and other various military vehicles that were being fitted with Praxi energy weapons.

"Where's all the aircraft?"

"That shits obsolete, bro. The flight systems and designs are incompatible with updates. There are helos around for transport, but that's about it. Come on, the good stuff is in the next bay," she said as we reached the other end of the hangar. Once again, we went outside, walked a short distance, and gained access with Maya's keycard. She flipped the light switch from a control panel on the wall and announced, "What the hell?"

"Where are they?" I asked as I rushed through a similar inventory of man-made vehicles from the previous bay. "Maya? Where are they?" I asked again.

"They're supposed to be right here! Two saucers and one pencil."

"Yeah, I remember you saying that very clearly. *We'll get into one of those saucers, blow the depot to hell, and zip off to CE.* Yet, here we are, and there's no ships!" I said as I slammed my palm on the hood of a jeep. "So, where the hell are they?"

"I don't know!" she shouted back as she shook her fists with teeth gritted. "In another hangar? Out on a mission? They could be anywhere."

"Hey! What are you two doing in here?" an MP startled us. "This area is restricted from midnight until 6 a.m."

"Sorry about that. I think I left my phone in a Humvee earlier today," Maya lied. "Can't seem to find it anywhere."

"You," he pointed at me. "I know you."

"I don't think so," I said as I kept my face lowered and tried to hurry by him. He grabbed my upper arm to stop me and got a good enough look to remember my image plastered on propaganda posters.

"Control, come back?" he spoke into his radio. I quickly gripped his wrist, spun his arm around his back, and pressed his chest against a Humvee.

"Midnight 2, this is control. Go ahead," the voice on the other end of the radio answered.

"I'm not going to hurt you unless you give me no choice," I said calmly as he struggled against my grasp. Maya unpinned his holster cover to remove his sidearm and stripped him of his radio while I kept my body weight pressed against his back. "We're not shooting him," I said sternly.

"No shit, genius. It's way too loud. What the hell are we gonna do?" she asked, and it was the first time I'd ever heard her voice inflect with panic.

"We'll tie him up. Get some rope," I said.

"Some rope? What do I look like to you? *Dora the Explorer?*"

"Okay, fine. Here, he's got cuffs," I pulled them off his belt. "Easy now. Into the front seat," I directed as I opened the door to the Humvee. I cuffed his hands to the steering wheel, and Maya removed her bandana to gag his mouth. "Now what?" I asked.

"We improvise."

"You told everyone to stick to the plan!"

"Midnight 2. You playing games on my airwaves again?" the radio voice asked.

"They're going to sniff us out. We have to move. Now!" Maya said as she rushed over to the case on the wall and rifled through the guard's keys until she was able to open it. "Check those crates for munitions. Get me something to work with."

"Grenades. Ammo. Small arms," I shouted to her as I sorted through the available inventory.

"Grenades are good. Hook me up," she shouted back as she scurried her way to the top hatch of a tank and unlocked the pad to gain access. "Come on, come on, come on," she pressed. I passed her a dozen grenades which she dropped down the hatch one by one. "Now get down and open the bay doors."

"I'm coming with you."

"No, you're not. I got this. Go back and release the hounds. I'll wait for you to start making noise before I take off. Hold their attention long enough to buy me some time, and then get our friends off the base and upload that evidence. And Chop..."

"Yeah?"

"Don't do anything stupid," she said as she lowered herself into that mechanical beast and pulled the hatch lid behind her.

I sprinted to the controls and tapped the button to roll up the bay doors. My heart was racing as fast as when we stormed Prius airspace, but this time the stakes were real. There was no time to waste zigzagging through the adjacent hangar, so I ran out in the open. I burst through the side door and tried to quickly organize everyone while being out of breath.

"What's happening?" Malik asked. "What are you doing back here?"

"The ships weren't there, and we were spotted. Open the bay doors!" I yelled to Alexis.

"Where's Maya? Is she okay?" Malik persisted.

"She's going for the triaxum and we need to give her some cover and then get the hell out of here."

"That wasn't the plan! She's going to get herself killed!"

There wasn't a second to waste arguing with Malik. The overhead doors were raised, and Maya needed our diversion. "This is the moment!" I yelled to the hundreds of prisoners who had been patiently waiting. "We're going to crash the gates and storm into the countryside. When engaged, don't bother taking any prisoners. Your enemy certainly won't!"

I wasn't sure what we were going to get out of those men. Had the system broken their spirits? Would they recognize their oppressors as such? Would they choose fear over freedom? Their actions left no doubt to these questions. They leaped at the chance to join the fight, and seven hundred and fifty warriors rose to the occasion. They followed me to the adjacent hangar where they armed themselves and commandeered the military vehicles. A disorganized fleet of chaos poured out of the hangar, some heading for the east gate, while others chose to open fire on the barracks and other buildings.

The alarms were raised, and the base came to life. High-powered floods lit up the grounds as thousands of soldiers were jarred out of their slumber and thrust into the middle of an active war zone. The quiet of the night was filled with small arms fire, screeching tires, warrior screams, and the metal thrashing of the chain-linked perimeter being tested.

"There she goes!" I said, pointing out Maya's tank which rolled in the opposite direction of the clash. "Let's arm up and get out of here. We'll follow the group crashing the gate and take the highways to CE." Malik, Emilia, and Alexis rummaged through the plethora of available arms while I matched a set of keys to one of the remaining jeeps.

Malik was the first to get into the battle. He took position using the hangar wall as cover and fired an M-16 across the airfield towards the soldiers who were rushing out of their barracks. Emilia followed his lead with a rifle of her own on the opposite side of the open bay but was far less effective in hitting her targets.

"Whoa! Look at this thing," Alexis announced as she lifted a silver tube out of a crate. She gripped the trigger housing and rested the back half of the device on her shoulder like a rocket launcher.

"Why don't you let me give that a try?" Malik suggested as Alexis joined him at his firing position.

"I got this," Alexis said confidently as she ducked around Malik and took aim across the tarmac at a WM jeep racing after Maya's tank. "Okay, this is the safety, I think," she narrated while flipping a switch, "which makes this the trigger." She fired a targeted wave of gravity and her body lifted off the ground and was thrown twenty feet backwards from the discharge. She slid across the concrete laughing hysterically at herself before coming to a rest at my feet. The wave hit the Jeep in the rear axle and caused the back quarter to tear from the rest of the vehicle and crush to the size of watermelon.

I helped Alexis to her feet and into the back seat of the running Jeep. "Behave yourself," I warned as she held onto her new toy. I took the driver's seat, pulled ahead, and invited Malik to the front and Emilia into the back.

The bay doors on every hangar opened as soldiers equipped themselves for battle. Enemy tanks and Humvees raced onto the airfield and began engaging with our untrained prisoner army. They fired upon each other in total chaos, most of them unable to distinguish friend from foe. I followed the line of vehicles that were crashing the perimeter fence, and we joined in the fire fight to escape the confines of the base.

Our vehicles were piling up as the front row rocked back and forth ramming into the fence. Our enemy was approaching from the rear, and we were about to get pinned into place with no escape before a tank broke through and created an opening in the perimeter. One by one, our convoy crept through the hole and sped out into the California wilderness.

Malik stood through the open top of our Jeep, rested his back against the roll cage, and fired towards the oncoming traffic. His M-16 was offering little resistance, so he curled his finger to Alexis to take control of her gravity launcher.

"Uh, you sure that's a good idea?" Emilia asked. Malik answered her by unleashing a gravity wave headfirst into a tank. The crunching of condensed metal was louder than any gunfire. The tank stopped on a dime with the entire front end squished to a point and the tracks buckled from the axle. Our Jeep hiccupped onto two wheels momentarily from the blowback of the discharge.

"Yeah! Get some!" Malik shouted as he ripped another wave towards a Humvee that capsized and rolled over twice.

"Come on, people! Come on!" I shouted pointlessly at the prisoners ahead of us making their way through the open hole in the fencing. Helicopters took to the sky like cowboys corralling cattle, and the vehicles that were clear split in every direction to search for an avenue of escape. The mass of disorder tilted in our favor until a silver saucer zipped to a hovering stop and pounded an energy surge which turned our small opening in the fence into a ten-foot-deep cavern in the Earth. A Jeep slid into the hole ahead of us, and our front tires sank to the point where the rear tires came off the ground.

"We're trapped. Get out!" I shouted.

Malik climbed out, pressed his back against the frame, and unleashed a stream towards the craft which did little other than move it off its point. "Guys, we might be in trouble here," he warned.

It became obvious that there was no path to escape on the ground. Within an hour, our entire company would either be caught or killed at this rate. "Back to the hangar!" I shouted while pulling a poor dead man from the driver's compartment of a stopped Humvee. "Get in! We! Are! Leaving!" I emphasized each word.

My crew piled in, and I mashed on the accelerator to race in reverse away from the carnage. Once cleared, I spun around, shifted to drive, and hustled back to the hangar with enemy vehicles in pursuit. "Into the chopper," I ordered. I ushered Emilia and Alexis around the 50-caliber mounted rifle into the passenger compartment, and Malik and I took the seats in the front.

"Buckle in," I instructed while going through my mental checklist of the knobs to turn and buttons to switch to prepare to take flight. I fired up the rotors and the staccato thumping seemed to pace with the accelerated beating of my heart. "Mom, you should see me now," I said to myself hoping she'd be proud of her son.

"You know what you're doing?" Alexis asked as I fumbled about, mimicking the patterns I had watched actual combat pilots go through.

"Sort of," I said as I raised us a few feet off the ground and attempted to navigate my way forward out of the bay. I tilted the nose a little too far forward, and the landing skids dragged across the concrete causing the craft to nearly spin out of my control before I tilted us level.

"Sort of?! You've never done this before, have you?"

"What gave it away?" I asked sarcastically as I gripped the controls and pressed forward. I turned the bird to the left and raised us to enough elevation to stay out of trouble from incoming ground fire. Maya was in the distance to the west where she had taken a firing position on the triaxum storage. She had already blown a hole in the building, and her tank was hopping with continued heavy munitions fire into the dilapidated structure.

I flew overhead to offer cover as Maya exited the top hatch. She looked upwards to notice her friends, yelled something we couldn't make out, and waved us off before sprinting towards the building with her arms full of munitions. She posted against the ruptured wall and began tossing grenade after grenade inside, before stepping over the rubble out of sight. I spun us around to face southwest and started making our escape towards the Connect Earth compound before our enemy could close in, leaving Maya behind.

"Wait!" Malik begged as he twisted around in his seat to look behind us. "They're on to her. She's going to get pinned down."

"She told me to go, and she waved us off," I said, refusing to look back.

"She made her choice," Emilia said with a cold demeanor. "Get us to CE before it's too late."

"Chop. Come on," Malik begged as he forced eye contact with me. In the grand scheme of things, Maya's life couldn't possibly outweigh the mission. She would gladly sacrifice herself in a blaze of glory for the cause. In a sick way, I thought that's exactly what she wanted. Malik's sad eyes pleaded for her life, and I knew we had to turn back. We were a team, and I couldn't bring myself to leave Maya behind.

I began a swooping curve back towards the base, and Emilia petitioned against my decision. "Maya knows how to make the hard choices, and she would never jeopardize the mission to save you."

"She's right," Alexis added. "We're clear of danger. We can't risk it."

"I don't care. She's one of us. I wouldn't leave any of you behind either."

A Humvee had parked, and a group of soldiers took a defensive position behind it to safely attack from. Maya was bunkered inside the damaged structure and was only occasionally returning fire. I increased speed, held the stick with one hand and launched targeted rockets with the other as we buzzed overhead. The smoke billowed behind us as I came around for another pass to assess the damage, only to discover that I had failed to strike the vehicle. The soldiers turned their attention in our direction, and I released another folly of rockets which went off-course as I dodged incoming fire.

"That's all the rockets!" I yelled as I realized what a horrible decision I'd made. "What do we do?" I asked in a panic as bullets screamed through the hull.

"Let me try!" Alexis shouted. She pulled the gravity launcher to her shoulder and leaned tight into her seat, with Emilia bracing behind her. I came to a dead stop to help steady her aim, and Alexis barked "Suck my lady balls," as she pulled the trigger. The wave went wide of her target, ripped a line of concrete to shreds, and sent a whirling kickback that spun our rear rotor into a tailspin. Warning sirens beeped as the stick jogged violently in my hands. I pulled back hard to keep the nose from diving, and regained altitude to the best of my abilities.

"Any other bright ideas?" Malik asked once I regained control.

"Pivot ninety degrees!" Emilia shouted as she pressed her chest against the mounted fifty-caliber rifle. She cocked the bolt into place and held steady until I had her lined with our targets. I kept the speed slow while flying by perpendicularly, and Emilia opened fire in five round bursts which cut through the soldiers flanking position and ripped holes in the Humvee. Six bodies hit the deck, and the seventh soldier abandoned his position and rushed towards the building. Emilia again took aim and sprayed a line of shells in his direction. The first few traced his steps, and the following hail peppered his backside.

Malik looked at me with wide eyes and pointed back, surprised, at Emilia. "Did you teach her that?" he asked with a laugh. "That was incredible!"

"Not her first time," Alexis said while playfully rubbing the back of Emilia's head. "Let's get our friend and get the hell out of here."

I was lowering our bird when Maya peeked out and cleared her corners. She was happy to see us, but her expression soured, and she pointed behind us. I didn't have time to react before the rear rotor crushed like a soda can and a wave of gravity fire toppled us over. The upper rotor blades spun into the ground as the helicopter skidded across the concrete on its side.

Malik unbuckled himself and began kicking at the cracked glass of the windshield. "Em? Alexis? You okay back there?" I asked as I unbuckled myself.

"A few bruises, but we'll be all right," Alexis answered as she tossed her headset and crawled up out of the smoking crash scene and helped Emilia behind her. I pushed my door open and was greeted by the barrel of a gun and Kai's evil smile behind it.

"My night just got so much better," Kai grinned with gapped teeth while directing me out of the crashed helicopter and onto my knees. "Risa, look who we got here."

"Got his pops and girlfriend too," Risa replied as the four of us were corralled side by side on our knees with a Praxi pencil craft hovering ominously overhead.

"What the hell are you doing here, Emmanuel?" one of the other soldiers asked as he patted down the front of Malik's fatigues.

"You guys are making a big mistake. You're fighting for the wrong side," Alexis interjected.

"I prefer the side that doesn't end up on their knees," Risa snarled.

"Risa! Seriously. Please take a minute to hear us out," Malik begged to no avail. "Kai! Please! The Praxi didn't hit us. It was a false flag."

Kai leaned down, nearly dropping one knee to the pavement in front of Malik. "What are you saying? The bomb dropped on London that killed your family wasn't the Praxi?" Kai inquired, which gave us the smallest glimmer of hope.

"No," Alexis answered faster than Malik could. "It was the World Military. They were under the surface of the OWG the entire time. They orchestrated everything and we have proof."

"Is that so?" Kai asked rhetorically as he kept his eyes fixed on Malik. "It's a good story, but it's got one massive hole in it. I *actually* know who hit all those cities. London especially."

"Who?" Malik asked.

"I did," Kai responded coldly. "I've wanted to tell you so many times. I really appreciate you giving me the opportunity to see the look on your face. And you," Kai turned his attention towards me, "we never needed your training or leadership. Every time someone referred to you as our great military leader, I bit my tongue."

"With what teeth?" I clapped back at him.

"You bastards. You son of a bitch," Malik raged with his fists balled against the concrete below.

"Ssshhh," Risa taunted before ducking behind Malik as bullets whizzed overhead from Maya's direction. Kai and the other soldiers took positions behind us and began returning fire without being positive of Maya's position.

"Give it up, Fontaine! Toss the weapon and come out slowly with your hands up," one of the soldiers shouted. Maya responded by firing a string of colorful metaphors in Spanish and a few more rounds towards anyone she could get a clean shot at, including the spacecraft overhead.

"These your friends, Fontaine? If you don't walk your tomboy ass out of cover in three seconds, I'm going to start putting bullets in them. Comprende?" Risa hollered.

"Don't do it, Maya! We're dead anyways," I shouted to her before Kai kicked me in the back and I landed face first on the pavement.

"I'm not playing with you, Fontaine. Toss the weapon, or I'm going to put your boy on ice," Risa yelled as she pressed her barrel tightly against Malik's cheek.

"All right. All right. I surrender," Maya responded as she threw her firearm. She raised her hands above her head and slowly climbed over the rubble. The soldiers quickly subdued her and threw her to the ground in front of us.

"I told you to go," Maya said to me as she shook her head in disappointment.

"No, you said '*don't do anything stupid,*'" I mimicked her accent.

"Yeah, and?" she said as she looked over the five of us on our knees, about to meet our fate. "This feels pretty stupid to me."

"Shut up," one of the soldiers threatened with his rifle. "Are we arresting them or blasting them?"

"Arrest sounds peachy," Alexis said as she pointed at him to signal his good idea. "In fact, if you fellas want to put us on a prison ferry to Prius, we'll get out of your hair. Seems like you've got better things to do around here."

"Let's hit them with the gravity wave and see what happens," Risa suggested with grim glee.

"What about our date, Risa? You and I have unfinished business," Maya pointlessly taunted. "You up for a fair fight?"

"I don't fight fair," Risa sneered back even though her ego was challenged. She signaled to the craft to land and looked to Kai. "Want to finish them off?" she asked.

"I'd love to," Kai responded as the others nodded along and he ran off to pilot the ship. They lined us side by side on our knees in the dirt and each took multiple paces back to watch like an execution viewing party, only with less tears and more twisted excitement.

Even as I was on my knees preparing for death, my final attempt to be a hero didn't feel like a failure. I acted with my heart and didn't have to pretend to be anyone else to rise to the occasion. I had done something good with no concern for earning the praise or status that I had long desired. There is no heroism without selflessness, which is a lesson I had failed to glean from my parents. I hoped that whatever lies the regime would concoct about me wouldn't be enough to fool my mother and father. When facing down certain death, I needed their approval and no one else's.

That was it. Our mission was a disaster, but at least we were going out together. Malik prayed. Alexis hummed. Maya cursed. Emilia gently took my hand, her face showing more expression than I was used to. There was a deep sadness and regret in her eyes. It was as if she had a million things to say to me, and only one breath remaining to draw from to speak her mind. Yet when she parted her lips, there were no words. She didn't need to say anything because I could feel her. Our communication was heightened like that of the Praxi. It was though I could sense a lesson learned from Gio in that moment. Intense personal contact with him facilitated an impassioned emotional exchange between us.

The low purr of the gravity cannon powering up was barely audible over the echoes of the nearby gunfire and shouting of the battle taking place. Kai took aim at the five of us, and Risa and our captors watched on with dark jovial excitement as we were about to be the subject of a twisted science experiment. I closed my eyes and gripped Emilia's hand tightly as the hum rose to a fever pitch from the craft preparing to fire upon us.

"Everyone, it's been a pleasure. I'll see you on the other side," I said as the devastating sound of the alien weapon was unleashed.

Chapter 16
Broadcast and Bullets
Alexis X

I had to take a physical inventory of my body parts after the thunder cracked from the cannon. My arms were still intact, and my head was in place. I ran my hands over my torso and down to my knees to find that everything was where it belonged. I looked up into the night sky at our attackers to find the enemy craft teetering on its axis and frozen in place. The structure was shaking violently as the hull started to rupture. Those seemingly indestructible materials collapsed in on themselves like a grape squished in a giant's hands. Kai's panicked face stared through the frontal viewer, and his blood painted the transparent surface red as his body was mushed by the crumbling structure.

The ship was crushed to the size of a small car as it shed the pieces that wouldn't fold up from gravity penetrating from all sides. The smaller it shrank, the more visible our savior became hovering closely behind the destroyed craft.

"Gio!!" Ranbir shouted as he popped to his feet triumphantly.

The soldiers watching on didn't get the show they had anticipated, and they were far too slow to react to their powerful attack ship being turned into a tin can. Maya and Malik were all over them before they could be bothered to turn their attention to us. Malik did his best to subdue Risa whom he tackled and held to the ground, but Maya wasn't so discerning in handling business. She quickly grabbed the base of a soldier's rifle, forced it to point toward the stars, and utilized her free hand to pull his sidearm from his belt. She fired a bullet under his chin and put two more into the back of the last man standing who was taking aim at Malik.

"Don't, Maya. She gave up," Malik pleaded as Maya pressed her handgun into Risa's face.

"This shit bag was going to have a laugh while we got crunched. Move," Maya barked as Malik positioned himself between Maya's vengeance and its target.

"No. We're better than them."

"They killed your babies, Malik! She doesn't deserve another breath."

"How about that date, Maya?" Risa attempted to work the situation the same as Maya had when roles were reversed. She didn't need to bargain for her life or manipulate her way into a fair fight with Maya though. Gio's calming presence was upon us, and not even Maya's iron will could survive.

The craft that saved our skin lowered to a few feet off the ground, and Gio dangled his head out from the lower hatch. We were collectively sharing the emotive joy of being together again, but it was his ridiculous smile that brought me the most cheer. His head disappeared up the port and then two of his legs swung out and he dropped to the ground to greet us properly.

Ranbir ran up to him, and there was palpable sadness between the two of them. "What are you doing here? What about your daughter?"

"I can't very well explain to my child that I left my friends in their time of need. My people will care for her until I one day join them with my conscience intact."

"There's still some triaxum in there," Maya spoke up. "More than enough to get you home. I'll grab the rest and start a fire," she raced back into the damaged building to retrieve it.

"Are we sure that's such a good idea?" I asked, which received confused looks from everyone. "Gateway. Bombs. Kaboom. None of this ringing a bell?"

"Oh, shit. Right. We sent one hell of a payload up there. The Jump Point could explode at any minute." Ranbir explained.

"The wormhole won't collapse because one door is closed. I could get through and still get home even after the explosion on your end," Gio expressed with happiness. "Not until my friends are safe, though."

Gio's smile unraveled and he turned his attention to Risa. He leaned down in front of her, and for a moment they stared at each other. Her bottom lip began to quiver, and tears streamed down her cheeks. She reached out to touch him and he placed one hand on the side of her face. I can only imagine what he said to her and what intense emotions she was experiencing from sharing the pain she had caused him.

It wasn't surprising that Gio would forgive her and offer some type of comfort, nor was it surprising that Malik would do the same. What was surprising, however, was Risa's inability to forgive herself. The moment Gio stood and turned away, Risa speed crawled ten feet across the pavement, picked up a discarded automatic rifle, planted the butt against the ground and the barrel against her chest, and leaned forward to hold the trigger down. Gio cried out an inhumane audible scream to stop her, but the damage was done. Risa's body flopped forward onto the weapon and her face was frozen in permanent sadness.

We would have been indifferent to her death if not for Gio. Even Maya seemed oddly moved when she returned with the triaxum to find her rival in a prone position. She walked over to Risa, leaned down to close her eyelids, and removed the WM patch from Risa's jacket. "You wouldn't want to fight me anyways," she said softly. Justice had been served.

"Let's get a move on," Emilia said as she drew our attention up the airstrip to a row of three tanks headed our way. "Come on, come on, come on," she hastened us, scurrying into Gio's ship.

The space was tight, but we all found a place to settle in while Gio took the helm. The approaching tanks signaled that they were on to us by launching a volley of fire in our direction, but it was no match for the gravity shielding which shrugged off the munitions like pestering insects. We turned ninety degrees without moving an inch in any direction and sped off over our attackers while torpedoing them with a wave from Gio's cannon that pushed them into a sinkhole through the crumbling concrete below. Gio zipped around and laid a similar blow to the damaged depot to finish the work that Maya had started. Within seconds of being airborne again, the first leg of our mission was complete.

"Southwest," Emilia guided us in the proper direction. As frantic and frightening as being caught in a war zone was, I remained more concerned about Emilia returning to Connect Earth. I wanted to believe that she wasn't the same untrustworthy person I had come to know. There were signs of her growth, but proximity to power is an addiction, and few had ever held as much as Emilia once did. If events broke a certain way, she might have to face down the temptation to salvage and even control the consolidation of power she had nurtured.

Maya, Malik, Ranbir, and I were all standing in the small space behind Gio's command console seat, and Emilia kneeled near him. Gio's middle appendage gripped the steering controls, while his free hand on the left and right adjusted dials and slid across electronic touch screens. Maya was uncomfortably close to Ranbir in that confined space, and I was face-to-face with Malik. The ship produced virtually no sound, and the silence among us was unnerving.

"Hi," I said awkwardly to Malik. He smiled and chuckled like a friend who knew me well enough to expect my awkward behavior.

"Hi," he said with a grin. "First time on an alien attack ship?" he played along.

"Nah. Mine's in the shop. It's got a stripped, uh, shaft hose." I could have kept the joke going for at least three or four more volleys back and forth, but our voices had given the green light for Maya to have a human moment.

"Look, I know I bust your balls, but you did good back there," Maya said modestly to Ranbir, inches from his face.

"No, you were right. It was stupid to go back. I nearly ruined everything."

"Would you shut up and take the compliment? It was brave, and I appreciate you coming back for me."

I reached over to Ranbir's jaw to move his mouth. "You're welcome."

"There she is," Emilia said as she pointed to Connect Earth in the distance. I turned my body so that my back was to Malik and leaned over Emilia's shoulders to get a look. The compound was a monstrosity the likes of which I had never seen before. We flew low over rows upon rows of tightly packed buildings that looked like fields of crops.

"This can't all be servers," I said lowly to myself.

"That's the farm," Emilia said proudly. "11.2 million square feet of raw computing power and data storage. It would be four times the size without the addition of Praxi tech."

"It's very impressive," I replied as I wondered if there was any way we could keep this marvel of technological achievement intact. The amount of good that could be done if that place was free of human and political greed was enormous. I chose not to speak that sentiment aloud for fear that Emilia would latch on and try to spin the situation in the direction I knew she was headed.

"Up there. The big one. Go to the roof," Emilia instructed as Gio navigated us into position over the main CE compound. "See those doors there? Be a doll and remove them for me."

Gio fired up his weapon, narrowed the attack point, and pulled the doors and their framing from the housing. "Good boy," she said while reaching over and scratching the top of his head like a puppy. "Okay, set us down."

The hatch opened below us, and one by one we dropped through the hole and made our way over to the entry point. I waited for Emilia and gave her a nod. "Lead the way. This is your show."

We followed her down the stairs until we came to a door where we stopped. "This is a programming and moderating level, and there shouldn't be anyone here at this time of night," Emilia explained.

"Why did you say that? There's going to be like fifty programmers in there now! That's how this shit always works."

"No more movie rules, Alexis. This should be a piece of cake," Emilia said as she cracked the door open. We were met with incessant chatter from all the cubicles and offices filled with the hustling of a work center on high alert. Emilia sighed deeply and rolled her eyes with frustration, and Malik pushed by her to try to control the situation.

"Nobody panic. There's been a small security breach. We need everyone to calmly and quietly make their way to the roof so that we can conduct a sweep of the area," Malik said as we followed him onto the office floor.

"It's an alien!" someone shouted, which caused everyone to join in the panic.

"Right. Yes. He's with uh, he's part of the... Maya? Do something terrible," Malik threw his hands up in defeat.

"Do your mercenary thing, Maya," I added.

"Onto the roof. Now!" Maya shouted as she waved her gun around but refrained from firing it. Her tempered display of power wasn't as effective as she had hoped it would be, and only scared the workers further. Some of those on the other end of the office floor made a break for the door to escape as the situation quickly got out of hand.

Seeing Gio spooked them, but hearing Gio calmed them. He addressed the crowd all at once, and the moment they could feel his good intentions and pure heart their demeanors changed. They lined up single file and marched their way towards the stairs, some of them stopping to touch him or share a moment of shared expression. The contrast between Gio's heightened ability and our primitive communication capabilities was stark. We could speak honestly to each other, but our experiences would rarely allow us to trust and understand our fellow humans.

Emilia dropped into a rolling office chair and pulled herself to one of the stations. She tapped away furiously as the screen jumped from one application to another. The CE login page pulled up and she punched in Ranbir's account name. "What's your password?"

"What? Why me?" Ranbir asked.

"Because you have sixty million followers, dummy. People trust you. They'll listen if it comes from you."

"I haven't been on Earth for months. My account probably isn't even active anymore."

"It's active," Malik informed him. "They must have hijacked your account after quietly removing you. Your account is always posting but you would never pick up your phone. They've been using Amir alone on their new ads and posters in your absence. He's like their mascot or something."

"Where is he? Is he okay?" Ranbir asked with his face lighting up to the sound of his little buddy's name.

"Come on. Stay on task. The password. Cough it up," Emilia snapped at Ranbir.

"It's embarrassing. Move over, and I'll type it in myself."

"Oh, hell no," Emilia laughed as she pulled the keyboard away. "Now I *really* want to know what it is."

"We don't have time for this," Malik warned in a sing-song tone, trying to rush us along and spare Ranbir's password pride.

"We can make time. I want to know what it is too. Is it *boobies*? It's *boobies,* isn't it?" I joked.

"Fine!" Ranbir capitulated. He leaned forward and whispered into Emilia's ear, and she twisted her head around to give him a disgusted look.

She tapped away at the keyboard entering the password, and asked "The 's' is a dollar sign?"

"Yes! You need a special character in the password. You designed the damn thing."

Emilia hovered the cursor over the password reveal button to taunt Ranbir for a moment before she hit enter with a devious grin on her face. "Your secret is safe with me, weirdo."

"Awwww. Come on," the rest of us groaned in unison.

"Are you sure the 's' was a dollar sign? And the 'I' is capitalized, right?" Emilia asked as the login attempt failed.

"Would you just let me do it," Ranbir pushed his hands in front of her to seize control of the keyboard and enter his password. Once again, access was denied.

"Penelope, you clever bitch," Emilia said softly to herself. "Maya, how many followers do you have?"

"Two hundred? Maybe two fifty."

"Malik? What about you?"

"I have no idea."

"You have no idea because it's somewhere between one and two million?" Emilia asked hopefully.

"No, I have no idea because I'm not a twelve-year-old whose fragile mental stability hinges upon a shallow social media follower count."

"Okay, okay. We'll read your manifesto later," I said, patting Malik's chest. "Don't look at me, Emilia. Your people throttled my reach. You better have another plan. This is the part where you do a bunch of cool hacker stuff and save the day."

"I can't do anything. This *was* the plan!"

"Well, we better think of something, and we better do it fast. The staff were probably burning the midnight oil because of the mess we made at Edwards. This whole place is alive right now doing damage control," Ranbir said.

"Maybe Gio can talk the entire valley onto the roof," Maya said sarcastically.

"I got it! Come on," Emilia said as she slid across the floor in her chair and leaped to her feet. We raced behind her out of the office, into the hallway, and onto an elevator.

"You going to fill us in?" I asked impatiently as we waited to descend to the third floor. Emilia reached over to start messing with my hair, and I slapped her hand away. "What are you doing?"

"I'm fixing you up a bit. Chill."

"You telling me to chill is going to give me a panic attack. The last time you *fixed me up* I ended up cuffed to a chair."

The elevator door opened to the broadcasting level. There was a monitor in the lobby playing the live feed of the news telecast taking place inside the studio. "We're recommending anyone west of Barstow or north of Lancaster to shelter in place. Do not open your door to strangers. Be on the lookout for anyone suspicious. Most of the criminal attackers met their fate at the hands of our brave soldiers, but we're getting reports that others have evaded capture."

"You always wanted to be on network news, right?" Emilia asked me suggestively.

"No way. I can't go on there. I'll freeze up. There are billions of people watching."

"It's like 3 a.m. There can't be that many people watching," Ranbir tried to console.

"Don't bullshit me. It's worldwide. The East Coast is waking up right now. It's midday overseas," my panic took hold.

"You did a podcast with thousands of viewers, yeah?" Malik asked as if they were the same thing.

"Millions. She had millions of followers on YouTube. Best damn podcast host on the planet," Emilia pumped my ego.

"Stop it. It was a home studio. You've never even seen the show."

"You've got to wake the fuck up before you go to sleep," Emilia quoted my late-night sign-off.

"All right. I'll give you that. You've seen it a couple of times. Big deal."

"Ugh, you stubborn mule. I watched your show all the time. Ever since you showed up at my OWG offices with your guerilla tactics. I checked you out. I binged your old shows and live-streamed the new ones. I admired your courage to swim against a powerful current." She paused in the middle of having one of her rare human moments. "I watched you eat ice cream and cry your way through a riot. You picked yourself off the floor and told your only viewer not to lose her humanity. I was too proud to get the message."

"Ho-ly shit. That was you. You're *Pro-Conspirator*." If I had ever experienced a cartoonish moment where my jaw hit the floor, that would've been it. "I have a stalker." I grinned, which drew a laugh from Malik.

"You can do this," Ranbir assured.

"Come on, girl. This is your thing, right?" Maya encouraged. "You've got broadcasts like I've got bullets."

"Whatya say, Gio? Can you use the force again to keep everyone docile?" I asked as Maya jiggled the locked studio door handle before shooting it twice and kicking it open.

"What is the meaning of this?" the floor producer asked as he attempted to stop us. "We're in the middle of breaking news here!"

"Yeah?" Maya asked as she confidently walked up to him with her trademark threatening swagger.

"I think you're about to be in the middle of a breaking nose," Malik said as he looked to Ranbir for the payoff of his pun.

"Ehhh." Ranbir twisted his open hand from side to side. "Needs work, but it's nice to see you've got your dad joke energy back."

Gio once again released his good vibes which would've been more effective if they weren't conflicting with the sound of the producer's face cracking from the butt of Maya's gun. He crumpled to the floor and everyone else froze in place. "Everybody, face the wall on your knees. There won't be any more trouble unless you start it," she warned.

The newscasters stood from behind their desk to survey the situation. The panic on their faces read like they couldn't feel Gio's calming words, and their live broadcast continued to roll. "Clock is ticking. This is your moment," Malik encouraged as he held the door open for me onto the enclosed sound stage.

I closed my eyes, took one last deep breath to compose myself, and approached the broadcast desk. I'd always wanted to sit in front of those cameras but could never tell the lies required to claim that spotlight. Or at least that's the virtuous lie I told myself to cover for my fear of the big stage.

"It seems we have some visitors on set this morning," the female news host said playfully, but the nervousness in her voice gave her away.

"Your show has been canceled. Get out." I pointed towards the door.

Neither of the two hosts would budge, and it wasn't a problem I was going to have to deal with. Malik whistled at Maya, and she tossed him a pistol. He stormed the stage like a wild bull, and I was sure glad he was on our side.

"Move it! Now! You people should be ashamed of yourselves. You were supposed to be the voice for the little guy and a bias-free check on power. But you're bought and paid for. You sold your souls to the elite establishment. We the people are done with your lies. Pawns no more to your propaganda. Do you have any idea what you've done? The Devil tempts me to put two in your belly, and let you writhe around in 5% of the pain you've brought onto others. Now get your butts off the stage and count your blessings that I'm a righteous man of God."

I looked to Ranbir who had taken position behind the main camera, and we shared a shocked smile as we nodded in a newfound respect for Malik. He ushered the newscasters quickly off the set, and I sheepishly walked around to the other side of the desk and took a seat.

"Okay. Hi. We're coming to you live from the Connect Earth headquarters," I verbally stumbled along as I stared blankly into the camera. I didn't know where to start and the pressure was weighing heavy on my psyche. The pause between my thoughts formulating into words was nerve-wracking. I was in front of millions, and I couldn't have possibly felt more alone.

"Alexis," I heard Emilia's voice from the booth over the intercom. "We're not doing the news. This isn't CEN. This is Conspiriousity, and you've done this a thousand times. I'm loading up the Area 51 footage for you. Be yourself," she encouraged.

"Right. This is Conspiriousity," I said with newfound confidence. "Strap on your tin foil hats and listen up, people. Everything you've been told is a lie. The Praxi didn't attack Earth, and we've got the evidence to prove it. Shadow governments orchestrated everything from the OWG unifying the planet into disarmament, to coordinated military strikes and subsequent counterstrikes. They wanted access to Praxi technology and minerals. They gained control over critical infrastructure and the world's military strength. They're using social media to control you."

"It's okay to take a breath every now and then," Emilia buzzed in. "I've got the video loaded whenever you're ready."

I breezed past Emilia's interruption without a second thought once I had found my groove. "Did you hear me? They're using social media to control you. Do you understand what that implies? They *need* to control you. These *elites* hold all the power, but they can't maintain their status if they must live in fear of the people overthrowing them. They want us distracted in arguments amongst ourselves. There's no time to fight them if we're too busy fighting each other. It's time for you people to wake the fuck up."

"Roll the tape, Emilia. Your neighbor isn't your enemy. Your government is. Have a look," I said as the film began to play. "This is never before seen footage from inside Area 51. We infiltrated the base and found the attack ships they used to hand out death on Earth hidden away from the public. We discovered the truth, and it cost us our freedom. Watch."

I offered no further commentary as the video replayed the events from my botched kidnapping. I looked from Malik to Ranbir to Maya to Gio through the glass. We were making the impossible happen, and there was a quiet relief in their eyes. The only person I couldn't see was Emilia in the control booth, and I hoped that she was experiencing a calming deep comfort of her own.

The bystanders huddled around the monitors outside the studio as they took personal inventory of their roles in the events that had transpired. The truth was smashing them in the face, and any of them with their souls still intact must have understood that they'd been culpable in millions of deaths and unleashing mass psychosis on the survivors.

"You see these markings here? This is the craft that attacked Chicago," my voice recanted on video as my image drew attention to the damage the ship took from a missile strike. I shared a smile with Ranbir behind the camera as we reveled in our victory instead of staying on point.

Time seemed to freeze as I noticed Penelope out of the corner of my eye. She had slipped into the studio undetected, and it was too late to do anything about it. I watched as she stood behind Gio, raised a pistol to the back of his head, and pulled the trigger. The execution happened in a split second, but I watched it play in slow motion with a million thoughts of terror fermenting in my mind.

The exit wound in his soft tissue left almost nothing remaining of his face as his body crumpled to the floor. Gio wasn't afforded a chance to sway Penelope's feelings, plea for mercy, or say a final goodbye. He risked it all to save mankind and was consumed by the worst of us. We couldn't properly appreciate his sacrifice or grieve his loss which we all felt partially responsible for. Penelope may have pulled the trigger; but human fear, greed, and weakness killed Gio the same as it had killed his kin.

The gunfire caught everyone off guard, and it was a surprised Maya who found herself staring down the barrel next. "Ah ah ah," Penelope warned as Maya's hand went for the weapon that she had set down beside her. "Kick it over here, butchy," Penelope insulted. "Now turn around, cross your legs, and face the wall." Penelope kept the gun pointed squarely at the back of Maya's head, but she was turning her attention to the rest of us.

The pain on Ranbir's face was gut-wrenching as he turned to see his friend laid out on the floor, but he kept his mental fortitude enough to rotate the camera in Penelope's direction before she haphazardly fired a shot into the wall next to Maya. "Don't be a hero, silly boy. Turn it off. And you," she glared in my direction, "Get over here. Sharpish," she said as she threatened to fire on Maya with any misstep from the rest of us.

"You," Penelope motioned towards Malik, "next to your little brother here," she guided him onto his knees beside Maya.

"No matter how evil you are, Gio never would have harmed you," Ranbir sneered. "He'd try to help you. Forgive you. Save you if he could, and you murdered him."

"Are you crying?" Penelope mocked. "Over this...*thing*? Pathetic. If it wasn't for weak men like you, there'd be no need for strong women like me."

I exited the enclosed broadcast set and truly didn't care if I lived or died at that point. "You're too late," I boasted as the door closed behind me. "The truth is out and killing us won't make a lick of difference."

"You ungrateful little twat. I should have let the General torture you. Or maybe I should have killed you myself. Lesson learned," she said as she pointed the gun at me, and I prepared myself once again to meet my end.

"Penelope! Stop!" Emilia's voice rang out across the studio in place of the gunshot I was expecting. She stood thirty feet from the rest of us holding a broadcast control tablet, and she stared down Penelope like a high noon showdown.

"Emilia? You're...with them?" she asked. "These pawns? These insignificant dolts? What have you become?" The disappointment in her voice was that of a mother whose daughter had failed to live up to expectations.

"I'm not with anyone. I've always been alone," Emilia replied coldly.

"Why come back here, child? You've ruined everything. Your new friends are going to die. You're going to die. The world I've built is going to fall into chaos."

"The world can be whatever you want it to be. I don't care. I just want CE back. I made it and it's mine. You can have everything else. I don't give a shit," Emilia replied.

"What are you saying?" Penelope lowered her weapon and raised an eyebrow.

"I didn't broadcast any of that," Emilia said with a condescending tone as if she was insulted that her mentor had underestimated her. "You think I learned nothing about leverage? Sure, some people in the valley may have seen it locally, but I didn't air it globally. There's no damage done that a little spin and a few coerced confessions from my *friends* here can't fix. Unless you don't give me what I want. One little press of a button, and our telecast will air your dirty laundry all over the world."

"I told you!" I growled with frustration. "I told you. I told you. And I told you," I said as I pointed at Ranbir, Maya, and Malik one by one. "I knew this would happen. Why does no one ever listen to me?"

"Because you're nothing. An outsider. A slob. A joke," Emilia insulted. "People respect voices with agency and power. You have so little of either that it's laughable."

I couldn't believe that I fell for her act. Everything she had done was to get to that moment. She must have known that Penelope would come, and Emilia had placed herself in a position to hold something worth bargaining for. I warned this would happen, but I doubted her betrayal would come to fruition the more I saw her human side.

"Don't do this, Emilia. This isn't you. You're not like her. She killed Gio!" Ranbir pleaded emphatically as he looked at our deceased friend. "He saved you more than once. Please. Don't do this to me again."

"This is exactly who she is," Penelope smirked. "The daughter I never had. I don't blame the rest of you fools, but I should have seen this coming. What exactly are you proposing, darling?"

"You turn administrative access over to me. I get my old office and position back. Full control of Connect Earth. I'll push whatever message and propaganda you want, but it must go through me. You get phony confessions of insurrection out of these four and then put them back on Praxi with proper measures to ensure they stay put this time." Emilia emotionlessly presented her terms.

"Absolutely not. I'm going to make an example out of them. There will be bleeding and crying and pleading. It will be public and painful. See if any of the sheep want to stare down the shepherd after they witness the consequences."

"No deal. They all live, or you can start shooting right now. Good luck putting out the fire when the truth burns through every home on Earth."

"Amir comes with us too," Ranbir added as if he had any agency over negotiations.

"The four of them, and the dog." Emilia rolled her eyes.

"Well, aren't you just the sweetest," Malik snarled sarcastically.

"Mary Poppins can't shoot us all. Can you?" Maya taunted Penelope.

Penelope took a deep breath and sighed in frustration. She was a woman who wasn't accustomed to things being dicey or out of her control. She held all the power to decide how things were going to go down, but Emilia had already made the choice for her.

"Fine. They get marooned, you get CE, and I get everything else. You better play nice, Emilia. They might be worlds away, but they'll never be out of my reach if I need to punish you." Penelope pointed to a broadcast staffer and curled her finger to draw the girl off the floor. "Be a doll and run down to the kennel on the second floor. Bring the dog so he can join the prisoners."

"I thought you'd see it my way," Emilia smirked.

"Screw this. Let's just rush her. For Gio," Ranbir angrily suggested as betrayal became his world for a second time.

"Are we voting? I vote no," I said quickly. There was no reason for any of the rest of us to die. The two snakes were both going to get what they wanted regardless, and a Praxi Island vacation sounded like a best-case scenario at that point.

"Don't do anything foolish. The four of you will be perfectly safe in no time," Emilia offered up as though she was doing us some grand favor. "Pull up the CE app, log into my old account, and enter the administrative passcode," she instructed Penelope.

Penelope moved the gun from her right hand to her left and began thumbing across the screen of her device. "Easy peasy. Now, delete that footage."

"Not so hasty. Forgive me if I have trust issues with you. We're going to burn out all future control. No tricks. No sneaky backdoor bullshit. Now, go into administrative controls and select *commands*."

"Your generation and these electronics," Penelope replied as she navigated her way through the labyrinth of settings and options. "All right, darling. Now what?"

"Enter 'GoodbyeBlueSky' into the command field as a single word and hit send."

"Done. Your baby is returned to you. Satisfied?" Penelope asked with a pleased smirk as she turned her screen for Emilia to view from across the room. We could do nothing but watch the transfer of power while hoping that we'd somehow survive the fallout of our assault on Earth. "Your turn. Delete that footage and provide proof. You're not the only one with trust issues."

"Yeah, about that..." Emilia trailed off as she looked over and gave me a wink. "I never sabotaged the broadcast. We played to a worldwide audience, and that feed has been running this whole time. Go ahead. Pull up the news on Connections. See for yourself."

The panic washed over Penelope, and her already overtly pale skin turned an even lighter shade of white. She frustratingly tapped at the screen of her malfunctioning device as she realized that she had been duped.

"What's the matter?" Emilia asked coyly. "Can't seem to get logged in? Network connection errors? Might have something to do with the fact that you just activated my doomsday device. Did I not mention that part?" she asked with a satisfied air.

"Emilia! What have you done?" Penelope raced towards Emilia with her gun pointed up. "You can have it! I swear. Don't destroy the power and influence you created. Reverse it. You can name your terms. Whatever you want."

The broadcasting staff began checking their malfunctioning devices as they sat on the sideline, and it was at that moment that I regretted having doubted Emilia. She had grown and changed for the better. Penelope may have gotten the best of Emilia when she was too drunk on power to see straight, but her vision was crystal clear now. She had outwitted her former mentor, and she was quite enjoying her checkmate.

"You won't destroy it. I know you won't. Emilia, stop this charade. You've had your fun and I give you high marks for it," Penelope pleaded as her control of the situation evaporated to nothing.

"You see, that's where you've got me all wrong. I won't dispute that we're similar," Emilia said as she closed the gap between herself and Penelope until the barrel of the gun was pressed lightly against her belly. "We're more intelligent than the others. We should be making decisions for those beneath us, whether they like it or not. The only real difference between us concerning that level of power is that you'll do anything to keep angles of control in play. You always had a backup plan for your backup plan, didn't you? Another level of manipulation to work. Hell, you'd share power for a time if it was necessary."

"And you wouldn't?" Penelope scoffed, pushing the barrel tighter against Emilia's sternum.

"If I can't have it," Emilia whispered in an almost sultry tone before dramatically pausing, "nobody can."

Penelope pursed her lips and looked at Emilia adoringly, even in her moment of defeat. She nodded her head as if to signify that she had been bested. Her eyes and half-smile conveyed a twisted level of respect. "Well done, Emilia. Well done," she said as her finger softly squeezed the trigger, and the echoing of gunfire caused us to flinch in shock.

Emilia fell to her knees and clenched at her bloodied belly. She toppled over onto her side and sprawled out on her back while Penelope took aim at her chest. She couldn't lock on to her target before Malik plowed into her hips and tackled her to the ground. Maya quickly joined him as the pair subdued Penelope and wrenched the pistol away from her.

Ranbir couldn't be bothered with Penelope. He sprinted forward and slid on his knees to Emilia's side. He held one of her hands in his own, and the other applied pressure to Emilia's wound. She didn't cry, whimper, or wince in pain even once. As odd as it was for someone in her condition; she seemed to be at peace, even as the blood darkened her military fatigues.

"Is Gio?" she shortened her worried inquisition for the wellbeing of her friend from the pain of death gripping her. Ranbir couldn't summon a verbal response. He shook his head *no* to deliver the heart-breaking news.

"Oh no. No, no, no," Emilia wept. "He has to get home. He's supposed to get home."

I joined Ranbir, kneeling on the other side of Emilia. She reached out for my hand, and I gripped her tight as the friend she had become. There was fear hidden behind her eyes, and she was struggling to maintain the unflappable composure she showed to the world. Emilia knew this was her end, and I could almost see the mental calculations of how much of her true self she would expose before she left this life.

"You should have seen your faces," Emilia's lips quivered while making light of her fate.

"Shh. It's okay. You're going to be okay," Ranbir lied, swallowing hard after speaking. With eyes glossed with tears and hands stained with blood, he still maintained his comforting presence. "You can't die. You can't," he choked up. "You've only just started living. You're going to be okay," he repeated.

Emilia could have said a lot. She could have had a personal goodbye with everyone. She could have shared her darkest secrets, her final thoughts, or professed her flawed love to Ranbir. She had no grand speech to give or any soliloquy of wisdom to impart. Emilia had only two words to speak on her deathbed, and once she delivered them, she smiled as though a weight had been lifted from her soul.

"I'm sorry," she choked out with blood now painting her lips red. "I'm sorry," she echoed, only softer. "I'm sorry," she repented one final time staring blankly ahead of us and the light evaporated from her eyes.

"It's okay. You're going to be okay," Ranbir persisted as she passed from this life. He ran his bloodied hand across her cheek and straightened her hair behind her ears. "It's okay. It's okay," he repeated before leaning down to kiss her forehead and close her eyes forever.

Ranbir didn't need to forgive her because deep down I don't think he felt that she owed an explanation or an apology. Maybe it wasn't for him though. Maybe her apology was for everyone. Maybe it was for herself so her soul could be at peace. Regardless, it was one of the few times I ever witnessed the woman behind the mask. She might have been hidden away all that time, or Emilia may have only discovered newfound humanity near her end.

There was no telling what was going on in the world outside those walls. Everyone was undoubtedly feeling the impact of Emilia's sacrifice, even though they might never know what she did for them. We toppled over the first domino of revolution but were too distracted with the damage to our new family to celebrate. We had won, but our losses turned the sweet taste of victory on our tongues into sour defeat.

Ranbir cradled Emilia's limp body in his arms and carried her towards the exit like a fallen soldier from the battlegrounds. He didn't bother looking Penelope's way as he practically walked right over her. His sadness was so great that even vengeance couldn't sway him.

Both Malik and Maya released their grip on Penelope and secured their weapons. Malik followed Ranbir's lead and carefully slung Gio over his shoulder. "What about her?" Maya asked as she carelessly waved her gun in Penelope's general direction.

"She's buried," I replied to Maya while staring down our defeated enemy. "The revolution is going to eat her alive. You hear me? There's not a lie you can tell that's elaborate enough to save you from what's coming. It's going to be barbaric and epic. You won't be able to control these people, and you'll wish you had never tried before the end. They're going to..." I hissed before the ringing of a single gunshot interrupted me.

The bullet entered the front of Penelope's forehead and exploded out the back. A strange, confused smile crossed her mouth as her body waved in a circular motion before dropping to the floor. Maya shrugged her shoulders at me, spit in Penelope's direction, and tossed her gun across the floor.

"Maya! I was doing a thing!" I complained.

"You've got your thing. I've got mine. It's not a competition or anything but," she said while nodding towards Penelope's corpse, "Bullets over broadcasts." While Maya's point was inarguable, I still felt that she gave Penelope the easy way out. No doubt remained within me that the people of Earth were finally awakened, and their retribution for the propagandists, militarists, and politicians would be swift and deadly. There's no telling what horrible fate may have awaited Penelope had she been arrested.

Maya collected an earring from Penelope as a final trophy and then followed to the exit to catch up with Ranbir and Malik, but I lingered behind. I peered through the glass at the empty broadcast stage where I had made my worldwide debut. I turned to face the now less-frightened news crew who were collecting themselves off the floor and processing the chaos and violence they had witnessed.

"This is a second chance for all of you. I doubt any of you dreamt of peddling lies and division when you wrote your first journal. Get back to your roots. It's your great responsibility to speak truth to power. To not only inform those who are in the dark but to serve as their voice as well. Hold each other accountable, because I can promise you this; If you don't check yourselves, I will," I warned harshly.

The staffer girl re-entered the studio as I was leaving, and carefully placed Amir in my arms while peering over my shoulder at the bloody scene behind me. "Hey, you. Hi!" I said warmly as Amir excitedly licked my face. "There's an old friend who's really going to need you." I walked out of the studio and followed the trail of bloody drops and handprints through the hallway, elevator, offices, and up the stairwell to the roof.

The sun hadn't begun to rise, but the night sky was at the point where it was about to lose the battle of light to daybreak. Maya was sitting alone, looking out over the CE compound. The incessant humming of electricity powering the massive server farm had been silenced, leaving us with the type of quiet Earth must have known before humans turned the volume up on everything. "You can actually hear yourself think up here," she noted.

"Where's the others?"

"In the ship," Maya said with her feet dangling over the ledge of the rooftop. "Hey buddy," she patted her lap as an invite to Amir. "You can sit with me anytime."

Ranbir and Malik dropped through the lower hatch after tucking away the bodies of our fallen friends. Both wore a solemn scowl, but the light returned to Ranbir's eyes when he noticed that he wasn't as alone as he must have felt. "Amir?" Ranbir asked. "Amir! Come here boy!" He beckoned with excitement while hunching down and waiting for his sprinting puppy to jump into his arms. "You're okay! I missed you," he jubilantly scratched the top of Amir's head while presenting his face for a tongue bath.

Ranbir sat to my left with Amir cradled in his arms and Malik trudged to Maya's right to join our side-by-side quartet. I felt the urge to sing, but there was no appropriate song for bittersweet triumph. Any notes of joy I had to belt out would taste acidic on my tongue. The world may have won that day, but there were no spoils of war for those of us on the frontline.

"They won't remember her the way we do," Ranbir lamented. "They'll never know the depths of Gio and Emilia's sacrifice. People will thanklessly go on with their lives, and it's going to be up to us to remind them. We're going to honor them by ensuring that their loss was not in vain."

"We'll remember them," I said confidently. "I know I'll never forget them, especially Emilia. She was a stone-cold killer, and no matter how big her exterior personality was, there was far more under the surface."

"She was a handful, wasn't she?" Malik echoed rhetorically. "Earth ejected her millions of miles away, and she fought her way back across the galaxy. She was willing to do it on her own if she had to. That takes a special kind of grit and stubbornness." Malik paused as his voice became shaky. "This war has truly claimed the lives of the best of us," he concluded as Maya consolingly put her hand on his knee.

The four of us sat side by side on that ledge for some time, sharing little besides the comfort of silence and comradery. I was confident in our victory but unsure how the world would receive it. We were unplugged for the first time in decades. There was no more internet or television, and people couldn't share their responses over text messages or posts on social media. If individuals were going to repair this world, they were going to have to leave their homes and engage in real human contact.

Could we learn to communicate like the Praxi? Would humans be able to put our collective house in order? Probably not, but I wasn't about to give up on trying, and I would no longer be alone in my efforts. My friends would stand with me, and so would everyone else who hadn't surrendered their hope for the human spirit.

The sun delivered the dawn of a new day over the eastern horizon. We looked to the sky as the stars eclipsed from sight and the purple glow in our atmosphere lessened as the day broke. Before it could fully give way to the light of the sun, the fading night sky erupted into colorful explosions. Maisie and Marcus entertained the people of Earth with a fireworks display the likes of which we'd never seen before. The ominous violet glow was replaced with sparking alloys careening off each other in every direction and a discharge of yellow and orange energy displacing from the structure as the Jump Point ripped from end to end.

"Woohoo!" Maya cheered while rubbing the back of Malik's head. He put his arm around her, and she rested her head against his shoulder.

"Those are my babies," Malik said proudly.

"We really did it, didn't we?" Ranbir asked rhetorically.

"We really did," I echoed. "You know, I dreamed of our first contact moment more times than I can count. I played out scenarios of being visited by benevolent aliens, violent aliens, and everything in between. Not once did my vivid imagination come anywhere close to reality."

"It took our first contact to make us realize that we weren't ready for *any* contact. We're going to slide back into isolation until we *are* ready. If ever," Ranbir said.

He was right. When the Praxi made contact, they didn't see us for what we truly were. They had been manipulated into believing that mankind had turned a corner. If their eyes had been bigger than their hearts, they would have seen us for the territorial, greedy, and dangerous creatures that we are. For all our technological and societal advancements, mankind was still an infant holding a rocket launcher. We weren't ready, we aren't ready, and we may very well never be ready.

"Our first contact was an isolating contact," I murmured. "Let's hope it won't be our last."

Afterword

Thank you so much for supporting an indie author! I hope you enjoyed the book as much as I enjoyed writing it. What a genuine pleasure it has been for me to entertain you for a few hours, and I hope I've earned your reading trust for the future.

None of this would be possible without readers like yourself who back independent writers. I don't have a mighty publisher with their advertising budget and connections bolstering me. My platform is small, my reach is limited, and I don't have any major publications lining up to review this book. I only have you, the reader, and I hope that's enough. I know you've already bought the book and given me so much of your time, but I have one last favor to ask of you. It would mean the world to me if you'd leave a review on Amazon. If you'd be so kind to post it on Goodreads or any social media platform as well, that would be amazing! Your support means everything to me, and I can't do this without you!

If you have any questions or comments about the book, or even just want to come and say hello; I'd love to hear from you! You can find me on Facebook as "Ash Remington," on Twitter as @AshRWrites, and on Instagram as "AshRemingtonBooks."

Coming Soon: The Contact Series: Book 2

ADDICTIVE CONTACT

Made in the USA
Las Vegas, NV
29 January 2024

85076090R00125